Masquerade

THE TRUTH ABOUT CASSANDRA

Laurie Brown

ZEBRA BOOKS
Kensington Publishing Corp.
http://www.kensingtonbooks.com

ZEBRA BOOKS are published by

Kensington Publishing Corp.
850 Third Avenue
New York, NY 10022

Copyright © 2003 by Laurie Brown

All rights reserved. No part of this book may be reproduced
in any form or by any means without the prior written consent of the Publisher, excepting brief quotes used in reviews.

If you purchased this book without a cover you should be
aware that this book is stolen property. It was reported as "un-
sold and destroyed" to the Publisher and neither the Author
nor the Publisher has received any payment for this "stripped
book."

All Kensington titles, imprints and distributed lines are available at special quantity discounts for bulk purchases for sales
promotion, premiums, fund-raising, educational or institu-
tional use.

Special book excerpts or customized printings can also be
created to fit specific needs. For details, write or phone the
office of the Kensington Special Sales Manager: Kensington Publishing Corp., 850 Third Avenue, New York, NY
10022. Attn. Special Sales Department. Phone: 1-800-221-
2647.

Zebra and the Z logo Reg. U.S. Pat. & TM Off.

First Printing: January 2003
10 9 8 7 6 5 4 3 2 1

Printed in the United States of America

A DANGEROUS DECEPTION

Anne whirled around to face Marsfield. "You seem to be laboring under a false pretense, confusing passion with a deeper, more abiding emotion. It so happens, I love the man I would marry."

Marsfield did not believe her. Refused to believe her.

"And he is not ugly. He is most handsome, and he is—"

Marsfield leaned over and kissed the tip of her nose. "Your eyes sparkle like the rarest emeralds when you are angry."

She took a half step back. "He is—"

He cut off her words with a gentle brush of his lips.

Shaking her head, Anne tried to concentrate on her story. The whole point of seeing him again as Cassandra was to make him believe she was beyond his reach so he would never seek her out again. But he was too close. She couldn't think when the familiar scent of his cologne fogged her brain and turned her knees to jelly, and the lightest taste of his lips made her hunger for more.

She took a full step back and bumped against the wall. He moved with her, giving her not an inch of respite.

"The man I love is—"

"Does he kiss you like this?"

Dear Romance Readers,

In July 2000, we launched the Ballad line with four new series, and each month since then we've presented both new and continuing stories set everywhere from medieval England to the American West—the kind of passionate, romantic stories you love best, written by the most gifted authors. At the back of each book, we'll tell you when you can find subsequent books in the series that have captured your heart.

First up this month is Pam McCutcheon, with the first installment of the charming new series *The Graces*. A fairy godmother is a very good thing for three sisters who need a little help when it comes to romance—and the women who pitch in, beginning with the **Belle of the Ball,** have quite a few ancient, and highly effective, secrets up their sleeves! Next, Golden Heart finalist Laurie Brown presents *Masquerade,* as a British operative meets the woman who steals his life story for her potboilers—and captures his heart in the process. Will he learn **The Truth About Cassandra?**

Talented newcomer Caroline Clemmons takes us to the sweeping Texas plains as she begins the story of *The Kincaids,* and introduces us to a man determined to find **The Most Unsuitable Wife**—who soon discovers a passion he can't resist. Finally, Marilyn Herr explores the paths taken *In Love and War* as a hard-headed man and an equally spirited woman catch up in the dramatic French and Indian conflict decide to follow **Where the Heart Leads.** Enjoy!

Kate Duffy
Editorial Director

To Brit,
who taught me to believe
in happy endings.

Prologue

October, 1854
Crimean War
Balaklava, Russia

"Cut it off and you die."

The surgeon looked down at his patient with war-weary eyes. "I'm trying to save your life, Captain Crosslee."

Stephen Michaels, Earl of Marsfield, tightened his restraining grip on the surgeon's arm. He tried to ignore the men in the surrounding beds of the filthy hospital ward and concentrate on the conversation. Confessing his real identity was not an option. Even though his title might get him better medical treatment, it would endanger his mission.

"The wound is suppurating," the surgeon said, frowning.

"It's not gangrenous."

The older man raised an eyebrow. "And where did you receive your medical training, sir?"

Marsfield gritted his teeth against the pain. If he didn't convince the determined doctor, he could well wake up minus his left leg. "I've seen enough in the last seven days to understand my own condition. I'll take the risk."

"This isn't one of your damnable card games, man." The surgeon was so upset his abundant gray whiskers quivered.

Mindful of his disguise as a ne'er-do-well cavalry officer, Marsfield shrugged. "I'm a gambler."

"This is your life, and you're holding a losing hand."

Marsfield wouldn't waste his breath explaining just how worthless an ante his life made.

"Even if the wound heals, you'll never be able to walk on it. You'd be better off with a wooden leg. Cut your losses and wait for the next hand to be dealt."

"I still say no."

"And I say you'll die within a fortnight. I can order—"

"Excuse me, sir." Private Kirby, Marsfield's batman, stepped between the two men. After dumping his armful of parcels on the foot of the bed, the feisty little man made an ostentatious show of a pistol nearly as long as his forearm. As the batman wiped the iron barrel with an oily rag, the doctor beat a hasty retreat.

"I've found a place," Kirby whispered. "Clean and quiet."

Marsfield sent a word of thanks heavenward for the little man who had somehow miraculously managed to find decent food and warm clothing in the cesspool aftermath of battle. When hell froze over, it would resemble Balaklava. Kirby had saved his life, and probably his sanity.

"I thought we didn't have enough gold left to rent a room," Marsfield said.

"You don't. And, Toby, he's old Colonel Danfries's bat, said there ain't a empty room for miles. But I got one o' my itches that told me to check it out for myself. Mighty discouraging until I got to talking with the manservant of some kind of rich Arab merchant or ambassador."

"Really?" Marsfield let his valet babble on, the raspy voice strangely comforting.

"Can't be real sure 'cause the Arab don't speak good English. As I take it, his master left him and his family behind in the rush to get out before the fighting started. Nobody wants to stay in that house, being as they's heathens and all. But they've got room, and they ain't even going to charge you."

"When something sounds too good to be true, there's usually a nasty hook under the bait."

Kirby looked away, but Marsfield waited in silence.

"We're to take them along when we leave Russia," Kirby finally mumbled.

"What?" Marsfield looked around to make sure no one had taken notice of their conversation. "You know that's impossible," he said, lowering his voice.

Undaunted, Kirby scurried about packing their pitiful belongings. "It gets you out of this hellhole, don't it?"

Suspicious, Marsfield asked, "Why would he believe you? What did you tell this Arab?"

"That you was an earl and knew people who could help him."

Marsfield stifled a bark of laughter. The dreaded title he'd recently inherited might well rescue him from the bullet he'd taken in the course of his career. A career he'd chosen, in part, to escape his estranged father and his precious earldom. A career that was, in all probability, ended. The gods of mischief and misrule were surely laughing at him now.

However, he would be more than happy to rid himself of this disguise. Taking orders and maintaining regimental discipline had never been his forte, but the persona of a carousing army captain had been necessary in order to enter a certain high-stakes poker game. He'd willingly lost a small fortune in exchange for information. Unfortunately, the enemy had staged an attack before he'd won his money back, and he had been forced to play out his military role, getting wounded in the process.

The latest information he'd gleaned needed to be reported personally to the director of Foreign Services at Whitehall. Marsfield would deal with the Arab when the time came. Right now, his main concern was staying alive long enough to leave Russia with all his limbs intact.

One

April, 1855
In the garden of Weathersby Manor
England

"A quick death is necessary." Anne Weathersby refolded the letter on its original creases and placed it in the drawer of her lap-held writing box.

"Oh no! I like Dunstan. He's—"

"Letticia." Anne's stern voice and glowering expression were meant to quell her sister's reaction before the young girl worked herself into a melodramatic scene. "You read his letter. Robert's coming home," she said, worrying her lower lip with her teeth. "He didn't say when to expect him, and the letter is dated weeks ago."

"But Dunstan—"

"Has served his purpose." In her secret heart, Anne admitted she'd miss him. Having a husband was so . . . convenient, even if it was only for Robert's sake. And she didn't relish playing the grieving widow, but there was no logical alternative.

Letty placed her hands over her ears. "I don't want to hear it. Dunstan is fun and exciting." She paced the narrow path separating the two marble garden benches, her half boots crunching on the shell-covered walk in tune with her agitated stride. "He gave us parties and weekend guests and a Christmas Ball."

Poor Letty. At sixteen she was so hungry for excitement that it made the ten years between their ages seem much greater. Anne rose and placed an arm around her sister's delicate shoulders. "Letty, dear, everyone at Weathersby knew it was only make-believe. We can't keep up the charade once Robert returns."

Letty sniffed. "I know. But when you read those long letters to us before you sent them to Robert, Dunstan seemed so real. As if he actually existed."

"That was the point." Anne handed over her handkerchief. "Allowing our brother to believe I had a husband to care for us, so he wouldn't worry. Now he's returning from the Crimea, and we'll go back to the way things were before Papa died."

"Boring, you mean." Letty plopped down on the bench.

"Now, dear, we have a very full life here. Our work with the orphans is rewarding. We—"

"Oh, yes. We have plenty of the three Rs—responsibility, respectability, and wretched boredom."

"Wretched starts with a W."

Letty crossed her arms and stared at the early blooming lilac bush that lent its heady scent to the small walled garden.

Anne stifled a sigh. Being mother and father to Letty these past three years had not been easy. If it hadn't been for the income from her stories, they would have starved that first year after paying off Papa's gambling debts. Well, perhaps not starved. She smiled at her own tendency to exaggerate. They'd closed the town house and retreated to the country, but all in all, she was proud of how she'd met the family obligations.

Adjusting her spectacles farther up her nose, Anne studied her sister's profile. Was she was being unfair to Letty because she herself had been a crashing failure on the marriage mart? Anne was too tall, too thin, and had a straightforward, no-nonsense manner. Her mousy brown curls and ordinary green eyes hadn't inspired any impassioned love sonnets. Letty, who had their mother's golden blond hair and vivid blue eyes, would do well in London.

"I think we can manage a Season for you if we aren't too extravagant," Anne said, sitting next to her sister.

The younger woman maintained her silence.

Aware that Letty practiced the quivering lower lip and sad-eyed expression in the mirror, Anne was immune to her sister's pouts. Everyone else bent backward to restore the girl's angelic smile. Yes, Letty would do quite well among the *ton*.

"You said that the last time."

Startled out of her reverie, Anne turned toward her sister.

"You said your last book would move us to London," Letty complained.

"The orphanage needed a new roof."

"Your orphans always need something or other."

"They are not *my* orphans. Helping the less fortunate is not only our duty, it's a reward in itself. Don't you remember their sweet, smiling faces during Reverend Pike's blessing ceremony?"

"I remember a horde of urchins who couldn't keep their grubby hands off my best white muslin. I still don't know if it can be salvaged." Letty sniffed and delicately touched her handkerchief to the corner of her eye.

Anne sighed. If her sister was willful and self-centered, she had only herself to blame. She'd spoiled the child since their mother's death nine years ago.

"I shouldn't have to remind *you*, of all people," Letty continued, "that it's your *duty* as my closest female relative to help me find a husband, and I certainly can't do that here."

Though Anne hated to admit it, Letty was right. Of the few eligible men within twenty miles, two were over sixty, one cared more for his horses than people, and the last was so slovenly even the vicar's wife refused to invite him to supper. They'd have to go to London to find a husband for Letty.

"With the proceeds from *Dora's Betrayal,* we'll open the town house. *Lucinda's Dishonor* should purchase a new wardrobe for you." Her sister's lack of reaction surprised Anne. "I promise. You will have your Season."

Letty snorted in a most unladylike manner. "Did you forget about Dunstan? You can hardly chaperon me wearing your widow's weeds." She turned and raised a finger in warning. "And don't suggest Binny as a substitute. She's dotty as a dormouse."

"She's just getting on in years and . . ."

Letty raised one pale aristocratic eyebrow.

"Binny was your nursemaid as well as mine. We simply cannot turn her out," Anne protested. "She has nowhere to go."

"That still leaves the question of my chaperon."

"Don't worry," Anne said. "I'll think of something. It's not as if I'll be in *real* mourning."

"Then you'll tell Robert the truth about Dunstan?"

"You know I can't do that. I've told him Dunstan is most generous. If Robert knows Dunstan is a sham, he'll wonder where I got the money to restore Weathersby Manor. You must remember your promise to never, ever tell Robert about my writing."

"What? And tarnish your pristine, oh-so-respectable old maid's reputation?"

Anne winced. Though at age twenty-six she'd been on the shelf long enough to become used to the term, the epithet still hurt.

"Besides," Letty said, "if your scandalous career were ever to be known, *my* prospects would be ruined."

Anne realized anew that Letty's world would ever revolve around herself. Shouldering the blame for not teaching her sister deeper values, she changed the subject.

"Shall we have a few gowns made in Weathersby to tide you over until we can visit a London seamstress?"

"Last week we had no money for a new dress."

"Well, I'm expecting a bank draft from Mr. Blackthorne any day now." She couldn't keep the pride from her voice. "I expect *A Maid's Revenge* sold quite well."

"Oh, speaking of your publisher"—Letty pulled a letter from her pocket—"I forgot to give you this."

"Letty!" Anne laughed and grabbed the letter. "This is it, the bank draft that will make your dreams come true." Before she could open it, Letty reached over and hugged her.

"You really are the best big sister in the world." Letty rose and waltzed herself around the garden. "I want a ball gown in pink tulle spangled with silver stars."

Amazed at how quickly Letty could turn her sulks off and on, Anne ripped open the letter and scanned the crabbed handwriting. With an effort, she maintained her smile despite her growing horror.

A Maid's Revenge had not earned as much as Mr. Blackthorne had advanced her against the sales, and he didn't want to publish *Lucinda's Dishonor.* He said the crucial scene in the gaming hall lacked the realistic details that brought a setting to life. A hollow emptiness yawned in the pit of her stomach.

Letty danced behind Anne to look over her shoulder. "How much is the bank draft?"

Anne quickly folded the letter. Oh dear, oh dear. She couldn't tell her sister the dismal truth. Letty was still such a child, still believed in happily ever after.

"How much?" she asked again, extending her hand.

Jumping up, Anne shoved the letter into her pocket and scurried out of reach. She forced a laugh, then hoped Letty hadn't noticed the too high, artificial quality. "If I tell, you'll spend every last farthing at the dressmakers."

"I'll try," Letty promised, hugging herself. "In fact, I'll

make a list of absolute necessities right now." Humming a lively tune, she danced her imaginary partner into the house.

Anne groped for the edge of the marble bench and sat down. What was she to do? The writing on her latest book was proceeding well, but there wouldn't be time to finish it, have it published, and garner any revenue before the Season started. She doubted, from the tone of his letter, that Mr. Blackthorne would even consider another advance.

Maybe she could rewrite the scene he disliked. Then he would publish *Lucinda's Dishonor*. Yes, that was it. If she convinced him some editing was all the book needed, she could still salvage Letty's dreams. She picked up her writing box. No. He could dismiss a letter too easily.

She must see Mr. Blackthorne in person. First thing tomorrow morning.

Anne set off for London even though the day promised to stay gray and rainy. Fifteen minutes down the road, she put the problem of her publisher to the back of her mind, and let the rocking of the old family carriage lull her into a relaxed state. She did her best plotting on long drives, and dealing with the Dunstan problem was rather like getting one of her heroines out of a troublesome situation. The familiar sound of Binny's snores from the opposite seat was a minor distraction. A two-hour nap on the trip would do the old girl good.

As she leaned over to tuck the lap robe around Binny's considerable girth, the carriage lurched to a sudden halt. Binny jerked awake and, waving her arms in panic, knocked Anne's hat askew. Anne was trying to right herself and calm the older woman at the same time when the coachman's trapdoor slid open.

"Sorry, Miss."

"Good heavens, Harvey." Anne sat back on the seat, her

hat down over one ear. The pins had fallen from her hair, loosening the frizzled mess. Now she would have to repin her hair before the hat would again sit properly. "What on earth happened?"

"Begging your pardon, but there's a man lying in the road. I figured you wouldn't be wanting me to just run him over."

She ignored the disapproving tone of Harvey's response. "Of course not," she said.

"Probably some poor drunken fool who couldn't find his way home from the pub last night," Harvey said.

"Please help the man to the side of the road." She patted Binny on the shoulder. "I'm sure we'll be under way soon." The older woman nodded and promptly resumed her nap.

Searching for her missing spectacles and hairpins, Anne put the delay out of her mind. Poor Binny stayed awake all night, every night, afraid of the ghosties and beasties, as she called the things that go bump in the night. Then she couldn't keep her eyes open during the day.

Anne found only two hairpins. Never one to worry overmuch about her looks, she quickly braided the troublesome mass of curls and tied the end with a ribbon from Binny's sewing box.

The carriage door opened.

"Pardon again, Miss," Harvey said, removing his hat. "We have a problem."

Somehow the unexpected news didn't surprise her. Binny stirred. Rather than wake her, Anne gave Harvey her hand and stepped out of the coach. When she started to walk toward the front of the carriage, he stepped in her path.

"What is it?" She strained to look around the coachman blocking her view.

"You shouldn't be seeing this, Miss. The gent's messed up pretty bad. Alive, but just barely. Likely a robbery gone bad."

She pushed past Harvey. She was no squeamish school-girl. Maybe she could help.

Standing by the man, who was lying in the middle of the road, she wished she hadn't been so brave. Little of his face could be seen for the quantity of blood. His dark hair was matted to his broad forehead. Long eyelashes she would have given her eyeteeth to posses fanned into dark crescents along the tops of his prominent cheekbones. Despite his condition, the width of his massive shoulders gave the impression of coiled strength. She knelt next to him and stanched the bleeding on the side of his head with her handkerchief.

"Get the water from the carriage," she said.

Cleeve, the footman, jumped to do her bidding.

"And that bottle of whiskey Harvey keeps under the coachman's seat," she called after him.

Cleeve shot Harvey a worried look, but the coachman calmly nodded.

"It's rum," Harvey said under his breath. "You weren't supposed to know."

She gave him a superior smile. "It was only a guess."

Anne did not pursue the subject, because the wounded man moaned and opened his eyes. She felt drawn into the sea-deep blue depths, felt a connection she'd never before experienced. The moment stretched as if time itself were at his command. His gaze seemed to ask her questions beyond her comprehension, to promise her delights she'd never known.

"Just hold on a little longer," she whispered to him. "We'll take care of you."

"He won't last long at the rate he's bleeding," Harvey said in a quiet voice.

Anne blinked back tears. Though a stranger, the man had touched her soul in some primal way that went beyond the usual bounds of human contact.

His hand twitched as if grasping for a lifeline. Instinctively, she put her hand in his. The strength of his responding grip surprised her, even as his eyes drifted closed.

"By the cut of his cloth, he looks to be a gent of quality," Harvey observed, squatting beside her.

Cleeve returned with the two bottles. "Do you want me to go for help?"

She tried to remove her hand so she could dribble a bit of rum into the man's mouth, but he wouldn't release her. Instead, he tangled their fingers together and tightened his grip. Harvey poured a capful between the man's teeth.

"Going for help will take too long." Anne tried to think logically, but the man's rapid pulse against her wrist forced her own heartbeat into a matching rhythm. "We'd best get him back to Weathersby," she suggested. "Mrs. Finch can care for him while someone fetches the doctor."

Harvey nodded and motioned to the footman to take the man's feet. "Give a hand, Cleeve. Let's get him into the carriage."

Anne tried to step out of their way, but the man wouldn't let go of her hand. When the coachmen lifted him, he stiffened as if he would fight them, then moaned and lapsed back into a stupor. Yet he did not release his grip.

The bandy-legged coachman and his young assistant tugged and dragged the awkward burden across the muddy road. The man's rigid hold on her hand forced Anne to walk at his side. Slipping and sliding, they managed to get the man to the carriage, but not without a number of painful groans, his and theirs.

Seated in the far corner, his head resting on her lap, Anne watched the coachmen maneuver the man's feet onto the other seat. She was unprepared for Binny's fright when she awoke to find a bloody body draped across the seat in front of her.

"Aaaagh," the old woman screeched. "It's the Cursed

Corpse of Thursten Marsh." She cowered into her own corner. "Risen from his unholy grave to kill us all. He'll—"

"Nonsense," Anne said in a calming voice. "Hush, now."

Still she wailed. "He'll suck our blood and laugh in fiendish glee."

A fit of hysterics couldn't possibly be good for the older woman. If Anne didn't do something, anything, to calm her, she'd have two patients on her hands. "It's not the Cursed Corpse."

Between the screeching, crying woman across from her and the bloody man in her lap, a woman with less fortitude than Anne Weathersby would have been tempted to slip into hysteria herself. But she was made of sterner stuff. What would calm Binny?

"It's only Dunstan." What in the world had made her say that! She shook her head in disbelief. Desperation had forced the first name that popped into her head to pop out of her mouth.

"Dunstan?" Binny whispered.

In the sudden quiet, Anne considered her response. It wasn't cricket to take advantage of the old woman's gullibility, but she *had* stopped screaming.

"Your husband? Dunstan?"

Of course, Binny had been told of the charade fabricated for Robert's benefit. All of the servants, long serving and well trusted, had been told, but the old nursemaid's memory wasn't what it used to be.

Anne took a deep breath. If she told the truth, Binny might lapse into hysterics again, so she reiterated the lie. "Yes, dear. My Dunstan."

"What happened to him?"

Warming to her story, she elaborated. "On his way home late last evening, robbers set upon him. A band of six cruel, greedy men. When dear Dunstan didn't have a rich purse, they beat him."

"Our poor, darling boy. Will he be all right?"

As the coach jockeyed back and forth to turn around in the road, Anne used her free hand to move a dark lock of hair off the man's bloody forehead. Could a man live after loosing so much blood? "I hope so," she whispered, praying she was correct.

Cleeve's frantic shouts as they approached the front door brought the two stable hands and old Finch the butler to the entrance. It took all five to get the wounded man, still gripping Anne's hand, into the hall. Binny hovered at his side, dabbing his cheek with her handkerchief.

Anne thought the man's complexion looked more ashen than before. *Don't you die on me,* she willed him with a little shake of his hand.

Everyone shouted and talked at the same time, the voices echoing off the walls of the manor's main entrance. She looked around and finally spied Mrs. Finch hurrying down the staircase.

"What happened?" the housekeeper inquired, calm amidst the chaos.

Anne couldn't answer because she also saw her brother behind Mrs. Finch. "Robert! You're home."

Robert ran the rest of the way and put an arm around her shoulders. "My God, are you all right?"

"I'm fine. Oh, I'm so happy to see you."

"You don't look so fine." He gestured to her bloody gown.

"No, no. This is his blood." She reached out to hug Robert, but only managed to wrap one arm around his waist. The man still held her other hand, and she couldn't break free. "When did you get here? How was your trip?"

"I've just arrived. Who is—?"

"Are you people daft?" Binny shouted, sounding like her old I'm-in-charge-of-the-nursery self. "No time for chitchat. We have a dying man here. Get Dunstan up to the east suite."

"D-Dunstan?" the housekeeper stammered, looking to Anne with wide eyes.

"Can't say this is the way I pictured meeting my brother-in-law," Robert said, peering over Anne's shoulder.

"This bloke ain't exactly a feather," Cleeve whined.

Binny urged the men forward by waving her bit of bloody handkerchief.

The entire staff's expectant gazes turned toward Anne. Although they had all been aware of the charade and had loyally agreed to go along with the fiction for Robert's sake, having a real Dunstan in the house was another matter altogether. She opened her mouth, but for once in her life could think of nothing to say.

"Anne is obviously in shock," Robert said, his brow furrowed.

"You men, get Dunstan up to the east suite," Binny shouted. "Mrs. Finch, get your medicine chest." She pointed to the stable hand. "You, saddle a horse and fetch Dr. Mullins."

The young boy turned took two steps and turned back. "Who?"

"That old quack Mullins died last winter—you remember, don't you, Binny?" Mrs. Finch said. "Besides, we don't need a doctor. We can deal with this ourselves."

"Nonsense. Fetch a doctor. Any doctor," Binny said, as if commanding men on the battlefield. The boy scrambled to obey.

Robert, looking pale, volunteered to get the brandy and quickly headed for the library.

Anne shook her head. She'd hoped the shy, sensitive young man in the shiny new uniform who'd left to defend Queen and country would have come back . . . well, stronger. That's why she had scraped together the money to purchase the commission he'd wanted. She turned to follow Robert, but was pulled to a stop by the man, who still had not released her hand. She tried to pry his fingers loose without success.

Anne felt a jerk on her arm and stumbled on the first step as the bizarre parade moved up the stairs. Binny led the way, calling for hot water, clean linen, and smelling salts. Harvey and Cleeve followed, carrying the wounded man, each complaining the other wasn't bearing his fair share of the weight. Anne was forced to walk at the man's side. Mrs. Finch trailed behind with her enormous box of herbs and potions.

Good heavens. She was actually escorting a stranger into her very own bedroom because he wouldn't let go of her hand. She couldn't tell her brother that this bloody man was not her husband, because then she would also have to tell him about her scandalous career.

The situation was worse than any her heroines had ever encountered. Oh, when would she learn to tell the truth?

What story could she possibly concoct to get out of *this* predicament?

Two

Once on Anne's bed, the stranger began to moan and thrash about.

"Hold him down," Mrs. Finch directed. Opening her medicine box, she retrieved the brown bottle of laudanum tonic.

"Hold him," Anne echoed, as he pulled her arm nearly out of the socket, jerking her forward. As she half sat, half lay across his chest, he stilled. Suddenly he released her hand and wrapped both his arms around her, pulling her until she was lying beside him. His strength surprised her.

She couldn't help but notice the sensations of her first time lying in bed with a man: The warm length of his body. Her breasts flattened against the hardness of his chest. She inhaled a deep breath and couldn't seem to let it out. A swirl of warmth settled deep within her body. Despite his condition—

Merciful heavens, what was wrong with her? The man needed medical attention. She struggled to free herself, but her movement caused him to groan and flail outward with one arm.

"Lie still for a moment," Mrs. Finch directed Anne. When she complied and the man quieted, the housekeeper tipped a spoonful of tonic between his lips.

The man opened his eyes, and Anne was again caught in their cerulean blue depths. Again she felt that connection. Could he read her wanton thoughts? Heat rushed to her cheeks. The moment stretched. Though she noticed the rhythm of his breathing as it slowed, it did not diminish her own shallow gasping. The warm circle of his arms slipped from her waist. His eyelids drifted shut, covering the gaze that seemed to plead with her to stay.

Mrs. Finch cleared her throat.

Anne jumped off the bed and stumbled back a few steps. The coachmen and Binny turned their gaze to other parts of the room. "I . . . I . . ." she stammered.

Mrs. Finch waved away any attempt at an explanation without turning in her direction. "Get his clothes off, boys. Let's see the damage and start stitching him up."

Anne fled the bedroom, but not before she caught sight of his naked chest. His symmetrical, sculpted chest, the intimate feel of which she'd never forget. How could she? It was the only time she'd ever lain with a man, even an unconscious one. In the cool darkness of the hallway, she rested her head against the wall and fought to regain her composure.

"Well, I've heard some interesting ploys to catch a man, but I must say, running one down with your carriage is a novelty."

Anne whirled to face her sister. "I did not run him down. We found him." She choked back a sob. "I think he's dying."

Letty crossed her arms and cocked her head to one side. "How convenient for you."

"Letty!"

"Oh, don't worry. I won't give away your precious secret."

Only the appearance of Binny and the upstairs maid saved Letty from the slap Anne itched to deliver.

"Make way. Bandages and hot water." Binny held the door for the maid, then turned to Anne. "I sent a bath to Letty's room. I'll bring you clean clothes so you can freshen up. Letty, go down to the library and try to keep Robert from drinking all the brandy."

"Drinking?" Anne looked at her watch brooch. "It's half past nine in the morning."

Binny just pursed her lips and made that disapproving clucking noise Anne remembered from the days when her father tried to drown his problems. Then the old woman followed the maid back into the bedroom.

"I'll see about this." Anne started down the hall, only to be stopped by Letty's hand on her arm.

"Shouldn't you change first? You look awful."

Anne's hand flew to her disheveled hair, and she glanced at her stained gown. "Of course." She turned toward Letty's room.

"I can handle Robert," Letty said. "I'm not as useless as you think I am."

Anne stopped in her tracks. She sighed, and her shoulders drooped. "I never said you were useless."

"You never trust me."

Though she'd wished many times for such a change in Letty, the girl could have chosen a better moment to assert herself. Fearing the opportunity to instill a sense of responsibility in her sister wouldn't be repeated, Anne decided to go against her better judgment. Turning around, she pasted a smile on her face.

"Thank you for offering to help. If you could talk Robert into a ride or a walk in the garden, maybe—?"

"I said I would handle him."

Anne nodded. "I'll be downstairs shortly."

"Take your time." Letty shouldered by her with a swish of her perfumed skirts. "You needn't bother to come down before luncheon. Robert and I will be busy."

Anne didn't move from her stance in the center of the hall. Overwhelmed by the events of the day, she fought the urge to escape to her writing desk. At least there, she controlled the world she created. Real life had suddenly become complicated.

Binny rushed out and grabbed both of Anne's hands.

"Marvelous news. Mrs. Finch says Dunstan will live. Now hurry," she added as she pushed Anne toward Letty's room and the waiting tub of hot water. Very complicated, indeed.

Anne pulled her chair into the afternoon sunshine coming through the bedroom window and opened her book. After reading the same sentence for the third time, she slammed the cover shut. Even her own room had ceased to be a haven. How could she relax with that man in her bed?

But anywhere else in the house was worse. Her lies, though well meant, had landed her in a terrible soup. Robert had grilled her for facts about her husband and details of the so-called attack on Dunstan. All through luncheon, Letty had taunted her with supposedly fond memories of Dunstan, and she'd even managed a few insincere tears when she expressed concern over his condition. And the servants, knowing the facts and going along with the fiction for her sake, stared at her as if she'd gone beyond the eccentricities expected of a spinster.

Setting her book aside, Anne stood and rolled her shoulders, stretching her tense muscles. She walked to the bed to check on her patient. Mrs. Finch and Cleeve had bound his wrists and ankles to the bedposts to keep him from thrashing about and reopening his wounds. She checked the soft cloths to make sure they weren't too tight. Leaning over, Anne brushed the stubborn lock of hair off the unconscious man's forehead.

"Who are you?" she whispered. Half his face was swollen and discolored, but the side nearest her was undamaged. With the white bandage around his neck, and the dark dressing gown they had placed over the borrowed nightshirt, she easily imagined how devastatingly handsome he would look in elegant evening clothes.

What would it be like to waltz with him? Oh, how well she remembered the feel of his arms. Her active imagination pictured a moonlit garden path strewn with fragrant rose petals. There would be music drifting on the summer breeze. She would reach up and lay her palm along his cheek.

Surprised by the rough stubble, she drew her hand back from his face. What in the world was she doing?

She returned to her chair, and stubbornly picked up her book. Imagining herself swooning in his arms! Why, the very idea! Thank heavens she'd regained her senses. Another minute and she might have actually kissed him.

Passionate kisses were all well and good for her heroines, but that had no relevance to her life. *She* had not reacted in such a ridiculous manner the one time she'd been kissed. Of course, he was a school chum of Robert's, and she merely ten years old. If memory served her right, she'd kicked him in the shins for his effort.

Oh, she could describe the kind of kiss that tingled to one's toes and left one weak and breathless, but her research had consisted of her own vivid imagination and of reading other authors, not in experiencing passion herself. Not that she would admit that to anyone.

The stranger moaned and turned his face toward her.

Against her will, her gaze fixed on his lips. Would they be warm or cool to the touch? She stood, hugging the book to her chest. He had a lovely mouth. The bottom lip was slightly fuller than the upper, giving him a sensuous, kiss-me look even in slumber. Maybe especially in slumber. How could she know? How could she resist?

She heard the doorknob turn. Plopping back into the chair, she flipped open her book and pretended to read.

Mrs. Finch entered and crossed the room.

"I think he's waking up," Anne said.

"That's too bad." Mrs. Finch wrung her hands. "We have to get him out of here before he sees any of us."

"Aren't you overreacting? I'm sure when I explain the situation—"

"The constable is looking for him."

Anne looked at the man lying helpless on her bed.

"He's a criminal?" She'd never met a real, live miscreant, even an unconscious one, but this man resembled her vision of a dark hero more than a villain.

"No. But . . ."

Mrs. Finch motioned the coachman into the room and closed the door behind him. Harvey stood with his back against the doorjamb, twisting his cap round and round.

"Tell her what you found out in town," Mrs. Finch urged.

"His friends have offered one hundred quid for the capture of his kidnappers. Constable Wilke is determined to collect."

"But we didn't kidnap him. We saved him," Anne said.

Harvey shook his head. "That won't matter to Wilke. He's got a burr under his saddle where me and Cleeve are concerned. Been looking for some way to take his revenge since last winter, when we proved he wrongfully arrested Cleeve's brother. Wilke would love to pin this on us and collect a reward to boot."

"We'll just explain—"

"And who will back up your story?" Mrs. Finch nodded toward the stranger. "Can you guarantee he'll be able to identify his real attackers? Will he swear it wasn't Harvey and Cleeve? Can you prove you haven't kept him here against his will?" She fingered the cloth that bound his leg to the bedpost.

"That's ridiculous." Anne pushed past the housekeeper and untied the knots.

"You're too late," Mrs. Finch said. "The doctor has seen him. As soon as he puts two and two together—"

"No one would believe that I—"

"Bah, no one'll believe *you* kidnapped him," Harvey

said. "But Wilke won't be so particular about me and Cleeve. Give him a ghost of a clue, and he'll be here lickety-split. And I don't fancy a night in the lockup."

Oh, no. Her servants arrested. She'd have to tell what really happened, tell Robert about the man she'd passed off as Dunstan. If the scandal reached the London papers, Letty's chances for a successful Season would be ruined. Anne had to do something, and quickly.

"We have to move him," she said.

"I'll rig up a stretcher," Harvey volunteered.

"Where are Robert and Letty?"

"She has barricaded herself in her room with a box of bonbons and *Godey's* magazine," Mrs. Finch answered. *"He* is passed out in the library."

Anne removed her glasses and massaged the bridge of her nose. "I'd hoped Papa's weakness had bypassed Robert."

"Right now, we have a bigger problem." Mrs. Finch tilted her head toward the bed.

"Yes, of course." She would deal with her brother later. First she would have to get rid of her guest. "We'll take him back to where we found him, but we'd better wait until dark."

Could she abandon him in the middle of the road? What if no one else came along? "No," she corrected herself. "We'll take him to the inn and leave him there." She paced the room as she planned. They would need to cover their tracks. "No. We'll take him closer to London. That way, no one will recognize us."

Mrs. Finch folded her arms and tucked in her chin. "I think you're too good at this. It makes me worry about you."

Anne stifled a smile. It was rather like pulling all the strands of a novel's plot together. Using her fingers, she ticked off all the people who'd seen the man. "Shameful as it is to trick her, Binny will believe it was a nightmare.

The rest of the servants can be trusted not to say a word, can't they?"

Mrs. Finch and Harvey nodded.

"And Letty can be bribed with a new hat or some trinket."

Mrs. Finch crossed her arms. "What about the doctor? And Robert?"

Anne paced the length of the bed. "I have it! We'll announce Dunstan has died, and we'll bury him tomorrow." When she turned, she noticed Mrs. Finch's shocked expression. "Oh, for pity's sake. We're going to put rocks in a coffin and bury it in order to fool Robert."

The housekeeper let out a relieved breath. Then her brow furrowed. "Won't he be suspicious if there isn't a laying out, and a vigil?"

Anne waved off her concern. "I'll explain that it was Dunstan's last wish to buried quickly."

"What about a minister?"

"Dunstan was an atheist." Anne looked at her watch pin. "Four hours until sundown."

Harvey left to attend to his tasks immediately, but Mrs. Finch paused on her way out. She nodded toward the man on the bed. "If he stirs again, give him another dose of the laudanum tonic like the doctor prescribed."

"Is that really necessary?"

"Maybe not, but it won't hurt him. That man will be a lot less trouble asleep."

Anne hesitated, then nodded in agreement.

"Oh, Harvey said his name is Marsfield," the housekeeper called over her shoulder as she left. "The Earl of Marsfield."

She turned to stare at the wounded man. *Marsfield?* Even rusticating in the country, she'd heard of his exploits. A gambler's gambler. He'd won the infamous stick wager, a thousand pounds on which stick dropped off one side of the Tower Bridge would pass under the bridge and come out the other side first. He was a noted pugilist, one of those men who settled their debts of honor in the ring since dueling had been outlawed.

And as London's most notorious womanizer, he'd had plenty of practice in the boxing ring. His name had been paired with the most beautiful women of the *ton,* married and single, as well as foreign royalty, stage actresses, and opera singers.

The wounded man moaned and rolled his head to the side, bringing her attention back to the danger at hand.

Marsfield. Gambler, pugilist, womanizer. In *her* bed!

This wasn't the first time he'd awakened in a woman's bed, but he usually remembered more of the night before.

Marsfield had known he was in a woman's bedroom even before he'd opened his eyes. A woman's room smelled different. He sniffed again. Freshly laundered sheets. Lilac, honeysuckle, and . . . a strange herbal, medicinal scent. A quick glance around the room had told him this wasn't one of his usual assignations. Not only was the room unfamiliar, the type was all wrong.

He smoothed the sunny yellow counterpane across his chest. Swags of white eyelet draped over the tester bed. Across the room, a small gold brocade chair and dark blue footstool were pulled close to a fireplace framed in blue and white Delft tiles and flanked by two large, overly full bookcases.

A woman stepped into his line of sight. Wearing a conservative green silk dress, she didn't appear to be one of his usual companions either, but the cruel morning light had revealed his folly on the rare occasion.

She stepped closer, leaned over, and peered wide-eyed at him, as if to see if he was really awake.

Now he could see why he'd been attracted to her, though she wasn't the flamboyant type of beauty that usually caught his attention. Neat and trim, his experienced senses told him her sensuality had been tightly bound, just like her hair. Her eyes sparkled like large empress-cut emeralds. The bright sunshine behind her highlighted the outline of her pleasing figure—

Sunshine! He bolted upright with a curse.

And cursed again as the pain brought back his memory of the night before. He squelched a flicker of disappointment that he'd not had a romantic assignation with this lovely woman.

No, he'd been doing nothing as sensible as seducing a green-eyed angel. He'd acted rashly, seen a chance, and had ridden like a madman though the night on unfamiliar roads. Not one of his finer moments.

This case had him chasing phantoms. Identifying the members of the business consortium who had supplied substandard goods to the war effort was not an easy task. But those men were just as guilty of murder as if they had lined up thousands of soldiers and shot them. And they would pay, as soon as Marsfield found them. With a groan he fell back onto the pillows.

"Where am I? And how did I get here?"

She jumped back at his harsh tone. "I . . ." She cleared her throat. "We found you. In the road. Don't you remember? You were attacked by highwaymen."

Marsfield shook his head to clear it, but the fogginess lingered. He didn't recall much about the night before or the incident itself, but he was damned sure it wasn't a random act of violence. However, letting everyone believe robbers were responsible would provide a reasonable excuse and thereby avoid the sort of questions he didn't want to answer.

"There are a good number of stitches in your arm, head, and neck. Your shoulder is bruised, and you've got a goose egg on your forehead the size of a cricket ball. All in all, you're lucky to have survived."

His head felt as if it was stuffed with cotton batting. De-

spite the grogginess, he noticed she hadn't answered his
first question. Where was he? She reminded him of a bird
watching a nearby cat. She fluttered her hands, smoothing
her hair and adjusting the waist of her dress. Her gaze flit-
ted away, then back again.

Not that women staring at him was all that uncommon,
but they were usually less obvious, hiding behind a fan or
some such flirtatious nonsense. He raised his hand to his
face. If the swelling and pain were any indication, she was
most likely staring at him in morbid fascination.

"Your face is just swollen," she said as if sensing his
question. "The doctor says you'll be fine in a few weeks."

Weeks? Here with her? As appealing as the prospect
sounded, Marsfield couldn't allow this ministering angel
with the intriguing emerald eyes to seduce him into staying. He had a job to complete.

"What time is it?" he asked.

"Quarter past two."

The last he'd known the first streaks of dawn had yet to
light the sky. He'd lost most of the day, and even though he
was sure his quarry wouldn't have waited to be questioned,
he might still find a clue or two. He forced himself to roll to
a sitting position.

"I feel like I was run over by the post coach. If you would
kindly have someone fetch my horse, I must be on my way."

"Wha-what horse? We didn't see a horse when we
found you. The robbers must have stolen it, too."

Marsfield muttered another curse under his breath. If he
was lucky, Apollo would have gone looking for a bucket of
oats and found his own way back to the stable. Perhaps he
could borrow one of her horses or catch a ride to the nearest livery. Marsfield turned to sit on the edge of the bed,
automatically keeping the sheet over his scarred leg. He realized he was naked beneath the unfamiliar nightshirt. Who
had undressed him? A disturbing, yet interesting, dilemma
he unfortunately did not have time to pursue.

"My clothes, then, if you please," he requested politely.

The sight of his one bare leg seemed to send her into a panic. She paled, and one delicate hand fluttered to her throat.

"You can't leave now," she said, scurrying around the bed and grabbing a small brown bottle. "Here, take this." She held out a spoonful of noxious smelling medicine. "It will ease the pain."

He wrinkled his nose. "I'd rather have a brandy."

"If you swallow this, I'll get one for you."

Marsfield looked at her, trying to judge the worth of her promise. Her nervous habit of touching her hair had caused several tendrils of wispy golden brown curls to escape the severe bun.

As if he were a recalcitrant child, she urged, "Come on. One big swallow."

Apparent amusement sparkled in her eyes, and his natural caution melted under the radiance of her smile. He opened his mouth. After she spoon-fed him, he gently grabbed her hand.

She shook her head, and tried to back away.

Marsfield held firm. "What's your name?"

"It's not important."

"It is to me."

She pulled harder on her hand. She must have realized he wouldn't release her until she answered because she finally whispered, "Cassandra."

Sensing her fear, he let her go. He owed her a debt of honor, yet he somehow knew she would be insulted by the offer of money. What price would he put on his life, anyway? He removed the signet ring from the last finger of his right hand, and held it out to her. "You saved my life. This is a token of my pledge to repay that debt."

"Oh, no. I couldn't." She took several steps back, shaking her head.

"Yes, you can. If there is ever anything you need,

anything I can do to help, you must call on me." He tried to stand and allowed another groan to escape.

She immediately stepped to his side and helped him to sit again.

His gambit had worked as planned. Before she could move away again, he reached for her hand. Placing his ring in her palm, he curled her fingers around it. "Take it, please."

He thought he heard her agree before the gentle darkness overtook him.

"I do not approve of such goings-on."

Anne wasn't sure if old Finch, the butler, referred to the whole Dunstan charade or to their being outside in the middle of the night. He frowned at his sister, the housekeeper, who was dressed as a dairy maid. He scowled at the wagon that would transport Marsfield to a discreet inn near London. And he glared at Harvey as the coachman loaded the borrowed milk cart.

There wasn't much old Finch *did* approve of.

As soon as Harvey finished making a pallet of quilts between the two rows of milk cans, Anne climbed into the wagon and seated herself near the front.

"What are you doing, Miss?"

"You can't be thinking of going along?" the housekeeper said, her tone echoing the coachman's dismay.

Anne intended to do just that. The plan was a good one, but she wouldn't allow her loyal retainers to suffer the prospect of going to jail as kidnappers if they were discovered with Lord Marsfield in their cart. She wrapped her brown wool traveling cloak tighter around her shoulders and tucked her feet, clad in serviceable walking boots, beneath the dark material.

"I'll be fine right here. If all goes well, we'll be back before first light and no one need know of our little adventure." And if it didn't go well, she added to herself, she would be there to tell Constable Wilke she was the one responsible.

Harvey crossed his arms. "This was not part of the plan."

"Yes, it was." She leaned forward so she could see his face in the lamplight. "I just didn't tell you, that's all."

"I wouldn't have agreed to help you if I'd known."

"Exactly," she replied with a sweet smile.

Just then old Finch opened the door for the men carrying out the makeshift stretcher. They stopped at the tailgate of the cart when Harvey raised his hand.

"Hurry up," Anne urged.

The confused footmen looked from Harvey to their mistress and back.

"Yes, hurry up," Cleeve whined from the other end of the stretcher. "This bloke has big heavy feet."

"She's not going to change her mind," Mrs. Finch whispered.

"Slide him in," Harvey said, throwing his hands up in defeat. He walked to the front of the wagon muttering about strong-minded women being the bane of his existence.

Within the hour Anne felt less than victorious. Her leg was asleep from the pressure of Marsfield's head. No matter which way she turned, one shoulder or the other was gouged by the handle of a milk can. And the incessant bumping of the farm cart and clanking of the cans as they traveled the rutted back roads had given her a headache. Through it all, Harvey and Mrs. Finch chatted away as if they were on a Sunday drive.

"Now, when we get to the inn, you let me do the talking," Harvey said to Mrs. Finch. "Your disguise will be more convincing if you duck your head and take small steps. Half of acting a part is getting the posture and the walk right."

"Just listen to yourself. What would a coachman be knowing about acting?" Mrs. Finch asked.

"Oh, I trod the boards some in my prime. Even appeared on the same stage with Garrick himself. 'Course, I was only a spear carrier to his Hamlet."

"You told my brother you were a seaman."

"Aye, I was that. But I didn't care for the sea. Too much water."

"So how did you wind up at Weathersby Manor of all places?"

"Well, I was visiting an old mate from my army days—"

"You were in the army, too?" she asked, disbelief in her tone.

"Do you want the story of my vagabond youth or do you want to know how I ended up at Weathersby?" After a silent pause, he continued, "I was visiting an old mate, when I spied this woman walking out of the bakery. I asked around and nearly kept moving on because I heard she was married. When I learned missus was an honorary title, being as she was the housekeeper at a fine house, I knew then and there my wandering days were over. So I followed her home and asked her brother for a job."

Anne sank lower and pulled her shawl up around her ears. Even though the two people in the seat were decades her senior, eavesdropping on their flirtatious banter made her feel old . . . and lonely. When Marsfield snuggled deeper into her lap, she wrapped her arm over his shoulder and laid her hand along his cheek. Would she ever have another chance to lie this close to a man?

She blinked away tears. Lack of sleep and tension were making her maudlin. Yes. That was it. Once she fixed this, life would return to normal. She'd see Letty had her Season, and somehow she'd help Robert.

Shifting her weight to her left hip, she tried to move around a bit in the limited space. If she could just stretch out her legs. Her headache would fade if she could put her head down for a few minutes. She wasn't lonely. She had a full, interesting life. She was just tired and uncomfortable.

Anne awoke as the cart rattled to a stop. The tailgate slipped open, and she blinked into the sudden light. A huge man wearing a white innkeeper's apron held a lantern high overhead.

"Well, well. What have we here?" he asked with a grin.

As the fog of a most pleasant dream lifted, Anne suddenly realized she was lying next to Marsfield, her head on his chest and his arms wrapped around her. She struggled to stand but her skirts had become entangled under his legs.

"I . . . we . . ." she stammered, searching her muddled brain for any plausible explanation. Curious onlookers gathered around the milk cart. So much for discreetly abandoning Marsfield.

Her plan had not included an audience. Nor had she expected to be caught in such a compromising position. How could she have allowed herself to fall asleep in his arms?

No time to dwell on her own scandalous behavior. Her first responsibility was to get her retainers out of danger. Once the injured man was settled in a room, she could slip away. She stumbled from the cart.

"My husband is hurt," she said, reeling out the story she had concocted in case they had been stopped on the road. She nodded to Harvey and Mrs. Finch as they pushed through the crowd, ignoring their gestures to remain silent. "These kind strangers gave us a ride after we were set upon by brigands. Do you have a room where my husband and I can rest while these good Samaritans continue with their delivery?"

"Of course," the innkeeper answered.

Anne whispered to Mrs. Finch, "You two drive on. I'll

meet you around the next bend in the road as soon as I can get away."

"No."

"Yes." She gave the housekeeper a firm push toward the front of the cart. The curious crowd soon blocked her from view.

Anne turned back to the innkeeper, satisfied she'd made the best of the unexpected situation. She'd no sooner finished congratulating herself when her relief was shattered.

"Come along, Lord Marsfield," the innkeeper said as he grabbed the unconscious man under the arms and lifted. "I've got your usual room ready."

"You know him?"

"Your husband stops by here now and again with his friends." He nodded to his assistant to grab the unconscious man's feet. "Just up one flight of stairs. My wife will bring you a pot o' tea and have you cozy in no time."

Anne glanced over her shoulder as the milk cart rattled out of the yard. Luckily, her servants hadn't heard the exchange and were well away from trouble. She, however, was about to walk directly into the lion's den. Or bedroom, as it were.

The innkeeper chuckled. "The missus is going to be jolly well pleased to meet you. His nibs here is one of her favorites. She's been telling him for years that he needed a wife and a handful of children to settle him down."

Anne's knees wobbled as she followed the burly innkeeper. This was not going according to her plan. She'd plotted a neat and tidy scene, just like in one of her novels, but somehow she'd lost control of the situation.

Her only hope was that the wicked Lord Marsfield had the decency to remain asleep for a while longer.

Three

"Lord love ya," Mrs. Parkins, the innkeeper's wife, said. She clucked and tisked as she handed Anne a steaming mug of tea. "Weren't you terrified? Did you see their faces?"

Anne hadn't thought she might be asked to provide a description of the robbers. She huddled deeper into the overstuffed wing chair and shook her head. Her fear must have shown on her face, because the woman patted her shoulder.

"You're safe now, dearie." Mrs. Parkins pulled a brick from the fireplace, wrapped it in a length of flannel, and tucked it under Anne's feet. "Crime these days! I tell the mister all the time it ain't safe anymore to travel the roads at night."

"Don't you be talking her ears off," Mr. Parkins called from the back of the room.

Anne knew the innkeeper and his assistant were undressing Marsfield and putting him into bed. Even though she refused to look, her vivid imagination supplied its own details as first one boot hit the floor then another. The sounds seemed inordinately loud in the small room. By listening to Mr. Parkins's directions and the swish of cloth, she knew when Marsfield's coat, pants, and shirt had been removed.

"Why, he's already bandaged," Mr. Parkins exclaimed.

The scandalous picture of Marsfield in Anne's head, the

thrumming heat it caused in her veins, did not serve her wits well. "We . . . they—*they* had some emergency supplies in the cart. The dairyman. And his wife," she stammered. "Under the seat."

"Aye," Mrs. Parkins said, nodding sagely. "I tell the mister all the time, 'tis better to be prepared than be left high and dry without a paddle." She went to the bedside and, after a short whispered conversation, shooed the men from the room.

Anne heaved a sigh of relief. Alone at last. She bowed her head in relief.

"He'll sleep for a while."

At the sound of Mrs. Parkins's voice, Anne jerked in surprise, spilling the last bit of tea. As the older woman rounded the end of the bed, Anne covered the warm, wet spot with her hand.

"Seems to me he'll be fine with a rest and some of my stew, but I've sent one of my boys for the doctor. Just to be sure."

Anne tried to smile in response.

"What's wrong, dearie?" Mrs. Parkins's eyes narrowed and drifted downward. "Do you have special cause to worry?"

She followed the woman's gaze and saw her own hand stretched across her belly. Suddenly, she realized that Mrs. Parkins thought she was pregnant. "No! Oh, no." She lifted her hand, ready to explain, but the spot had dissipated into the dark plaid pattern. She jumped up. "It's not that. It's—"

"All in good time," Mrs. Parkins consoled. She nudged Anne back into the chair and sat down on the footstool. "His lordship is a fine figure of a man." She lowered her voice to a conspiratorial whisper. "I couldn't resist a wee look-see."

Anne leaned back and closed her eyes. What would Marsfield have said if he woke up to find Mrs. Parkins peeking under the covers? She willed her cheeks to stay pale and, with effort, swallowed the giggle that threatened.

"And quite vigorous, ahem, in his bachelor days. Not that we allow any of *those women* here. I've my three daughters to look out for, don't you know? As I always tell the mister, keep your house like you mean to live in it."

Anne nodded even though she had no idea what the woman was rambling on about. "Mrs. Parkins—"

"As I was telling his lordship the last time he was here—"

"I think I'd like to rest a little now, if you don't mind."

The older woman jumped up. "Listen to me going on. Do you need help with your stays? I was an upstairs maid before I married the mister."

"No. I'll just sit and rest my eyes until the doctor arrives. Thank you."

Mrs. Parkins threw up her hands. "I forgot all about the doctor. He always likes a bit o' warm posset when he gets here." She rushed to the door. "You just holler if you need anything."

"That won't be necessary. Thank you for all your kindness."

Mrs. Parkins waved off the heartfelt gratitude as she backed through the door and pulled it shut.

In the sudden quiet, Anne warned herself to count to ten before she made her escape. One. Two. Was Marsfield really all right? Three. She stood and laid the plaid blanket over the arm of the chair. Four. Five. What if the jouncing ride in the cart had caused further damage? She peered through the shadows at him. Six. What if she'd given him too much laudanum?

Seven. She didn't hear him breathing. She should at least check on him. Eight. Just to make sure. Her feet seemed to step toward the bed of their own accord. Nine. She wouldn't want to worry the rest of her life that she'd left him for dead.

Ten. Anne stood beside his bed.

The candle on the nightstand remained unlit, and firelight softened the purple of his bruises. Even relaxed in sleep, he exuded energy, like a sleek jungle cat prepared at all times to protect himself. Her vision of a handsome hero come to life.

What would his child look like? A little girl with his thick dark curls and enchanting clear blue eyes. She placed her hand on her stomach. But that firm chin and noble nose should be reserved for a son. Suddenly, she realized what she was doing and jammed her hand into her pocket. How long had she been woolgathering? Seconds? Minutes? She spun away from him to flee.

Before she took a step, she felt Marsfield's ring in her pocket. Her original plan had included returning it, yet in the confusion she'd almost forgotten. She turned back.

Where should she leave the ring? If she left it on the nightstand, he might not see it. She could put it in a pocket of his clothing, but it might fall out and be lost. If it was her family heirloom—not that she had any, because her father had sold everything of value—if it was *her* ring, she'd want special care taken. She'd have to put it back on his hand.

That meant she would have to first free his hand from the bedcovers. Not wanting to drop the ring, she shoved it on her thumb. Because the ring was sized for his little finger, or maybe because her hands were large for a woman, the ring exactly fit. Grasping the very edge of the cover, she lifted and folded the sheet back at his waist.

Her imagination had been right. They had removed every stitch of his clothing. Yet even her wildest dreams hadn't been equal to this close-up view. Against the stark white of the bandages on his shoulder, his skin appeared tanned, as if he worked outside without his shirt. Or was that his skin tone? Would the tan appear all the way down? She held her hands still, inches from the smooth planes of his chest, felt the heat his body generated. Her lungs began to ache, and she let out the breath she hadn't realized she'd been holding.

His hand remained hidden under the bedcovers. She could pull his arm out or . . . heaven help her . . . lower the sheet even more. Was she as brave as Mrs. Parkins? Did she dare a wee look-see of her own?

Suddenly, his arm shot out, wrapping like a steel band around her waist. He pulled her onto the bed. Her squeal of surprise as she landed sprawled across his chest caused him to chuckle. She felt the reverberations against her breasts.

Her second time in bed with a man. The same man. Only this time he was awake. With a predatory, hungry look in his eyes.

How long had he pretended sleep? Had he known she stood calf-eyed at his bedside? Oh, no. He had seen her ogling his chest. She ducked her head in mortification and pushed with all her might to break his hold on her.

"Easy, darling." Marsfield grunted when her flailing hands hit a sore spot. He kicked one leg free of the blanket and wrapped it over hers to strengthen his hold. With little difficulty, he anchored both of her hands in the small of her back with his right hand. She suddenly stopped fighting him.

"Let me go. Please."

He rotated his shoulder, testing for pain. Though he knew it wasn't as bad as earlier, he couldn't remember what *earlier* meant in this case. And there was something else . . . He looked around and recognized the familiar room. He looked at the woman in his arms and didn't have a clue who she was.

"Since Mrs. Parkins doesn't allow whores, you must be a thief." From her indignant stare, he'd obviously insulted her. Nothing was making much sense, and his usually dependable brain was as fogged as if he'd drank an entire bottle of brandy. No matter how he'd gotten into this situation, he wasn't one to let a prime opportunity pass him by. Using his free hand, he lazily traced a line down the curves of her body. She felt just right settled between his thighs.

"Though if you are a thief, I must say you've missed your calling." He chuckled again at her outraged indrawn breath. What was he supposed to do? She'd shown up in his room when he obviously had been sleeping alone.

"Let me go or I'll scream," she said through clenched teeth.

Sweeping back the hair that had fallen in her eyes, he cocked his head to one side to get a better look at her face.

"That would bring Parkins and his brood of strapping sons pounding up the stairs. For some reason, I don't think you want that." *Any more than I do,* he added to himself.

"Then let me go because you are a gentleman."

"Darling, whoever told you that will go to hell for lying."

She wiggled, trying to free her hands.

"Keep that up and you'll see just how much of a gentleman I'm not," he grumbled.

At least that had stilled her. What was wrong with him? A slip of a woman—fully clothed, mind you—put a little pressure on his cock, and he was ready to explode like an inexperienced youth. He shifted to one side.

Her movements had also caused her bodice to pull lower, giving him a good view of the creamy swells of the tops of her breasts. By lifting his head slightly, he could reach the satiny skin with his lips. And his tongue.

"Please . . . stop."

Marsfield looked up at her. Though she held her body rigid, she'd closed her eyes, tilted her head back, and was gasping shallow breaths through open lips. Such delectable lying lips. She no more wanted to stop than he did.

"Look at me." He hadn't meant it to sound like a demand, but unexpected passion roughened his voice.

She snapped her head down. For a moment he was shocked by the familiarity of her emerald eyes. No, if he'd met her before, surely he would remember. Looking deeper, he fancied he saw buried passion. But he also saw fear, uncertainty . . . and pain. He immediately released his iron hold. Yet he was no fool. He used the movement to capture her in a firm embrace. With one hand he guided her head down for a gentle kiss. Passion dictated another. And another.

Easy, old boy. One of his secrets of successful lovemaking was to let the woman set the pace.

He tilted his head for better access. She tilted hers. He parted his lips and she parted hers, like an adult version of follow the leader. He flicked her lips with the tip of his tongue. She tasted of honeyed tea, peppermint candy, and . . . and something unique. Mystery? Magic? Whatever its name, it proved a powerful aphrodisiac.

She responded by wrapping one arm around his neck. The other hand she threaded through his hair. All his warnings to himself to go slowly went up in flames when her passion ignited.

In the midst of the next deep kiss, he rolled her over. Cradling her head between his hands, he asked her name. Her eyes flew open.

"I can't just keep calling you darling, can I?" He kissed the tip of her nose. "Well?"

She looked around as if in a sudden panic. "I must go. My . . . I have someone waiting for me." She pushed with both hands on his chest.

Whoever it was, let him wait. A long time. Marsfield was willing, and confident he could change her mind. He nuzzled her neck and nibbled the sweet lobe of her delicate ear.

"A few more minutes," he whispered.

She shifted sideways to allow him better access to her neck. Oh, yes. He would make her forget whoever waited for her.

Marsfield felt the sharp blow to the side of his head. Fighting the engulfing darkness in vain, he remembered another pair of treacherous emerald eyes. Cassandra!

Be she thief, tart, or angel of mercy, she would pay for this night of perfidy.

Anne couldn't lift him, but by wiggling sideways, she managed to slip from beneath his suddenly unbearable weight. Standing, she set the candlestick back on the nightstand and straightened her clothing. How dare he . . . how dare he *maul* her like that? She looked over her shoulder at the naked man sprawled across the bed, the blanket and sheet tangled around his legs. Good heavens, even his back was muscular and attractive. The sight of all that bare skin caused a rivulet of warmth to shimmer through her insides. She had to leave.

Sounds from the hallway caused her to hesitate. The doctor and Mrs. Parkins would be coming upstairs any minute. Anne looked back to the bed.

Setting her lips in a grim line, she stomped back to the bedside. The man was a libertine and deserved the worst for taking advantage of her, but . . . deep unexpected relief coursed through her when she heard his soft snores. She refused to examine her own part in this fiasco, or how she had enjoyed, encouraged his kisses. With a growl of embarrassed frustration, she yanked the blanket free and threw it over him. Heaven forbid he should catch the ague. She tucked the blanket around his shoulders.

Marsfield was much more cooperative when unconscious.

Mrs. Parkins returned moments later with the doctor. After examining Marsfield, the doctor pronounced he would be fine with a few days' rest, though he predicted a monster of a headache in the morning. As soon as they left her alone again with Marsfield, Anne gathered her traveling cloak and bonnet from the hook by the door, and slipped away.

Only later, as the coming dawn lightened the sky and she stumbled along the rutted road to meet the dairy cart, did she allow her tears to fall. Even then she wasn't sure if they were tears of relief or regret.

Marsfield held one hand to his throbbing head while the other slid along the wall as he made his way down the steep staircase. He rounded the corner and entered the taproom. Squinting against the early morning sunshine flooding through the open door, he made his way to the bar. Dressing had been difficult, but at least the room had been fairly dark.

"Good morrow to you," Mrs. Parkins chirped. She and her husband were polishing tankards for the day's trade. "And how's your wi—?"

"I'm looking for a woman," Marsfield said. His anger and the need for quick answers made the request brusque and rude, a tone he would not normally use with old friends. He swallowed despite his dry throat. "A stranger who—"

Mrs. Parkins crossed her arms over her ample bosom and puffed out her cheeks. "I always say, if a man tends his garden at home, he needn't be buying a pig in a poke."

Shooting pain stabbed behind his eyes when he tried to decipher the meaning behind the mixed platitudes. He gave up and leaned one hand on the bar. The other arm he held out at shoulder height. "Dark blond or maybe light brown . . ."

Mrs. Parkins opened her mouth.

"This be man's work," Parkins said before she could speak. He spun her around by the shoulders and pushed her through the kitchen door. Resuming his polishing, he nodded to his guest.

"A woman—" Marsfield said.

"It may not be my place to interfere, but I've known you since ye were a lad."

"The woman—"

"Despite what you see, I am a man of the world. Sowed my wild oats I did, same as you. But there comes a time—"

The thunder of an arriving coach echoed through the taproom. Marsfield felt as if each hoof struck the back of his head.

"—the fragile flower of young womanhood—"

He leaned both elbows on the bar, rested his head in his hands, and tried to block out Parkins's babbling. All he wanted was information pertaining to the woman who'd saved his life, then nearly killed him with a candlestick. If he could just get his mouth and his pounding brain to co-operate. "What I need—"

"Aye, son. We all have needs, but marriage is—"

The commotion of several men entering the taproom saved Marsfield from further confusion. *Saved* being a relative term due to the additional pain caused by the noise reverberating between his ears. Unable to hold back a moan, he closed his eyes. He didn't know whether he wanted to kill her or kiss her, but at this rate, he'd never catch up with Cassandra.

"Marsfield!"

He turned and squinted at the last two people he wanted to see this morning, Anthony Burke and Davis Preston, agents-in-training and his erstwhile assistants. Why

Whitehall assumed he needed them on this case was beyond him. Do his footwork, indeed. He hadn't been out of service for *that* long. The last thing he needed was two overeager young pups who were more hindrance than help.

"Can't imagine how you found your way here," Burke said. He walked over to stand at the bar. "We thought F—" His breath came out in a *woof* as Marsfield jabbed him in the side.

Preston leaned one arm on the bar at his other side. "We thought you'd been kidnapped, drugged, interrogated," he whispered. Though he looked around the room as if checking to be sure he wasn't overheard, he seemed thrilled at the prospect of the imagined mayhem.

Marsfield turned around and, resting his elbows on the bar, pressed his throbbing temples with his fingertips. Typical young aristocrats. They acted as if innkeepers and servants were just part of the furniture. If these two were ever going to be of any real service to the government, they had a lot to learn. Preferably from an experienced agent other than him.

"Unfortunately, we were forced to leave the task of locating you to the local constabulary," Preston said, lowering his voice.

"Preston and I are meeting Captain Jones at the Buccaneer's Rest at noon." Burke offered the information with a smile, like a small boy offering a dandelion bouquet to his nanny.

Marsfield stifled a frustrated groan. What did these boys know about buying intelligence from a scurvy reprobate in a seedy waterfront hellhole? He could just picture them strolling into the disreputable tavern, plopping a bag of coins on the table, and leaning forward with eager faces, oblivious to the fact that anyone in the place would kill them for their boots alone.

Damn. He hated playing nursemaid. Yet he knew from

his experience of the last few weeks he wouldn't be able to talk them out of the meeting. He'd have to go along to save the two young fools from their own folly. Marsfield pushed himself upright and headed for the carriage. "Let's go."

He consoled himself with the knowledge he'd followed cold trails before. Cassandra would not escape him this easily.

Four

October
London

Anne paced an erratic path in Blackthorne's small office as she waited impatiently for her editor to finish reading. Her black crepe skirts brushed piles of manuscripts and stacks of books, stirring up dust. The musty paper odor mixed with the sharp smell of ink from the presses in the back room.

She flipped the bothersome widow's veiling over her shoulder. Oh, she had regretted her lies and the mock funeral more times than she could count. She'd proven quite good at playacting with long sad sighs and faraway stares whenever Robert was in the room. And she'd avoided his probing questions about her late husband by hiding her face and breaking onto loud choking sobs. But her acting skills had cost her. Robert had believed the fiction of Dunstan's death so well, she'd been forced to rusticate in these stupid widow's weeds for six whole months before she convinced him to bring her and Letty to London.

The six-month mourning period required for a sister-in-law had postponed Letty's Season, but now the girl was *Season-ing* with a vengeance. Even if Anne, still in her year of full mourning, couldn't attend dances and balls with Letty, there was shopping, teas, social calls, shopping, carriage rides in Hyde Park, shopping. It had taken three weeks for Anne to escape her demanding sister in order to meet with her publisher.

Anne's latest manuscript, *Gypsy Princess,* finished over the long boring summer, had earned enough to provide her sister a reasonable wardrobe. Scant weeks into the Little Season and already Letty was being hailed as one of the year's beauties. The flood of invitations necessitated additional trips to the dressmakers and milliners and glovers and boot makers. Blackthorne simply had to buy *Lucinda's Dishonor,* written and ready to go to print. It all boiled down to that one pivotal scene he had not liked the first time she'd submitted the book.

Blackthorne flipped the last page, looked up at her with a frown, and shook his head. "It's still not right," he said. "Actually, not even close."

How could a simple description sway his decision?

"But Mr. Blackthorne, my readers don't know what the inside of a gaming hall looks like."

"Never underestimate your readers," Blackthorne said.

"What if I change it again? Make it right. Then will you publish my manuscript?"

Blackthorne leaned back in his chair, causing his rotund belly to protrude above his desk. He stroked his snow-white beard and scowled at the ceiling. His Father Christmas appearance had led her to trust him with her first scribblings, but behind that cherubic facade lay a sharp mind and an autocratic temper.

His chair creaked and thumped as he sat forward to return her stare. "Yes. *If* you can present that scene with authority and realism, I think the rest of the book is adequate."

Anne ignored the word adequate and pulled a chair to the side of his desk. After seating herself, she opened her reticule and pulled out a pad and pencil. "Now, if you would please describe the inside of a gaming hall to me, I'll bring you the edited pages next week."

"Me?"

"Of course."

"Now listen here, young woman. I neither frequent such places, nor would I subject your innocence to a graphic recitation of the details if I did. What kind of man do you take me for?"

She gritted her teeth and counted to ten before responding. "If you haven't been there, how can you judge the accuracy of my description?"

Blackthorne shifted his gaze around the room. "I have it on good authority."

"Excellent. Give me the name of your expert, and I'll question him."

"I should say not. It's bad enough that I allowed you to talk me into publishing the work of a gently bred young woman in the first place. I refuse to be a party to an interview that would mean the total destruction of your reputation. Why, the very idea!"

She gripped her pencil until it broke in half. In the past few years, living in the country and making her own decisions, she'd almost forgotten the illogical standards men referred to as the voice of reason.

"Then how am I to know what changes to make?"

Blackthorne stood, signaling the end of the meeting. "My conscience is clear in refusing you the necessary information."

Anne also stood.

"However, if you obtain the details on your own . . ." He tipped his palms up and shrugged his shoulders.

As she stormed out of his office, she noticed the grin on the skinny, pimple-faced youth who acted as Blackthorne's secretary. He'd probably heard every word through the open door. He probably agreed with every bit of the old man's sanctimonious blather. She yanked the concealing veil over her face. Men! Unseen now, she stuck out her tongue at him before she walked through the outer door.

She climbed into the waiting carriage so quickly, the footman had no time to assist her. Her ire lasted halfway to Grosvenor Square. "I'll show him," she fumed.

"Show who? What?"

Anne had been so wound up in her anger, she'd forgotten poor Binny, left asleep during the appointment.

"Nothing. I was just thinking aloud."

Binny attempted to cover a wide yawn. "I do so love a nap in the carriage. Are we having a nice drive?"

"Just lovely," she said, forcing pleasantness into her voice. It took exactly two minutes for Binny's head to fall forward, cushioned by her several chins and frothy lace jabot.

Anne twisted her black lace handkerchief into a knot. Oh, yes. She would show Blackthorne she could get the information without his help. But how? Obviously, she'd have to interview someone who frequented a gaming hall—or gaming hell, as some referred to them.

Lord Marsfield came immediately to mind. His saturnine visage popped into her head easily, as it had so many times over the past six months. He most certainly would know the information she needed. And he did owe her for saving his life.

But Marsfield had awakened strange unsettling feelings in her, feelings that had taken months to relegate to the dark of night and her dreams. What if he remembered her? No, she couldn't risk seeing him again.

She would have to think of another source for the needed information. Robert? Out of the question. He, unfortunately, knew the details all too well, but he would demand to know the reason why she dared ask such preposterous questions.

Harvey? He'd led a varied life before coming to Weathersby. When the carriage stopped for traffic, she tapped twice on the roof with the tip of her closed parasol.

The little trapdoor beside the driver's seat slid open. "Yes, Miss?"

"Harvey, have you ever visited one of the gentleman's gaming halls?" she whispered, so as not to awaken Binny.

He gave her a quizzical look before answering in the negative. "I never had the blunt."

"Thank you. Drive on."

He gave her another strange look before disappearing from her sight. The carriage lurched forward.

She searched her brain for other possible sources. She had a few friends from her time in London years ago. Did any of them have brothers? She gave up that line of inquiry as useless, because she could hardly renew a tenuous relationship and immediately drop her scandalous questions. Yet the pressing need for money did create a certain urgency.

It was a sad commentary on her life, but she knew no more than a handful of men. She held up her hand. Robert. Harvey. She bent down two fingers. Cleeve? Too young. Another finger down. Old Finch? That possibility was laughable. That left her thumb. She dug into her reticule, pulled out the ring and placed it on her thumb, just as she had that night in the inn.

Marsfield.

The now familiar ruby-eyed eagle on the elaborate crest stared back at her. Despite all her self-admonitions to return the ring anonymously, she'd kept it. Kept it close to her at all times.

Marsfield was the answer. The only answer. She must have known all along she would one day return his ring to him in person, that she would take him up on his pledge to repay his debt. Had she secretly hoped for an excuse to see him again? Without further useless soul searching, she tapped on the roof to give the coachman Marsfield's direction.

Marsfield stuck the cigar in his mouth and leaned over the edge of the large copper tub to pour another finger of brandy into his glass. Settling back into the warm cocoon, he rested his head on the high curved back. Another hour of this and his aching body might forgive him for the past three weeks of punishment. Days in the saddle, nights on the hard ground, unpalatable food, worse drink. And for what? He raised his glass and let the smooth smoky flavor wash away the sensory memory of rotgut whiskey. A wild goose chase, that's what.

First months on the continent, working his old underground contacts for information, and now this. Was it supposed to have been some kind of test? Oh, the director was devious, all right. As the head of covert operations at Whitehall, he had no official title and no official duties, but his invisible web reached wide. Was the old spider testing Marsfield's assistants? Or was it to see if Marsfield himself could still come up to snuff?

No matter the reason, he had thrown himself into his work to blot out the frustration caused by his six-month search for the elusive Cassandra. If it hadn't been for the fact that Mr. and Mrs. Parkins had seen her, talked to her, believed she was his wife, even Marsfield would have started to believe she was a figment of his imagination.

He closed his eyes and instructed his body to relax. Later, after a dinner of his favorite foods, cooked to his exacting specifications, he would try to puzzle out the director's motives. Marsfield tried to ignore the buzz of conversation off to his left, but the boys had started another of their interminable inane arguments.

"Ten pounds says the Elgin marbles are the most popular exhibit."

"Save your money, Burke. I just told you the British Museum itself says the Egyptian Room is the most visited," Preston said.

"That doesn't mean everyone likes it best."

"Don't you lads have homes?" Marsfield sat up and glared toward the tiled window seat, where the two young bloods flipped cards into a hat placed between them. Damn it all. When he'd reconstructed this room in the style of a Roman bath, he hadn't intended to entertain in it—at least not this sort of company.

"Of course we do," Preston answered. His innocent expression implied he'd totally missed Marsfield's sarcasm.

"Then go home." Marsfield enunciated clearly, as if speaking to the dimwitted.

Burke pulled his inordinately large pocket watch out of his vest pocket. When he flipped open the top, the chimes played *God Save the Queen*. "Can't. Not yet. Only half past two o'clock."

"It's not that we're loath to leave your witty conversation, old boy—"

Marsfield settled back into the tub with resignation. As long as the steamy water was having the desired effect on the cramped muscles of his left leg, he didn't suppose it mattered if the inane chattering set his teeth on edge.

"If we arrive home too soon, we'll be coerced into escorting our respective sisters to whatever intolerable entertainment is the *affaire du jour*," Preston concluded.

"Lady Asterbule's musicale," Burke supplied.

"How do you remember things like that?" Preston asked.

The other young man shrugged. "Just do."

"So go," Marsfield muttered. "Make your mothers happy. Dance with a pretty girl. Make *her* mother happy."

"Timothy Asterbule did mention that one of the new crop has the face of an angel," Burke said. "He seems quite smitten with her blond hair and blue eyes. And the dimple in her chin."

"Timothy is smitten at least three times each Season," Preston snorted.

"Must admit, he does have an eye for the crème de la crème."

"Maybe we should see this paragon for ourselves."

"Good idea," Marsfield grumbled. Now maybe he could have some quiet. The boys gathered their hats and gloves and left arguing about Timothy Asterbule's qualifications as a judge of beauty. He wondered if he'd even been invited to Lady Asterbule's musicale. Of course he had. The Earl of Marsfield was invited everywhere. But then, of course, everyone hoped he would refuse.

A bark of rueful laughter escaped before he settled back to relax. He'd spent far too long blackening his reputation to expect society to forget in the span of a few short years.

The soft click of the door latch brought him to full awareness, even though he didn't betray it with so much as a flicker of an eyelash. He recognized the near silent tread and opened one eye. "What is it, Gaines?"

The taciturn butler held out a silver tray with a letter on it. "Sorry to disturb you, milord. The delivery boy said it was urgent."

Marsfield recognized the seal and opened the letter. In bold thick strokes of the pen, the director came right to the point, requesting a meeting this evening. At Rose's Garden, London's most elite brothel, of all places. Who knew the old spider had a sense of humor?

Was this most recent *summons*—for it could be called nothing else—another test? Marsfield glanced at the fireplace to be sure the note had burned completely. A test of his ability to blend unobtrusively into any environment. Is that why the director chose a brothel?

Blending in went beyond appropriate clothing, speech, and manners. It meant having a plausible and apparent reason for being in the place one wished to infiltrate. A tradesman could enter an unfamiliar pub if his cart broke down across the street. A pickpocket could cross into another territory if coppers were chasing him. He'd used both ruses effectively in the past.

What plausible scenario could he use? An interesting puzzle. Why would a man, namely himself, who'd just last session argued in the House of Lords for the closing of all brothels within the city limits, attend one of the premier parlor houses? Why, indeed?

Sure to meet acquaintances, Marsfield would need a cover story adequate to convince even his critics in the House. There were some who claimed his reformation a sham, a pretense to curry favor with the mothers of eligible females.

True, the idea of marriage and a family didn't give him the disgust it once had. However, he wasn't one to shape his principles on the nattering of old women. In fact, he would readily admit to enjoying a romp with a willing woman, no strings attached. But he'd seen the depraved extent jaded tastes could stoop to, seen the damage done to innocent young lives.

Wasn't that why he'd volunteered for this job? He would have preferred a duel to settle the score, but this way he would also prove he could still function as an agent. Even if he'd intended to retire from the service, it still grated that he'd been cashiered due to his injury. Damn, he needed another drink.

"No reply, Gaines. Thank you." He reached for the bottle. Because Gaines did not exit, he asked, "Is there something else?"

"Yes, sir. You have a caller." He again held out his tray, a lady's white calling card centered on the shiny surface.

Marsfield hid a smile as he stated the obvious, "I'm not currently receiving."

"The widow is quite insistent, sir."

"Well, I don't intend to leave this bath until dinner, if then. Her petition for whatever charity she's sponsoring will have to wait until another day."

Gaines raised an eyebrow in response. "She asked me to give you this." He held out a thimble-sized, golden object between his thumb and forefinger. "I will tender your regrets. Sir."

There was just the slightest disapproving hesitation before the word *sir.* Gaines dropped the object with a dramatic flourish and turned to leave.

Just before it plopped into his bath water, Marsfield recognized his family crest on the piece of jewelry.

"No! Wait." Marsfield plunged his hands into the water, forgetting his cigar until the lit end fizzled out. "Damn." He tossed the soaked stub away and continued searching beneath the surface. If that was what he thought it was . . .

The dimensions of the tub, though large by any standard, did not leave a lot of room for maneuvering his long legs. He touched the object, but it skittered away in the swirling watery tempest.

If the object was really his ring, that could mean only one thing.

"Aha!" He cornered the object with his big toe. As soon as he held it in his hand, he knew. Surging to a standing position, he raised his fist high in triumph. "My ring." He turned to Gaines. "Show the woman in."

Gaines pulled himself even straighter, if that were possible. "Sir?"

Marsfield looked around. He stood stark naked in his tub with most of the water splashed outside its confines. He lowered his arm and cleared his throat.

"Into the parlor. Please show the woman into the parlor." He stepped out of the tub as if his irrational actions had not taken place. "And tell her I'll join her shortly."

"Very good, sir." Gaines bowed and retreated without cracking a smile.

Marsfield wrapped a towel around his waist and rushed to get dressed. Cassandra. The woman who had haunted his dreams. Unbelievable. After all his searching for her, Cassandra had come to him. He stopped at the door of his dressing room. It suddenly occurred to him to wonder why.

* * *

Anne sat on the very edge of the sofa, her back properly ramrod straight, her gloved hands folded neatly in her lap. Only the gentle tapping of one foot betrayed her nervousness.

"May I serve you a refreshment?" the butler asked.

Not wanting to remove her concealing veil or fuss with the awkward chore of drinking tea with it on, she declined. "Thank you just the same."

"Very well, madame. His lordship will join you shortly." He backed through the massive double doors, bowing and pulling them closed in one smooth motion.

"Why did you go and do that?" Binny said. "I could use a spot o' tea to brighten me up." She looked around the elegantly appointed parlor. "I'll bet they serve tasty biscuits. Maybe even chocolate ones?" she added, hope evident in her voice.

Any other time and place, Anne would have indulged her old nursemaid. But not here, not when Marsfield could arrive any minute. She needed Binny to do her usual poor chaperon act and fall asleep.

"My business with Lord Marsfield will only take a few minutes. You just relax."

Binny continued her examination of parlor furnishings. "Excellent paintings. Tasteful bric-a-brac." She wiggled deeper in the overstuffed wing chair. "Comfortable. Yes, I'm quite comfortable here."

Anne crossed her fingers and remained silent.

"No restless spirits," Binny mumbled. "Safe. Safe," she said with a sigh as her head drifted toward the padded wing of the chair.

As the ormolu clock on the mantel ticked the minutes away, Anne wound the strings of her reticule around her fingers, then unwound them. Almost six months had passed since she had seen him. Of all the ways she'd dreamed of meeting him again, she'd never imagined she'd be hiding her identity behind dowdy widow's weeds.

Would he even remember giving her the ring, promising a favor in return? Wind the strings. Unwind the strings. What could be taking him so long? She wanted to see him, yet at the same time she wanted to run out the door. Once this interview was over, once she had the information she needed on the gaming hall, she'd have no reason ever to see him again. Her stomach clenched tight as the doors whispered open. She stood and turned to face Marsfield.

His presence filled the room. Though dressed casually in a midnight blue coat, blue and gold striped waistcoat, buff trousers, and high Hessian boots, he looked elegant. On any other man, the complex knot of his ascot would look foppish. On Marsfield it accented his virility.

If she'd thought him handsome before, without the bruises and swelling he was devastating. He'd been out in the sun without a hat, his tanned skin at odds with the ashen face she remembered so well from their first meeting.

But the stunned expression was the same: As if he didn't recognize her, didn't have the vaguest idea why she was in the same room with him.

"Lord Marsfield," she said with a slight nod.

He held up the ring for a moment before placing it back on his finger. "I presume we've met before, but you have me at a disadvantage."

He had forgotten her. All for the better, she decided. She gathered her wits, deciding to deal with her disappointment later.

"Please, may we sit?" she asked, motioning to the two Queen Anne chairs at the far side of the room.

Marsfield glanced at the sleeping chaperon and seemed to understand her intent. He led the way and held a chair for her. Once she was seated, he sat facing her across an empty chessboard. So close she noticed the damp ends of hair curling over his pristine linen. So close she smelled the soapy clean fragrance of his recent bath. She found it easier to concentrate if she stared at a spot beyond his right ear.

He seemed willing to let her speak first, though his curiosity was obvious as he tried to peer though her veil. Since there was no point in inane trivialities, she decided on the direct approach.

"I have returned your ring in order to ask for the promised favor."

She sneaked a quick peek at his face. He nodded. Calm as could be, as if this sort of thing happened to him every day. She felt the piercing warmth of his gaze and averted her eyes. Blood rushed to her cheeks. Thank heaven the heavy veil shielded her.

"Perhaps we should start with your name and how you came to be in possession of my ring." He smiled, exhibiting indulgence and forbearance, as if she were a child asking for a piece of licorice.

A jolt of irritation stiffened her spine. After all, he was the one who had pledged his gratitude, not her. "My name is Elizabeth Gordon," Anne said, assuming her aunt's name as she'd planned and assuming her haughty mien for good measure. "Lady Decklesmoor to you, you impertinent pup," she added.

He dipped his head in acknowledgment, yet remained calm, his manners impeccable.

She knew with sudden certainty that this man would no more describe a gaming hell to her than he . . . than he would fly to the moon. Yet she needed to sell *Lucinda's Dishonor,* and without his help she would never be able to complete the book to Blackthorne's satisfaction. "You gave me the ring."

"*I* did?"

"Yes. For saving your life." She cautioned herself to

stay as close to the truth as possible. "We found you injured and lying in the road. We carted you home and had
the doctor patch you up. Then, because I am a widow living alone, we installed you at an inn to recover."

"You said *we*. Does the name Cassandra mean anything
to you?"

Her heart sang. He remembered her after all. She stored
that gem away to examine later. Just now she had to concentrate. She nodded toward her sleeping chaperon. "Mrs.
Edwina Binns is my companion. *We* found you."

He twisted the ring around and around his little finger.
"And Cassandra?" he insisted without looking up.

"Ah . . . you mentioned that name several times in your
delirium, as I recall. I assumed she was a . . . someone of
your acquaintance. By the references you made, that is.
You were quite feverish."

Marsfield sat back and shook his head as if shaking off
his reverie. "Well, delirium and fever being what they are,
I guess I can't expect my memory of the time to make
sense."

"Most certainly not." She smothered a pang of disappointment that he could dismiss their meeting with such a
cavalier attitude. She hadn't been able to do the same.

"Do you suppose the innkeeper and his wife were also
feverish?" he asked.

Lord help her, she'd forgotten all about them. She
should have realized he would have asked them questions
the following morning. Her brain whirled like a carousel
to find a plausible explanation.

"I remember meeting Mr. Parkins for a few moments.
And dear Mrs. Parkins insisted on bringing me a cup of
tea. Nice woman, but she couldn't seem to say a straight
sentence. Quite confusing. Is she addlepated or just scat-
terbrained?" Anne said a silent apology to Mrs. Parkins,
because she had liked the woman.

Marsfield chuckled. "I've had a few conversations with

her myself where I wasn't sure we were discussing the same topic."

"Exactly. And I specifically didn't mention my name. My reputation was at stake, as I'm sure you understand. A widow must be above reproach."

He sat quietly for a few moments. "What color is your hair?" he asked suddenly.

Anne pictured her Aunt Elizabeth. "Brown," she said without hesitation. "Well, it was dark brown when I was younger. I must admit a little gray can be expected with age."

"You mentioned a favor."

She breathed a sigh of relief. He had believed her lies, finally. Yet she hesitated. So much depended on her success. Interviewing a witness wasn't nearly as effective as actually seeing a place with her own eyes, immersing herself in the sounds and smells. What if he never even noticed the kind of details she needed?

Suddenly, a bold and daring scheme popped into her head. She presented the plan to Marsfield before she had a chance to talk herself out of it. "My . . . nephew has recently exhibited an intense interest in gambling. So much so that I fear the somewhat limited Decklesmoor inheritance is in jeopardy. Therefore, I'd like you to show him around a gaming hall."

His bark of laughter startled her. He clapped a hand over his mouth when she shushed him. They both looked toward Binny, but she only snuggled deeper into the cushions without waking.

"Isn't that rather like putting the lamb in the wolf's den to show him where the danger lies?" He smiled, and it reached all the way to his eyes.

She focused on the spot over his shoulder again and forced herself to breathe normally. "Not at all," she replied after a moment. "If the lamb had a wise and powerful ram at his side to *show* him the dangers without putting him *in* danger, then the lamb would learn the ways of the wolf without risk."

"I'm not sure I like being compared to an old, smelly ram."

"It was your metaphor."

He nodded acknowledgment of her riposte. "What if I would rather be the wolf?"

"The wolf is also offensive."

Marsfield smiled. "Not all women would find a wolf so."

Aware their verbal jousting had reached a new level, she nodded. "And, it is my understanding, that a . . . shall we say, a less than discriminating female might be considered by some to be lacking in intelligence and therefore not entirely to blame for that singular lapse in judgment."

"Choosing a mate is rarely a matter of intelligence."

"I am forced to agree with your observation."

Marsfield sat back with a grin of triumph.

"However," she continued, "common behavior is rarely considered an achievement."

He waved at the chessboard. "Do you play?"

"Why?" she responded, unsure of where the sudden shift in topics was headed.

He stared at her with narrowed eyes. "Perhaps we shall engage in a game one day. For some reason I think you play rather well." He slapped his thigh as if that had clinched his acceptance. "Good. Then I shall do as you request."

Anne stood. "Thank you." She pulled one of her aunt's cards from her reticule as she walked to the nearby secretary. "This is my direction," she said as she scribbled the address on the back. "I appreciate—"

"I shall call for him this evening at nine o'clock."

"Tonight?" she squeaked as she whirled around to face him. When she'd hatched this plan only moments ago, she'd hadn't thought about how much work it would take to disguise herself as a boy. She shook her head. She needed clothes, and—

"It will have to be tonight," he said, voice firm with authority. "For whom shall I ask?"

He stepped to her side, and she was forced to look up at him. He seemed much taller and broader than she remembered, but then of course she'd never stood so close to him. Lain next to him in her bed, on him, under him—

"What?" She blinked as she tried to get back into the thread of his conversation.

"When I call? On whom should I say I'm calling?"

"Ask for An—" She caught herself and coughed to cover her slip of the tongue. "Andrew. My nephew. That's his name. Andrew. My nephew."

"Very well." Bowing with old-fashioned courtesy, he brushed his lips across her knuckles.

Even through her gloves, a frisson of electricity sizzled from her hand straight up her arm. She jerked away and hurried to the parlor door. Whipping it open, she'd gone several steps before she remembered Binny. Turning back, she roused the older woman, grabbed her firmly under the arm, and marched her outside before she had time to truly awaken.

Marsfield stood at the window and watched the carriage pull away, disappointment a sour taste at the back of his throat.

Expecting Cassandra, he'd been shocked by the woman's attire, until he remembered Gaines had referred to his guest as a widow. Yet he'd held out the faint, foolish hope that the widow and his dream woman would be one and the same.

But the Dowager Decklesmoor was much older than Cassandra, a woman sure of her place and her importance. She also seemed taller than Cassandra, though he couldn't be sure. It was just an impression. Cassandra had fit his body exactly, and since no other woman had ever met that criteria as well, he had no height to make a comparative judgment.

It was painfully obvious the woman he sought was a figment of . . . of what? His deepest needs? His secret desires? Marsfield scoffed at his own fanciful musings. Lady Decklesmoor had been right. He had been delirious.

Then why had he sat there and let her charm him with her wit? For all her stiffness, he'd enjoyed the woman's sharp tongue and conversational banter. But widows in mourning held no appeal for him. Certainly not.

However, he had been obliged by his debt of honor to agree to her request, as ridiculous as it might be. At least it gave him the solution to one of his problems. The formidable dowager Lady Decklesmoor's nephew was the perfect cover for his meeting with the director that evening. Maybe it wasn't to the letter of his agreement with her, but Marsfield was willing to wager the nephew would gladly give up gaming in favor of the other attractions Rose's Garden offered.

Five

"Cut it off."

"Oh, no, miss. I haven't got the heart."

Anne looked in the mirror. Mrs. Finch held the long braid of hair in one hand and a huge pair of scissors in the other. Unshed tears glittered in the older woman's eyes.

"I don't see why you can't send Cleeve to the gaming hall like Harvey suggested," Mrs. Finch said.

"We've already established Cleeve doesn't know how to play cards. If the situation comes up, I can at least hold my own at whist." No offense meant, but it would take more than a few hours of gaming lessons to pass Cleeve off as a young gentleman.

"You could teach him. Do this a few weeks from now."

Months would be more likely, and she didn't have the luxury of time. She needed to get the edited pages to Mr. Blackthorne as soon as possible. With typesetting, printing, and binding, it would seem like forever until she started seeing any revenue as it was. The emergency fund she'd spent years building pound by pound had slipped like water through her fingers into the waiting sponge of London merchants. Besides, there was no guarantee Cleeve would be a reliable resource for the kind of details she needed to write the scene. No, she must do this herself.

"Everything will be fine," she assured her servant. "It's only hair, and it will grow back. Now, please hurry. We have so much to do, and it's already near eight."

She took a deep breath as Mrs. Finch applied her shears to the braid. Anne's head suddenly felt so light she almost fainted. Not from the shock of seeing her hair cut, but because the binding around her breasts restricted her breathing more than the tightest corset. She grabbed the edge of the dressing table as an anchor and managed to keep her head upright.

"Just a few more snips," Mrs. Finch said, sniffling.

Anne swiped her brush a few times through the short mass, even more unruly now that the weight of the long braid had been removed. Turning left and right, she studied her reflection. "Thank you, Mrs. Finch."

The housekeeper wiped her eyes with her apron. "I can't believe I cut your beautiful hair."

Letty walked up behind Anne and held out the coat she'd altered. "You look ridiculous."

Anne smiled at her sister's reflection. "Well, you'd better hope this disguise fools Lord Marsfield, or you won't have that fancy costume you want for the masquerade."

Flouncing over to sit on the bed, Letty stuck out her bottom lip in a pout. "For whatever good it will do. I never have any fun. I can't dance because we're in mourning for Dunstan, and Robert always makes me leave early because he has other plans."

Anne struggled into the coat. Letty had been prattling on the same subject for the last two hours. If they hadn't needed her additional skill with the needle to complete the alterations of Robert's clothes in time, Anne would have sent the girl away.

"And don't tell me again that I can always take Binny." Letty stuck out her lip in a pout.

Anne walked to the cheval mirror and adjusted the cuffs Letty had just shortened. "Not too bad," she said, turning a full circle. "Not bad at all."

Letty sat up. "Except you still walk like a girl and stand like a girl. This is never going to work."

Anne struck a pose with one knee cocked and a fist on her hip. Wearing pants felt strange, but liberating rather than inhibiting. Probably because the entire outfit, including smallclothes, weighed less than one of her petticoats with its yards of material.

"Harvey is going to give me some of his acting tips. Mrs. Finch, please tell him to meet us in the library."

The housekeeper, still sniffling, nodded and left.

"If you had to steal Robert's clothes, you should have chosen something more fashionable," Letty said.

"It's not as if I'm going to Almack's." Anne fussed with the cravat. "Besides, I think he would have noticed if one of his new coats had gone missing. Gads, how do you tie one of these bloody things?"

"At least you're beginning to talk like Robert." Letty joined her sister. Slapping Anne's hands away, she tied the cravat into a fancy knot.

"Where did you learn to do that?"

Letty shrugged. "Last night Budgie Willingham described his knot to me in detail." She rolled her eyes. "His idea of entertaining conversation."

"Well, I thank Budgie, and you for listening to him." She looked in the mirror, patted the knot, and turned to face Letty. "Chin up. Your six months of mourning will be over in a few days, and then you'll be allowed to dance, and you'll have a beautiful costume for the masquerade ball—while I still have another six months of wearing that hateful black, and then another year of half mourning."

"If you would just tell Robert the truth, you could be my chaperon instead of him."

"You know that's impossible. And I'm holding you to your promise not tell him."

"But he's embarrassing. He stumbles and slurs and makes a fool of himself."

Anne bit her lip. She should be able to do more for

Robert, but she didn't know exactly what she could do to help him.

"He'll come around when he sees the error of his ways," she said to Letty in a reassuring tone.

Except she wasn't sure he ever would. Their father had drank and gambled away a fortune, and nothing she had ever said to him had made a difference. All she could do was try to make up for his deficit. Reminding herself that she could only work on one problem at a time, she forced a smile. "Why don't you go ahead and dress for your evening, dear? Where are you off to tonight?"

"Lady Asterbule's musicale."

"That sounds like an interesting evening."

Letty laughed. "Not as interesting as yours."

"This is serious research. There are things a writer can only describe from experience."

"What if Robert recognizes Marsfield as the husband you supposedly buried?"

"He won't. Robert saw him for only a few minutes, and Marsfield's face was swollen and covered with blood. Believe me, he looks far different now." Anne remembered with a thrill the handsome man as he had looked in his parlor.

"I can tell from the sparkle in your eye you're looking forward to this evening."

"Nonsense. I'm a respectable, responsible person. I'm doing this in order to have money for your wardrobe."

"You can't fool me. At least be honest with yourself. Inside all that stiff binding, you're dying for a little adventure."

Anne pondered Letty's words as she gathered her top hat, gloves, and cane. Where had her sister gotten such a notion?

She looked into the mirror once more. Tonight plain ordinary Anne Weathersby would visit a gaming hall in the company of a wicked, handsome man. Just the thought of seeing Marsfield again caused a shiver of anticipation. How well she remembered that night in the inn—the strength of his arms, the feel of his lips. She gave herself a stern glare.

He'll not be kissing you tonight, you silly goose. So just get that out of your head.

But the vivid memory of Marsfield's searing kisses would not go.

Marsfield stifled a huge yawn and glanced at the clock on the mantle. Eight-thirty, and he was ready to call it a night. He looked at his stocking feet, propped on another chair. The *ton* would laugh to see him now, sitting here by the fire like a gouty old man rather than out on the town as any disreputable thirty-three-year-old rake should be. Nowadays he received more satisfaction from a well-worded appeal to the House than betting on a winning horse.

Closing his book, he set it aside. He wasn't old. He was weary. The boys thought it fashionable to ape his blasé attitude, but in truth, his ennui went soul deep. There was very little he'd not already done or seen. At this point in his life, he wished he could forget many of the things he'd seen, forget a few of the things he'd done that he was less than proud to claim.

Damn. He was getting maudlin.

He stood and yanked on the bellpull. At least this evening's diversion would get him out of the house and maybe into a better frame of mind.

"Kirby," he yelled for his valet. Where was he?

The little man skidded around the door, holding on to the frame. "Aye, Cap'n," he said between gasps.

Marsfield pursed his lips together to keep from smiling as the valet sank dramatically onto the settee, one hand on his heart. Even though Kirby managed the wardrobe with proper care, he'd never mastered the expected respectful behavior of a valet. "If you were at your post, you wouldn't have to run up three flights of stairs."

Kirby sat up. His large black mustache quivered.

Marsfield knew what that meant. Kirby had a secret and was dying to spill it. Marsfield sighed. He knew more household gossip than any other peer in London because he listened out of courtesy to the little man who had saved his life. And he had to admit, amid the dregs there was sometimes a golden kernel that had helped his previous investigations. Servants knew more than anyone gave them credit for. Kirby must have spent the afternoon in the pub frequented by the other valets in the city.

"Out with the news," Marsfield said with a stern look that fooled neither of them.

Kirby bustled around the room laying out shoes, tie, coat and other accessories. "Lady Asterbule is expecting her dear boy to snag an heiress this Season."

Marsfield turned this way and that as he was helped into his attire. Kirby needed no encouragement to continue.

"But 'dear boy' is infatuated with a simple country miss. Very mysterious, that. The beauty seems to have come out of nowhere. Only rumors about her portion, mind you, but they've put up in Grosvenor Square—you know, that house that sat empty for ages. The servants are uncommonly tight-lipped, suspicious in itself. We figure a lease, but even that would take a full pocket. Beauty and money. 'Dear boy' will have to move fast to catch this one."

Marsfield reassessed his earlier conclusion. With all this gossip about the Asterbules, Kirby must have stepped out with one of their maids. He trusted that same maid was not currently giving her lady a similar rundown on his household. He nodded absently, letting his mind wander until Kirby mentioned something of real interest.

"—havey-cavey, I say. No one knows where the family gets their money. The father a wastrel, the brother was a military man. At Sevastopol, Alma, Balaklava, and Inkerman. A career mover, a real up and comer, then suddenly he decides the army is not his cup o' tea and he sells his commission. Now, here's the sister on the sharp edge of fashion."

Unexplained wealth was one of the clues Marsfield was following to find the villain. Contacts in the military would also have been necessary to the culprit. Although his gut had told him his old enemy Lord Fain was the guilty party, Marsfield hadn't yet been able to prove it. He had to check out every lead. "Who is this paragon?"

"I didn't catch the debutante's name. But if you're interested, I'll be happy to—"

"I'm sure I can manage an introduction on my own, Kirby." The boys would not only know her name, but where she'd been invited. At last they could prove useful. He would attend one of those events himself and charm the necessary information out of the young chit. Then, if warranted, he would investigate the brother.

"I'm glad to see you taking an interest. You've been mooning over that . . . that woman—"

"What are you—"

"Begging your pardon, sir, but you know I speak my mind. That Cassandra woman you've been having me investigate. Even if she really existed, she'd be beneath your regard, sir."

He waved off his valet's concern. "That is quite—"

"Course, I was relieved when your interest gave you cause to send your mistress her walking papers. Never liked—"

"Kirby! That is quite enough."

"Yes, milord."

Now he'd hurt the little man's feelings, but, damn it, his

private life was not a matter he wished to debate. "As far as I'm concerned, we never had this discussion."

"Yes, milord."

"Send word to Arif Sadiq's shop that I will call on him tomorrow morning."

Kirby sniffed his acknowledgment.

Marsfield smiled. Though the two men would never be friends, they had come to tolerate each other. Marsfield could never repay his debt to Arif, whose knowledge of Eastern medicine had made his life tolerable. With the use of exercise and massage techniques, the Arab had restored almost complete use of his leg after his battle injury.

Marsfield had not visited his friend for a treatment in some time and would enjoy not only a massage but also a cup of the dark, strong coffee and sweet pastries Arif's wife made. The shop, a successful combination coffee shop and apothecary that marketed exotic spices and potions to the *ton*, was also a good place to pick up information.

"Thank you, Kirby. You may have the rest of the evening off."

Marsfield turned and strode down the hall. Now that he had another lead, he was anxious to follow it. He wished he could cancel his current engagement, but it was too late to send word to the director of a change in plans.

A few minutes before nine, his carriage pulled up to the address Lady Decklesmoor had written on the back of her card. A properly forbidding butler answered his knock. The usual polite greeting ritual was interrupted when one of the side doors along the hall opened and an eager young boy bounced out as if he'd been playing hide and seek.

At least his companion for the evening was prompt. As the butler handed back his cane and hat, Marsfield looked the boy over. What was Lady Decklesmoor thinking? This lad was no more than fourteen or fifteen, pale and on the thin side. Strange blue-tinted spectacles. Even a tad effeminate with his narrow shoulders. Of course, few boys that age had grown into their manhood as yet. Maybe later he'd suggest a regular routine of boxing to build the boy's upper body.

"Good evening," he said with false joviality.

"Good evening, Lord Marsfield."

Gads. The boy's voice was still cracking. Marsfield couldn't take a bloody child to a brothel. Reformulating his plans for the evening, he tried to think of an excuse to give Lady Decklesmoor.

"Is your aunt at home? I would like to pay my respects."

The lad cleared his throat and said in a deeper voice, "She bade me give you this."

Marsfield took the proffered letter. Excusing himself, he stepped to one side to read it. After the usual salutations, Lady Decklesmoor mentioned that Andrew wore the darkened spectacles because of sensitivity to bright light brought on by his childhood illness. She gave the boy's age as seventeen and blamed the aforementioned illness, never specifically named, for his less than manly physique and for what she thought he might perceive as the lad's lack of social polish.

Marsfield was more intrigued by what the letter said between the lines about the aunt. Her handwriting was neat, each letter perfectly formed, as if a demanding headmistress would grade her on her penmanship. Her word choice indicated education, yet the lack of flowery phrases hinted at a sensible manner. All quite in keeping with his earlier impression. It would be interesting to someday see her face, to see if she looked like her voice and handwriting.

In closing, Lady Decklesmoor thanked him for his kindness to her nephew in such a clever way as to hint at his obligation without saying it directly. With his debt of honor weighing heavy, he refolded the letter and placed it in his breast pocket.

Well, the boy would have to become a man sooner or later.

"Shall we?" Marsfield said, clapping Andrew on the shoulder and heading toward the door.

Because Anne knew the contents of the letter, she'd used the time to repeat the litany of directions from Harvey: slouch a little, hands loose at her side or in her pockets, feet apart, chin out. Then, because she wasn't paying attention, the slap on her shoulder staggered her sideways.

She grabbed her reading spectacles to keep them on her nose. Harvey had painted the inside of each lens with her watercolors, insisting it was necessary to hide her long eyelashes and change the appearance of her eye color. Now, everything had an azure blue tint. She had to squint to see clearly past arm's length.

Anne recovered her balance and followed Marsfield to his waiting carriage. Her disguise had passed the first test. A quiver of excitement replaced her nervous butterflies. She was really going to get away with it! She lounged back on the seat, as she'd seen her brother do a thousand times. She even propped her foot on the facing seat.

"If that shoe is muddy, I'll tan your backside."

His deep rumble brought her to attention. Her foot thumped to the floor.

"No, sir." Her voice too high, she coughed and lowered her tone. "I mean my lord. They're clean." Just in case, she removed her handkerchief and wiped the seat across from her.

"Listen, Andrew. As a favor to your aunt, we're to be companions for the evening. You may call me Marsfield. However, I am not your school chum, and I expect a certain degree of respect for myself and my property."

She bristled. He was dressing her down as if she were

a misbehaving child. Of course, she rationalized, she was pretending to be a young boy. Maybe his reaction was natural. She sought to change the subject.

"Yes, sir. Will there be whist? At the gaming hall, I mean. I'm rather good at whist, you know."

"I think you'll find the games quite interesting, though I doubt you'll be playing whist."

"Oh." That exhausted her knowledge of gambling, other than the usual parlor board games played for trinkets. "I suppose that's why my aunt arranged for us to attend together. So that you'd be available, should I need advice."

The man responded only with an oblique stare that made her feel as if he could see beneath her disguise to her quivering nerve endings.

Seeking to end the uncomfortable silence, she said the first thing that came to her mind. "On the rules, that is. I think one should always learn the rules of the game before commencing play. A gentleman would never advise another gentleman on his wager, would he?"

Suddenly he chuckled. "Out of the mouths of babes. That is actually quite good." He reached into his breast pocket and pulled out a small notebook and gold encased lead pencil. He flipped open the notebook and wrote for several seconds.

"What are you doing?"

"Writing down that bit of wisdom."

"A gentleman never advises—"

"No, no. Custom and wisdom are hardly synonymous." He snapped the notebook closed and returned it to his pocket.

She recognized the crux of her own argument with him the last time they'd met, but that still didn't tell her why he'd written it down. "Do you have a faulty memory? I have heard that as one gets older—"

"There is nothing wrong with my memory," he snapped at her. He turned away to signal the subject was closed.

Her innate curiosity overcame her discomfort with his
slight show of temper. Ignoring the dictates of her polite
upbringing, she persevered as she thought a curious young
boy would. "Then why do you make notes of an ordinary
conversation?"

His sigh of resignation told her he was humoring her as
one would a small child who didn't know better than to
pester his elders with endless questions.

"It is a habit I began as a young man. When I hear or
read something I think will be a useful life lesson, I write
it down. Thus, when I have a decision to make, I can usually find the appropriate advice close to hand." He looked
straight into her eyes. "Does that satisfy?"

Her colored glasses did not hide the intensity of his stare.
She quickly looked away. The uncomfortable silence grew
as the coach rattled over the uneven cobblestones. He hadn't
written anything down during any of their previous conversations. Finally, she couldn't stand the silence any longer.
"What exactly did you write down?"

Marsfield jumped as if he'd forgotten she was there.
"Pardon?"

"After all, if you are going to quote my noteworthy
words, I should at least be aware of what you wrote."

With a sigh that denoted his grudging agreement, he retrieved the notebook, opened it to the appropriate page,
and handed it to her before turning back to the window.

She held the notebook closer to the lamp and read:

*October 14th, London, in the carriage, young Lord
Decklesmoor said, without being aware of the univer-
sal wisdom of his words, "One should always know the
rules of the game before commencing play." To that I
would add the stakes.*

The words seemed rather inconsequential to her. If
she'd known he was in the habit of taking notes, she could

have prepared something spectacular, like . . . she turned back a page to see what others had said.

She received quite a shock to read:

Number 7. Qualities of the Perfect Wife: should have a pleasant laugh but not be too easily amused so one does not weary of her constant giggling.

Now thoroughly intrigued, she skimmed several pages of business notations, looking for more qualities of the perfect wife. Stopping when she found another numbered heading, she read:

Number 5. On retaining a Mistress: make love in unusual places, novelty keeps the relationship interesting, cross reference #3 On gaining a Mistress, the element of surprise.

With eager anticipation she found another:

Number 4. On retaining a Mistress: should circumstances force you to cancel or delay an appointment, an apology combined with a sentimental token, a scarf she admired in a shop window, the first bloom of the season, will atone for her suffering. However, a gift of value added to the above will assure her future silence on the matter.

A few pages further:

Number 8. Qualities of the Perfect Wife—

The notebook was snatched out of her hand.

"You were not invited to read the entire book," Marsfield said, returning it to his pocket.

Caught snooping, she mumbled an embarrassed apology. "But you must admit, my words seem rather out of place."

He raised one eyebrow.

"Well, those notes about your mistress for one."

"And you don't see the relationship between a man and woman as a game with rules and stakes?"

"Certainly not."

"Then, of course, you are quite young. Do you yet long for the romantic love idealized by Sir Walter Scott? A Juliet to your Romeo? Or even that of Browning, who makes a public fool of himself over his wife?"

"You don't believe in romantic love?"

He leaned back and crossed his arms. "If I remember correctly, at your age I was more interested in the physical aspects of love."

Anne realized she'd expressed school*girl* sentiments, endangering her disguise. She took a deep breath to calm her nerves and ended in a coughing fit because her bound breasts left little room for her lungs to expand.

He looked at her with curious stare. "Have you ever been physically intimate with a woman, Andrew?"

She choked on a gasp of air. Feeling a bit faint, she bent forward. He leaned over and clapped her on the back a few times.

"I take that as a no," he said, calm as could be.

She nodded and forced herself to breathe slow and shallow. He wanted to discuss physical intimacy with her. If she didn't think quickly, all would be lost. She tried to remember if her brother had had a romantic interest at sixteen. Oh, yes. The fair Yolanda. Of course, now she was quite rotund, had five children and as many dogs, but back then Robert had died a thousand deaths for want of the older woman.

"There's this girl. She smiles at me one minute and ignores me the next. She'll walk with me in the garden and let me steal a kiss, then return my note the next day unopened."

She tried to think of what Robert would have done in a

situation like this. "As a man of experience and, dare I say, some reputation with women, can you offer any advice on the subject of women? I don't understand why they do what they do."

Marsfield chuckled. "I think understanding is beyond the scope of mortal man. However, predicting a woman's behavior is not. Through diligent study"—he straightened the lapels of his coat—"most diligent, I assure you, I've compiled ten principles which, when followed, guarantee success."

"Success? As in they fall in love with you?"

He gave her a quizzical look. "My goal was never quite that lofty."

It took her a moment to derive his meaning. "Oh."

"In fact, I find emotional attachments . . . inconvenient."

"I see." And indeed she did. His reputation as a libertine was well deserved. She dismissed the niggling idea that his boast hinted at sadness and loneliness. Doubtless, she was projecting her own feelings into his response. Would his method work in reverse? Could a woman make a man fall in love with her?

The well-sprung carriage rolled to a smooth stop.

"We're here. And let's keep this discussion between us gentlemen, shall we?"

"But, sir—"

"Can't have the women thinking there is an infallible method to getting them to succumb, now can we?"

The footman opened the door and let down the steps. Marsfield motioned her to precede him.

She hesitated. "Sir, I would like to know your principles."

"Don't you think it would be better to learn them on your own, in your own time?"

"Oh, no. You see . . . it's Yolanda. She acts like she doesn't know I'm alive."

He smoothed his gloves and picked up his hat. "We'll talk on the ride home. Just now . . ."

Marsfield waved his hat toward the door. She had no choice but to disembark. He stepped down behind her and told the coachman to return in two hours.

She would have preferred to stay in the cozy carriage and talk more, but, remembering her original purpose, she noted the discreet facade of the large stone building. It looked pretty much like any residence on a quiet side street. Somehow she'd expected a noisy, dirty waterfront location.

Well, this was a gentleman's gaming hall, after all. Already she was accumulating valuable information. A solemn butler opened the door and she followed Marsfield inside.

As they handed over their hats, cloaks, and gloves, she strained to look around Marsfield's bulk. The large entrance hall with its black and white tiled floor was flanked on either side by elegant curving staircases to the upper floor. The only furnishings were a red velvet covered settee and two Greek statues on chest-high pillars. Even squinting through her colored glasses, she could tell the statues were nude.

Through the double door to her right, she glimpsed what looked like an ordinary drawing room. Curious. She'd expected a low ceiling, smoky crowded rooms, and the sounds of drunken revelry at the very least.

"Marsfield."

Anne turned at the sound of a woman's voice. Then she couldn't help but stare as the large woman sailed across the foyer, arms open wide, her prodigious half-bare bosom leading the way. Her perfume reached Anne long before the woman stepped straight up to Marsfield and engulfed him in an embrace.

"You rogue. Never thought to see you in the enemy camp."

Anne looked at him over the top of the woman's obviously dyed red hair. Why, he was actually blushing.

He placed his hands on the woman's waist, set her away from him, and bent over to look her straight in the eye. "Rose, you know as well as I that piece of legislature was aimed at panderers of the worst sort." He chuckled when she brushed his hands away. "Believe me, if I could have legally done so, I would have publicly excepted the Garden from any move to force its closing."

"Well, it's all water under the bridge, since it didn't pass and I'm still here." Rose tilted her head and raised one thin, arched eyebrow. "Yet I am surprised to see you."

Marsfield reached around and grabbed Anne by the arm, forcing her to stumble to a stance before the other woman. His hands on Anne's shoulders held her in place.

"Madame Rose, may I present my young friend, Andrew Gordon, Viscount Decklesmoor."

She cringed at the use of her cousin's name and title. Andrew was practically a monk. If he ever heard of her gambling in his name . . .

Marsfield finished the introductions, then said, "I brought Andrew here for his time-honored initiation."

Rose smiled broadly. "Welcome to Rose's Garden." She reached out to touch Anne's cheek. "Why, he doesn't even shave yet."

She backed up a step. "I shaved," she grumbled in her deepest voice.

Rose patted Anne's cheek. "When? Last month?" She laughed at her own joke. "But that's quite all right. We have a special room for the youngsters. Nothing fancy or foreign." She leaned toward Marsfield and whispered, "We call it the nursery."

Anne bristled. She resented that woman's patronizing manner. Besides, she needed to see the real thing, high-stakes gambling, not some trumped-up playground. She straightened her waistcoat with a tug. "I think I can hold my own in regular play."

Rose looked to Marsfield for a response.

He placed a companionable arm across Anne's shoulders. "May I suggest the Moorish Room," he said.

She felt his deep voice rumble and resonate down her spine to pool at its base. His hand on her shoulder, his arm, the length of his body next to hers, radiated heat, deep beckoning heat that made her want to turn toward the source, to get closer still.

Rose smiled and nodded. She clapped her hands twice. Two young women scurried into the hall from the door to the left.

"Andrew, this is Daisy and Petunia," Rose said as she encouraged the girls to stand in front of Anne. "Girls, this is Andrew's first time." Both girls giggled. "Would you escort him to the Moorish Room, please?"

"One moment." Marsfield slipped something into Anne's pocket. "For upstairs. We'll meet back here at half past eleven. Good luck."

She was stunned by his brief, all too brief, touch on her hip. Even through the layers of clothes, the warmth of his fingers caused heat to spread from her hip across her stomach and lower. Placing her hand over her pocket, she traced the shape of a coin. For luck. How considerate of him. She'd treasure the coin, never spend it. She croaked out a thank you.

One girl took each of her arms, and Anne felt a distinct chill when she stepped away from Marsfield. They steered her up the staircase on the left. She looked over her shoulder to see if Marsfield followed, but all she saw was his back as he and Rose disappeared into the drawing room. For a gentleman's gaming hall, there certainly were a lot of women present.

She looked from one girl to the other. Up close, she could see their heavy makeup. They were not as young as she'd originally thought. And their clothes were scandalous. Why, the material was so thin she could practically see though it.

The truth dawned on Anne slowly as she ascended the stairs. She pulled to a sudden halt as if struck by lightning. Oh, my God! Rose's Garden wasn't a gaming hall. Marsfield had brought her to a brothel.

Daisy and Petunia giggled and tugged on her arms.

"Wait." She needed to think. If she ran back down the stairs and sought out Marsfield, would she catch him with Rose in . . . well, she didn't know what, but she was sure she didn't want to find out, either. She should just sneak out the front door. And do what? Huddle on the doorstep for two hours until Marsfield's carriage returned? She didn't even know where in all of London she was. She'd brought money to gamble and could use it to hire a hack to take her back to Grosvenor Square, but what if no hackney cabs came down this quiet street?

However, money was still the answer to her problem. As soon as they were somewhere private, she would pay these two silly women to leave her alone. Then she could meet Marsfield later as if nothing . . . well, as if something had happened. She let the two girls pull her to the top of the stairs and down a short hall. Giggling again, they opened an ornate door and shoved her inside. She stumbled several steps into the darkened room. The door closed behind her with a loud click.

She removed her colored glasses in order to see better in the dim light. The ceiling and walls were draped with gold and green and red silk fabric to create the illusion of an exotic tent. Thick Persian rugs covered the floor. To her left sat a green and gold chaise, flanked by an ornately carved chair and a small table holding fruit and wine. On the right, a platform draped in more silks was covered with dozens of plump, tasseled pillows. She felt her eyes widen to saucers. In the middle of the pseudo bed lay a nearly naked woman. Her long dark hair covered more than the skimpy transparent veils she wore.

"My name is Jasmine." Her voice was husky and heavily accented. She threw one arm out and patted a nearby pillow with her other hand. "Welcome to my casbah."

Anne couldn't find her voice. Her mouth opened and closed like a newly caught fish floundering in the bottom of the boat. She took a step backward, searching behind her back for the doorknob.

Jasmine plumped a tapestry-covered pillow, then laid back on it, arranging herself artfully to expose and entice. "Come over here."

Ann searched along the wall, but all she touched was material. Where was the bloody doorknob? "I've got money," she managed to croak out.

With the grace of a jungle animal, Jasmine stood and sidled close. "Let's make you a little more comfortable." She reached out and undid several waistcoat buttons with ease.

Anne slapped her grasping hands away. "Wait." Then she had to cover her cravat. "Stop." Then her shirtfront. "Listen to me."

Jasmine reached for the buttons on Anne's pants.

"Oh, for Pete's sake, I'm not a man."

"What do you mean?" Jasmine said, all trace of her foreign accent gone. She grabbed Anne's chin and turned it back and forth. She let go and stepped back, placing her hands on her hips. "How'd you get past Rose?"

"Lord Marsfield introduced me." Anne took a deep relieved breath. "What's that odor?"

"Sandalwood incense," Jasmine pointed to the corner where a small brazier burned. She looked at Anne with a calculating gaze, then shook her head as if answering her own question. "Are you one of those society women slumming to see what they're missing?"

"No."

"When Rose hears about this, she's going to hoist Marsfield up by his—" Jasmine reached behind one of the hangings, pulled out a dressing gown and put it on. "She doesn't like to be taken for a fool."

"No. Wait. He doesn't know."

"Doesn't know what?"

"That I'm a woman. I fooled him into thinking I'm a boy."

Jasmine sat on the chaise. She poured herself a glass of wine. "Honey, I've seen Lord Marsfield, and he is one fine specimen of a man. Why in the world would you want him to think you're a boy?"

"It's a long story."

Jasmine pointed to the chair. "I'm a good listener."

She hesitated. "Isn't that a little cliché? The prostitute with a heart of gold?"

"Who said anything about heart? You've got two hours, paid in advance." Jasmine chuckled. "Listening is easier than what I usually do to earn this much money."

"You mean you won't tell Marsfield?" Anne sat on the edge of the chair.

"Look, I don't ever give back the money. What do I care how he thinks I earned it?" Jasmine narrowed her gaze. "You're not one of those do-good reformers, are you?"

Anne shook her head. "Do you have a gaming room? Marsfield was supposed to take me to a gaming hall."

"You did all this to gamble? Pardon me for stating the obvious, but you might want to find another interest. You haven't got the luck to be a gambler."

"No luck is right." Anne groaned and leaned back.

"Rose allows very little gambling here. Slows the trade, you know."

Now what? Anne doubted she could talk Marsfield into another excursion. Maybe she could change the setting of the scene. Would Blackthorne buy a scene in a brothel?

She hadn't realized she'd been mumbling aloud until Jasmine said, "What are you planning? Rose doesn't like scenes."

Should she tell? After all, this woman wasn't likely to be shocked, wouldn't look down her nose at Anne's secret career. Maybe the woman would even give her a tour.

"I meant a scene in a book. I'm a writer. This disguise was supposed to get me into a gaming hall so I could accurately describe the setting of the scene."

"What's your name? I mean, it's obviously not Viscount Decklesmoor, like the reservation card said. What have you published?"

She introduced herself by her pen name, Cassandra Drummond, and recited the names of her books.

Jasmine jumped off the chaise so fast she nearly tripped over one of her veils. Then she ripped aside one of the hangings, whipped open the door, and ran from the room.

Anne blinked back her disbelief. Was it possible? Were women novelists considered so low that she'd been snubbed by a prostitute?

In moments, Jasmine was back, dragging the formidable Rose with her, and followed by Daisy and Petunia. She pointed an accusing finger at Anne.

"That's her!"

Six

Rose stomped into the room and plopped down on the chaise. Jasmine, Daisy, and Petunia stood in a row behind her.

Anne shrank back in the chair to get as far away from Rose's hard stare as possible. They didn't lynch novelists, did they?

"I'm sorry, I—"

"What happened to Marianne and Roderick?"

"Who?"

Rose heaved a deep sigh and the chaise groaned. "Marianne Malone and Roderick Winters from *A Maid's Revenge*. If you're the real author, you must know what happened to them."

Anne smiled. Even though her books usually ended with a kiss and an implied a happily-ever-after ending, she'd always imagined more than she actually wrote.

"They were married in secret by the old vicar, took a ship to Charleston, South Carolina, in the United States, built a lovely plantation, and had five children. Three boys and two girls."

Rose looked back over her shoulder at Jasmine. "See, I told you they would never stay at his estate with his dragon of a mother."

Jasmine wrinkled her nose and pulled a face at Rose. Then she looked across at Anne. "What about Kate and Reno? Oooh. Oooh. Melissa and Valdric. What happened to them? Valdric is my favorite. I've always had a weakness for swashbuckling pirates."

Suddenly, the three women standing behind the chaise were all talking at once, arguing about which hero they liked the best. Rose held up her hands and requested silence. She nodded to Anne, giving her the floor.

"I can't believe you remember them. I wrote those stories years ago." She smiled at them. "Thank you."

"We're ardent devotees," Rose said. "I've read *A Maid's Revenge* at least four times."

Jasmine held up two fingers, Daisy three.

Petunia held up one finger. "I'm still learning to read," she whispered. "Thanks to Miss Rose."

Rose waved off the shining gratitude in the girl's eyes. She faced Anne. "Miss Drummond—"

"Please call me . . ." Anne paused and gave a self-conscious laugh. "My real name is—"

"We don't need to know your real name," Rose interrupted. "We understand the necessity and the market appeal of a pseudonym."

"Ain't that right, Martha?" Jasmine said as she punched Petunia lightly on the arm.

"You would know, Sharon Mary Kathleen." Petunia flicked her hand in Jasmine's face. Jasmine grabbed the end of her nose.

Rose held up her hand and cleared her throat. The scuffling behind her stopped. "To us you are Cassandra Drummond," Rose continued, as if she'd taken no notice.

"Then please, call me Cassandra," Anne said.

Rose nodded with the regal grace of a duchess. "I would be honored if you would attend me in my private parlor." She stood and motioned toward the door.

When the three women behind Rose gasped, sighed and nodded in unison like a well-rehearsed Greek chorus, Anne realized the significant honor of the singular invitation. She stood and bowed as deep as any courtier.

"I also would be honored if you would consent to auto-graph my copies of your books."

"The honor and the pleasure are mine." Like the gen-tleman she was dressed as, Anne offered her arm to the madam.

The chorus applauded, giggled, and followed as the un-usual couple left the room in grand style.

Marsfield sat across the empty gaming table from one of the most powerful, yet unknown, men in the country. They traded the usual gentleman's chitchat regarding horses, sporting events, and the hunting season until the scantily clad servant girl had taken their orders, served their drinks, and left the room. He rose and checked the door to make sure no one listened at the keyhole.

The director chuckled. "Don't trust anyone, do you?"

"No, John." He sat and sipped his drink. "Not even you."

"Most especially me?" He gave Marsfield a sly look over the rim of his own glass.

"If you want to play games"—Marsfield swept his hand over the green baize tabletop—"I can have appropriate equipment brought."

John shook his head. "You never did appreciate the thrill of intrigue, the—"

"I find nothing entertaining about soldiers dying need-lessly."

John snorted. "This isn't about individuals. This is pol-itics, knowledge, power. The power of knowledge that can cause the resignation of a prime minister, affect the fate of nations."

Marsfield raised one eyebrow. "You claim to have forced Aberdeen's resignation?"

John studied his fingertips.

This time Marsfield snorted. "Florence Nightingale's

reports from the front raised the hue and cry. The people's abhorrence of his mismanagement of the war supplies brought down Aberdeen."

"The people, as you so grandly refer to them, are an unruly mob most concerned about their next meal and pint, devoid of logic and easily swayed by emotional appeals."

"The people are represented by the members of Parliament."

"Exactly." John leaned forward. "And my point still stands. Present company excepted, of course."

"Naturally. Or I would have to call you out for that insult." Marsfield grinned to show the thought gave him pleasure, and he had the satisfaction of seeing the director squirm. "You're lucky dueling has been outlawed." He raised his glass in salute and drank.

"And you're lucky I respect your abilities enough to ignore your rudeness," John grumbled. He rubbed his forehead. "This case has dragged on too long. Palmerston is getting antsy."

"How is the old boy doing?"

"Good job as P.M. Putting together a sanitary commission to set standards for military hospitals—"

Marsfield interrupted, "I know his professional credits. I meant personally. He seemed a bit under the weather the last time I saw him."

"Running himself ragged. Won't last long at his age."

"Really?"

"Two, three years. He knows it, too. That's why he's anxious. Aberdeen may have faced his responsibility, but Palmerston wants justice. He wants the scum who made fortunes off the misery of our soldiers, but the culprits are hidden behind a morass of legal paperwork and complicated ownership mills." He looked at Marsfield. "We'll settle for ruining them socially, economically, anything short of breaking the law."

"But first you have to find them."

John smiled. "That is why we have you, Lord Marsfield. If it were easy, I wouldn't have wasted my best agent—"

"Former agent. Remember, you wrote me off even before I made it home."

"The doctor's report said if you survived, you'd never walk again."

"Apparently, the doctor was wrong."

John shrugged. "Hindsight is always perfect. If you feel I treated you so badly, why did you accept this assignment?"

"Maybe just to prove I can do it."

After a bark of laughter, John shook his head. "I could have used those two new young men. They have access to the same social circles you do."

"Is that why you saddled me with their care?" Marsfield ran his hand through his hair. "Not that I'm making so much progress that they're slowing me down."

"Come, come, dear boy. Even you had a mentor when you first took the field."

He hadn't thought of Jackson in a long time. "Whatever happened to old Jack? Is he still on that island in the South Seas?"

"Spends his days fishing, swimming, sunning naked on the beach with a harem of nubile natives."

Marsfield leaned back and crossed his arms. "My guess is you're spying on the missionaries. Tsk, tsk, low even for you, John. Either that or you're getting shipping and trade reports from Jack."

The director grinned. "Good call, but too easy a deduction to be impressive. And I'm not ashamed, as you seem to think I should be. It's a good deal for both of us."

"Well, I'm not interested in any of your deals."

"I haven't offered any." John held out his hands, pulling one cuff away from his wrist, then the other, as if to show he had nothing up his sleeves. "Now let's get to business. Any new leads?"

"One. I'll start on it tomorrow."

"So the trip up north proved fruitful?"

"Hardly." Marsfield scowled. "And I can't think what you really expected me to find during that little jaunt into the wilderness."

"Even a journey of one destination has many goals," the director said with an inscrutable expression.

The earl snorted his disgust, but he knew from experience that meant he would get no answers to any further questions.

"This new lead," Marsfield said, letting a slow smile spread across his face, "is local." He couldn't resist the less than subtle dig. The old fellow would hate that there was something inside the city he didn't know about. "Impoverished gentry. A soldier who served in the Crimea. A sudden unexplained fortune."

John scooted his chair closer to the table. "Who?"

Marsfield made his face a blank.

"Come on, man. This could be the one we need. Pull the right thread, and the whole cover-up will unravel like a badly knit sweater. Tell me, and I'll put my men on it right away."

"You said I was the best agent for this job."

"You can't expect to do this alone."

"You gave me two assistants."

"Blast it." John pursed his lips into a tight line. "At least tell me your bloody source."

He wasn't fooled by the director's conciliatory tone. Under normal circumstances, John would have his source in the bowels of Whitehall, spitted and grilled before daylight. But this hand, Marsfield had an ace up his own sleeve.

"My source is Kirby." Marsfield resisted the urge to crow in triumph when the older man's shoulders slumped in defeat. They both knew the valet would never betray his employer.

"You'll keep me posted of your progress?" John asked.

"Haven't I always?" Marsfield looked at his watch and stood. "By the way, I put this entire evening on your tab." He opened the door. When the servant scurried over, he ordered cigars, a bottle of brandy, and a cribbage board. Returning to his seat, he said, "We have to kill time until eleven-thirty in order to keep the subterfuge intact. Pound a point and no cheating."

"Just out of curiosity, what did you tell Rose?" John shot him a sly look. "You haven't exactly been on her list of favorites lately."

"I brought a young friend along for his first experience in the Garden. He's up in the Moorish Room as we speak."

"You charged two hours with Jasmine to my tab? Gads, ten minutes was probably more than enough for the boy's first time."

Marsfield chuckled. "Then let's just say you paid for his first *and* second time." He poured fresh drinks and dealt the cards.

Except for their clothing and the time of night, Anne could have been in a normal parlor on a normal social call. Well, except for the oversize bed visible through an arch to the rear. And maybe the lush paintings on the walls of naked men and women copulating in every conceivable location and position, many of which she was sure must be impossible. She'd lived in the country, after all, and was not totally ignorant. But like that? In the British Museum? In a carriage?

Even the tea service was decorated with a Greek design of naked men and women cavorting around the rim. After slopping tea into the saucer when she tried not to place her lips on the depicted . . . torso of a man, Anne gave up trying to normalize the situation.

She'd never been anywhere remotely similar.

But she relaxed when the first half hour of conversation centered on her books. She really was honored to meet people who liked her characters, her stories. Daisy and Petunia left reluctantly for appointments, but Jasmine and Rose brought out their well-worn copies of her books for her to autograph.

Rose entertained her with amusing stories of her world travels in her first career as an actress. She'd appeared on the great stages of all the grand cities of Europe, had visited the Orient and even seen the pyramids of Egypt. Her travels had given her the ideas for the theme rooms of the Garden.

Soon Anne felt comfortable enough that her innate curiosity asserted itself. She couldn't bring herself to ask the questions she really wanted to ask, questions about Lord Marsfield, so she asked about the paintings. Rose and Jasmine were more than happy to fill in the huge gaps in Anne's knowledge. More than once she put her hands to her cheeks and felt the heat of an intense blush, but she wasn't as horrified as she'd have thought. Shocked at times, yes, but mostly the revelations fascinated her. Here was an aspect of the relationship between a man and a woman she would never otherwise know.

"We have rooms with peepholes. You can watch if you'd like," Rose offered. "The guests don't mind. It excites some men to think someone is watching."

Anne felt her mouth hanging open and shut it with a clack of her teeth. "I don't think so," she said, shaking her head. "Your etchings were quite educational." She shifted to a more comfortable position.

The paper in her pocket rustled against the arm of the sofa. She withdrew it and unfolded the small packet, expecting to find some kind of good luck coin.

"What have you got there?" Rose and Jasmine leaned forward in their seats.

"I'm not exactly sure." Anne held up the object. "Marsfield slipped it into my pocket."

Jasmine giggled, but Rose huffed and grabbed it out of Anne's fingers. "You will never need to know. Just forget it."

"What if he asks me about it? What is it? Please?"

Jasmine whispered something to Rose. After several hushed comments back and forth, Rose shook her head and Jasmine left the room.

Rose cleared her throat. "There are several incurable diseases which are transmitted through sexual union. Many women in our profession are infected. My girls are clean, checked by a doctor regularly, and trained to spot the symptoms in our guests before intercourse. I'm torn between being insulted by Marsfield's actions, and being perversely pleased that he'd start a young man on the right path."

"This is a sheath," Rose continued, holding up Anne's gift. "This one is made of silk, covered by a thin coating of rubber, rather like a mackintosh. Trust Marsfield to purchase only the best quality. A man wears this to protect him from infection. It has the additional benefit of protecting the woman and preventing pregnancy."

Anne looked from the silk disc to the picture on the wall behind Rose and back to the disc. "I don't understand."

Rose chuckled. "This sheath has been rolled in preparation for quick application."

Jasmine returned. "I brought the largest one I could find." She laid a carrot approximately ten inches long and several inches around on the tea table. "I trimmed the top and bottom."

"I will demonstrate." Rose stood the carrot on one end. "Hold this near the bottom," she directed her guest.

Anne scooted forward in her seat and grasped the vegetable. Her fingers barely circled the base.

Rose held the small circle over the top. "Let's pretend this carrot is a man's erect penis—"

Anne dropped the carrot and jumped back with a squeal.

The three women looked at each other in a moment of shock before erupting into spasms of laughter. Anne could not help but laugh with them.

Catching their breath, Rose and Jasmine looked at each other. "Virgin," they said in unison.

Anne stopped laughing mid giggle. "Of course, I'm a virgin."

"We didn't mean it as an insult," Jasmine said.

"Not at all," Rose added. "It's one of our pet peeves that society uses virginity as a club to browbeat young women into fearful submission. Virginity is a physical fact. It is not an excuse for a woman to be ignorant of her own body or that of her husband. All women would have a better chance at a happy marriage if they were given more instructions than simply to close their eyes and think of England."

"Isn't a woman's husband supposed to teach her all she needs to know?"

Jasmine shook her head. "Sadly, most men know less about a woman's sexuality than the woman herself. It's the rare man who pays attention to what a woman likes, what she needs." She shrugged. "Of course, I can only judge by my own experience. Maybe it's different for a wife."

Anne sat deep in thought. The situation tonight had pointed out to her just how ignorant she was regarding men and women, and the physical relationship between them.

Rose insisted they try again. Anne held the carrot upright between her thumb and forefinger.

"Not like that," Jasmine said. "A man won't get no pleasure from a tentative touch. Let him know your hand is there."

Rose gave Jasmine a sideways glance and a little shake of her head.

"Besides," Jasmine continued, "the carrot will tip over if you don't have a firm hold."

Gripping the vegetable firmly, Anne hoped she wasn't blushing. She would never be able to look at an ordinary carrot in the same way ever again.

Rose fitted the disc over the tip. "Then you just unroll it, rather like rolling a stocking up your leg." Rose stopped after about three inches when the sheath started to rip. "The carrot you brought is too big."

"The carrot is the right size. It's the sheath that's too small," Jasmine quipped. She looked at Anne with a twinkle in her eye. "Tell Marsfield next time you need a bigger one. That'll take him down a peg or two."

The joke went over Anne's head but Jasmine and Rose seemed to think it was hysterical. She didn't have time to ask for an explanation because they were interrupted by a knock on the door.

Petunia slipped into the room. "Lord Marsfield said to tell you the carriage is waiting."

She looked at the clock. It was quarter to twelve. She jumped up. "Oh, dear. I'm late. You're not going to tell him about me, are you?"

"Of course not," the two women said together.

"Thank you for a most enjoyable and educational evening." She took a step and stopped. "I don't think I can do this. I'm too embarrassed."

Rose removed the sheath from the carrot, folded it and stuffed it back in Anne's pocket. "Nothing to be embarrassed about. Now, plaster a big, cat-got-the-cream grin on your face, and let Jasmine and me do the talking." She took Anne's arm and started toward the door.

Jasmine took her other arm. "Just nod and grin. It'll be fine."

Anne pulled them to a stop. "But what about in the carriage on the way home? What if he asks me questions?"

"La, child. Just keep grinning. Stare off into space a

lot." Rose gave her a playful slap on the arm. "You looked at enough of them pictures to answer a few simple questions, didn't you?"

She nodded.

A panel in the wall slide open.

"I just wanted to say good-bye," Daisy said, stepping into the room. The panel slid shut.

Anne blinked, but no one else seemed surprised to see the girl appear out of nowhere.

Rose looked at Anne's expression, and chuckled. "She used the escape passage to save time."

"The what?"

"When I had this house built, oh, more years ago than I care to remember, I had a few . . . enemies, other madams who were in the habit of kidnapping my best girls. So I had an escape passage built with secret doors in each room. Now it's only used as an access to the peepholes."

"And to get around quickly without being seen," Daisy added.

"Well," Rose said. "I guess you have to be on your way."

"Wait a minute." Jasmine stepped in front of Anne. "We can't have him leave as neat as when he came in." She pulled on Anne's shirt until it hung out slightly, undid her tie and retied it in a loose bow, and mussed her hair. "Where are your spectacles?" She placed them on Anne's nose and tipped them a tad askew. "There. That's better."

Rose looked her up and down with a discerning eye. She shook her head. Then her face brightened and she snapped her fingers. "I know what she needs; a bulge. Bring me my sewing basket," she instructed Jasmine. "Drop your pants," she told Anne.

In the space of a few minutes, Rose had stuffed several socks inside one another and pinned the contraption to Anne's small clothes so that it hung down inside the leg of her trousers.

"I . . . I don't know about this. It feels too weird."

"This is the clincher for your disguise, honey. A man will check out the competition's equipment."

"A woman, too, once she knows what she looking for," Jasmine added. They stood back together to admire their handiwork.

"What do you think?" Rose asked.

"Well, she fooled you without the bulge in the first place. I have the excuse of it being rather dark."

"And I was distracted by Marsfield." Rose rolled her eyes and shook her head. "You'd think I'd know by now not to let a man take my mind off business. Well, this would have fooled even me." She reached over and patted the sock. "At least for a little while."

"Thank you." On impulse, Anne leaned over and kissed Rose's powdered cheek. "I don't have many friends, but I feel like I have made four new ones tonight. Thank you."

If she hadn't been so sure nothing under the sun could shock Rose, she would have sworn she saw the older woman blink back her surprise.

"If you really want to thank us," Jasmine said, "you could put us in one of your books."

Anne smiled. "I just might do that."

Rose made a grand sweeping gesture with her free arm. "Open the door, Daisy. It's show time."

Anne stopped mid stride. Marsfield, standing in the hall and looking toward the stairway, was framed by the doorway molding, the picture of a London gentleman out for the evening. The epitome of handsomeness. Her memory, her newfound knowledge and her vivid imagination conspired, stripping him naked. He turned to face her, the personification of virility.

She gasped. Unable to take a deep breath, she panted in an attempt to get enough air. Her heart pounded, but her blood had turned to warm honey, pooling low in her stomach. Her knees buckled, yet pressure under her elbows kept her upright. Without knowing how she moved, she stood a few feet from him. Blinking in the bright light of the overhead chandelier, she saw his scowl. He wasn't supposed to be frowning. Where was the desire? The look of love?

"It's about time," Marsfield said.

Her world snapped back into focus with a click as distinct as the lid of his pocket watch closing.

"Don't blame Andrew, Lord Marsfield," Rose cooed. She turned her back on him so he couldn't see her wink. "Andrew was a most . . . enthusiastic pupil." She mouthed the word smile and pinched Anne's cheeks. "We were just trying to wear him out."

Anne pasted a smile on her face, but she was sure it looked more sickly than satisfied. She stumbled a step, but Jasmine kept her standing by supporting all her weight.

"I think we succeeded," Jasmine said through gritted teeth.

Marsfield raised an eyebrow. He looked to the open door of Rose's private parlor as if just realizing they hadn't descended the stairs. "You didn't like the Moorish Room?"

"Oh, milord." Rose patted her hair. "Let's just say we . . . discussed several of the great romantic locations of the world."

Jasmine giggled as if on cue.

"Do you need help into the carriage?" Marsfield asked Anne.

She shook her head. The erotic drawing on Rose's wall of the couple making love in the carriage was fresh and clear in her mind. Before tonight, she never would have thought that . . . in a carriage! Oh no, she couldn't be in that small cozy space, alone with him, knowing what she now knew. She shook her head again.

"Good." He swirled his great cloak over his shoulders. Bowing over Rose's hand, he thanked her for an enjoyable evening. The solemn butler opened the door, and Marsfield exited with long brisk strides.

"I can't," Anne whispered, not taking her eyes off his retreating back. "You're wrong, Rose. Too much knowledge is dangerous. I keep imagining him naked."

Two handsome, well-dressed young men entered the still open door, but she took little notice of them.

"She's got it bad," Jasmine said.

"I've got what?"

"Nothing." Rose shot Jasmine a quelling glance.

"I could take a hack," Anne suggested.

Rose shook her head. "You'll have to face this sooner or later. It's only nerves. Actors get them all the time. I was taught to picture the audience naked to quiet the butterflies, but in your case . . . every time you picture him naked, force your imagination to add something funny, like a silly hat."

"What good will that do?"

"Believe me," Jasmine said, "it's difficult to get sexually aroused by a man wearing your Great-Aunt Matilda's go-to-meeting hat with the giant pink posies and two bluebirds perched on top."

Anne was willing to cede to their superior knowledge.

"If you ever need anything," Rose called after her, "you can count on us."

She blew each if them a kiss. "Thank you."

Pausing on the outer stoop, she took as deep a breath as she could with her breasts tightly bound. Only a twenty-minute ride and she'd be home. Surely she'd survive twenty minutes. Crossing her fingers for luck, she stepped forward.

The carriage door yawned wide, like the opening to a black pit of sin.

Seven

Anne slid on the smooth leather seat of the carriage as far into the corner as she could. She looked out the window, intending to concentrate on the passing view, but the darkness outside, conspiring with the light from the crystal lamps inside the carriage, turned the finely tempered glass into a mirror, giving her the dubious choice of looking at either Marsfield or his reflected image. She closed her eyes.

Without sight, her other senses ignited in the cozy darkness. The familiar clop-clop of the horse's hooves and city sounds faded into the background of her awareness. She heard the gentle rhythm of Marsfield's breathing. The perfume of the brothel that clung to their clothes was soon overpowered by the pervasive odor of well-cared-for leather and horses. Yet she easily identified his scent. Tobacco and brandy. The woodsy-spicy tang of his cologne. Something she couldn't name that was uniquely him.

Her imagination recalled Rose's engraving of the couple using the privacy of a carriage to indulge their passion. Only in her mind's version of the scene, the woman was herself and the man was Marsfield. The more she tried *not* to think of it—

"My apologies for being insistent about leaving. I don't care to keep my cattle standing in the night air."

Something in his smug tone told her it wasn't so much an apology he offered, but a rebuke for her tardiness. His sanctimonious attitude didn't sit well with her. However, her aggravation wiped the scandalous pictures from her mind.

"When we stop, I shall tender my regrets to your horses."

He only raised an eyebrow in response.

She gathered her wits to engage him in conversation so as not to think about . . . those other thoughts.

"If I were one to write in a notebook of my own, I should note under the heading of qualities of a gentleman to emulate, while it is abhorrent to be inconsiderate of animals, it is acceptable to be rude to people."

"A gentleman accepts a well-meant apology with dignity."

"And a gentleman's horse?" She noticed his dimple flash an appearance before he masked his amusement. The fact that he enjoyed their verbal jousting gave her a warm tingle.

He brushed a nonexistent piece of lint from his coat. "I can't say an elaborately worded apology would have no effect on a horse, never having tried it myself. I must confess I usually opt for the mundane apple or lump of sugar to atone for their suffering and reward their silence."

"Do you treat your horses as well as you treat your mistresses or is it that you treat your mistresses as well as your horses?"

"I beg your pardon?"

"Your advice on horses sounded suspiciously like appeasing an offended mistress." At his befuddled look, she pointed to his breast pocket. "Number four."

He retrieved his notebook. After reading the appropriate passage, he chuckled. "Similar wording aside, I can't say I've ever given a diamond-studded collar to one of my horses."

"Or an apple to your mistress?"

He snorted a laugh and looked toward the ceiling as if

appealing for patience. "My boy, you truly know nothing about women if you think one would be satisfied with such an apology."

She bristled at his condescending manner. How she longed to give him a proper set down. If she revealed her true identity, he would see how insufferable he sounded. But she wasn't foolish enough to cut off her nose to spite her face.

"I know more than you think." Searching for some other way to disturb his complacency, she remembered her new friends' laughter at his expense. She pulled the ripped condom from her pocket. "Rose said to tell you I need a larger size next time."

He nonchalantly waved away her boast. "Put that away. Remember, a prostitute is paid to make you believe you are the world's best lover."

"And a mistress is not?"

"No. Well, yes," he said with a thoughtful look. "Though it's probably more in the manner in which she is treated than in the essential services offered. It boils down to the basic nature of a man to want what every other man desires but cannot obtain. To acquire a sought-after mistress is a conquest; to retain one despite her many other offers, a victory. Hence, the occasional need to appease her."

Since that gambit had failed, she searched her memory for any incident related to her by her brother that would further her case. Unfortunately, Robert had never mentioned a mistress. "I once gave a box of chocolates to a girl to apologize for calling her a dimwit."

"And she forgave you?"

"She stopped smacking me with her fan every time I came within arm's reach."

"Ah, there's the rub. I would be searching for a much different reaction. And I would get it."

"You're quite confident. One might even say smug."

He shrugged his shoulders as if it was of little importance. "My method has proved itself."

"So you say."

"A fact does not lose veracity because you are unaware of its existence."

Clearly, she would need more ammunition to fight this verbal battle. "If that is true, I would be interested in reading the rest of your principles."

"You would ask a champion to divulge his fighting techniques? A magician to reveal his secrets? Sorry. You'll have to blunder through and learn your own lessons."

She lounged back, draped one arm across squabs and propped her feet on the facing seat. She plastered a superior, know-it-all smile on her face. "Obviously, you are not as confident in your method as you proclaim."

"Nonsense."

"A method that has been tested by only one man can hardly be presented as scientific fact. Perhaps it's successful because . . . because you dress well. The credit could belong to your tailor."

"That's rubbish, and you know it."

"Maybe. But there are other factors that surely contribute to your success that must be taken into account."

"Such as my boot maker? Hah!"

"Well, you are wealthy." She looked him up and down with a critical eye. "Besides dressing fashionably well, you're reasonably attractive. You're punctual. Clean. And you have all your teeth."

"I'm flattered. I've never had my attributes catalogued quite so succinctly."

She allowed her lips to curve upward ever so slightly and nodded in his direction.

Marsfield loosened his collar. "I myself might have listed sophisticated, intelligent, and skilled in the ways of satisfying a woman."

"Your ego has proved my point for me."

Despite being seated, he executed an elegant bow in her direction. "I shall send around a fair copy of my list."

Her euphoria in winning was short-lived.

"And I will watch with interest as *you* put my principles to use and prove my method yourself."

She choked on her surprise. "That's impossible."

"Why?" He looked her up and down critically. "You're reasonably attractive and intelligent. And you have all your teeth. Everything else can be learned or acquired. We'll start tomorrow."

"I can't. I . . . I . . . my Aunt Elizabeth has made plans."

"Of course, I will send a letter of explanation to her. I'm quite sure she'll be suitably grateful I have taken her nephew under my wing."

"No. No, I'm sure she would never agree."

"Of course she will. Not that I would threaten her, mind you, but she'll naturally consider what a public snub would do to her social standing." He assumed a haughty expression. "Being an earl does have certain prerogatives."

Great heavens! What had she done now? Her pride in her wit had put her family at risk. Aunt Elizabeth would never forgive her if she became a social pariah. Not to mention what it would do to Letty by association.

If only Anne could buy a little time, she could arrange a plausible disappearance for the young man she pretended to be. Death, though preferable, was impossible because the real Lord Decklesmoor lived and breathed at his remote country estate.

Perhaps a Grand Tour. That was it. Tomorrow she would send a polite note, thanking Marsfield for his interest, and informing him that Andrew would be leaving for the continent. Immediately. Movement from the corner of her eye caught her attention.

Marsfield rubbed his hands together. "This may prove diverting as well as convenient."

"Pardon?"

"Sorry. I was thinking out loud."

Convenient? Why would he think of a young man tagging along, aping his behavior, as convenient? "What do you mean?"

"Pardon?"

"You mentioned you would find it convenient."

"Oh, that. It's nothing."

Now she knew he had meant something by his comment. "Tell me, or I won't agree to test your method."

"That would be your loss."

She copied his nonchalant shrug.

"Very well. But I don't want this known." He looked around as if to be sure they were alone. "I have decided to seek a wife."

Marsfield in the marriage mart! Mothers of the *ton* would swoon in combined dread and anticipation. The social world would be turned upside down.

"Close you mouth before you catch a fly. It isn't that bloody unusual. Every man, even you, my boy, gets married eventually. And you can wipe that silly grin off your face."

Her smile broadened. She rubbed her hands together in an imitation of his earlier action. "This could prove diverting."

The carriage rolled to a smooth stop, forestalling further conversation.

She alighted, bounded up the front stairs of the Grosvenor Park house, and turned to tip her hat good night.

Marsfield opened the side window. "I'll call for you tomorrow at four. We'll start with a visit to my tailor."

Before she could recant the deal, the window slammed shut and the carriage pulled away.

"Hell," she said for the first time in her life. She had lied her way into another mess. "Bloody hell."

* * *

Marsfield settled back into the seat, satisfied with his evening's work. He'd set the proper wheels in motion so he could follow the recent clues into the drawing rooms of the *ton*. Andrew would provide a plausible excuse for entering the very social scene he'd avoided like the plague for so many years.

All was going rather well, yet he felt unsettled. There was . . . something he couldn't put his finger on. His instincts said something wasn't quite right, and he'd learned to trust his instincts. Was it just the slow progress of the investigation frustrating him? No, he didn't think that was it. He had no doubts as to its eventual outcome.

He reviewed his discussion with the director, but couldn't identify a cause for this vague, off-kilter feeling, as if the world had shifted the tiniest bit on its axis.

He could identify one problem. His own uncharacteristic loose tongue concerned him. Saying he intended to look for a wife had been a brilliant cover of his earlier verbal faux pas, but the fact remained, he'd made the slip. For a man whose life had often depended on his being in control of himself and the situation, this development was disturbing indeed.

First the widow, then the nephew. What was it about the members of that particular family that caused him to let down his guard?

Anne unlatched the lock, then paused to remove her shoes before she eased open the front door just wide enough to squeeze through. She didn't want to wake anyone. She didn't want to explain her disheveled appearance, explain how she'd come to smell of perfume rather than the expected odor of cigars and liquor Robert usually wore home.

She stepped inside. Cleeve, whose job as footman included watching the door for late arrivals, had propped his chair in the corner and was fast asleep.

After nudging the door closed inch by agonizing inch, she tiptoed through the hall to the foot of the staircase. The blood-curdling shriek caught her by surprise.

Her shoes flew out of her hands as she windmilled her arms to regain her balance. The silk stockings she wore seemed to give her feet a life of their own as she quick stepped to find a purchase on the smooth marble floor.

Cleeve awoke with a yell. He jumped up so fast, the chair he'd been using bounced off the wall and skittered across the floor to bark her in the shin. She grabbed the chair for balance and wound up on her knees, draped over the seat. Something flew over her head, and she heard a dull thud. Cleeve collapsed straight back, like a felled tree in a logger's dream.

She shoved the chair aside and scrambled toward him.

"Leave him alone," someone shouted.

A blow to her rump knocked her flat onto her stomach. The breath left her body in a whoosh as she slid across the hall and into a decorative four-foot-tall wooden pillar. By reflex, she curled into a ball and covered her head as the vase, flowers, and the stand that had supported them crashed to the floor.

"Get up, you scurvy little thief."

She peeked around the peony that had landed on her elbow and blinked the room into focus. "Binny?"

The old woman, dressed in her beribboned mobcap, faded red plaid dressing gown, and yellow galoshes, stood like an avenging Valkyrie with a cricket bat raised over her head.

Recognition dawned on her wrinkled face. The bat clunked to the floor.

Anne stood and gingerly picked her way through the glass shards. By the time she reached clear floor, the entire house staff, each brandishing his or her weapon of choice, surrounded her. "Please, everyone, calm down."

Cook lowered her heavy skillet, and Harvey tucked his

pistol into the waistband of his hastily donned trousers. Mrs. Finch stood a fireplace poker against the doorjamb leading to the library. The housekeeper tightened the sash of her serviceable blue serge robe, then held the neckline closed with one hand.

"I'm sorry for waking everyone," Anne said.

Finch, still dignified, though dressed in his nightshirt and pointed nightcap, brandished his ancient blunderbuss under her nose. "Who are you? What are you doing sneaking into this house?"

"Put that down before someone gets hurt," Harvey said, grabbing the barrel.

Finch wrestled for control. "I'll not let him steal from my family."

"It's all right, Finch." Anne reached for his shoulder to reassure him, but slipped on the wet floor and wound up grabbing his arm to keep from falling. As she dragged him down with her, the ancient weapon went off, exploding buckshot across the chandelier and ceiling.

At the sound of the shot, Harvey grabbed Mrs. Finch, pushed her to the floor, and then protected her with his body. In the resulting hailstorm of plaster chunks, crystal slivers, and bits of candle wax, the cook put her pan over her head, muttering about her weak heart and that girl being the death of them all.

Before the dust had a chance to settle, Anne sat up and visually reassured herself that everyone was all right. Finch refused Mrs. Binns's offer of a hand up. Harvey helped Mrs. Finch to her feet, and the butler glared at them both. They, in turn, helped Cleeve to his feet. The young man already had a goose egg forming on his forehead. Dazed, he kept blinking at Anne as if trying to bring her image into focus. But he knew his own name, the name of the Queen, and the date. Aside from having a whale of a headache in the morning, he seemed none the worse for wear.

Mrs. Binns giggled.

"What are you laughing at, you barmy old biddy?" Finch asked.

"You," she replied. "You stiff-necked old coot. In thirty years, I've never seen you mussed." She smiled. "You look a fright."

There was silence except for a few discreet coughs.

Finch bent to retrieve his nightcap from the floor, smoothed back his sparse hair as he stood, and set the cap firmly on his head. He looked directly at Mrs. Binns. "They lock up scatterpated fools."

"They put mules in traces."

Anne, used to their bickering, stepped between the two. "Now, now. We've all had a scare." She waved her arm to indicate the entire group. As her gaze followed the motion of her hand, she noticed everyone was covered in plaster dust. She tried to suppress a smile. "They all look a fright."

"You don't look so grand yourself," Mrs. Binns said.

Mrs. Finch set Anne's shoes beside her feet, urging her to beware of the glass on the floor.

As she stepped into her shoes, she inspected her own wet, soggy garments that had leaves, flower petals, and the occasional sparkling bit of crystal glued on by sodden plaster dust. "It's the latest look." She assumed the pose of an elegant gentleman. "Do you think it will catch on?"

Suddenly, everyone was talking at the same time, making fun of each other's nightclothes, arguing over their choices of weapons, and reenacting the part each one played.

"You are all crazy," Letty called from the last stair step. "I could have been killed."

In the silence, her heels clicked across the hall floor as she stomped its length to face her sister.

Anne noticed that even in the middle of the night, Letty was impeccably groomed and fashionably attired for the occasion. Her neat braid was tied with a light blue ribbon the very color of the lace at the neck of her nightdress. Her brocade dressing gown of coordinating darker blue matched her high-heeled slippers.

"I thought you were asleep," Anne said.

"With this racket? You must be joking." Letty held out one arm, and with her other hand pointed to the satin cuff. "Look at that."

Try as she might, Anne couldn't see anything.

Letty stuck her finger through a tiny hole, making it several times larger. "This is a bullet hole. Inches from my heart." She turned and pointed at Finch. "That fool nearly killed me."

"No such thing." Anne grabbed her sister's hand and tucked it through her arm. "Stop overreacting," she hissed from the side of her mouth. "He fired at the ceiling."

"I was on the landing. He aimed straight at me."

With a few simple movements of his head, Finch set everyone scurrying to clean up the mess.

Anne pulled her sister toward the stairs. She took her by the shoulders and gave her a small shake. "What is the matter with you? The gun went off by accident. Why were you hiding in the shadows?"

Letty wretched herself free. "I heard a scream." She crossed her arms and stuck out her bottom lip. "I was afraid."

"The intelligent action would have been to stay in your room with your door locked. As you saw, the servants defended you."

"Not me. It was you and your house they were defending." Letty sniffed and stomped up the stairs.

Anne ran after her. "Not so." She caught up with her on the landing where the stairs split to the east and west wings.

"They love you," Letty said. "They support your wild schemes, like tonight. Just look at you. They keep your secrets, defend you, even lie for you." She stuck out her lower lip. "They wouldn't do that for me. They hate me."

"Everyone loves you."

"They tolerate me because you make them do it."

She turned her sister to face the large framed mirror that reached from one side of the landing to the other. "You're so beautiful, how can anyone fail to adore you? Your lovely smile brings sunshine into our lives."

Letty fluffed the lace at her collar and tested a sweet expression on her reflection. "I do have a nice smile, don't I?"

"The nicest."

"I did receive a dozen cards today. Four nosegays, six poems, three boxes of candy—"

"And a partridge in a pear tree?"

"And a handkerchief embroidered with my initials, which of course, I returned as being too personal. I hardly remember meeting the gentleman."

Anne suppressed a twinge of jealousy. In her entire two Seasons, she hadn't received that much attention all told, much less after one evening. "That was the proper thing to do."

"You shall have to tell me of your adventure. I'm sure it was quite fascinating."

"It was . . ."

Letty covered a yawn. "Maybe tomorrow. Lord Asterbule is taking me driving in the park tomorrow, and I don't want to have unattractive dark circles under my eyes."

"Yes, of course. Good night." As Letty resumed her way up to her room, Anne turned and checked the front entrance. The floor was spotless and everyone had returned to bed except for Harvey, who had assumed Cleeve's position by the door. Before she had a chance to thank him for his earlier actions, she noticed his chin droop slowly to his chest. The familiar light under the door to the library showed that Mrs. Binns had returned to her solitary guardian duties against the forces of evil that haunted the hours of darkness.

In her own room, Anne found a pitcher of hot water, a light snack of fruit and biscuits, and a pot of sweetened chocolate beneath the tea cozy. Despite her usual ablutions, the comfort of her oldest cotton nightdress worn to silken softness, and the warmth of her down coverlet, she couldn't fall asleep.

Her sister was right. The evening had been fascinating—the first real adventure of Anne's normally staid life. Not that her life was boring. No, it just wasn't . . . adventuresome.

Tonight, she'd become one of her brave heroines. She'd flaunted convention by dressing as a boy and risked her reputation by riding alone with man in a carriage—not to mention the trip to Rose's Garden. Why, she was probably the only woman of her acquaintance who had actually seen the inside of a brothel.

Rising from her bed, she wrapped a heavy shawl around her shoulders and poked the fire to life. Then she retrieved her writing supplies.

Eight

The first pearl gray shadings of dawn were visible through the fan-shaped window over the front door. In spite of her lack of sleep, Anne's step was light and energetic. Her bedroom slippers made no sound on the carpeted stairs. No sense waking the servants just because she was hungry.

She'd spent the entire night transforming the troublesome gaming hall scene in her recent manuscript. Blackthorne, editor extraordinaire, had been correct in his assessment. The scene was pivotal in the hero's development, and changing it to a brothel setting made it even stronger. And she'd included Rose and Jasmine as characters as a thank you for their kindness. Now she couldn't wait for the day to begin so she could see her publisher and present him with the amended pages.

As she skipped down the last three steps, the front door banged open. Robert stumbled in, supported under one arm by his childhood friend, country neighbor, and gambling cohort, Geoffrey. Both were singing a raunchy ditty, of which Robert had apparently forgotten half the words.

Harvey sprang from his seat by the door where he had been napping. By stepping under Robert's free arm, the coachman kept his drunken master from tripping over his own feet.

"Halloo," Robert said. He narrowed his eyes and peered

closer at his savior. "Where's Cleeve? He always puts me to bed."

Harvey did not seem to have any trouble understanding Robert's slurred speech. "I'm here to do the honors, sir. Let's get you to your room now."

Though her first reaction was to slip away, Anne decided to stay. Robert should know she wasn't fooled by his patent excuses. Her witness to his condition would be valuable when she confronted him later with his unacceptable behavior. She stood on the last step, blocking their way upstairs.

The three men noticed her presence and came to an abrupt halt. Robert's shocked reaction nearly knocked his supporters down. He made an effort and, straightening his waistcoat, stood tall and tried not to weave.

Momentarily freed of his burden, Geoffrey made an elegant leg, executing an old-fashioned courtly bow. "Miss Anne." He eyed her from neck to ankle. "You're looking well this fine evening."

His insolent perusal of her dishabille and the unholy glint in his eye made her feel as if he could see right through her modest night wear. She'd forgotten she wasn't dressed to receive callers. Crossing her arms, she thinned her lips into a severe line.

"Good morning," she said, with the emphasis on the second word. The stench of their evening's revelry reached her nostrils, and she fought the urge to step back. Nor did she step forward, because the height of the single stair gave her the advantage of looking down her nose at them. She glared at her brother. "Robert."

He leaned away from her disdain and would have toppled backward if Harvey had not stepped behind him to support him under the arms.

"Don't be angry, Annie," Robert said with an ingratiating smile. "Look!" He pulled large crumpled wads of money out of each pocket. "We're rich."

"You're drunk."

He shrugged one shoulder with such force it caused him to lurch sideways. Harvey managed to keep him standing, but only by wrapping his arms around the younger man's chest.

Robert looked up at her, his puppy-dog-brown eyes pleading for understanding. "I always win when I'm drunk."

"We will discuss this later," she said, stepping to one side. She signaled Harvey with a movement of her head, and the servant half walked, half carried Robert past her and up the stairs.

Geoffrey leaned one elbow on the nearby newel post. "A proper hostess would invite me to stay for breakfast."

Proper? What would he know about proper? Whenever Robert was not around, Geoffrey made most improper advances toward her. If only she could kick him in the shins as she had when she'd been a child. She tightened her crossed arms and raised her nose a fraction of an inch.

"Breakfast will not be served for two hours."

"I can think of several ways we could . . . entertain each other to while away the time."

As he spoke she followed his gaze and realized he was staring at her bosom. She also realized the position of her arms had pushed her too small breasts into voluptuous mounds. She dropped her hands to her side.

Finch appeared in the hallway, dressed in his usual somber livery. "Is there anything I can do for you, miss?" he said, his voice modulated and face expressionless, as if this were a normal afternoon call.

She shot him a look of gratitude, though he didn't betray his understanding with so much as a blink.

"Thank you, Finch. This gentleman was just leaving."

"Very good, miss." The butler walked the length of the hall, opened the door, and stood by the open portal like a sentry.

"Your trusted minions protect you well. It will not always be so," Geoffrey whispered for her ears only.

A shiver of dread snaked up her spine.

He noticed and chuckled. After another elegant bow, he slapped on his hat and sauntered from the house whistling the same raunchy tune he'd been singing when he entered.

She sank to a sitting position on the steps, suddenly exhausted.

"Bloody hell," she whispered. This time the obscenity came easily to her lips.

Marsfield poured the last bit of coffee into his cup. Before ringing for a fresh pot, he glanced at the clock and decided to wait. Though his usual routine started unfashionably early, this morning he'd risen well before dawn after a night of fitful slumber. Organization and order always soothed his spirits. He'd already finished a mound of personal correspondence, including the notes that would rearrange his schedule for this afternoon, drafted a new piece of legislation to be presented to the banking committee of the House of Lords next month, and had caught up on his reading of the latest scientific journals.

At the stroke of seven, the door to his office opened. His man of business stopped on the threshold with a look of distress on his face. "Excuse me, your lordship. If I'd known you were here, I would have knocked."

"Quite all right, Bartholomew. No offense taken. Come in. Come in." The flustered secretary had been his man of business ever since he'd assumed the earldom and had worked for his father for several years before that. Marsfield laid the stack of journals on the corner of his desk.

"These can be catalogued and filed. These"—he added his personal notes, folded and sealed with his wax and crest—"are to be delivered this morning." Onto those he laid the usual invitations to society's amusements. "Send my regrets." On the top he put six more engraved invitations, stacked crossways to differentiate them from the rest. "And accept these."

"Accept them, sir?"

He ignored the man's look of surprise. "Yes, of course."

"Yes, of course," Bartholomew echoed, looking around the room as if he didn't quite understand how he got there, didn't quite know what to do first.

Marsfield ducked his head to hide a smile. No doubt his man felt as if he'd stepped into someone else's shoes. This wasn't their normal, well-established order of business. And he'd never accepted invitations of that sort before.

Even though Marsfield didn't usually enter the office until eight o'clock, he knew Bartholomew's morning routine included a lengthy visit to the kitchen below, where he would drink coffee and chat with the housekeeper. At first Marsfield had suspected a romance, not that he would have been displeased, but the affair had never progressed beyond the morning ritual. At least, not to his knowledge. Perhaps they should salvage as much of their routine as possible.

"Bartholomew? Before you get started . . ."

"Yes, your lordship?"

"I realize this is an imposition, and not one of your regular duties, but I would appreciate it if you'd fetch me a fresh pot of coffee from the kitchen. The staff is undoubtedly very busy right now."

"It wouldn't be an imposition at all." He jumped up and very nearly ran from the room.

"And Bartholomew?"

"Yes, your lordship?"

"Don't be in a hurry to return. I could use another hour of solitude to finish this project. We can resume at eight o'clock, if that is convenient."

"Absolutely, sir. Eight o'clock."

After Bartholomew left, Marsfield leaned back in his

chair, propped his hands behind his head and his boots on the edge of his desk. Did Bartholomew desire the plump and competent Mrs. Knowelton? Did she long for ordinary looking Bartholomew to sweep her into his arms, to stroke her with his ink-stained fingers?

Bloody hell. Now he was playing cupid for his loyal servants. What was wrong with him? He may have started thinking of others, but the woman he pictured in his mind was his own private romantic vision. Cassandra.

This time, she stood in a field of daisies, a breeze blowing her wild dark blond curls around her angelic face. She smiled, and the warmth of it reached to melt his hardened heart. The look in her eyes told him she knew how well her diaphanous gown enticed him. The gentle wind molded her dress against her body, then plucked it away, teasing him with the momentary shape of her thigh or the glimpse of a defined nipple. The picture was indistinct, fuzzy, yet he remembered with clarity the feel of her against his body, her curves fitting perfectly—

He sat his chair forward with a thump. He grabbed his pen with a determined swipe. Damn it! He'd accepted that the Cassandra he remembered was a figment of his imagination or, at worst, the personification of some deeply denied need or desire. Whatever she was, she was not real. So why did she continue to haunt his dreams? Hell, his waking hours, too. He shifted in the chair. His body didn't realize his brain had conjured her out of thin air.

Maybe he should reconsider taking on another mistress. For some reason, the prospect didn't hold the appeal it had in former years.

Since he'd accepted he would marry, perhaps he should act on the decision sooner rather than later. Maybe that was an subconscious reason why he'd slipped and told Andrew marriage was his reason for returning to society.

Would a wedding put to rest his romantic fantasies? Most likely not. As a logical man and a member of the aristocracy, he knew marriage had nothing to do with romance. A society wedding was a business agreement disguised by flamboyant ceremony and pompous ritual.

However, that particular contract would have the benefit of release for his frustrated urges. And relief would, hopefully, diminish the frequency of his daydreams.

He took out his notebook. While he made the promised fair copy of his instructions for obtaining a mistress to send to Andrew, he also copied his requirements in a wife as a reminder. He was a man of logic and would chose his bride in a befitting manner.

He set the finished copies aside.

As long as he was forced to attend society functions to further his investigation, it wouldn't hurt to look around. He'd heard the newest crop held a fair number of beauties. Now he sounded as shallow as his young so-called assistants, Burke and Preston. Damnation.

Bartholomew returned and Marsfield threw himself into a determined frenzy of work.

The day that had started so badly did not improve for Anne. Not only had Mr. Blackthorne been unavailable to see her revised manuscript today, the normal myriad duties of running a house had been disrupted by one domestic crisis after another. The butcher's boy delivered the wrong order and cook set off to straighten the butcher's hair, leaving her assistant to burn the toast and undercook the eggs.

Because Cleeve had been given the day off to recover and Harvey was out making arrangements for the repair of the ceiling and chandelier, only Finch was available to help when Mrs. Binns dropped off to sleep in the middle of breakfast and fell off her chair, twisting her ankle. In his efforts to raise the hefty woman, Finch strained his back and couldn't straighten up. After he was treated by the doctor, Anne ensconced the pair on opposite ends of the parlor couch and instructed them to rest.

Then Letty had insisted she needed new gloves for her afternoon carriage ride with Lord Asterbule. Attempts at reason had produced only a stubbornly set chin and one pitiful tear. When Anne agreed to accompany her, she hadn't realized it would take her sister two hours to find the perfect pair of gloves.

She'd planned to take Robert to task for his gambling while his embarrassment at facing her this morning was still fresh in his mind. Unfortunately, Robert had risen while she was gone and left the house in the company of another gentleman. Probably Geoffrey, from the description provided by the workmen on the scaffold in the hall. They had overheard the gentlemen discussing Jack's boxing gym.

Luncheon was inedible because cook had not returned. When she finally did return at one o'clock, it was to announce that she and the butcher were to be married as soon as her replacement could be found. Anne opened a bottle of champagne to toast their good fortune—in the parlor, of course, so Mrs. Binns and Finch could stop arguing long enough to raise a glass.

When a messenger delivered the packet from Marsfield, she escaped to the quiet of her room with a whisper of thanks to a benevolent Almighty.

She glanced through the two lists, smiling because he'd also included his requirements for a perfect wife. The bold strokes of his pen enraptured her. She could hear his deep voice in her mind as she read the words. The third piece in the packet was a personal, the type of informal stationery one used to correspond with a friend. His crest was engraved on the front.

She ran her finger lightly over the familiar eagle, the same image as on his ring, correct even to the two tiny red eyes. Her breath came in shallow puffs; her heartbeat raced.

Silly woman. What was she expecting? A love letter? Mentally shaking herself, she flipped the note open and read the ordinary verbiage of one gentleman to another.

Will call for you at three o'clock. This is earlier than we discussed, but there is a pair of blacks scheduled to go on the block this afternoon. You will enjoy the auction.

She shook her head at his presumption, but he was right. She probably would enjoy the excitement of Tattersall's, never having been to the noted auction barn before. It was said the finest horseflesh in the world could be seen. However, she couldn't go with him. She already had the research she needed. One evening disguised as Andrew was sufficient adventure for her. As she withdrew a sheet of her stationery to write her regrets, she realized the delicate beige rose parchment wouldn't be used by a young man.

Since her brother was out, she decided to pilfer a few sheets of his personal stationery.

Anne didn't make a practice of entering her brother's rooms, which were located in the opposite wing of the house from her own. Hoping she wouldn't run into Martin, Robert's valet, she eased through the door.

Martin had been with Robert only since they'd returned to London, and none of the household servants liked or trusted him. By the condition of the room, he was lazy as well as self-important and condescending. Robert's clothes lay everywhere, the bed was unmade, and his shaving water hadn't been emptied.

Martin was another matter she should probably discuss with Robert. Fighting the urge to tidy up, she walked straight to her brother's writing table for the object of her errand.

She moved aside a chair in order to open the desk drawer, and in so doing noticed a deep blue coat of superfine draped over the arm of a chair. If she *had* been going to Tattersall's, that would have been her choice of apparel, with . . . she looked in the large wardrobe. Yes, the tan chamois pants and the maroon silk vest with the embroidered clock pattern.

She removed her choices and held them up to herself in front of the mirror in his dressing room. With a white shirt and a high-pointed collar—

The rattle of the latch on the door leading to the servants' stair startled her. Good heavens, what could she say if Martin caught her going through her brother's closet? She scurried into the hall and raced back to the safety of her own room.

Leaning against the closed door, she caught her breath. That had been a close call. Only then did she realize she'd forgotten the paper she'd gone to fetch. And she still held her brother's clothes clutched to her chest.

Could she pass for a boy in the light of day?

Even as she shook her head at the ridiculous idea, she laid the clothes on her bed, smoothing out the wrinkles and adding the freshly laundered shirt and cravat she'd worn the night before. Harvey had said people saw what they expected to see unless one gave them a reason to doubt their own eyes.

Marsfield hadn't seen through her disguise, and he was the most intelligent man she'd ever met. Jasmine, with all her vast experience, had thought her a man. Or, rather, they had both thought her an inexperienced boy. They had seen exactly what they expected to see.

She glanced at the clock on her writing desk. One hour and a half to alter the clothes and learn a sufficient amount to convince Marsfield she knew her way around a horse barn.

Did she dare?

Nine

Anne finished shortening the second sleeve and snipped the thread with her tiny sewing scissors. Today's preparations were proceeding quickly because only the coat sleeves and pants had to be shortened. Her hair and disguising spectacles were set to go. The linen and accessories from yesterday would serve.

Harvey insisted on a refresher course in walking, standing, and sitting like a man. She strode around the room while Mrs. Finch continued sewing, and Harvey pontificated on the finer points of horseflesh evaluation.

"A horse high in the withers won't make a good saddle mount, because the rider will always feel as if he's leaning forward a wee bit. Don't stand so stiff and straight. Loosen your shoulders. Slouch a little."

"Her posture will be ruined," Mrs. Finch said around a mouthful of pins.

It wasn't her posture Anne was worried about. She sat and propped one ankle on her other knee. The effect was somewhat comical, considering she was wearing an afternoon tea dress of muslin with dainty roses embroidered around the hem. She ignored Mrs. Finch's shudder.

"It's hopeless," Anne said to Harvey. "I'll never remember all this. I'll make a fool of myself for sure."

He shook his head. "You'll do fine. Just examine different parts of the horse with a thoughtful frown on your face. After all, you're not buying, Marsfield is. And he's reputed to be an excellent judge of horses."

"What if he asks me what I think?"

"The ultimate questions of a horse's worth cannot be determined by its size or proportions. Is he a goer? Will he respond to his rider or driver? In other words, does he have heart?" He chuckled. "I once lost a guinea on a horse that looked no better than the poorest moth-eaten hack because he ran like the wind and refused to let another horse get in front of him during a race. He was all heart."

"And *you're* teaching her about horses?" Mrs. Finch said.

"I was much younger when that happened. I'd like to think I have better judgment now."

"How can you tell?" Anne asked.

"I don't bet on losing horses," Harvey said.

"No. How can you tell if a horse has heart?"

"There's just something about the way he looks back at you when you look him straight in the eye." He shrugged. "It takes years of experience."

"I don't have that much time," Anne said with a groan.

"You don't need to answer the question in order to sound like you know about horses. You just need to ask it."

She glanced at the clock. "Eek. It's twenty to three."

"Done," Mrs. Finch said, holding up the tan pants.

Anne grabbed them and ran for her dressing room.

With Mrs. Finch's help, she bound her breasts and donned her boy's clothing in eighteen minutes flat. After snatching up her hat and gloves on the way through her room, she descended the stairs and ran toward the front door just as the hall clock began to chime.

A carriage bearing Marsfield's crest pulled up. She didn't want anyone to come to the door. Then she might have to explain either the scaffolding in the hall or the bickering that could be heard coming from the parlor. She continued running down the front steps. The footman opened the carriage door. Unable to slow her forward motion in time, she practically launched herself into the vehicle.

She stumbled across the feet of two additional and unexpected bodies in the carriage. With mumbled apologies for stepping on his toes, she plopped into the empty space next to Marsfield on the forward-facing seat.

"Punctual, I see," he said, unruffled by her clumsy entrance. He snapped his watch closed and returned it to its pocket.

"I didn't want to keep the horses standing."

He looked at her with a raised eyebrow. "They barely came to a full stop."

The intended sarcasm in his tone was totally mitigated by the flash of his dimple. In his amusement, his expressive eyes turned the brilliant color of a clear May sky. She pictured a lone eagle soaring in joyous freedom in the wild blue expanse. She had to turn away.

That brought her to face the two other occupants. After giving his coachman the signal to go by tapping his cane on the ceiling, Marsfield formally introduced Preston and Burke.

There was a moment of awkward silence.

"Are you purchasing or just looking?" Burke asked.

"Interested in any particular horses?" Preston asked simultaneously, as if they were as nervous as she was.

She pushed her spectacles up. At Weathersby they hadn't purchased a new horse for years. They had two gentle ladies' mares that were swaybacked and long in the tooth, but sufficed for their undemanding needs. A pair of aged geldings pulled the ancient family coach. The only other equine was a plow horse she hoped would live through another planting and harvest.

Remembering to keep her voice pitched low, she answered, "Just looking. I've been mostly in the country. We keep only the usual saddle mounts and plow horses."

"Do you ride to the hounds?" Burke asked.

Now what could she say? What kind of country-bred aristocrat didn't ride to the hounds? In her teens she'd been invited to a few hunts, but her father had handled all the affairs concerning the horses. After her mother's death, she'd little free time while she raised Letty and Robert. The fine stable they once maintained had been sold to pay her father's gambling debts. She pushed on her spectacles again. "I've not often had the opportunity."

"Health reasons," Marsfield explained.

Burke and Preston nodded in acceptance. She shot Marsfield a grateful look.

"I'm quite looking forward to Tattersall's," she said. "Heard the horseflesh offered for sale is the finest available."

The two young men looked at each other in confusion.

"My oversight," Marsfield confessed. He apologized. "I assumed you would know I meant Squire Humphrey's annual auction. But you won't be disappointed. It has gained quite a reputation over the years and attracts some excellent merchandise."

"And quite the crowd," Preston added, with an elbow to Burke's side.

Before she could worry about that little byplay, Marsfield steered the conversation toward the horses that would be offered at the auction. All three men were passionate about their cattle and the rest of the ride proceeded without any more inquisitive questioning. In fact, she barely had to speak at all.

They parked the carriage among a long line of similar conveyances and tromped across a muddy field to an area of makeshift corrals. The area was crowded, and the group soon split up. Preston and Burke were both interested in a particular stallion and didn't want to waste time looking at the matched pairs. They arranged to meet at Marsfield's carriage in two hours.

Anne accompanied Marsfield as he walked aimlessly

through the crowd, stopping to examine a horse here, talking to a seller there, and passing the time with a friend. She'd been introduced to more men in one afternoon than in her entire life.

There were a number of women present, but they mostly stayed in their carriages parked around the perimeter of the field. She occasionally caught a glimpse of fashionable dress as they visited back and forth, but mostly she kept her attention on Marsfield's conversation—and on where she put her feet.

He stopped to study a pair of dappled grays. Marsfield examined their teeth, felt their fetlocks, and smoothed his hand over their withers as the seller iterated the horses' finer points.

"What do you think?" he asked her.

She put her chin in her hand and furrowed her brow. "Of course, the ultimate question is, do they have heart?"

"Quite so," he agreed, and steered her away with a hand on her shoulder.

"All right, it's time to look at the blacks." He started in that direction at a slow pace.

"I don't understand. If they're the only horses you're interested in buying, as you said in the carriage earlier, why didn't we go there first?"

He gave her a quizzical look. "Not much of a horse trader, are you?"

She could only shrug.

"If the seller knows how much you want a particular item, he will jack up the price. If you have demonstrated interest in other similar items and can present that you are willing to walk away from his deal, that's a bargaining chip in your favor."

She nodded. "I see. The economic principle of supply and demand at its most basic level."

He smiled. "I would say its most basic level is in human relations. This is your first lesson. Horse trading is an example of the number one principle of how to attract a woman. Express interest, but also indicate that there are others of equal interest."

She returned his smile. Women had been using the same technique for eons. "I get the point." She quoted his notes. "Principle number one: Do not let the woman of choice know you are interested."

"Exactly. Now, while I'm talking to the seller of the blacks, I want you to make yourself scarce after a few minutes. Go for a refreshment, go to the jakes, or . . . whatever. Make something up."

"Why?"

"Your disappearance will be a convenient excuse to leave at the time most suitable to my purposes."

"I want to hear what you say, how you handle him."

Marsfield set his jaw, but he also took a deep breath that puffed up his chest. He was obviously not immune to the subtle flattery.

"It would be educational for me," she added.

"Yes, yes." He shook his head as if not believing he was relenting. "You can circle around and eavesdrop, but stay out of sight."

"Certainly."

The plan worked smoothly. The vendor had only begun to point out the fine shapes of the horses' heads when she excused herself to look at some other horses nearby.

Watching her step, she nearly bumped smack into Geoffrey and Robert. She ducked around a large white mare in the nick of time. What was Robert doing here? He was supposed to be at the boxing gym. Surely her brother would have no trouble seeing through her disguise. And Geoffrey? She didn't even want to think what his recognizing her could mean. Bending over to look between the horse's legs, she waited with bated breath for Robert's shoes to pass by.

His shoes stopped on the other side of the white. Robert

and Geoffrey discussed the relative merits of the horse. Any second one of them could walk around the animal to complete their inspection, and catch her. Backing away, she turned and fled.

She was soon lost in the maze of equipment, mud, and excrement, yet she feared using the main aisles. Her best plan of action was to make her way to the perimeter and wait for Marsfield at his carriage—if she could find it. She was so turned around, and she felt as if she had walked for miles.

Robert's old boots, even with paper stuffed in the toes, were rubbing blisters on her heels. Anne found a hay bale and sat down to rest her poor abused feet. What she wouldn't give for a basin of hot water steaming with fragrant herbs and a pair of soft satin slippers. She remembered to sit like a man, spreading her feet apart.

The movement dislodged a large field mouse from his hiding place of loose straw, and she wasn't sure who squeaked louder, she or the animal. Anne jumped up onto the hay bale. Though the mouse disappeared in a moment, she took a few seconds longer to catch her breath.

When a hand reached up to help her from her perch, she automatically took it and stepped gracefully down.

Then she realized her mistake.

She snatched her hand back, but from the look on Preston's face, it was too late. "I . . . climbed up there to . . . to see if I could spot Marsfield's carriage," she stuttered.

Preston crossed his arms. "Perhaps, but methinks there is more to the tale, *Andrew*. Though I'm sure that isn't your real name."

"Bloody hell," Anne groaned, sinking back down onto the hay bale. The jig was up, and it was time to pay the piper. Her only recourse was to appeal to Marsfield for mercy. Not for herself—her reputation was shredded beyond redemption—but for her sister. For Letty's sake, Anne would beg and plead.

"Go ahead," she said to Preston with a wave of her hand. "Fetch Lord Marsfield and I'll confess the whole sordid story to him."

Rather than leave, Preston pulled up another hay bale and sat across from her.

"Now it's getting interesting," he said, an unholy glint in his eyes. "You're saying Marsfield doesn't know you're a woman?"

She nodded, and he hooted with laughter.

Suddenly he stilled. "Are you trying to blackmail him or something? Is this some crazy ploy to trick him into marriage?"

"Nothing like that," she assured Preston. But the only way she could convince him she didn't have matrimonial designs on his friend was to tell him the whole, if abbreviated and edited, story.

When she was done, Preston slapped his hands on his knees. "This is too good to be true. Stuffy old Marsfield fooled by a slip of a girl. I love it."

"He is neither stuffy nor old," she said bristling. "And I would prefer not to be called a girl if you use that tone."

Preston apologized. "But you must admit, he doesn't have a sense of humor."

"I think he's witty."

"Not the same. Have you ever heard him laugh out loud?"

"No, but I hardly know him."

"Then you've never been on the receiving end of one of his sanctimonious, know-it-all stares."

"Well . . ."

"Aha." Preston pounced on her words, or lack thereof. "Then you know what I mean."

She had to admit she did.

"Then you must see the humor in this situation. I can't wait to see the look on his face when he finds out the truth." Preston rubbed his hands together. "Man oh man, it will be so good to be one up on him for a change. Please say I can be there when you tell him."

"I have—rather, had, until now—no intention of his ever finding out the truth. Once I had the information I needed, Andrew was simply going to go on a Grand Tour and never come back. I'd planned on sending Marsfield a note to that effect tomorrow."

"You can't give up now."

"I have more information than I could use in a dozen books, thank you very much." She didn't relish the idea of facing Marsfield near as much as Preston apparently did. But then, he would only be a spectator at the crucifixion. She would be the one on the receiving end of his wrath.

"Nonsense. There's much more to see."

She shook her head.

"I'll help you," he offered. "Burke will, too."

"Burke?" she choked.

"Sure. This is too rich not to let him in on it. We can go to Vauxhall Gardens. The areas respectable women never see," he said, wagging his eyebrows.

She hesitated, but shook her head.

"What about a tavern? You could use that in a book, right? I know a great seedy dockside tavern with pirates, robbers, and all sorts of miscreants that defy my limited powers of description. You'll love it."

The offer was almost too tempting to resist, but she had to say no. She'd fooled everyone so far, but if Preston had seen through her disguise, it was only a matter of time before she slipped up in front of Marsfield. The risk was too great.

"Thank you," she said. "If I get through the rest of today, Andrew is going to retire." She stood and straightened her coat. "Now, which way is Marsfield's coach?"

* * *

She spotted Marsfield ahead, leaning back against his carriage, his arms and ankles crossed in a relaxed manner, as if he owned the world. Burke was slouched next to him, his expression glum. She gave Preston a brilliant smile and sauntered toward Marsfield, hands in her pockets, humming the raunchy ditty Robert and Geoffrey had sung the night before.

"Did you buy the blacks?" she asked as she approached.

"I'm satisfied as to their value. My man will handle the transaction if an agreement on the price can be reached. What have you two been up to?" Marsfield asked.

The question was casual and offhand, but she noticed Preston's face blanched to the color of his stark white collar.

"I don't know about the rest of you," she said, drawing Marsfield's attention, "but I've had wonderful time listening to everyone. It's been most educational," she added with a wink at Marsfield. He would, she knew, misconstrue the meaning of her truthful statement to reflect the light of their own previous conversation, however that worked to her advantage.

Her stomach growled loudly. She laughed at Preston's embarrassed expression and resultant blush. Did he think women never got hungry?

"Obviously, I'm famished. Isn't anyone else hungry?"

"I've made arrangements for us all to dine at my club before we take you out gaming," Marsfield replied to her question.

She wasn't to go directly home after all. Marsfield had made additional plans. Despite her earlier protestations to Preston that she was ready to end the masquerade, the anticipation of spending more time with Marsfield held a certain appeal she refused to analyze.

The inside of a gentleman's private club—and a gaming hell, all in the same night! And in Marsfield's company. Her stomach did a little flip-flop, which she attributed to not eating a proper meal all day.

Burke cleared his throat. "There's a respectable pub right down the road. I could do with a pork pie and a pint myself."

"Capital idea," Preston agreed. "A pub is just the thing. Your club is much too stuffy and high in the instep."

"Nonsense," Marsfield contradicted. "Not that I'm adverse to decent pub fare on occasion, but I refuse to accept it when I have an excellent meal waiting."

Her stomach growled audibly again. "What time will supper be served?"

"Gads," Marsfield said with a chuckle. "You're as bad as Burke and Preston. I'd swear they eat every two hours like suckling babes." He waved off their objections to his reference. "We'll stop on the way, but I expect each one of you to do justice to the meal tonight, or the chef will be insulted."

She nodded in unison with Preston and Burke.

Marsfield opened the carriage door himself. As the others piled in, he removed his glove, stuck two fingers to his lips, and produced a piercing whistle. Immediately, two men detached themselves from the knot of liveried servants and trotted toward the coach. He gave them directions and climbed into the coach.

"I wish I could do that," she said.

The conversation on the short ride centered on the mechanics of whistling. To her delight, she could produce a thinner, weaker imitation of his original example by the time they pulled in to the inn yard.

As she disembarked, Anne noted the sign of the Green Goose seemed familiar. She followed Marsfield as she tried to shake off a strange feeling of déjà vu. Though she'd never been here, she'd stopped at a few inns in her lifetime, she reasoned. One inn yard looked pretty much like the next.

Didn't it?

Ten

As Marsfield led the way into the inn, Preston excused himself for a minute and dragged Burke along the path that led to the rear of the building. Anne followed Marsfield, looking around, trying to identify a specific reason for her uneasiness.

Marsfield spoke to a plump and blushing girl at the door. He declined the use of a private dining room because both were currently in use and he professed to be in a hurry. He had no objection to a table at the back of the dimly lit public room.

After a short wait, during which Marsfield asked general questions about the auction and Anne answered in as few words as possible, they were shown to a table. He took the seat against the wall. She sat to his left. Burke and Preston joined them, sharing the bench facing them across a small table, thankfully clean, though distressed by years of hard use.

The waitress appeared immediately and dipped an awkward curtsy. "Lord Marsfield, it's good to see you."

Mrs. Parkins! Anne wanted to sink into the floor and die. He'd brought them to the very inn where she'd pretended to be his wife last April. From what she knew of Mrs. Parkins, the woman would have no qualms about confronting the earl about any chicanery brought into her inn.

Ann rose to run, but her path was blocked by a group of laborers just seating themselves at the next table. Then she realized running would do no good. Marsfield knew where she lived. Perhaps she should confess all before she was unmasked.

Marsfield rose and kissed the innkeeper's weathered hand as if she were a great lady.

Mrs. Parkins slapped at him with her dish towel for his efforts, but she giggled like a schoolgirl. "Sit down. No need to waste your charming ways on me. The mister is already fetching your favorite brandy."

"The boys were hungry, and I knew your pork pie would be just the thing."

"If I'd known, I'd would've made you some special, but all I've got is shepherd's pie, chicken pasties, and beef stew." She looked around the table. "What'll it be, boys?"

Anne sat slowly and let out the breath she'd been holding. Mrs. Parkins either hadn't recognized her or had decided not to say anything. In turn, Anne decided to brazen out the situation. She looked at Preston and Burke and copied their relaxed pose by crossing her arms on the table.

She hadn't attended to the discussion of the meal selections, so when they ordered chicken pasties all around, she nodded in agreement.

A young girl brought three foaming tankards of ale, a bottle of brandy and glass, and set them on the table.

The boys each grabbed one and took a long swig. Anne had tasted ale before and found it not unpleasant. She'd never been much inclined to imbibe spirits, what with the males of her family's inclination to become overly fond of drink. However, the day was unusually warm for October, and she'd walked miles and miles around the corrals. She copied their actions and took a long drink.

"This is me daughter, Sophie, what'll be serving you, so I want you boys to behave yourselves."

"We know, Mrs. Parkins," Burke said. He removed his handkerchief to wipe the foam from his mouth.

Preston wiped his mouth on his sleeve like most of the other patrons. "No hanky-panky," he said.

Mrs. Parkins gave a curt, satisfied nod. As they left, the girl looked back over her shoulder at the young men and smiled.

Anne laughed at the dour look on their faces.

Marsfield laid his hands open on the table. "You said food. You didn't mention other appetites."

"You know me," Burke said. "Always ready for a little slap and tickle." Then, as if he'd just realized what he said, he glanced at Anne and ducked his head.

Anne guessed Preston had taken the opportunity earlier to tell Burke of the situation. He certainly hadn't wasted any time. She knew this was a defining moment. If she wanted to make it through the evening to see the gentleman's club and the gaming hell, she would have to do something to put Burke at ease.

"Yeah, Marsfield," she said, jabbing him the arm with her elbow. "Weren't you ever young?"

He grunted in reaction. "I'm not old. I'm discriminating."

"Well, that's one word for it." She heard a titter of laughter from across the table.

He turned in his chair to face her. "And you'll keep your sharp elbows on the table, if you know what's good for you."

She stuck her chin out at a belligerent angle and raised her fists. "Or what?"

The boys howled with laughter. The fact that they knew she was a woman probably fueled their hilarity.

She kept her attention on Marsfield's eyes. He could control his expression, but to her, their changeable color was a clear window to his emotions. She loved that May sky color they turned when he was amused. Of course, she was looking through her blue tinted glasses. What if she'd read him wrong? She pushed at her spectacles as if they offered her protection.

Marsfield merely rolled his eyes. "This is what comes of being raised by your aunt. You make a fist like a bloody woman. If you'd hit me, you'd have broken both your thumbs."

She looked down. "I haven't had much opportunity . . ."

Suddenly contrite, Marsfield apologized. "I forgot. Health reasons?" he asked with kindness and sympathy.

She nodded and flicked a glance at the boys, who had buried their noses in their tankards.

Marsfield held up his hands and demonstrated making a fist. "Curl your fingers as tightly as you can. The thumb wraps around the fingers between the first and second knuckles, making a parallel line."

His hands, so elegant and expressive, became powerful, lethal-looking weapons.

"Now, you try it."

She copied his example, but her fists were puny, weak imitations. He held up his hand palm open and, at his insistence, she hit him several times until the food was served.

"Good job," Marsfield said, slapping her on the back before he turned his attention to his plate.

She caught herself on the table edge before she fell face first into her food. Good heavens. That wasn't a plate. It was a platter. Two huge pasties, each the size to feed a family of six, framed a mountain of mashed potatoes containing a lake of gravy deep enough to launch a boat. Even if it were possible for her to eat it all, she wouldn't be able to walk for a week.

She looked up at the serving girl. "Thank you."

The girl polished several pieces of silverware on her apron before reaching over to lay them by the plate. Anne was shocked to feel the young girl's breast brush her arm. Her gaze flew back to the girl's face, and she received a smile and a wink in response.

"I think she likes you," Preston chortled.

Burke choked on a swallow of ale.

"I'm taking Andrew to the boxing gym tomorrow," Marsfield said, as if he'd missed the entire incident.

Anne was glad for the change of subject, and she wasn't concerned about tomorrow. Regrets could be sent and that would be the end of the matter. Surviving today took all her concentration. Aping the actions of her companions, she tried to eat her food as quickly as the others consumed theirs.

Preston plastered a serious expression on his face. "I'm sure boxing lessons will be most helpful to Andrew. Burke and I can come along. Sparring partners and all that. Couldn't hurt us to go over the basics again. Might be quite interesting." He silenced Burke's giggle with a warning twitch of his elbow.

"Bloody hell," she said under her breath.

"Chin up, mate," Preston said, looking directly at her. "We've both been on the short end of Marsfield's tutorial stick for some time now. We won't make fun of you, and we can help you be a better man."

She smiled her acknowledgment of his wit.

"What do you mean tutorial stick?" Marsfield pushed back from his plate. "I only offer advice when and where sorely needed."

"In the pedantic manner of an Oxford don forced to teach level fours."

"Yeah," Burke agreed, even though his mouth was full.

"I didn't ask to have you two attached to my coattails."

She looked back and forth across the table. But she didn't understand the unspoken communication that seemed to be taking place beneath the text of the conversation.

Preston and Burke were the first to break eye contact.

Marsfield looked at his watch. He stood abruptly and tossed several coins on the table. "My tailor is expecting Andrew. I'll meet you at the carriage in five minutes."

She'd forgotten the about tailor, the original errand of the day which Marsfield had mentioned last night. She watched him as he stepped up to the bar to have a few words with Parkins, the beefy innkeeper she remembered. How could she cry off the tailor, yet gain admittance to his club later in the evening?

Burke excused himself to the jakes. The fullness of her bladder urged her to follow. It might prove awkward, but it wasn't like it would get better if she submitted herself to a carriage ride after drinking two pints of ale.

"Don't worry," Preston whispered. "I'll be there to help you."

"At the necessary?"

He looked confused. "At the tailor."

"Oh. Right." Silly. Of course, he'd meant the tailor. He hadn't heard the workings of her mind, her internal lament of longing for simple chamber pot. "Well, one problem at a time," she said.

He laughed and shook his head, as if suddenly realizing her problem. "You are a wonder, whoever you are."

"Andrew will do fine."

"Well, Andrew, come on. I'll make sure the path is clear."

With Preston standing guard, she managed in the cramped outhouse with a modicum of trouble. It was certainly much easier on the ladies. She longed for a private room where she could freshen up. So far in her masquerade as a man, that was the only advantage to being a female she'd found. She fumbled with the still unfamiliar buttons on her trousers and tried not to breathe. When that didn't work, she tried humming to take her mind off the smell.

By the time Marsfield joined his little band at the carriage, Burke was curled asleep, the hat over his face only slightly muffling his snores. Preston was quietly teaching her the raunchy words to the tune she'd been humming all day.

Marsfield pronounced Burke the wisest, as the ride would take about an hour and they were planning a late night. He propped one foot on the door's railing, tipped his own hat forward, and then crossed his arms. Preston shrugged and followed suit.

As the carriage pulled onto the road, she looked out the window at the receding sight of the inn. She watched as Mr. Parkins dragged Sophie out of the taproom by the ear. When a turn in the road blocked the view, she leaned back in the seat.

So Marsfield had noticed the girl's flirtatious behavior. But rather than participate in the jocular teasing of the boys, he'd taken the father aside for a quiet word. This showed Anne another unexpected facet of the complicated man the *ton* described as a notorious rake.

In fact, it had surprised her to think he'd not noticed. He seemed so aware of every detail around him. But then, why had he not seen through her disguise?

The answer was not pleasant to face. Even if she had been wearing a dress, she wasn't the kind of woman Marsfield would notice. She was too tall and too thin for him to find attractive. Therefore, she must be just as easy to see as a man as it would be to see her as an unattractive woman. Hence, he never bothered to look close enough to notice any small slips she might have made.

Her line of reasoning made logical sense. Even if it hurt, she had to accept it.

After tonight, she would likely never speak to Marsfield again. If they met at some society function years from now, they would meet as strangers. She tried to picture herself and him, gray and stooped over, but the scene that came to mind was the two of them dancing in a moonlit garden.

She glanced at Marsfield to find him staring at her, through her, with a strange expression. Discomfited, but unable to think of anything to say, she tipped her hat over her face and pretended to sleep.

Marsfield shook himself from his reverie. Damned daydreams. He took his hat off and placed it in his lap. He closed his eyes, pretending to sleep. How utterly embarrassing. He'd been thinking of Cassandra, and his body had reacted like a bloody schoolboy's. He willed his body to relax—his entire body.

He needed a woman. That was it. How long had it been since he'd given Beatrice that generous parting gift? Six months. It felt like years. Some doctor had theorized that the backup of male juices produced insanity. Well, he was living proof.

He needed a woman.

The problem was, he wanted Cassandra.

Eleven

Anne stood on the dais. She turned this way and that and raised and lowered her arms as instructed. She'd been measured for a dress just last week, and if she squinted, she could almost imagine the officious assistant crawling around her feet on his knees was pinch-faced Madame Solange.

Marsfield and Burke were at the far end of the long narrow room, seated on a sofa going over the fabric samples with the tailor while an assistant took notes. Yet another assistant served wine and biscuits. Preston stood at the foot of the dais, one hand holding the elbow of his other arm, his glass raised for easy access. His back to the others, he seemed fascinated by the process of her getting measured.

The officious assistant jotted down another measurement on the notepad strapped to his left wrist. Suddenly, he looked up at her with wide eyes. He knew.

He opened his mouth and turned.

Anne held her breath. Preston must have been waiting for that moment, because he caught the tailor's gaze, slowly shook his head, and placed one finger over his lips. He moved his hand slightly, and she caught a glimpse of a folded ten-pound note.

The assistant tailor discretely nodded his understanding and agreement as he stood. The money practically jumped from Preston's fingers and disappeared into the little tailor's pocket. But his hands shook as he measured her inseam.

She gritted her teeth, but still a giggle escaped.

Marsfield looked over at her.

"I guess I'm ticklish," she said, then cursed herself for such an inane statement.

"Nonsense," Preston said. He walked over to join the group at the other end of the room, at the same time blocking their view of her. "I am the soul of wit, and have been entertaining Andrew with the latest *on dits*. You know I find this ritual most tedious when the clothes aren't for me."

The assistant finished his measurements and scuttled out of the way. She took the moment of relative privacy to cool her burning cheeks with her ice-cold fingers. She joined the others just as Marsfield began to order formal evening wear, riding clothes—

"No. I told you I can't afford this."

"I'm buying," Marsfield said.

"No, you're not," she said.

"The clothes are a gift."

"I can't accept them."

"You might as well," Preston said. "I would if I were you."

Furious, she rounded on Preston. "Well, you're not me." Turning back to Marsfield, she said in a deceptively quiet voice, "May I speak with you privately?"

The tailor and his assistants disappeared. Burke and Preston followed when Marsfield jerked his head toward the door.

"Thank you for the generous offer, but I cannot accept your gift. I have sufficient funds to purchase my own wardrobe, limited though it may be, and I would prefer not to be beholden to you for the very clothes on my back."

Marsfield took a sip of his drink. "Are you quite through?"

"Yes. I think so."

"Then it's my turn. We have agreed to conduct a scientifically accurate experiment in order to prove that I'm right. Therefore, I have a vested interest in assuring the variables that would skew the outcome are eliminated. Providing you with the proper wardrobe needed to attract a mistress is simply eliminating that particular variable."

"All this to prove a point. There isn't even a monetary gain to be made from winning."

"A principle can be worth more than money."

Oh, she hated it when he assumed that superior, insufferable, smug attitude of his. "Said like a man with more money than sense."

He shrugged. "I believe I have sufficient of both."

"Lord Marsfield, it will cost you a great deal to find out you're wrong."

"Lord Decklesmoor, I can easily afford to prove I'm right."

But *she* wasn't talking about money.

"You can't expect to dine at my club in what you're wearing. I arranged to purchase a nearly completed suit originally intended for someone near your height and weight. Alterations will be completed within the half hour."

Bloody hell. He must have planned all this before she'd even been invited to supper. Not that she was actually invited. Commanded was more accurate. Oooh, if only she didn't really want to see the inside of his club and go to that gaming hall.

He was right. She couldn't go dressed as she was. Even if she could filch some of Robert's evening wear, it would take her and Mrs. Finch longer to alter them than the army of tailors Marsfield must have enlisted to complete the job in thirty minutes.

"I will purchase the evening clothes. That is all."

"And the riding suit," Marsfield insisted. "If we are to make the circuit in Hyde Park, you must be suitably attired."

She had no intention of riding with him. She would appear quite ridiculous perched on a sidesaddle wearing pants. But she could see the determination in the set of his jaw and the stormy gray, winter-sky color of his eyes. If she could alter Robert's clothes for herself, her new clothes could be made over to fit him. Vowing silently to include to cost of the clothes in the farewell note she intended to send Marsfield, she relented to his purchases.

"Excellent." He stood, walked across the room, and pulled on the bellpull for service. "We'll pick you up in one hour."

Her sudden panic must have looked like confusion to him, because he explained further.

"Rather than my waiting here for you and then your waiting at my house for me to change—"

The officious assistant who had measured her rushed in to stand at attention at Marsfield's side.

"Simpson here will provide everything you need. The dressing rooms are well appointed, and a barber can be fetched if you wish a shave."

She shook her head.

He tipped his head from side to side, peering at her cheeks. "No, I suppose not. Last week, you say?"

Had she? She couldn't remember. The tiny kernel of panic she felt at Marsfield's announcement that he was leaving her took root and grew. She realized she had always felt safe when he was near, but she couldn't allow herself to become used to that luxury. Once this evening was over, she would never see him again. As he gave instructions to the tailor's assistant, she nodded absently.

"One hour," he reminded her.

Then Marsfield was gone.

She clenched her jaw to keep from crying out. She wanted to scream for him to wait, to run after him and cling to his strong, protective arms.

Simpson indicated another door. "This way, er, sir." His voice cracked, and his outstretched hand trembled.

His nervousness boosted her confidence just enough that she managed to force her stiff legs to move. She followed the tailor into the unknown.

Simpson showed her to a sumptuous dressing room, mumbled for her to make herself comfortable, then beat a hasty retreat, shutting the door a tad too firmly. She half expected to hear the turn of a key so she couldn't escape and wander around this males-only kingdom, as if she'd contaminate it with her presence. Not that she had any desire to wander.

She examined the room, making mental notes in case she ever needed to use such a setting in a novel. One wall held three long panels of mirrors, the two sides cleverly attached to swing out so the viewer could see their sides as well as their front. Letty would love one.

Along the back wall, a mahogany sideboard held an artfully arranged collection of cologne bottles and aftershave lotions. There were pots of hair pomade and jars of cream, brushes, combs, and shaving paraphernalia. She was a bit surprised to learn men had nearly as many cosmetic items as women did, but that didn't stop her from examining each one.

The cabinet below contained a well-stocked bar. She read a few labels and recognized names meant to satisfy expensive tastes, but they were of little interest to her.

In the corner, a washstand held a ceramic bowl decorated with hunting scenes. She sat in a leather chair which would have looked at home in a well-decorated library. Investigating the accompanying smoking stand, she found an assortment of cigars and cheroots in the humidor. She fingered one. What was the appeal? She was tempted to try one.

A knock on the door startled her. When Simpson asked if she was decent, she stifled a nervous giggle. She stuffed the cheroot back in the container, assumed a casual pose in the chair, and called her permission to enter.

He sidled in, set a pitcher of steaming water on the washstand, added three pristine white towels, and laid a small stack of fresh linens on the sideboard, all without looking at directly her.

"I will return in twenty minutes with the rest of your clothes," he said as he bowed out.

For a moment she sat frozen in place. She noticed her reflection in the mirrors. Three young men grinned back at her with a cat-got-the-cream look. She was going to get away with it. The nebulous ordeal she'd dreaded had not materialized. She jumped up and shed her coat. Off came the choking cravat. She wanted to crow at her success, but she settled for humming the now familiar raunchy ditty.

Stripped to her chemise and bindings, she washed and donned the new smallclothes, whisper smooth against her skin. She added the thick black silk stockings and attached them to the knee garters. Slipping her arms into the white shirt, she savored its crisp smell as she fastened the studs up the front. She struggled with the cuffs and gave up. She would need Simpson's help.

Exactly on time, he knocked on the door. Instead of coming in, he opened the door a crack and shoved the clothes through. She thanked him. Hanging the coat on a peg, she donned the pants. Another knock sounded and she called for Simpson to enter.

Preston, already dressed in evening clothes, followed him through the door. "I thought you might need some help, so I sent a runner for my clothes and dressed down the hall."

Although the door remained open, the room suddenly felt stuffy and overcrowded. Preston took charge as if he did this sort of thing every day, and Simpson reacted to his directions with a grateful look and increased efficiency. He pushed her into the chair and combed her hair as Preston knelt and fastened her cuffs.

"A touch of pomade, don't you think, Simpson?" The man jumped to carry out Preston's suggestion.

"I don't think—"

Preston hushed her objection. "Something severe is more masculine. The pomade will darken your hair, thereby making your too delicate eyebrows recede from attention."

She nodded her acquiescence, but it wouldn't have mattered. Simpson now had a master to serve and had already begun to comb the goo through her curls. Preston directed the finishing touches of her outfit. He chose an uncomfortable collar with stiff points and a cravat that wound around her throat several times.

She immediately felt the chafing on the back of her neck. "I can't turn my head."

"Turn with your shoulders to look to the side."

"Isn't there something else?" She looked meaningfully at his floppy collar and cravat in the avant-garde style he'd denied her.

"We need to hide your lack of an Adam's apple."

She resigned herself to the stiff neck she would undoubtedly suffer tomorrow.

He then directed Simpson in engineering an elaborate knot in her cravat that pushed her chin up with its bulk. "To camouflage your graceful swan neck," he said.

Simpson helped her into the cream brocade vest and black coat. He swirled a black opera cape around her shoulders, flipping one edge back to reveal the crimson silk lining.

Preston handed her a top hat, charcoal gray gloves, and an ebony walking stick. He stepped behind her and steered her by the shoulders to stand in front of the three-way mirror.

The transformation astounded her. Gone was the rumpled little boy look. An elegant man about town stared back at her.

"Bravo!" Preston said.

Simpson retrieved Preston's cloak and accessories from the hall and ushered them out as if glad to be rid of them. Because it had started to rain, they waited just inside the shop door for Marsfield's carriage.

"Thank you for your invaluable assistance," she said.

Preston made a deep bow. "Always happy to help a lady in distress." He pronounced it *dis-dress,* in a pun of her skirtless apparel.

"It is my impression you'd more likely de-dress a lady yourself." She was pleased to see he had the gallantry to laugh at her poor joke.

"I do have a favor to ask," he said.

"As one gentleman to another?"

"Of course. Don't tell Marsfield I was here."

"Won't he know that as soon as he arrives?" she asked.

"I mean, don't tell him I was here early and helped you dress. If you're successful and become his—"

"Whoa, right there. I told you before, this isn't a ploy to capture his attentions. Are you insulting my intelligence? If that were my aim, I'd be smarter than to dress as a man."

"You've captured my attention," he said.

Egad. The boy was developing a *tendre* for her. "That's very sweet of you Preston, but I'd rather be your friend."

His usual expression of slightly amused ennui returned, as if a serious thought were the last thing to enter his mind.

"How droll. It never occurred to me one could have a female friend."

She patted his shoulder. "It will do you good. I'll help make you a better man."

He looked up and opened his arms as if appealing to heaven for guidance. "She is either the veriest innocent or the best actress I've ever had the privilege to meet."

"Why do you say that?"

"You spout double entendres with the naïveté of a well-born lady."

She pulled herself to her full height. "Well, I am certainly not an actress."

"More of my bad luck."

"Pardon?"

"If you're a lady, and I don't doubt you are, then I'm obliged to protect you. It's part of the gentleman's oath. You didn't know about the oath?"

"No," she said in a mock serious reply to his teasing.

"Oh, yes. Vows, signing in blood, and all that. So you see, I have to do everything I can to protect you and your reputation, though I'm afraid that might be a sticky wicket when all this gets out."

"It won't get out," she promised. She diverted his attention from the subject with another question. "Your oath doesn't require you to protect actresses?"

"Heavens, no. Just the opposite. A willing actress is to be ravished on demand. We gentlemen are nothing if not the servants of the fairer sex."

The door opened and Marsfield stepped in. They had been so engrossed in their conversation, they'd forgotten to watch for his carriage.

"I was afraid there was a delay," Marsfield said.

If she'd been expecting a compliment on her attire, she would have been disappointed. He merely gave her a satisfied nod.

"Not at all, old man." Preston put his arm around Marsfield's shoulders and steered him toward the door. "Andrew and I were just discussing the ravishment of actresses." He winked over his shoulder at her. She followed to the carriage with a light heart, confident that, with her new friend's help, she would do fine this evening.

Burke joined them almost immediately and the group set off. Marsfield seemed preoccupied during the ride, but the boys carried the conversation, including her in their varied discussion. Only she seemed to notice Marsfield's lack of attention.

Marsfield would have to change the plans for the evening. The director wanted another meeting, something about a Scottish connection and a new lead. Again he had chosen the place and the time without consideration of anyone else's schedule or preference.

However, in this instance, Marsfield had been thinking earlier that very day he needed a woman. He'd even wondered if Beatrice would allow him back in her bed on such short notice. He's dismissed the idea because he didn't happen to have any diamond bracelets lying around to appease her outraged sensibilities. Never mind the fact that the idea of seeing her again held little appeal. Perhaps the meeting place chosen by the director would prove beneficial in more ways than one.

Marsfield considered taking Andrew along, but decided against it. The boy had looked decidedly pale several times that afternoon. Perhaps he wasn't fully recovered from his illness and needed extra rest. Marsfield certainly didn't want to face the Dowager Lady Decklesmoor if his social agenda caused the boy to suffer a relapse. No, he would tell Andrew he'd changed his mind and decided on an early night.

Marsfield passed the word to his assistants. In their eagerness, supper, which should have taken a leisurely two hours, was completed, including dessert and a sip of after-dinner liqueur, in forty-five minutes.

By nine o'clock Marsfield dropped off Andrew at his house.

Twelve

Anne stepped inside her door and blinked back her surprise. It was as if she'd been caught in one of those newfangled kinescope machines where everything sped by clackity-clack, as if someone turned the crank too fast.

White-coated waiters had served each course, then taken it away before she'd barely had a chance to taste it. She'd had three sips of soup and two bites of fish. Four bites of beef because she'd learned to chew faster. She'd cut her pear and grabbed a slice as the waiter removed her plate.

She glanced at the grand hall clock. Nine o'clock. No one had acted as if anything was out of order. Burke had shoveled his food as if someone would take it away from him, which they did. Even her silent appeals to Preston had produced only a slight nod in response.

And Marsfield! What was his problem? He hadn't looked her way once. Hadn't spoken to her. What conversation there was in the few seconds between courses consisted of his inane comments on the weather. There wasn't a single moment without a servant hovering close when she could ask for an explanation.

She'd assumed they were eager to get to the gaming hall, but in the carriage, she had summarily been informed their plans had changed.

Then she'd been dropped off at her door.

The rejection hurt.

Take A Trip Into A Timeless World of Passion and Adventure with Kensington Choice Historical Romances!
—Absolutely FREE!

Let your spirits fly away and enjoy the passion and adventure of another time. Kensington Choice Historical Romances are the finest novels of their kind, written by today's best selling romance authors. Each Kensington Choice Historical Romance transports you to distant lands in a bygone age. Experience the adventure and share the delight as proud men and spirited women discover the wonder and passion of true love.

4 BOOKS WORTH UP TO $23.96— Absolutely FREE!

Take **4 FREE** Books!

We created our convenient Home Subscription Service so you'll be sure to have the hottest new romances delivered each month right to your doorstep — usually before they are available in book stores. Just to show you how convenient Zebra Home Subscription Service is, we would like to send you 4 Kensington Choice Historical Romances as a FREE gift. You receive a gift worth up to $23.96 — absolutely FREE. You only pay for shipping and handling. There's no obligation to buy anything - ever!

Save Up To 30% On Home Delivery!

Accept your FREE gift and each month we'll deliver 4 brand new titles as soon as they are published. They'll be yours to examine FREE for 10 days. Then if you decide to keep the books, you'll pay the preferred subscriber's price. That's all 4 books for a savings of up to 30% off the cover price! Just add the cost of shipping and handling. Remember, you are under no obligation to buy any of these books at any time! If you are not delighted with them, simply return them and owe nothing. But if you enjoy Kensington Choice Historical Romances as much as we think you will, pay the special preferred subscriber rate and save over $7.00 off the bookstore price!

We have 4 FREE BOOKS for you as your introduction to
KENSINGTON CHOICE!

To get your FREE BOOKS, worth up to $23.96, mail the card below or call TOLL-FREE 1-800-770-1963 Visit our website at www.kensingtonbooks.com.

Take 4 Kensington Choice Historical Romances FREE!

❤ *YES!* Please send me my 4 FREE KENSINGTON CHOICE HISTORICAL ROMANCES (without obligation to purchase other books). I only pay for shipping and handling. Unless you hear from me after I receive my 4 FREE BOOKS, you may send me 4 new novels - as soon as they are published - to preview each month FREE for 10 days. If I am not satisfied, I may return them and owe nothing. Otherwise, I will pay the money-saving preferred subscriber's price plus shipping and handling. That's a savings of over $7.00 each month. I may return any shipment within 10 days and owe nothing, and I may cancel any time I wish. In any case the 4 FREE books will be mine to keep.

Name _____

Address _____ Apt No _____

City _____ State _____ Zip _____

Telephone ( ) _____ Signature _____

(If under 18, parent or guardian must sign)

Terms, offer, and prices subject to change. Orders subject to acceptance by Kensington Choice Book Club. Offer valid in the U.S. only.

KN112A

4 FREE
Kensington
Choice
Historical
Romances
are waiting
for you to
claim them!

(worth up
to $23.96)

See details
inside....

||..||..||...||||..||..||.|.|.||..|.||..||.|..||..||.|..||...||...|

KENSINGTON CHOICE
Zebra Home Subscription Service, Inc.
P.O. Box 5214
Clifton NJ 07015-5214

PLACE
STAMP
HERE

It was too early to go to sleep. Was this what she would feel like after Letty married? Alone. Lonely. She fought back the tears that threatened because Cleeve sat at his post by the front door watching her. Never, not even in her two dismal Seasons without suitors, had she felt rejection so keenly.

A single note on the silver salver addressed to Lord Decklesmoor caught her eye. With a nonchalant air, she walked to the table where callers left their cards. She recognized the stylized rose embossed on the corner and ripped the note open.

Hope this reaches you. We're sending it by way of Marsfield's coachman. Please stop by whenever you have a chance. We have a surprise for you.

There was no signature, but she knew who had sent it.

"Cleeve. Ask Harvey to bring the coach. I'm going out."

"But, miss—"

She assumed her haughtiest expression. "Are you arguing with me?"

"No, Miss Anne, but Harvey took Miss Letty and Lord Robert to the reception at Whitmore House. He'll be waiting to bring them home."

If she wanted to see Rose and Jasmine, Anne would have to travel alone at night in a hackney cab. A daunting prospect. But then she'd dared so much in the past two days, what was one more thing?

"Fetch a hack, Cleeve."

"Andrew! My darling boy."

Rose rushed out to meet her as soon as she was announced, and enveloped her in a fleshy embrace. Anne hadn't realized until that moment how much she needed that hug.

"My, my. Don't you look fine?" Rose twirled Anne around in a circle. "Quite the debonair young man." She winked. "Come right in."

"This isn't a bad time for you?" Anne asked as they walked toward Rose's parlor.

Rose whispered something to the butler, then shut the door. "Oh, no, dear. Until the midnight soiree, what little business there is the other girls can handle. I'm so glad to see you."

Jasmine, Daisy, and Petunia rushed in, and there were more hugs and kisses all around.

"Now for your surprise," Rose said.

"That's not why I came tonight. I . . . to tell the truth, I was feeling down and needed a visit with friends."

"Then this is perfect." Rose waved and the other women lined up by the fireplace. She pushed Anne to sit on the sofa facing them, and sat beside her.

Jasmine, in the middle, cleared her throat and stepped forward. "We, the members of the newly formed Cassandra Drummond Admiration Society, wish to thank you for all the pleasurable hours of reading you have given us through your talent."

"Do you have an admiration society, dear? We thought maybe we should add a number or something," Rose interjected.

Anne shook her head, her throat almost too constricted to speak. "I'd never even met one of my readers before I met you."

"Ahem," Jasmine said. "As duly elected chairwoman, I hereby call this meeting of the Cassandra Drummond Admiration Society, Unit Number One, to order. Our first item of business is a suitable thank you."

"We've been talking about this all day," Rose interrupted, obviously excited.

Jasmine put her hands on her hips. "Rose, if you wanted to be chairwoman, you know we would have elected you."

Chagrined, Rose sat back in her seat and clasped her hands demurely in her lap. "My apologies, Madame Chairwoman. Please continue."

Jasmine nodded with regal aplomb.

Anne opened her mouth to protest the very idea of a gift, but at Jasmine's severe look, she closed it again.

"We had many fine suggestions from our charter members, including a most excellent one to commission a statue of Valdrick and Melissa in a passionate embrace. For your garden," she added.

Anne widened her eyes to keep from cringing at the thought of explaining that piece of artwork to her brother.

"However, we finally agreed that since we wish to honor your talent, it would be most appropriate for us to use our talents for your benefit."

Anne blinked. Since she had not the vaguest idea what they were talking about, she had no idea what to say.

"You, Miss Cassandra Drummond, are the recipient of a Garden beauty makeover. Rose has been transforming common weeds into exotic flowers for years—"

"You should have seen Daisy when she got here."

Jasmine shushed Petunia. "After we get through with you, you'll catch the husband of your dreams, your very own happy ending."

"I don't know what to say." A tiny flame of longing, deeply buried and long ignored, burst to life in Anne's heart. A husband. Not someone like Marsfield, of course—that would be like wishing for the moon—but a solid, kind man. Maybe a squire. The dream of a family of her own flared, but she quickly squashed it.

"I've always been plain. That's why I'm able to pass as a man. There's nothing you can do—"

"Just put yourself in our hands," Rose said.

Anne must have agreed, because the next thing she knew, she was hustled out a hidden door in the wall of Rose's parlor, down a short hall, and into a bathing chamber.

"First, let's get that goo out of your hair," Rose said.

The four women undressed her with the ease of long practice. She balked at the removal of her chemise. She'd always bathed with it on when Mrs. Finch attended her in her bath. But these women brooked no shyness.

Left in peace for a few minutes, Anne luxuriated in the ceramic tub large enough for two. Blushing, she realized it had probably held two people on more than one occasion. In fact, the walls were decorated with pictures of couples bathing in various shapes and sizes of tubs and pools. Good heavens, two in a hip bath? Impossible. She looked closer. Well, if they sat like that, maybe.

Those were her last moments of repose. The four women returned, soldiers in the hopeless battle to make her beautiful, armed with a wild assortment of sponges, brushes, bottles, and jars. She was sloughed, scrubbed, rubbed, oiled, and creamed. Concoctions were washed into her hair then washed out. A secret facial recipe opened her pores; another closed them again.

When she was finally allowed to exchange the terry robe for underclothes, they brought out a French chemise so sheer she could see through it.

"I . . . I can't wear that. It's transparent!"

"Of course it is. That's the point," Jasmine said.

"It'll be fine," Rose assured her. "No one will see it. But you'll know you're wearing it. There's nothing that makes a woman feel more desirable than sexy unmentionables. It'll give you a glow. You'll see."

"Give me the ague, you mean." But she raised her arms so they could slip it over her head. The new corset was of an unfamiliar shape. Though she'd never needed one with her slim waist, she'd always worn a corset, as every proper woman did.

"It's my own design," Rose bragged.

As Jasmine tightened the laces from behind, Anne felt the corset pushing up on her breasts, and looked down to see them generously mounded, ready to spill from her chemise.

"Oh, my."

"I call it the Little Wonder Corset. I've applied for a patent so I can market them. My retirement nest egg."

Anne turned this way and that. It wasn't any more uncomfortable than any other corset she'd worn. Her breasts, which a normal corset made appear almost nonexistent, now appeared full and voluptuous.

"I predict you're going to be a very rich woman," she told Rose with a grin.

Then came sheer stockings trimmed with lace and fastened with wicked red garters. Two petticoats provided the bulk necessary for the skirt, but because of the sheer panel inserts, they concealed little.

Next she sat at a dressing table. The oval mirror had been covered so the final effect would be a surprise. Daisy had been chosen to do her makeup because she had the lightest touch. Petunia, a whiz with hair, took her turn by adding a switch of matching hair and swirling it around Anne's head like a coronet.

"Now for the pièce de résistance," Rose announced. Everyone scrambled to line up by a curtained alcove. She pulled a cord to reveal an emerald green moiré satin dress just the color of Anne's eyes. The simple, elegant lines of the bodice were not spoiled by excess decorations, but a single deep red velvet rose captured a long sweep of overskirt up on one hip.

Anne clapped her hands together in delight. "It's the most beautiful dress I've ever seen."

The other women smiled and nodded at each other. They were just as pleased with their gift as she was.

"Jasmine designs and sews all our clothes," Petunia said.

"With help," Jasmine allowed. "I used to be a seamstress before I realized I could work half as hard and make ten times as much money doing what came naturally."

Anne held the dress up to her waist with one arm and swirled the skirt around in a circle. "I can't believe you made this so quickly—today."

"Oh, it was mostly put together already. We're about the same size, so I just made a few design changes to suit you and voilà, instant custom gown."

"I can't accept it. You were making it for yourself."

"Nah. In truth, I don't know why I was even making it." She fingered the sumptuous material. "I just loved the fabric. I wasn't making it for myself, that's for sure. Even though I've always wanted a green dress, I'm purple."

Rose explained. "I give each woman a color to go with her name and complexion, and that's the only color she wears. That way there are no fights over clothes, and if a gent can't remember a name, I just ask what color she was wearing. We've never had a green."

"I guess there aren't any green flowers."

"It's not that. There are quite a few types of flora that have green decorative bracts that may accurately be referred to as flowers."

"Parsley always looks like a flower to me," Petunia said.

Rose patted Petunia on the cheek. "I think you're getting over your shyness, my dear. And now that you say so, I agree. But who wants to be named Parsley? Besides, the woman in the green dress? It's just too obvious."

Anne was still confused and said so.

"You know the expression, the woman in the green dress?"

She shook her head.

"Green dress? Green from rolling around in the grass?" Jasmine hinted.

She shook her head.

"It's a euphemism for a promiscuous woman," Rose said with an impatient sigh. "See, too obvious."

"Oh, dear. Green is my favorite color. I have several

green dresses. But none as beautiful as this," she added to Jasmine. "You didn't mean—oh, dear."

"Not at all. No one infers anything negative about a *lady* in a green dress. Small difference in words, big difference in meaning."

Anne acknowledged she must be right, because she'd never heard the expression before. They helped her into the dress. As Jasmine fastened the row of tiny buttons down the back, Anne kept tugging at the bodice. Between the low neckline and the Little Wonder Corset, half of her breasts were exposed. Rose slapped her hands away. Anne pulled the puffed sleeves up, and Rose pushed them down to bare her shoulders.

Finally done fussing, they turned her to face another wall. Daisy removed the coverlet that had been draped over the large mirror. For the second time that night, Anne barely recognized her own reflection.

"I feel like Cinderella," she said, turning around and around. "And you are all my fairy godmothers."

Anne gave them each a hug and whispered her thanks for each of their special talents. Then she couldn't resist turning back to her reflection.

"I can't believe it." Anne danced in a wide circle, trying to see the dress from every angle.

"Unfortunately, Cinderella, we don't have a ball to send you to, but we do have an evening soiree starting in fifteen minutes." Rose waved her hands in shooing motion. The others quickly removed their aprons and rushed to the mirror to primp.

"Thank you. I know you have a business to conduct so I'll just go—"

"Nonsense. You're going to the soiree."

Anne nearly choked. "I couldn't . . . do what you do."

"What a ninny. Of course you won't. You'll just walk around the room. Talk to a few men."

Anne shook her head with so much force a loosened

wisp of curls sprang over her forehead. She blew it out of her eyes. "I'm not good at social chitchat."

Rose smoothed the strand of hair back into place. "Let them do the talking. You need to see how men will react. You won't really believe yourself beautiful until you experience unbridled male admiration."

"Once you know you're beautiful, it won't matter what you're wearing, your own special beauty shines through," Jasmine added.

"Believe it," Petunia added, her serious face intent. "I didn't at first, but it's true."

"But won't they think—?"

"So what if they do?" Rose said, sweeping away the objection with a brushing motion. "Nothing happens downstairs that doesn't happen in the best parlors all over London, except the gentlemen make appointments for later. No one is allowed to leave the parlor for the first half hour. By that time, we'll have bundled you home in a cab."

"We'll all be there to help you," Daisy added in her tiny, modest voice.

Anne looked back to the full-length mirror. Such a shame to be all dressed up and have no place to go. A shame to waste all their efforts by going home to an empty, lonely house.

Suddenly, she agreed to their outrageous scheme. She crossed her fingers that she wasn't inviting disaster.

Thirteen

Anne dug in her heels, stiffened her legs, and hesitated at the door to the salon. She would have turned and run the other direction as fast as her high-heeled shoes would let her, except Rose and Jasmine each held one of her arms in a firm grip.

"Smile," Rose said. "Remember, you are beautiful."

"At this point," Jasmine muttered, "I'll be happy if she remembers to breathe."

Anne let out the breath she'd been holding and sucked in another deep measure of oxygen. What a change from the quiet and relative security of Rose's private quarters. The room had been decorated to give credence to the name Rose's Garden.

The large chandelier, in the shape of a stylized sun, beamed light up to the blue painted ceiling as well as down on the trellis motif wallpaper. The furniture was an eclectic mix of armless chairs upholstered in grass green brocade, comfy looking sofas covered in tan velveteen, and several scattered groupings of brown leather wing chairs. The plush carpet had been woven in a clever pattern to resemble flagstones. Two fireplaces, one at each end of the long room, kept the chill night air at bay. One corner had been cleared for dancing, and on the musicians' balcony a string quartet played a soothing composition.

The design of the room and its earthy colors provided

the perfect backdrop for Rose's flowers, the women in their bright silks and satins. They mingled among the men, who looked like so many black crows encroaching upon the garden. The occasional man wore peacock colors of his own, and one old fellow wore full court dress, including a powered wig and buckled shoes.

"Good evening, gentlemen," Rose said in a loud voice.

Every man in the room, and it was crowded, turned to greet her with similar sentiments. Those who had been sitting stood, and then, all standing, they bowed almost in unison. Rose and Jasmine each executed an answering deep curtsy. Not only did they pull Anne down into a curtsey with them, she had no free hand to cover her bosom, which was quite exposed to view.

Suddenly released, Anne popped up to a standing position, fumbled her fan open, and plied it at a rapid speed in the vain hope of cooling the blush that spread heat from her brow to below the edge of her bodice. She peeked over her shoulder. Daisy and Petunia, grinning from ear to ear, blocked her exit route.

In a smooth motion, Rose flipped open her fan of ostrich feathers that had been dyed to match her peony pink gown.

"Smile," she hissed at Anne from behind its screen. Then she made a grand sweep with the fan. "Welcome to my garden of beautiful and exotic flowers from all over the world."

Jasmine again locked her elbow through Anne's. The full petticoats under the woman's shiny purple skirt pushed against Anne's dress. The rustling fabric provided a tactile reminder of how little she wore beneath the green satin. Daisy, in her signature yellow gown, stepped to her other side, thus completing a pose suitable for framing, and spoiling any escape schemes Anne harbored.

All of the women in the room remained at motionless attention, and Anne aped their lack of movement with ease. Rose completed her grand entrance with a slow walk across the room. She paused occasionally to greet a friend, to receive a kiss on her pudgy bejeweled hand or on her freshly powdered cheek or even planted full on her painted cupid's bow mouth. When she reached her destination, the old gentleman in court dress had the honor of seating her on her throne, a garden bench padded with mossy velvet cushions and placed under an arbor covered with live honeysuckle and fresh pink roses.

"Please, gentlemen," Rose called. "Enjoy yourselves."

That must have been some sort of signal, because the activity immediately resumed and increased in fervor. The deep rumble of male voices, sounding to her like the warning of an approaching storm, was broken repeatedly by the crystal tinkle of women's laughter. The almost overpowering smell of various floral perfumes mingled with that of imported liqueur and the smoke from expensive cigars. Yet another odor, not unpleasant exactly, but new and strange, lent an underlying note of excitement.

Jasmine and Daisy guided Anne to a spot at the left side of the double doors. Her guards flanked her and a large potted fern protected her back. For a few minutes, she observed the scene. Everyone behaved with the best of etiquette. Snippets of conversation reached her ears:

"—terrible weather for this time of year but—"

"—my tailor said this knot is all the rage in—"

"—the House? Surely, Aberdeen's men won't—"

"—always bet on the black horse. That's my system. It never fails."

The social small talk repeated the same tittle-tattle found at any gathering she'd endured during her own Seasons. The stiffness of fear faded from her limbs. When a kind looking gentleman with gray hair walked over, she returned his smile in an almost natural manner.

He introduced himself. Well, that was different than the formal world, where an introduction had to be made by someone known to both parties. She considered this eminently more sensible. Jasmine introduced herself and Daisy. She also introduced Anne as Emerald.

"Ah, an exquisite jewel among the beautiful flowers," he said.

He bent over Anne's hand and brushed his lips along the knuckles. Though his hands were cool, the heat of admiration in his eyes did not seem feigned.

A young man, barely out of short pants, she assumed, ran up and shouldered the older man aside in his eagerness to meet them. He introduced himself as Percival Hartmoor, grabbed her hand, and had it halfway to his mouth when the first gentleman pushed back.

"Back to the nursery, puppy. I found her first."

Anne was relieved to have her hand back. Hartmoor had looked ready to take a bite out of it.

"La, Edward," Jasmine said with a coy smile.

Jasmine stepped between the two men with an such an easy grace that it seemed like a natural movement made to allow another person into their conversational group. She tapped him on the arm with her fan and stuck out her bottom lip in a pretty pout.

"It may have been ages since you've been here," Jasmine continued, "but I'm sure you remember Rose doesn't allow arguments."

Edward chuckled and placed Jasmine's arm through the crook of his elbow. "How's my favorite little flower? Shall we stroll over by Rose and check her appointment book?"

As he steered her away, Jasmine gave Anne an apologetic look over her shoulder. "I'll be right back," she mouthed silently.

Petunia stepped forward to take Jasmine's place and Hartmoor's friend, hovering about four feet away, finally gathered enough courage to approach.

"Ba . . . Ba . . . Balderson," he stuttered. "Th . . . that's my name."

Anne was gratified to see neither of her companions laughed or made fun of his ovine manner, which matched his tightly curled, light blond hair. If this had been a typical drawing room, she doubted the young debutantes would have shown the same forbearance. In fact, she decided after just a few minutes of conversation, the two pairs—Hartmoor and Petunia, Balderson and Daisy—would get along like fish and chips. She encouraged the couples to dance.

The girls, mindful of their guard duties, demurred in favor of conversation. But when a lively waltz began, Anne noticed four pairs of eyes take turns peeking at the dancers. She assured them she would be fine, and pushed them toward the dance floor. With help from the two boys, Daisy and Petunia finally relented, if Anne promised to stay just where she stood. She assured them she would be fine.

As soon as the girls were sweeping around the dance floor in the arms of their ardent admirers, Anne took a step backward toward the door. She smiled at Petunia and took a step back. She waved at Daisy and took another step back.

Anne had to be getting close to the door. She applauded after Hartmoor twirled Petunia through an intricate pattern of steps. She took another step back, right into a body.

Heavy hands around her waist kept her from tripping on her skirts and sprawling on the floor. With a squeal of surprise, she spun around.

"Hello."

Anne regained her balance and stepped out of his reach.

"Here I've been wondering how to approach you without using a line you've heard a thousand times, and you solved the dilemma for me in a most unique way."

The insolent manner with which the stranger eyed her from head to toe and back again unsettled her. She flicked a quick look over her shoulder.

He put his hands out toward her waist and moved toward her. "Shall we give our names to Madame Rose?"

Anne was nothing if not a fast learner. She used her folded fan in the same manner Jasmine had earlier, but she gave him a snapping crack across the knuckles. "La, sir." She watched him rub the hand she'd smacked into his other palm. "You can speak to Rose if you want to." Lord knows what the woman would tell him. Unfortunately, he stood his ground with a scowl on his face, effectively blocking her exit.

"I was told to circulate," she added in an innocent voice. He looked crestfallen. Her small victory stoked her confidence. She spun on her heel, walked up to the nearest man, and introduced herself.

Her original intent had been to engage someone near the door in conversation until the coast was clear. Once out of the parlor, she would make her way back to Rose's rooms, change her clothes, and leave the same way she'd arrived. That was her honest intention.

But something magical happened on that Cinderella night.

First, a man laughed out loud at a small witticism she made. Then she received a sincere compliment on her statuesque height. Though she never strayed far from the door, her ears were compared to delicate seashells, her mouth named a rosebud, her brow hailed as patrician, her nose admired in an extemporaneous poem, and her chin made the subject of euphemistic limerick even she understood. Her favorite was the old army colonel who looked straight at her breasts, harrumphed through his bushy mustache, and said, "Nice knockers."

This sort of attention had never been paid to her before, and she was hooked. Before long, her walk loosened to a hip-swaying saunter. She used her fan to admonish, to flirt, and to entice. She laughed at their jokes and compliments alike. She promised nothing. In fact, she went out of her way to make sure they understood she wasn't available. Her aloofness only served to increase their adoration.

She thought about Marsfield's first principle and the law of supply and demand. This probably wasn't exactly what he'd envisioned. She smiled.

Marsfield lounged back in his chair and sipped his drink. "Why do you want to pin this on the Scots?"

"It's a good lead."

"And it would be politically expedient to point the finger away from London."

The director shrugged. "I think you should follow it up, though. Take Preston with you."

"I just returned from tromping around the wilds of Scotland. Send someone else."

"Grouse hunting at the MacClaren estate is not exactly what I would call hardship duty. Besides, I haven't anyone else available who could pull this off."

Marsfield swirled the brandy in his glass, watching the smooth motion and releasing the pungent aroma. He had a few leads of his own to follow right here in town, and he was convinced the trail would eventually reveal his old nemesis, Lord Fain, as the villain behind the consortium.

But he didn't have to personally do the legwork. Right now, a few weeks in the fresh air might serve to purge his brain of his unrealistic obsession with Cassandra. No other woman had ever distracted him so thoroughly or for so long. Distance might give him some welcome perspective.

"Why Preston and not Burke?" Marsfield asked. "Why not both?"

The director's closed expression did not register any surprise at the question.

"There is room for two gentlemen to join the duke's invited party. Any more would require a change in the arrangements and call attention to the substitutions. Mac-Claren's pool of investors is large, but his hospitality is not unlimited."

Marsfield refrained from commenting. As he expected, the director spoke to fill the uncomfortable silence.

"We're grooming Preston. The experience will stand him in good stead."

"And Burke?"

"To be honest, and I think I owe you that much—"

"And more." Marsfield hid a triumphant smile behind the rim of his glass when the director squirmed in his set.

"We recruited Burke in order to have him unknowingly assist us in recruiting his best friend. Truthfully, I don't expect Burke to stay the course. He's too dogged, too hesitant to act before he's thought everything through at least three times."

"I was much the same at his age."

"And it almost got you killed, if I recall correctly. If it hadn't been for Jack—"

"Isn't that what mentors are for? Preston's tendency to jump to conclusions can be just as dangerous."

"He'll mature."

"And Burke will gain confidence as he makes good decisions and learns to trust his instinct."

"Climb down off your soap box. This isn't Speaker's Corner in Hyde Park, and there is no injustice for you to rail against. Both men will be given an equal chance."

But not necessarily equal opportunity, Marsfield added to himself. He decided to take a hand. "When is this hunting party?"

"The duke and his guests are leaving at nine tomorrow morning from his town house."

"You don't give much warning."

The director smiled. "It took me a while to wangle the invitation."

"I don't suppose you want to share what you have on the duke that finally convinced him to snub two of his intimates in our favor?"

"Certainly not." The director chuckled. "I didn't tell him you would be attending. Right now, he's sweating that I'm going to stick him with an uncouth Bow Street Runner."

"And you didn't know if I would agree."

"I didn't know at the time I'd be forced to ask you." He finished his drink in one gulp. "Once your connection to us is known, your usefulness is compromised."

"I'm no longer *connected* to you. Remember?"

"I feel it only fair to warn you. If the culprit is one of the duke's friends and he realizes we used him to gain the evidence necessary to ruin that friend . . . well, the duke could become a powerful enemy."

"You warn me after I agreed to go?"

The director smiled with satisfaction at his successful manipulation. "Of course. I know you're a man of your word."

Marsfield wasn't particularly worried about the duke. The director didn't know of the school-yard incident that had made Marsfield and the duke friends even though they no longer shared the same interests. Marsfield wasn't one of the sycophant toadies who surrounded the duke, but his unexpected addition to the hunting party would produce nothing less than a genuine welcome. He could have relieved the director's trepidation with ease, but he chose to let the old spider worry.

Yielding to the temptation to retaliate for the gross lack of consideration, Marsfield decided to give the old man a few sleepless hours by pointing out the obvious. "You, of course, run the same risk of making a powerful enemy."

"That's a risk I take every day."

The director may have acted nonplussed, but Marsfield was satisfied his jibe had hit the target and would cause the intended damage. He replaced his glass on the table and stood.

"You will, of course, excuse me. Since I'm to leave in the morning, I must complete my other business rather more quickly than I'd intended."

He chuckled in response. "Business or pleasure?"

Marsfield stopped at the door and turned. "When a man attends to his pleasure with the same exacting attention he applies to his business, he is both rich and satisfied."

"Or exhausted," Marsfield heard the director mutter as he left.

Anne worked her way around the room, stopping for a few moments to share her exhilarating experiences with each of her friends. Taking the thinning crowd as her cue to leave, she headed in the general direction of the door. When she stopped to offer the requested opinion on the cut of one man's coat, she felt a prickle of unease.

She scanned the room, hoping the first man she'd met had not returned. Petunia and Daisy were nowhere in sight. Rose was nose to nose with the old gentleman in court dress. A sense that someone stared at her sent a shiver of dread crawling up Anne's back. She craned her neck, looking for Jasmine.

Her friend waved to her from the hall. Jasmine signaled instructions by pointing at Anne, then making a walking motion with two fingers, and pointing to Rose's private rooms. Then she pantomimed getting undressed, much to her escort's amusement. And obviously to his arousal, too, because he picked her up and carried her toward the stairs with a comic leer. Jasmine's pretended distress kept Anne smiling as she made a beeline for the parlor doors.

Three steps shy of a safe exit, she noticed the man standing against the wall. Though the fern hid his presence from most of the room, she recognized the relaxed pose—arms and ankles casually crossed—just as he had waited by the carriage only yesterday.

Yet there was a difference. His stormy eyes glinted hard like cold gray slate. And his mouth looked different, his generous lips stretched into a thin, taut, disapproving line.

What was Marsfield doing here?

Not waiting to find out, Anne fled. But it wasn't the hounds of hell that chased her across the entrance hall of Rose's Garden.

She wasn't that lucky.

Fourteen

Marsfield pushed himself away from the wall. Enough. He had watched her bewitch every man between the ages of eighteen and eighty. She might call herself Emerald now, but he knew Cassandra when he saw her. He ought to. She'd haunted his bloody dreams for months.

She was as gorgeous as he remembered, though not in the usual prissy china doll style so currently admired by the *ton*. She had a striking beauty all her own that was more than the sum of her individual features. Graceful and elegant, yet with an enticing air of *sans souci*. He wasn't the only man to appreciate her. Obviously.

He could tell by the look on her face the instant she recognized him. Surprise he expected. But fear? What was she trying to hide—besides herself?

Already on the move to intercept her, he also saw the decision to run in her expressive eyes. Unfortunately for him, a couple with attention only for each other blocked his path, giving Cassandra the precious seconds she needed to slip out the door ahead of the lovers. Pushing through the couple, he mumbled an insincere apology. He doubted they even noticed, but he didn't look back to see. His gaze never strayed from his target.

Anne scooted into Rose's parlor and slammed the door. But her sigh of relief came too soon. There was no key in the lock. Yet she had no doubt Marsfield would follow her here. Picking up her skirts, she draped them over one arm. She tore through the parlor, throwing everything she could get her hands on into the path behind her. Anything to slow him down. She would explain the damage to Rose later.

She bypassed the door to the bedroom and headed down the other hall, the one they had used to get to the bathing chamber. She knew the door directly across from the bedroom led to the stairs, because it had been open earlier. She hesitated.

Marsfield had no compunction about barging into Rose's private rooms in pursuit of Cassandra. If he'd had any question about which way she'd run, the path of destruction she left in her wake gave him a clear answer. Rather like what she'd done to his life. He kicked debris out of his way. He shoved at an upside down chair and it slid to the other side of the room. Taking a short cut, he leaped over the sofa.

And landed in a pool of something slippery. The resulting undignified sprawl would have hurt little more than his pride, except he smacked his elbow on the carved wooden cupids on the back of the sofa. Ow. Damn their gilded butts.

She heard a thump and a yelp of pain from the room behind her and paused. Yet still he came after her. Choosing the unknown evil over the known, she ran up the stairs, hoping to put some distance between them.

He reached the hall and stood rubbing his funny bone. The patter of high heels on bare wooden stairs gave him the direction she'd taken. The servants' stair was behind the first door he opened.

The stairs led to another hall lined with closed doors. This was the floor with all the theme rooms. If Anne's memory served her right, the main staircase leading to the front door was at the far end.

Heavy footsteps pounded up the stairs behind her. She'd never make it all the way down the hall. If she could find an empty room, she could use the escape corridor Rose had told her about. Every room had a concealed door that led to it. His footsteps sounded louder, closer. Just pick a door. Any door.

She counted off three doors for luck, turned the knob, and sidled through the opening.

He mounted the stairs with determined strides. The only door at the top of the stairs opened into another hall. He looked both directions. Cassandra had disappeared.

Anne barely noticed the fishing nets, seashells, and gaudy paper flowers that identified the Caribbean Room. Masses of plants gave the room a jungle feel, and real sand covered the floor. A large palm tree in the corner curved its trunk to accommodate the ceiling, its fronds hanging over a bed shaped like a boat. She recognized Jasmine and her escort. Anne's cheeks flamed with embarrassment. If Marsfield hadn't been outside in the hall, she would have turned and run. No, if Marsfield hadn't been outside, she wouldn't be in this untenable situation.

"Where's the secret door?" she whispered to Jasmine, trying to ignore the man who sat on the boat-shaped bed. He wore a tricornered hat with a large purple plume and had a black patch over his left eye.

Jasmine walked across the room, unconcerned that she wore nothing but a wisp of some filmy material tied around her waist and a large flower behind one ear.

"The door," Anne whispered. "Hurry."

"What's going on?" Jasmine asked as she pulled downward on the decorative fretwork of a wall sconce. A piece of bamboo wood paneling creaked aside. "You need help?"

"Shhh. I'll tell you later." Anne put a finger to her lips.

From outside in the hall, slow, firm footsteps crept closer.

"You haven't seen me," Anne whispered, and ducked through the secret door and into the narrow escape passage.

She hesitated, so turned around that wasn't sure which way led to the main staircase. Remembering the old instruction that if one was lost in a maze one should keep turning right to find the way out, she turned right.

Having lost sight of her, Marsfield used his other well-honed tracking senses. A trace of her exotic perfume lingered in the air. He followed past a door, then backed up when he lost the scent. Hoots of male laughter and a woman trying to shush him came from inside the room. Simple reasoning told him the expected activity was not taking place inside that particular room. He banged the door open.

"I say, this is the most fun I've had in a hound's age," said a man sitting cross-legged in the middle of a boat.

Marsfield asked, "Have you seen—?"

"She went that way." The man pointed at the closing bamboo wood panel.

"Now see here," Jasmine said, grabbing at Marsfield's arm.

"Stay out of it," Marsfield said. He stuck his foot into the quickly diminishing opening to prevent it from latching shut.

"I'm getting Rose," Jasmine said and ran out of the room.

With a grunt of effort, Marsfield shoved the panel back into its pocket, probably breaking the mechanism in the process. As if he bloody cared. He squeezed through the opening and followed Cassandra to the right, pausing only long enough to remove his shoes.

The escape passage was not a straight shot, due to the imaginative renovations on the rooms. It varied in width from a bare three feet to areas wide enough for a table and chairs. For the clients who used the peepholes, Anne deduced.

She rounded one empty chair left in position facing the inner wall. Rose had said she made those particular arrangements only when all parties were aware of the conditions, but Anne didn't understand the appeal.

But then, she'd known practically nothing about sex until two days ago. She was learning at an astounding speed, yet knew she'd barely scratched the surface.

Because she was still a virgin. And at her age she was likely to die in that blessed, bloody state.

Anne searched for an exit through a room that wasn't occupied. She couldn't quite bring herself to use the peepholes, though she was thankful for the dim lighting they provided. The doors were clearly marked from this side. She listened at each room for a second before moving on.

She found a narrow winding stairway, and with a sigh of relief scurried down. Gad, why was the hallway so warm? Her pulse raced from the effort of running. Her fan still flopped from the band around her wrist, and she caught it up to cool the flush from her cheeks as she listened for a few seconds at room after room. Muffled voices in each room told her business was brisk. If she had a choice, she'd rather not interrupt another couple while they . . . she ran from door to door on her tiptoes so as not to betray her presence.

Once again the hall narrowed. The skirt she held bunched over her arm took up a good two feet of space, so she had to squeeze along the wall. She listened at the next door. Hearing nothing, she put her hand on the latch. Still, she hesitated. Angling her head, she listened for any telltale sounds of pursuit. Quiet. Her skirt slipped down her arm, and she hiked it further up. She put her ear back to the door. Counting the seconds, she decided if there was no sound by the time she reached ten, she was going to look through the bloody peephole.

Marsfield stopped and listened. Sensing she was near, he placed his shoes on a nearby chair. Keeping as close to the wall as possible in order to minimize the chance of a creaky floorboard betraying his presence, he eased toward the point where the passage narrowed. He remained concealed by the portion of the room that extended into the hall.

He peeked around the corner.

The sight nearly stopped his heart.

Cassandra stood facing the other direction, her skirt wadded over one arm, her ear to the door. He had a clear view of her long legs from the ridiculous high heels along the sheer stockings to the red garters and above. Her wickedly daring chemise revealed as much as it covered.

His heart pumped the tattoo of his desire, sending blood pounding to his loins. His shaft rose in homage to the view.

Then she stepped back and bent at the waist to look through the peephole drilled at chair height.

Surely he'd died and gone to heaven. Marsfield leaned so far to the left that his head nearly touched the far wall. More blood pumped to his loins, making him rock hard and leaving his brain grasping for a coherent thought. He could no more stop her name from leaving his lips than he could turn away from the sight of her delightful derriere.

"Cassandra."

Anne had been listening so intently for any sound that the breathy whisper echoed as loud as a pistol shot. Her hands seemed to fly to her mouth of their own accord, and because her fan was tied to her wrist, it smacked her on the forehead. She dropped her skirt, accidentally hitting the latch on the door, which swung open. She staggered back, catching the heel of her shoe in the hem of her petticoat. Hopping on one foot in order to jerk the heel free, she stepped on the ridge that outlined the bottom of the doorway and twisted her ankle. She fell through to the other side.

Marsfield lunged to catch her, but he had been leaning too far to the left. In his unbalanced state, he succeeded only in stretching out full length on the floor. Ahead of him, through the door, he saw her still form lying on the cold tiles.

Oh, God. He'd killed her.

Marsfield half crawled, half stumbled to her side. This was what his unbridled lust had done. "Please don't be dead," he whispered.

With a gentle touch, her turned her over. *Let her live and I promise I'll . . .*

What could he promise that would be worth her life?

He took up her hand and leaned over to listen for her breathing. Chafing her wrist, he felt her pulse, strong and steady. A bit on the rapid side, but that was understandable.

So close. He'd been dreaming of her for months, day and night. And now here she was. So close that her delicate perfume enveloped him. He could not resist. He placed his lips on hers.

...

...

...

Fifteen

Anne let Marsfield believe she was dead. Maybe not the kindest thing she had ever done, but at this moment in time, definitely the safest. She'd let her body go limp. Her corset helped keep her breathing shallow, though it did make her a little light-headed. If only he would leave to fetch Rose, everything would be all right.

But he was kissing her. Gently. A lingering touch of his warm, soft lips. Tender, caressing. She knew in that instant: She loved him. The Marsfield she had come to know, even though he didn't know her, even though he saw her as the rigid widow, the troublesome boy, and the disreputable Cassandra. She knew him and she loved him.

No. Her better sense denied it. Impossible. But her heart refused to listen to her brain.

Her circulation system was malfunctioning, sending all her body's warmth to pool at the apex of her legs. What with the lack of oxygen, it was no wonder she erred and allowed a tiny sigh to escape.

Bloody hell. Now he knew she was alive.

Marsfield asked her to open her eyes. She did not.

With a gentle touch of his fingertips, he examined her head for bumps. He ran his hands down her arms. Warm, caressing hands. She mentally steeled herself against his touch, warned herself not to react. If only he would leave to fetch help instead of manhandling her limbs. With difficulty, she managed to keep her breathing shallow and her eyes closed.

"Time to wake up, Cassandra." He tapped her lightly on her cheeks. He reached under her skirt and petticoats, running his hands along her calves.

She gritted her teeth and refused to open her eyes.

"Searching for injuries," he explained.

Ha! Then he moved his hands higher, cupping her knees and rubbing the soft spot behind them. And higher, kneading her flesh to feel the bones beneath. Touching places no man had ever touched.

When he reached her upper thighs, she smacked him upside the head with her fan.

"That is quite enough," she said.

"Ow." He grabbed his ear and sat back on his heels. Then he grinned at her. "It was worth it."

She sat up and straightened her skirts. "I find your touch insolent and unbearable."

"No, you don't. You like it."

"And how would you know?"

He sniffed arrogantly and grinned like an idiot. "I can tell."

She didn't understand the man. Now he had decided to play the fool. Well, she'd had enough of this farce. She was going home. She tried to rise, but her exertions of the day, combined with lying on the cold tile floor, had stiffened her muscles. Before she could stifle it, a groan of pain escaped her lips.

"Wait." He stood, slid his arms beneath her shoulders and knees, and picked her up.

"What are you doing? Put me down."

"Stop struggling or I'll drop you." He staggered under her weight.

She believed him. She wasn't exactly tiny. And she knew from experience the mosaic tile floor was hard. Her better sense prevailed and she stopped fighting him, but she crossed her arms and stiffened her body.

"Relax and put your arms around my neck."

"Not bloody likely."

"Tut, tut. Such terrible language to come from such a pretty mouth." He staggered again and her weight shifted.

With a squeal of fear, she grabbed him around the neck. The idiot had nearly dropped her.

When she saw his satisfied smirk, she knew she'd been manipulated. But being curled in his strong arms was a delicious sensation. He made her feel cosseted. The ease with which he carried her made her feel delicate, womanly.

She looked around. From the decor, she knew they were in the Egyptian room. Friezes around the walls displayed dark-haired women with one breast bared and men wearing short pleated skirts carrying palm and feather fans on long sticks. Their jobs were obviously to provide a cooling breeze for the numerous couples pictured engaging in amorous activities. Very detailed pictures. Just a month ago she would have been shocked senseless. That she could peer at the nearest friezes with shameless curiosity only showed how depraved she had become. Good heavens. Was that physically possible? She felt her cheeks flame and averted her gaze.

The far corner of the room was draped with gauze hangings nearly concealing a platform covered with silk pillows. Steam rose from the dominant feature of the room, a six-foot by eight-foot tub of water sunk into the floor. Steps led down on one end, and a system of braziers on the other not only heated the room but also pumped a bubbling stream of steaming water over an erotic tile mosaic. A padded bench framed the pool along on each side.

He carried her toward the water.

"What are you doing?"

"A soak will ease your aches."

He stepped down the first two steps, apparently without concern for his clothes.

"No."

He stopped.

"It'll ruin my dress."

"You could take it off," he said with a leer.

"Not bloody likely."

He shrugged and she gripped him tighter just in case he had thoughts of throwing her into the water. "Please," she whispered.

"Since you asked so nicely." He backed up and set her on one of the benches instead. "Lie down."

"What are you doing?"

Firm hands on her back pushed her down on her stomach. When he began to rub at her sore muscles, the sensation was too pleasant to resist. Just a few minutes. Then she would leave. She straightened her legs and snuggled into a more comfortable position.

"That's it. Relax."

"Mmmmm."

"Breathe deep."

His strong fingers worked the kinks from her shoulders, spread their warmth up to her neck and into her hairline. Then he worked his way back down to her waist.

When his hands continued down her spine to the curve of her derriere, she came to her senses. Swinging her legs away from him, she sat up facing the pool. Her fan fell from her wrist to the bench and her bodice fell into her lap. She clutched it back up. He'd undone all the buttons. She shot an accusatory glare back over her shoulder.

He held up his hands as if in protest. "Magic?"

His unrepentant grin not only spoiled the image of beleaguered innocence, it caused a flame of warmth to ignite low in her belly. This was the teasing, charming side of Marsfield that had earned him his scandalous reputation.

No wonder women couldn't resist him. She had to get out of here. Now.

Because he stood behind her on the other side of the bench, her only escape path was the narrow lip of the pool. She stood. Her ankle throbbed and threatened to give way. Suddenly, the room seemed to swirl. She flailed out with her arms as she tipped toward the water. He grasped her hand.

Her body leaned out over the pool, her feet perched precariously on the edge. She twisted and grabbed his arm with her other hand.

He had one knee on the bench. He hardly seemed to notice the strain of holding her weight by one hand, and he held her there.

"Pull me up."

He quirked an eyebrow.

"I can't swim."

"I rather like the view from here."

She followed his gaze. Her bodice had fallen away unheeded, and her position pushed her breasts so high in the Little Wonder Corset that the edges of her nipples showed. She looked over her shoulder at the expanse of water.

"There is a price to be paid for saving one's life. And I know just the price for yours." He pinched his chin with his free hand. "Ah, but then I owe you for saving my life, don't I?"

Anne had stepped neatly into a trap. If she admitted Cassandra had saved his life, then what would he say about the widow who had already made that claim and had foisted Andrew on him?

"I don't know what you're babbling about. And saving a dress is not the same as saving a life. Pull me up."

He leaned forward an inch. "But you can't swim."

Her stomach flip-flopped. Yet she couldn't dare admit her chicanery. Letty, the real Aunt Elizabeth, the real

Three lives ruined. That would be worse than any cost he could name.

"What's your price?" she asked, knowing he wanted something or he wouldn't have hesitated to drop her into the water.

"The rest of the night. Stand up your other appointments and spend the night here, with me."

He thought she worked here. Well, that was a logical conclusion. She'd been prancing around the parlor, acting like a courtesan. He would know soon enough she was untutored in the ways of love.

Then again, maybe not. Rose had said that once a man's blood became heated, he paid little attention to details. She had the friezes around the room to use as examples, a picture primer even a dimwit could follow.

It all boiled down to one point. The real cost would be her virginity.

Not that that particular prize had been much sought after. And if she faced reality, this would probably be her one chance to be with him. After she went back to being plain Anne Weathersby, he wouldn't give her a second glance. She would have this one memory to cherish as she played the old maid aunt to Letty's and Robert's children.

Though her love would remain unrequited, she would have tonight. Never his love, but just this once, his body. Was that so terrible of her? *Yes,* her fear seemed to say. *Don't bring disaster on yourself,* years of proper breeding screamed in her brain.

If she could fool him, act the courtesan, then she would have this one night with him to remember the rest of her lonely life.

He let her slip another fraction of an inch, getting her attention. His expression was shuttered, his eyes looking more gray than blue.

"Is it ... .cult a decision?" he asked, his voice

"No." She looked him straight in the eye. "I agree to your conditions."

He pulled her up with such exuberance she flew over the bench and into his arms. He wrapped his arms around her and held her close. "You took your sweet time making up your mind."

The pressure of his lips cut off her response.

She remembered the lessons in kissing he had inadvertently given her that night in the inn—remembered well, because she'd relived that scene in innumerable dreams.

Nibbling, teasing, exploring kisses. Tongues entwining and dancing free. He cradled her head in one hand while his other arm held her pressed to his chest.

She rubbed the back of his neck and ran her fingers up into his hair. What next? She was supposed to be experienced and aggressive. With her other hand, she reached around his back to run her fingernails down his spine. Copying a picture on the wall, she cupped one cheek of his firm buttocks in her hand.

He moaned into her mouth.

The sound vibrated to the center of her being. She sensed the heady power his desire gave her. Instinctively, she pressed forward with her hips and urged his body closer with the pressure of her hand.

Then he broke the kiss and chuckled. "Easy, darling. We have all night." He reached around, moved her hand and stepped back, ducking his head out of her embrace.

She answered with a pout.

"First things first," he chuckled. Putting his hands on her waist, he guided her to a seat on the bench. Kneeling in front of her, he reached for her foot and removed her shoe. He ran his thumb up and down her instep and then massaged the top of her foot and ankle.

Would he expect her to do the same to him? This step was not in any of the pictures she had seen. If he expected it. . . . Still clutching her bodice in place, she raised her skirt a few inches to better see his hands. She glanced at his feet, and when she saw his lack of shoes, she realized why she hadn't heard him sneaking up on her. She braced her free hand on the edge of the bench. If she had known how good this would feel . . .

He gave her other foot the same attention, being extra gentle around her slightly swollen ankle. "Does it hurt?"

Lots of feelings swirled around inside her right then, emotions she couldn't name, sensations she'd never felt before. But pain? No. She shook her head.

When he pushed her skirts up higher, she resisted the urge to slap his hands away and cover herself. She didn't think she would be able to parade around half-naked like Jasmine, but if she planned on maintaining the persona of a prostitute, bashful was not an option.

He leaned over and kissed her knees, then smiled up at her. "I have a fondness for red garters, but—" He pulled one knot free with each hand and threw the ribbons over his back. As he smoothed the stocking down her left leg, he kissed her knee again, flicking out his tongue to lave the skin. "I like the taste of your bare skin better."

He paid the same homage to her right knee. A warm lassitude spread through her limbs. Her blood turned the consistency of honey.

Suddenly, he stood. Before she had a clue what he was about, he grabbed her by the waist, hauled her up, and stood her on the bench. He held her there until she gained her balance.

"It's time to get rid of that pesky dress."

He reached up, but stopped when she shook her head. Spreading his hands in a gesture of submission, he stepped back and leaned against the wall in the casual pose she now knew so well.

"Have it your way," he said, his voice husky.

He sounded put out with her. Now he expected her to stand there on the bench and strip off her clothes. She didn't think she could do it. She looked at his eyes to judge the extent of his anger. Their color told her he was amused by her actions. Amused! How dare he laugh at her feeble attempt at seduction?

She released her bodice, and it fell forward to her waist, displaying her Little Wonder Corset and sheer chemise. His eyes darkened to midnight blue. The color of his passion.

His reaction not only emboldened her, it changed something inside of her. Awakened something sleeping. She was no longer the shy virgin. She was a siren, a vixen. Never taking her gaze from his eyes, she shimmied out of her dress and held it out at arm's length.

As her reward, he pulled himself from the wall and stood straighter. She smiled and looked deep into his eyes. Midnight blue was her new favorite color. She dropped the dress with a dramatic flourish.

He stepped toward her, but she stopped him with a raised hand and a shake of her head. She pointed to his shirt. "You're overdressed."

He ripped the shirt from his body, heedless of the studs that scattered, and threw it aside.

She took a moment to admire his chest. Oh, yes. Her memory had not failed her. Her fingers itched to smooth the warm planes. She undid the bands of both petticoats and slowly slid them over her hips, dropping them to pool in a froth of lace at her feet.

"Venus rising from the sea," he whispered.

She undid the first two hooks of her corset before she remembered what the effect of removing the Little Wonder would be. She turned her back to him. She didn't want to see his face when his expression fell in disappointment. She sank to her knees.

She felt his hands on her back, undoing her laces with the same practiced ease he had used on her buttons. He tossed the corset aside and smoothed the skin on her sides and stomach where the stays had left telltale ridges.

"I hate those things," he whispered in her ear.

She closed her eyes. He wouldn't say that once he knew.

He knelt on the bench behind her, straddling her feet and calves. He reached up and pulled a pin from her hair.

"No." She curled forward to take her head out of his easy reach. If he removed her false coronet of hair, he would know her secret.

He ran a finger down her spine. "I'll agree for now." He followed that movement with his mouth. "I can see certain advantages," he whispered against her skin.

He placed his hands on her shoulders and pulled her back against his chest.

She didn't resist him. She couldn't play at being a courtesan and continue to hide her inadequate breasts. There was really no point in delaying the inevitable. He would learn the deception of the Little Wonder and turn from her in disgust. She willed away her tears. At least her precious virginity would be saved. Without conscious thought, she rested her head in the crook of his neck.

He slipped his hands across her shoulders. Skirting her nipples, he trailed his fingers down the outside of each breast. He kissed her neck below her ear, licking and nipping. He captured her earlobe between his teeth as he cupped her breasts in his hands.

"Perfect," he said. "See how they exactly fit my palms?"

She opened her eyes. Did he say perfect? She raised her head, straightened up, and looked down at his hands.

He chuckled behind her. "I didn't mean that literally."

The contrast of his lean brown fingers against the sheer white of her chemise entranced her. He circled her nipples with his fingertips, closer and closer. Her nipples formed hard little buds in anticipation. She waited, holding her breath, the tension in her body mounting. He gently grasped the buds and rolled them between his thumb and forefinger.

A bolt of electricity shot downward from her breasts to the apex of her legs. She raised up on her knees and arched her back, pushing her breasts into his hands. He moved quickly, wrapping one arm around her waist, saving her a tumble into the pool.

He widened his kneeling stance on the bench.

When he snuggled her back to his chest, she felt the evidence of his arousal. She tried to move away, but he'd changed the position of his hands, and she wound up pressing her stomach into his hand.

With his left hand he stimulated her right breast, at the same time, his arm around her middle held her close.

To her consternation, he explored her lower body with his other hand. He slid his fingers through the slit in her pantalets. She nearly cringed with embarrassment when he touched her . . . down there, and found her damp.

"I knew you liked my hands on you."

He sounded pleased.

Though he still held her back against his chest, she twisted her head to look up at him just as he found what he had been seeking. Her eyes widened in shock and she made a little 'O' of surprise with her lips. Before she could protest, he covered her mouth with a deep kiss.

With the coordinated movement of his tongue and fingers, he played a rhythm that spoke to the core of her womanhood. She wasn't exactly sure what he was doing . . . down there, but it made her feel intoxicated yet sensitized, lethargic and yet energized. Matching him hungry kiss for hungry kiss, she climbed toward some goal, something she craved but could not identify.

Twisting her body slightly to the side, he removed his hand from her breast momentarily to position her arm behind her head and around his neck. He slid a finger inside of her, and she jerked back, her derriere rubbing his hardness. He groaned into her mouth. Murmuring something, he slid another finger into her. She didn't even try to comprehend his words. Her knees seemed to slide wider apart of their own accord. He resumed the dancing pressure on her most sensitive nub and yet, at the same time, slid his fingers in and out.

His thumb, her distracted brain finally deduced. Thumb there, fingers inside. Her last conscious thought.

She was no longer herself. She became the wild, passionate Cassandra he expected. The woman he wanted. Gripping the back of his head, she savaged his willing mouth with her tongue. She pushed her breast against his hand. Her hips gyrated in lascivious response to the tune he played with his magic hands, her derriere grinding against his hardness. *More, more,* her wanton woman's body demanded.

An earthquake shook her. She wrapped both arms around his neck to anchor herself, clinging to him for safety.

Then the world exploded.

Catapulted from the top of a mountain, she stretched to embrace the stars. She cried out as fireworks burst around her, as she became part of the pyrotechnic wonders.

And she collapsed with a shiver as the sparks slowly winked out one by one.

He cradled her in his arms, rocking her as the last tremors left her body. He crooned meaningless sounds, and smoothed back a tendril of hair that had escaped over her ear. He kissed each of her eyelids, her forehead, her chin.

When she stilled, he stepped away and laid her on the bench. He was certainly in a hurry to leave once he had played the gallant to her sniveling collapse. Her sensibilities returned, and she curled into a ball. She squeezed her eyes shut in mortification. She'd let him—she'd begged him—

Suddenly he picked her up. "I knew you liked my touch."

She opened her eyes, and her heart skipped a beat. His eyes were still midnight blue. His self-satisfied grin said he was pleased with himself, as well as with her.

"The face of an angel and a body made for sinful, passionate pleasures," he murmured.

She tried to imagine what Jasmine or Rose would do. She put her arms around his neck and gave him a hesitant coquette's smile in return. "For your sinful pleasure," she whispered.

He chuckled and his dimple flashed his amusement. "Yes, it is my turn, isn't it?"

Whatever he meant by that, her heart sang with his approval. She would do anything—

A squeal of surprise escaped her lips as her derriere touched the water. She climbed higher in his arms as he continued down the steps, deeper into the warm water.

"You can't mean to . . . to bathe . . . together . . . at the same time?"

"No."

Her relief was short-lived.

"I mean for you to bathe me. Remember, it's your turn to pleasure me." He waggled his eyebrows in a comic leer. "And if you're lucky, then I'll bathe you."

His promise reactivated that little curl of warmth which was becoming familiar in his presence. He loosened his hold on her and she tightened her grip. "Remember. I can't swim."

He bit his lower lip. "I'm standing on the bottom."

She looked around. The water came to his chest. It would not be much higher on her. "Oh."

He burst out laughing.

She smacked him on the shoulder. "Saved my life, did you?"

"I saved your dress. That deserves some gratitude."

She pushed out of his arms, then had to flounder for her footing when he let loose of her. He'd taken advantage of her under false pretenses. She brushed aside the fact that she, too, was sailing under false colors. He moved to lean against the side, both elbows propped back on the rim of the pool. She faced him with her hands on her hips.

"You, sir, are a cad."

He smiled, his lips thin. "I never claimed to be anything else, Cassandra. Honesty simplifies matters, and because I prefer my life uncomplicated, I always tell the truth." He looked at her meaningfully. "Unlike some I could name."

Like he told the truth to Andrew about his plans for the night? She crossed her arms and returned his stare.

She had to admit he hadn't exactly lied. He'd just said his plans had changed. What did he think she was lying about? He couldn't possibly be referring to—no. He would have mentioned something specific, like Andrew, or called her by her real name. No. He was bluffing, fishing for information. She only had to play out the charade, then escape back to her old life, and no one would be the wiser. No one would be hurt.

"Be honest, darling," he urged. "Admit you want me as much as I want you."

So that was it. Even the notorious rake was not immune to the eternal conundrum of a man who paid for his pleasures, a man who was forced to wonder whether or not the prostitute faked her enjoyment. She looked at him and immediately changed her mind. No, this was not a man who doubted his appeal or his abilities. She searched her memory for a clue to his intention.

Bloody hell. He had skipped right to the tenth principle on his list. *Once your mistress admits her attraction to you, the power of the relationship rests firmly in your hands.*

He wasn't going to play his precious games on her. She looked him up and down with the same insolent leer he'd used earlier.

That's when she noticed he was naked. Completely

nude. Somewhere along the line he'd shed the rest of his clothes, and his bare torso, his bare . . . legs were visible beneath the clear water. He was so large . . . there. Virginal fear gripped her stomach and twisted. She turned and ran, the water slowing her desperate movements.

He lunged for her, splashing into the water when he missed.

She looked around in panic. She couldn't run down the hall in a chemise made transparent by water, yet her dress was on the side of the pool furthest from the door. The bed was only a few steps away. She skated on slippery feet toward the corner of the room, grabbed a sheet, and flung it around her shoulders. She turned toward the door.

She hit the bed with a whoosh as the weight of his body pressed the air out of her lungs.

He looked down at her, combing back his wet hair with his fingers. "I find your eagerness flattering, but the bed, Cassandra? I expected something more adventurous from you."

"Get off me, you oaf. I can't breathe."

He slid his weight down her body, insinuating his hips between her legs. He leaned to one side and rested his elbow on the bed, his head in his hand, seemingly content to stare at her. The intensity of his gaze made her uncomfortable.

"Now what?" she finally asked.

He laughed. Not a chuckle, not a snicker, but deep loud laughter. And she felt the vibrations resonate deep within her.

"Oh," he said when he caught his breath. "I think if we wait a moment, something will come up."

Sixteen

Marsfield stared down into her lovely face. What was it about Cassandra that enraptured him so? Beauty, yes, but he'd known many beautiful women. Yet most had left his heart cold. And none had dominated his thoughts as she had.

Except for her extraordinary eyes, her features were much the same as many others. Well, her mouth was very kissable, and her ears and the soft skin of neck beckoned him, and . . . the explanation of his fascination lay elsewhere.

She was a walking contradiction. Innocent air and wanton actions. Blushing and brazen. One second clinging, the next pushing him away. She had him feeling like a toy bandalore, traveling up and down the entire length of its string, spinning into the palm of her hand, then out of reach and back again.

He picked up her hand and kissed each knuckle of each finger. Her hands were smooth and unmarked by the hard manual labor that usually drove a woman into her chosen career. Yet the well-shaped nails were clipped short and blunt, like those of a seamstress or maid.

She was an enigma. As well spoken as any lady, her word choices indicated education, except when she was cursing like a sailor. He chuckled to himself. That was another thing. She made him laugh. He had never laughed while making love before. More confusing still, he'd never wanted to make a woman laugh with him while making love.

She jerked her hand away. "I don't know what you find so amusing."

He retrieved her hand and continued his ministrations. "I find you deliciously amusing," he said into her palm. He licked the length of her love line and flicked his tongue on the spot known as the mound of Venus. She shivered in response.

He moved his mouth to her wrist with a sense of wonderment. He'd never known a woman so responsive to his every touch. When he kissed the inside of her elbow, she giggled and pulled her arm away, inspiring him to find other ticklish spots. He followed her collarbone with kisses and nuzzled her neck, producing a sigh from her parted lips.

And he was inspired to find her other erogenous spots. He definitely wanted to touch all of her sweet spots. Kiss them. Taste them.

The promise of what awaited him hurried him lower to pay homage to her perfect breasts. He circled one aureole with his tongue while his fingers mimicked the movement on her other breast. Her nipples tightened. He grazed the nub with his teeth, then laved it smooth with his tongue, repeating the processes when she moaned and arched her back in response.

He paused to look at her face. Her eyes were closed, her magnificent emerald eyes. He felt the need for her to see him. For her to recognize he made her feel this way, not some other lover. The thought of others worshipping at her altar twisted his gut.

"Look at me, Cassandra."

She opened her eyes wide. "Marsfield?"

He saw her confusion, her passion, and in those deep emerald depths he saw her wonderment. Her surprise. Had no other lover taken the time to awaken her senses?

He knew from his earlier experience she could come to climax quickly, but had they all been so clumsy as to not enjoy prolonging the ecstasy?

Though he ached with the need, he vowed he would let her set the pace. "Tell me what you want," he prompted with an encouraging smile.

She smiled back at him. A vixen lover's smile.

"More," she whispered.

She laughed and threw her arms around his neck. She found his lips with a soul-stealing kiss.

"More," she demanded against his lips.

He was more than willing to oblige.

Anne lost track of time, of space, of the universe. Her world became that bed, his arms, and his lips. His talented lips and his magic hands. She reveled in their touch. She tried to remember to repeat his actions on his body, but she kept losing track of the mechanics in the delicious sensations.

She kept climbing that mountain, reaching for the stars. But whenever she would feel she was getting close, he stopped. She would stick out her bottom lip. He would laugh and do something outrageous like rip off her camisole or flip her over to place nipping kisses on her derriere. She laughed, rolled away, and directed his kisses back to her pouting lips. Or her breasts. She did like that.

He slipped lower on her body. She didn't know what he intended, but in this short time she'd learned to trust him in the matter of her pleasure. He knew more about her body than she did. He trailed lazy kisses down her ribs, counting and outlining each with his tongue. He circled her belly button. She stretched forward to smooth his hair back.

He paused to look at her. She couldn't think of anything to say. Her heart was too full. This was the man who'd paid his debt of honor to a prickly widow, who'd befriended a sickly boy. Even though he thought her one of the prostitutes, that was her doing, not his. She knew him. And she loved him, trusted him. She smiled her feelings.

Her smile of encouragement gladdened him. She was an adventuresome and experienced lover, truly his match.

"Close your eyes and lay back on the bed," he said.

He ran his hands down her thighs and pulled on her knees until she bent her legs.

"Relax."

He massaged her thighs, pressing down until her legs lolled on the bed. Spread wide just as he wanted. When he directed his kisses lower, he felt her sudden quiver of anticipation. Good. She knew what pleasure awaited her. Suddenly, he was in a hurry. He'd waited long enough to taste her.

He scooted to the edge of the bed, pulling her with him and stripping off her pantalets in the same smooth motion. Kneeling on the floor, he dived his head downward and latched onto her tiny bud. Her body rose off the bed and she cried out in intense pleasure.

Anne cried out in intense disbelief. He couldn't mean to kiss her there? Oh, no. He did. She tried to close her knees, but he held her legs open with his elbows. She dug her heels into the edge of the mattress, and succeeded only in raising her hips off the bed.

He moved, and somehow her legs were draped over his shoulders. Oh, no. This was too embarrassing. She'd never expected—shivers of pleasure expanded into tremors. She gripped the coverlet in her fists. Oh, no. His tongue flicked and licked and swirled. Oh, no. Yes. Oh, yes. The fireworks exploded and still he didn't stop. Oh, my heavens. Now she was climbing the mountain while the fireworks continued.

"Please," she pleaded, unaware of what she begging for.

He replaced his mouth with his thumb, but still held her with her legs over his shoulders. "Please, what? Tell me what you want." He rubbed her sensitive nub with a little more pressure.

She arched her back with the intense pleasure. "I don't know," she sobbed between panting breaths.

He rose to an almost standing position, taking her with him. Because she had only her head and shoulders on the bed, it was not difficult to scoot her several feet with the pressure of his chest. He then lowered her body enough to surge into her as they both fell to the bed, scooting her another few feet forward.

She stiffened and then scrambled as if to get away from him. He held her firm with his weight. He grabbed her chin and forced her to face him. Tears had gathered in her eyes.

"What's the matter?"

"That hurt."

What? He hadn't done anything to hurt her. "Where?"

She gave him a look of disgust. "I'm a virgin, you bloody numskull." She slapped him on the shoulder. "And that hurt."

He looked at her in shock. But it lasted only a few seconds. Surely she didn't expect him to fall for that old trick. He ignored the tiny stab of disappointment that it couldn't possibly be true.

A tear escaped her luminous eyes. What an excellent actress she was. He forced a laugh.

"Good try, Cassandra."

She gaped at him. "You don't believe me?"

"I may have been born at night, but I wasn't born last night."

She closed her eyes and thinned her lips to a tight line. Of course he didn't believe her. Her series of lies and misdirection had led him to believe her a prostitute. She'd wanted him to believe that. And yet it hurt that he did. The old saying that she'd made her bed and now had to lie in it suddenly had new meaning.

"Though you're much tighter than I'd expected." He moved in short stokes to accommodate her small size.

She squirmed as if to get away from him, but the movement only served to enflame his already tortured patience.

"You're so big," she blurted out.

He smiled at her expression of mock surprise. Damn if she hadn't bewitched him, although she overacted the part just a bit. If he didn't know better, he might mistake her expression for one of horror. Without withdrawing, he rolled them both over so she sat straddling him.

"I'll let you set the pace," he said.

Anne decided she'd had enough and moved to get off him, but he grasped her thighs and held her in place. The small up and down movement caused her to express a little "oh" of surprise.

"Just ride me like your very own private stallion," he said.

She looked down at their joined bodies and swallowed visibly. "I've only ridden sidesaddle before."

He hooted with laughter and, at her confused expression, rolled forward to pull her in his arms. She lay on his chest and he held her close as he continued to chuckle.

She relaxed. The pain had passed quickly, though she was still very aware of his fullness inside her. Not as uncomfortable as before. Actually quite nice once she got used it. Maybe she would stay a little longer. She snuggled in his comfortable embrace, and the movement of her hips sent a delicious sensation rippling along her insides.

And Marsfield stopped laughing with a deep intake of breath.

She experimented with another movement, sliding up an inch and back down. After a few more small, tentative movements, he pushed her to a kneeling position. Bracing her arms on his shoulders, he surged up with his hips. She rode him high off the bed. Then, when he had settled back on the mattress, she raised her body away from his and then slowly settled back down.

She tipped her head back at the intense pleasure, and he groaned his. He reached for her breast with one hand; his other cupped her mound. He played her sensitive nub, and she danced up and down his shaft to his erratic rhythm. Slow. Fast. Smooth. Fast. Faster.

With a growl, he grabbed her thighs and pinned her to him as his hips surged upward. He rolled them both over so he was on top, holding most of his weight on his arms. He watched her eyes as he drove into her body, a slow steady beat of long smooth strokes.

She watched his midnight blue eyes as she raised her hips to meet each thrust.

Suddenly his tempo increased.

She wrapped her legs around his body.

"Come with me, Cassandra," he panted, his voice roughened.

She was confused for a moment. Oh, over the mountain. He could go there, too? Several deep, fast strokes, and she felt the tremors quake her insides. Then he arched his back, driving into her, a look of tortured ecstasy on his face, a cry of triumph on his lips.

His reaction amazed her, humbled her, and sent her over the mountain to the land of exploding fireworks with him.

He collapsed on his side next to her, turning her body in the process so they lay facing each other. He ran his finger along the line of her chin and around her mouth. She kissed the tip of his finger, and he brought the kiss to his own lips.

"Silent, my sweet?" he murmured.

She was afraid if she opened her mouth words of love and gratitude would pour out. Instinctively, she knew he wouldn't want to hear them. She shrugged one shoulder.

"You are a jewel. Most women feel the need to talk after making love. Incessantly."

She shook her head.

"Give me a minute to recover."

She nodded.

"We still have the rest of the night." His look promised more delights to come. Then he rolled onto his back and closed his eyes.

"Don't leave," he whispered.

Seventeen

Anne stared at her lover. He lay so near the heat from his body still warmed her. He looked younger when he slept. Somehow vulnerable. Her heart melted. He'd asked her not to leave. Her lover—yikes.

Of course she had to leave. As soon as possible.

Moving at a snail's pace despite the need for haste, she slipped off the bed, then turned back to cover his sweat-sheened body with the coverlet so he wouldn't catch a chill. Unable to resist, she placed a kiss on his forehead. She found the sheet on the floor and wrapped it around herself.

Hoping the main hallway would be deserted, she eased open the door and slipped out. Rose sat on a small gilt-edged chair, guarding the door in her sleep.

Anne touched her on the shoulder. Rose woke immediately.

"There you are, dear. I thought you might need some help. Being it was your first time and all."

"How did you find me?" A terrible thought occurred to her. "You didn't—"

"Of course I didn't use the peepholes." Rose stood and stretched. "Oh, these old bones are not what they used to be. I didn't have to peep. You left the passage door wide open."

Anne felt the blush stain her cheeks and ducked her head.

Rose put her arm over Anne's shoulder and propelled her down the hall. "We respected your privacy."

"Then how did you know he—"

Rose looked at the sheet she was wearing. "I didn't think you voluntarily stripped for him."

Despite her embarrassment, Anne couldn't allow Marsfield to look the villain in Rose's eyes. "Actually, I did," she confessed, expecting censure.

Rose chuckled. "Good for you."

"But—"

"Come along. I have a nice cuppa tea waiting. If you want to talk, that's fine. Or if you don't, that's fine, too. Every woman reacts differently to losing her virginity."

Anne was suddenly grateful for Rose's experienced presence. Not that she wanted to talk, but it was nice to know someone was nearby to listen, someone experienced in case she had questions.

"Right now, I just want to go home," Anne said. "I never want to see him again."

"You might change your mind after you've had a chance to think about it."

Anne shook her head. "I won't. I can't. He must never know who I am."

Rose ushered her through the parlor and into her bedroom.

"Your gentleman's clothes are behind the dressing screen, and there's hot water in the basin." Rose gave Anne a affectionate pat on the shoulder and a little shove. "Go on. I'll pour while you dress. Then, after some strong tea to brace you up, one of the girls will see you home."

Anne washed her face and hands. She folded the cloth and placed it on the sore spot between her legs. The stinging faded with the warmth. Not that it was unexpected, but she was still shocked to have the cloth come away stained with blood. Evidence of the extreme step she'd taken. Step? Giant leap into an abyss was a better description.

She wanted to get home as quickly as possible. Without bothering to take the time to bind her breasts, she slipped on the man's shirt and trousers. She bundled the smallclothes into the waistcoat and tied it in a knot. While she wrestled the coat on, she slipped her bare feet into the shoes.

The front door of the parlor banged open.

Anne crouched behind the screen, making herself as small as possible.

"Marsfield," Rose said, as calm as if an irate earl burst into her parlor every day. "I was expecting Jasmine, but you're welcome to join—"

"Where is she?"

"Upstairs with her last customer, I imagine."

"You know who I mean."

"Petunia? Daisy?"

"Cass—Emerald. Where is Emerald?"

"I've only just come downstairs myself."

Anne moved a few inches to the left so she could peer through the crack between the panels of the dressing screen. Marsfield's presence dominated the parlor. He'd donned his pants, but his shirt gaped open for lack of fastening studs. She cringed back from his thunderous expression.

"Quit carrying coals to Newcastle, Rose. You know the whereabouts of all your girls at all times. Now here's your last chance to tell me the truth before I tear this place apart, room by room. Where is she?"

"She's not one of my girls."

Anne didn't understand how Rose could remain so calm in the face of Marsfield's fury.

"She was in your parlor, working the crowd," he snarled. "I saw her there."

Rose shrugged. Seating herself on the sofa, she picked up her cup of tea. "There are times when a female member of the *ton* needs an outlet for her baser instincts. I have, on occasion, obliged if the price was right."

"Are you telling me Emerald is a society woman slumming for a few thrills?"

"I'm allowing you to draw your own conclusions."

"She was a virgin. God knows how, but she was. I saw the blood on the sheets."

Rose managed a creditable trill of laughter. "Did you know I was a virgin forty-three times? Alas, now I'm too old for it to be believable. I did rather enjoy it."

"Are you telling me she used a cheap whore's trick on me?"

"I'm telling you no such thing. And it isn't cheap, believe me. A good virgin costs more than a coach and four."

Anne covered her mouth with her hand to stop the giggle that threatened. Rose was marvelous. Telling only the truth, but leading Marsfield down the garden path of her choice.

"What's her real name?" he demanded.

"I never asked. Actually, I told her I didn't want to know her real name. Professional reasons, you understand."

He looked long and hard at Rose as if to judge her veracity. Evidently, he believed her.

"Where does she live? How can I find her?"

Rose sighed. "We've only met here. For obvious reasons, I don't call on her."

Marsfield turned and stomped toward the door. He stopped and turned back. "If she ever comes here again, I expect to be notified immediately."

"If Emerald ever again seeks a lover here, I will send a runner," she promised.

Marsfield stared at Rose, who then crossed her heart and spit between her fingers. Marsfield nodded his acceptance of her word and left. Through the still open parlor door, Anne watched him take his hat and overcoat from the butler with the same casual grace he would have exhibited if he'd been wearing shoes.

* * *

Anne sat at her writing desk. She'd expected today to be different, expected to feel different in light of her momentous experience last night. For that was what she'd decided to call it. Not her downfall, or her ruin. Her momentous experience.

But the sun had risen as before. Cook had burned the toast and sausages. Binny had fallen asleep in her oatmeal. Cleeve had gotten into a fistfight with the footman next door. Old Finch could still not stand up straight, but insisted on returning to his duties, pain being preferable to another day in the parlor with Binny. Robert had not yet arisen. And Letty had refused to eat or come out of her room until Anne had agreed to accompany her on a carriage ride in the park this afternoon. An ordinary morning.

Yet she should feel different. Thinking it might help her to make a list, a lesson she'd learned from Marsfield, she took out a fresh sheet of stationery. She looked at the other paper she'd laid to the side. In the light of her momentous experience, every item on Marsfield's list now held new meaning.

Suddenly an idea seized her. Once she started writing, the words seemed to flow from her pen. A new story based on his principles for finding a mistress. Not her story, no. That was too personal. Yet a story loosely based on her adventures with Marsfield. The heroine was beautiful, self-possessed, and articulate. Everything Anne herself was not. By the end of the story, the hero would fall madly in love with her. Still, it was very different from her other efforts. Because of her momentous experience.

The sound of a carriage stopping in front of her house roused her from her work. Marsfield had been so much on her mind that she ran to the window hoping to see a tall, elegant man enter. Bloody hell, she couldn't even see the markings on the carriage.

She ran to the top of the stairs and looked over the railing like a giddy schoolgirl.

Preston leaned over and placed his card in the silver salver held at approximately knee height by poor bent-over Finch.

"I'm here to see Andrew—Lord Deck—a young woman—uh." He took a deep breath. "To be frank, I'm not exactly sure who I'm here to see. I'm a bit confused."

"I understand completely, sir," Finch intoned. "If you'd care to wait, I'll see if any of the previously mentioned persons are at home."

She ran down the stairs to save poor Finch the trouble of coming up. "Preston, how nice to see you."

Preston's mouth hung open.

"Thank you, Finch. Please ask Mrs. Finch to bring tea to the parlor."

"May I suggest the library, miss?"

"We shall take tea in the parlor," Anne said in a firm voice.

"You'll be sorry," Finch muttered in an ominous tone to Preston as he shuffled away.

Anne waited for the inexorable long minutes it took poor Finch to travel the length of the hall. Then she turned to Preston.

"Is this about Mars—?"

"Marsfield sent me."

They'd spoken at the same time.

"Please continue," she said. "No, wait. Come in here."

She practically dragged him into the parlor. Binny lay sprawled on the couch, her injured foot on a stool, her head tipped back, her ample bosom covered in biscuit crumbs. Loud snores emanated from her open mouth.

"Never mind her. Continue."

Preston stared at the old woman in morbid fascination. "Who is she?"

"Mrs. Binns, my chaperon. Now about Marsfield."

Preston choked. "Your chaperon?"

"You can't expect me to entertain a gentleman alone."

"I'm beginning to think there's nothing I can't expect from you."

"Preston, I thought we were friends."

"No. I offered friendship to a plain girl dressed passably as a boy." He looked her up and down, and shook his head. "You cannot be that boy."

"I'm the same person in a dress or in pants."

He shook his head. "No, you're not," he whispered.

Binny roared to life. She flailed around until she came to a standing position. Grabbing up her cricket bat, she whirled around to face the intruders.

Anne calmly introduced them to each other. "Preston has come calling." She had to give the man credit. He blinked at few times at the sight, but he didn't hide behind her or run screaming from the room.

"You're not one of those ne'er-do-well scalawags after our Letty, are you?" Binny asked, her eyes narrowed and shrewd.

"No, ma'am," Preston said in a hurry.

"Well, then." Binny put down her bat. "Everything's fine." She resumed her place, and presently her snoring.

"I presume that means your name is Letty."

"Oh, no. Letty is my sister. It's her first Season."

"And that means you are?"

"Sorry." She held out her hand to shake like a gentleman. "Anne Weathersby."

He took her hand and turned it over to kiss the back. "Miss Weathersby. I am honored."

"Please call me Anne. We're still friends, aren't we?"

"Yes."

She noticed the hesitation in his voice, but didn't give him a chance to elaborate. Placing her arm through his, she walked him to the settee by the window. Since he did not once turn his back on Binny and her cricket bat, she gave him the seat farthest from her chaperon.

"You said Marsfield sent you," Anne prompted.

Preston leaned over as if to whisper. She stopped him just in time.

"If you talk in a normal tone of voice, Mrs. Binns will ignore you. If you whisper or shout, she'll wake up. Or if anyone mentions f-o-o-d." She wanted to be fair and warn him just in case, even though she had hoped for quite a different topic of conversation.

Preston straightened his tie. "Thank you. I'll try to keep my voice normal. As I was saying, Marsfield—"

The door opening interrupted him. Mrs. Finch brought in the tray and sat it on the table before them. "Your—"

"Shhh." both Preston and Anne said. She pointed to their companion.

Mrs. Finch nodded. "Your t-e-a, Miss."

"Thank you, I'll pour." She turned to Preston. "L-e-m-o-n or s-u-g-a-r?" She could not suppress a giggle.

"C-r-e-a-m, please," he answered.

She handed him his cup. "You were saying?"

"Yes. Marsfield sent me to tell Andrew he has gone grouse shooting in Scotland and will be away for several weeks." He smiled. "He also said we'd begin your boxing lessons when he returns. I can't wait to see that."

"Scotland?"

Marsfield had made love to her and then gone hunting the next day as if nothing had happened. He hadn't even tried to find her.

"Yes, Scotland." Preston shook his head. "It makes no sense to me, either. This sudden change of plans is very unlike him. Marsfield is so methodical about his schedule. And he took Burke with him."

Anne was barely listening. Not that she'd expected Marsfield to knock on her door, but she now realized she'd hoped. And shattered hopes hurt.

"Would you?"

"Would I what?" she asked.

"Pay attention to what I'm saying, obviously."

"Sorry."

"I said I'm at loose ends without Burke. Would you like to go to the British Museum this afternoon?"

"I would love to, but I can't. I already have plans for the afternoon."

He gave her with a strange look. "I rather thought you'd set your cap for Marsfield."

"I've already told you I'm not chasing Marsfield. I'm well past the marriage mart. We're in town for my sister's Season. Marsfield and me? Impossible."

He chuckled. "You would certainly upset his well-ordered life."

"Not only do I have no desire to upset anyone, Marsfield wouldn't give a plain woman like me a second glance."

"Are you fishing for compliments? You're not a plain woman."

"We're friends, Preston. There's no need for you to play the gallant with me. Save your flattery for someone who doesn't own a mirror."

"You are defiantly an original." He stood. "May I call on you again?"

"I'd like that very much."

He kissed her hand and showed himself out.

Mrs. Finch arrived on his coattails. "Miss Letty says she cannot possibly go on a carriage ride in the same hat she has already worn four times."

Anne sighed. "I guess I'm lucky she hasn't noticed it's the same carriage we've been using for the last five years."

"Then don't let her read today's paper. The Countess Mongraith has had her horses dyed to match her latest carriage outfit."

Anne leaned back and closed her eyes. How much would that cost? Money. The bane of her existence. They weren't halfway through the Season, and she had few financial reserves left.

If she could avoid Letty, who would insist on being consoled for her disastrous lack of a new bonnet, Anne would still have the afternoon free to take her edited manuscript to Mr. Blackthorne as she had planned.

"Do you think you could fetch my hat and coat without Letty seeing you?" Anne asked Mrs. Finch. "Also the manuscript on my desk. I have an urgent errand to run."

She tapped Binny on the shoulder. "Wake up, dear. We're going for a carriage ride."

"I'm awake," Binny said. "And I can spell."

Mr. Blackthorne sat down at his desk and unwrapped the package containing her manuscript.

"Stop pacing," he growled. "You know I hate it."

"I'm uncomfortable watching you read."

"Then go look out the window. I need to concentrate."

Anne stood with her hands clasped at her waist, but she didn't really see the street scene before her. Her attention was focused on the papers rustling behind her back.

"The new chapter begins on page one hundred seventy-five," she said in a helpful tone.

"Yes, yes," he muttered.

He sounded distracted. That could either mean he was engrossed, which was good, or it could mean he was indifferent, which was bad. She couldn't resist a peek over her shoulder.

What was he reading? Oh, no. That was her rose beige stationery, not her writing paper. She rushed to his side. He was reading what she'd written this morning, the story about her and Marsfield. That was her own fantasy, and she'd never intended for anyone to see it. Mrs. Finch must have packed it up in the package with her manuscript. She made a desperate grab for the pages, but Blackthorne moved them out of her reach.

"You don't want those," she cried, reaching over his head in vain. "They're not part of the manuscript."

"But I do want them," he said. "This is an excellent start. I love it. How soon can you finish?"

She shook her head. "It's not for publication."

"Nonsense. This is the best you've ever done."

Anne refused to give in to his flattery.

"I know," he said. "We'll add pictures. There's this starving cartoonist whose work would be perfect, and I can get him for pennies per drawing. And he's quick."

She shook her head.

"I see a slim volume," Blackthorne continued. "Dark blue cover with gold lettering. We'll call it *A Lover's Manual, How to Get a Mistress, Based on the Scandalous Affair of Lord X.* And just to appease the sensibilities of the fuddy-duddies, we'll subtitle it *Rules of Misbehavior Not to Follow.*" He rubbed his hands together. "This will make publishing history. Two weeks. I'll need your copy in two weeks."

She shook her head. "You don't understand. I couldn't—"

"We won't need much copy. I see the principle in bold across the top of the page. Then your story to illustrate it. In the style of an exposé or maybe a confession. Ten, twelve pages each. Then the cartoon. It'll sell like umbrellas in a thunderstorm."

"But I can't—"

"Trust me. I know when something will sell. I'll double your usual royalty. And I'll guarantee one thousand copies."

She tried to do the math in her head and came up with . . . a lot of money.

"An extra five percent royalty if you can have it ready in two weeks."

She supposed she could. On a decent day, she could write five to ten pages. If she did nothing else and worked from dawn to midnight, maybe fifteen. The lure of so much money was tempting. Adding to Letty's dowry would increase her chances of a good match. The orphans could use an education fund, and she could give Binny and poor old Finch a comfortable retirement settlement. It would be so nice not to have money worries.

And it wasn't as if anyone would know it was really she who wrote it.

"On one condition," she said.

"Name it."

"You pay that artist one pound per drawing and a royalty."

"Now you're giving away my money."

"That's the condition."

"All right. One percent royalty. But I want you back here in two weeks, stories in hand, to meet with the artist for your first sitting."

"Me?"

"Who else? We don't want word of this to leak out until we're ready to go to market."

"But the heroine must be a ravishing beauty for the story to work. Not only do I not fit, I shouldn't want anyone to recognize me."

"Don't worry, the artist will change your face. Now, what about Lord X? Hmm. I've got it. We'll only show him from the back. Every picture, only the back. Heighten the mystery. But we still need a model. How about my assistant?"

Anne frowned and shook her head.

"I see your point," he said. "Even from the back. Well, I'll think about it. Hmm." Blackthorne raised his chin and scratched under his beard. "Someone we can trust implicitly."

"With broad shoulders."

"Yes, yes. Well, we have two weeks. You'd better get to work, young lady."

Eighteen

Marsfield unwound the red ribbon from his fingers and returned it to his breast pocket. He picked up the folded *Times* from the carriage seat opposite. Even his attempt at reading had not stopped Burke from talking nonstop. The boy was different when Preston was not around. Burke not only thought every decision through multiple times, he remembered and could verbalize every iteration. Marsfield had begun to long for Preston's repressive presence before they'd reached the outskirts of town. As if he needed additional proof, this was an example of the disasters making rash decisions could bring.

On the other hand, Burke provided prima facie evidence that a man could dither a decision to death.

"Listen, Burke. What say we catch a few winks? I didn't get much sleep, and I feel a headache coming on."

"Capital idea. I hardly slept myself. Short notice and all. My valet and I were up most of the night deciding what to pack. At first I'd thought the houndstooth jacket. It's my favorite. But Yarnell pointed out, quite rightly I must admit, that it's so noticeable I wouldn't be able to wear it above a time or two without comment."

"Burke—"

"Say, I do hope your man won't mind doing for us both."

Kirby would probably strangle the young man before

the three weeks were up . . . if Marsfield didn't beat his valet to the task.

"I would have brought Yarnell if there'd been room. He has quite the way with a cravat. He suggested the herring plaid jacket, saying it would be perfect for any weather, but I've never been all that fond of the color. Only bought it because Preston insisted."

Marsfield could easily imagine the reason. Shopping with Burke had to be a form of torture the Inquisition would have found appealing.

"About that nap—"

"We decided on the bottle green for jacket number one—"

"Burke."

"Sir?"

"Sleep."

"Do you think that's such a good idea? I always get a crick—"

"Arrrgh." Marsfield grabbed two of the small pillows Kirby had thoughtfully provided and, placing them over his ears, leaned into the corner. It was going to be a long three weeks.

So why didn't he send his regrets and turn around? Because he'd accepted this futile assignment. Because . . . Marsfield faced the real issue. He was running away. It was not an easy admission, even to himself.

Cassandra had gotten under his skin. For years he'd disdained emotional involvement as the solace of the unintelligent masses and inflicted poets, and yet he'd succumbed to her charms. He, who had kept his relationships with women free of the messy entanglements of love, had lost control and had begun to care, to hope.

He'd even decided to make her his mistress. Oh, how she would have laughed if he'd offered his protection. Fortunately, he'd been saved that embarrassment by her timely disappearance. Back to her society life. What a fool he'd been. The clues were right in front of his face. He'd seen them, noted them, and yet he'd allowed his loins to rule his brain as if it had been his first sexual experience.

At this very minute, she was probably waking up in her elegantly appointed town house. Despite his distaste for her duplicity, his staff reacted to the mental picture of her stretching in satisfaction and contentment under a lace and satin coverlet. That lazy, I've-got-a-secret smile courtesy of his humiliation. Admitting a woman had gotten the better of him didn't sit well.

Let her have her moment of triumph. Check was not checkmate. One battle did not foretell the outcome of a war. She would know he had entrée into society. All of Rose's customers did. What she didn't know was that his scorn for aristocratic approval provided him with the audacity to approach her in public. Perhaps he would offer his protection after all.

Wouldn't that set her back on her ear? In front of her friends, her . . . husband? No. He didn't think she was married. A wife wouldn't have the freedom to stay out all night. In her case, any husband with a grain of sense would have her watched constantly.

Yet Cassandra was no schoolroom miss. Even with a Season or two of polish, the average chit wouldn't have the opportunity or the aplomb to carry off such a charade. No. He'd bet his money on a widow. A widow well past her mourning.

Now he had two reasons to reenter society, two quarries: The villain behind the consortium that provided substandard goods to the front, and the scandalous woman he knew as Cassandra, though he now doubted it was her real name. He was actually looking forward to his return. Grouse in Scotland couldn't hold a candle to the game he would be hunting in London.

* * *

"My back is killing me," Preston said.

"At least you don't have to keep your face in this asinine adoring expression," Anne said through gritted teeth.

Preston pulled a monkey face, and she couldn't stifle a giggle.

"Pa-leeze," Bernard called from behind his easel at the other end of the studio. "Blackthorne wants this page today and we only have another hour of decent light."

"An hour," Preston groaned. "My feet are killing me."

"I think my foot is asleep." She had been seated on a hay bale for this horse auction vignette. With her head tilted to one side, she gazed up at her admirer, while at the same time holding up her skirt to display her ankle, held out for his inspection. She wiggled her toes. The hidden support was a great improvement over holding up her leg to achieve the effect Bernard desired, but it tended to make her foot go to sleep.

"At least you're sitting," Preston said.

"This hay bale is not exactly comfortable."

"More so than this fence." Preston leaned against the section of wooden rails that had been brought in to serve as an additional scene prop. Both elbows rested back on the top rail, and his ankles were casually crossed. "I can't imagine why I allowed you to talk me into this mad scheme."

"We're friends," she reminded him. "And doing favors for each other is part of friendship."

"You forgot to tell me this particular favor involved staring for hours on end at your red garter—"

"I have a fondness for red garters."

"So do I, but I would never consent to stare at Burke's leg, friend or not."

"I should hope this a less onerous duty," she teased.

"Good," Bernard called from behind his easel. "Hold that twinkle in your eye."

"Only slightly less," Preston moaned.

"Really?"

"It's a matter of degree and situation. A bonbon in itself is not onerous, but tie a starving man's hands behind his back, wave the bloody thing under his nose, and tell him he can't have a taste, that is a cruel form of torture."

She wasn't sure she wanted the direction of this conversation to continue. "Preston, I—"

"Don't say it. If Marsfield were not in the picture—"

"Who says he's in—?"

"Come on. Any fool can see you're in love with him."

"Me in love with Marsfield?" Anne sputtered.

"You practically glow when anyone so much as says his name."

"Good glow," Bernard muttered. "I like the glow."

"I do not glow. And if you don't discontinue this ridiculous pretense, then I shall be forced to recant my friendship."

"Very well."

"Excellent."

Anne suffered through several minutes of silence. It would hurt to loose Preston's friendship. Over these last few weeks, he'd proved an entertaining companion and understanding confidante. She hadn't told him about Rose's or her meeting with Marsfield there, though he seemed to sense there was more to the story.

"I'm sorry," she finally said.

"For calling me ridiculous?" Preston grinned.

"Noooo," she said, shaking her head.

Bernard stomped over. "Head position, head position," he muttered. He took her face in his hands and tilted it to its previous pose, then stomped back to the other side of the room.

"We're friends," she said. "And it was wrong of me to trivialize that by threatening to remove my regard."

"I accept your apology. And since we are still friends, I'll tell you that I heard from Marsfield."

"Hold that glow," Bernard called from the other side of the easel.

Anne ignored Preston's smirk. She did not *glow* whenever anyone mentioned Marsfield's name. With difficulty, she pretended disinterest in Preston's news.

He, in turn, changed the subject. "Did you read in the *Times* that they've cast a bell at the Whitechapel Bell Foundry weighing thirteen and a half tons? They're already calling it Big Ben after Sir Benjamin Hall."

"No," she said, staring over Preston's shoulder with the stupid adoring expression Bernard found so appealing.

"Have you read Burton's *Pilgrimage to Mecca* yet?" Preston asked. "Quite makes one want to travel to far-off, exotic locales. But then, if one isn't prepared to suffer hardships and to embrace the native culture to the extent Sir Richard seems to enjoy—and I'm not prepared to do either—then what is the point?"

"No point," she agreed through gritted teeth.

"Exactly. Oh, I heard of this fabulous love charm. Guaranteed to work. You take the hair off the belly of a goat, tie it in nine knots, and conceal it in the room of your beloved. You'll be married—"

"Preston." Blast him for testing her patience.

"Yes?" He plastered a blank expression on his face.

Bloody hell. He was going to make her ask. For Bernard's sake she retained her sweet, insipid expression.

"Tell me what Marsfield said in his message, or I shall wring your popinjay neck."

"How can I refuse such a sweetly worded request?"

She threw her reticule at him.

He caught it in the air just before it hit him in the face. "Temper, temper."

"Peo-ple." Bernard rushed over and reset their positions, all the while muttering about the indignities of having to work with nonprofessional models.

"Well?" she said after the artist had returned to his place on the other side of the room.

"It seems that on the last day of shooting, Burke fell while climbing out of the blind and broke his leg. It will be a week or two until he's able to travel, and then he'll have to make the trip home in easy stages."

"And Marsfield's staying with Burke? Admirable."

Preston laughed. "His letter said he didn't have a choice. Feared for our boy's life if he was left without a protector. Burke can be . . . shall we say aggravating in the best of circumstances."

"I never found him so."

"That's because you seem to thrive in a environment rife with aggravating people."

"I knew there was a reason we seemed destined to be friends," she said.

"Not so. I've insinuated myself into your good graces for only one reason."

"My scintillating company?"

Preston grinned. "Anticipation of the entertaining scene sure to ensue when Marsfield discovers the truth."

"He won't. Not unless you tell him."

He laid his hand over his heart. "I've given you my word of honor as a gentleman."

And she trusted his word.

"But that doesn't mean Marsfield isn't going to find out the truth," Preston added.

Anne didn't want to be in the same room—in the same country—if he ever did.

Nineteen

There must be a mistake. Anne dropped her hands into her lap and blinked her eyes. She focused her gaze on the ordinary, familiar objects of the library. The books still stood in orderly rows like dutiful soldiers, the two leather chairs still flanked the fireplace, and the ormolu clock still ticked a steady beat on the marble mantel. Taking a deep breath, she raised the bank draft and looked at the number again. It still read ten thousand six hundred ninety-six pounds and eight shillings.

With shaking hands, she set the bank draft aside to scan Blackthorne's letter. Skipping through his mushy praises, she scanned to the details of the sales report. Two incidents had pushed the sales to record figures. The lending libraries had banned *A Lover's Manual* as indecent, causing anyone who wished to read a copy to purchase one. And a bookseller from New York City had purchased six thousand copies for export to the United States. Blackthorne had already used every scrap of paper and binding leather available to him and was only waiting on supplies to begin the fourth print run. Based on his current requests and inquiries from other foreign booksellers, he expected the figure to double or even triple before the end of the year.

He closed his letter with, "Congratulations on your resounding success."

"Astonishing is perhaps a better word," she said aloud.

She retrieved a piece of ledger paper from the desk and proceeded to recalculate all of his figures. Editor extraordinaire he might be—and an excellent salesman, it seemed—but his accounting skills were somewhat lacking. There remained a niggling doubt in the back of her mind that he'd made a huge mistake.

There was a knock on the door, and she absently called, "Enter." Before poor, stooped-over Finch had a chance to announce him, Preston burst through the doorway, waving a piece of paper. Finch followed.

"What exactly is this?" Preston demanded.

"Thank you, Finch," Anne said, ignoring her friend for a moment. "Please ask Mrs. Finch to bring tea." After the butler shuffled out, she turned to Preston. "From what I can see, what with you waving it around like a flag in gusty wind, it appears to be a bank draft."

He held it between a thumb and forefinger inches from her nose. "And what is this supposed to be for?"

"One thousand sixty-nine pounds, three shillings and tuppence. But that's wrong."

"You bet it's wrong—"

She looked over her notes. "Blackthorne underpaid you by one penny."

He crossed his arms over his chest and stared down at her. "Why would Blackthorne send me a bank draft?"

"That's your fee for modeling. I had him put it in the contract."

Preston sat in the nearest chair with a thud. "You *paid* me to model for the pictures in your book?"

"Not me. Blackthorne."

"Amounts to the same thing."

"Does not. Besides, you deserve something for your trouble."

"I did it out of friendship."

"I know that. And I appreciate it, as your friend. Blackthorne, however, shows his appreciation in pounds and shillings."

"And pence." He placed the draft on her desk. "I don't want your money."

She slid it to a spot in front of him. "It's not my money. And I don't want your money."

"Then give it charity," he said, pushing the bank draft back toward her.

She pushed it toward him. "It's yours to keep."

He pushed it back to her. "Then it's mine to give."

Anne realized from the stubborn set of his jaw she wouldn't win the argument.

"I thank you," she said with a gracious smile. "There's an orphanage near Weathersby that is in desperate need of a new building. Where they are housed now is an affront to decency. I'll mark this for the building fund and see you receive proper credit for your generous donation."

"I'd rather it be anonymous." He put his head in his hands. "Do you know absolutely everyone is talking about your book? The possible identity of Lord X is the biggest item to hit the gossip mill since . . . since nothing. This *is* the biggest."

"So it seems." Anne pressed her lips together to keep from grinning in triumph. Her book was a success. A shivery thrill shook her insides.

"If word of this . . . this modeling gets out, not only will my reputation be in shreds, but Marsfield will bloody well kill me."

"Marsfield has nothing to do with the book."

He gave her a look that said she must be bordering on lunacy.

"All right, he was the original model for the hero, but no one knows that. No one will be able to identify him as Lord X because it's fiction, Preston. I made it all up out of whole cloth. A fictional affair between a fictional man and a fictional woman."

"Everything?"

She fought the urge to roll her eyes. "You were there at the horse auction. Did Marsfield make love to me on a hay bale? And at the pub? I wasn't even wearing a dress for him to slip his hand underneath the skirts."

"I've read the book, you know. Seems quite real."

"I think you mean realistic. And I'll take that as a compliment to my writing skill rather than a smirch on my personal reputation."

"Are you telling me you and Marsfield never—"

"I'm not telling you anything." She felt the blush creep up her throat. "And I hope you're not asking what I think you are, because . . ."

"I won't ask." He stood to leave. "I don't need to."

She ducked her head to hide her tears. "Please don't think less of me."

He walked around the desk and stood silently until she looked up.

"I think I feel sorry . . . for both of us. I know you must love him if you . . ." He swallowed visibly. "I hope he comes to his senses soon. I'd hate to have to call him out."

"Don't be ridiculous. He doesn't even know it's me. I—" She stopped at his look of surprise. Bloody hell, now she'd have to tell him about Cassandra, or else her friend and her lover would wind up meeting at dawn with pistols drawn.

"Please sit."

She started with her imaginary husband Dunstan, and though she didn't tell him about her second trip to Rose's, by the time she'd brought him up to date, Preston was laughing so hard that he held his sides and had tipped over sideways to lie on the sofa.

"It's not that funny," she finished.

"No, but the look on Marsfield's face when he finds out will be. I can just picture it."

"I keep telling you, he won't find out."

Preston only shook his head. Coughing and blinking, he finally sat up and managed a straight face. He rubbed his eyes with the palms of his hands and took a deep breath.

"I'm holding you to your vow of silence," she said. His mirth miffed her for some reason she didn't care to analyze.

"Of course," he said with an affronted air. "You'd best not make a mistake in his presence that will give away your duplicity."

"It hardly matters, since I don't intend ever to see him again."

"But you must. That's the main reason I came over today. He sent word 'round this morning that he arrived late last night. Tomorrow he's taking Andrew to the boxing gym and out gaming. Just think, the gaming hall—the research you originally wanted."

"I no longer need that. I rewrote that scene . . . another way."

"You might need it in the future. For another book."

She stopped to think. With the fortune she'd earned and was still earning from *A Lover's Manual,* she would never need to pen another book. The very thought wrenched her gut. She liked writing. And her only other option was to resign herself to respectable spinsterhood, something she realized she wasn't ready to accept.

Even if Marsfield found her out, he would hardly make public an affair in which he looked to play the dupe. Besides, if she'd managed thus far, she could fool him one more time. Preston undoubtedly overestimated the risk of discovery.

When she agreed to accompany Preston in her disguise, she ignored the smirk of satisfaction on his face. Her heart fluttered at the thought of seeing Marsfield again, and she tried to ignore that also.

Tomorrow would have to be the last time.

* * *

"But I can't go if you don't go."

Anne put down her book. Letty had been pacing the parlor for an hour waiting in vain for their brother to arrive and escort her to the Featherstones' masquerade. "Mrs. Binns—"

Letty stomped her foot. "No. I'll be mortified when she falls sleep and snores louder than the band or tips her chair over backward or—"

"Then you must wait for Robert." She reopened her book.

"What if he doesn't show? Please, Anne. I was so looking forward to this ball, to showing off my beautiful costume that you bought me."

Letty did look lovely as the Fairy Queen. Her hair had been arranged in a mass of loose ringlets with silver threads woven throughout. Ruched silver ribbons encrusted with glass beads covered the waisted bodice. Wings of gossamer tissue were glued to a wire frame and attached to the costume between her shoulder blades. Seven layers of white tissue tulle had been draped over a silver underskirt, each layer a few inches shorter than the last, each Van Dyke point on the hems accented with a glass teardrop. She shimmered and glittered—and pouted.

"I can't—"

"Yes, you can. There's always a row of widows in the chairs against the wall, lined up like black crows on a fence."

"If I'd only known how appealing the prospect would be—"

"Wouldn't it, though? You could listen to the music, watch the dancers."

Anne sighed. Sarcasm and irony were lost on Letty. "It's only been six months since Dunstan's death. I can't—"

"He wasn't a real husband. You can keep your veil on. I've seen that before. No one will ask you to dance."

"That veil is hot and uncomfortable. To wear it inside for hours—"

"Two hours. I promise we'll leave after two hours. No more. Please."

Anne knew better than to look at Letty's face, but she did it anyway. Two tears shimmered on the girl's cheeks, matching the glass beads on her gown. How grossly unfair that Letty could do that without her eyes getting all puffy and red, without her nose running. On the few occasions Anne had indulged herself in a good cry, her face had remained blotchy for days.

The minute Anne agreed to go to the masquerade, Letty brushed the tears aside like yesterday's crumbs.

"You change your clothes as quickly as possible," Letty said with a radiant smile. "And I'll have Harvey bring around the coach."

Anne sat between the Dowager Countess Farnsworth and the Dowager Baroness Brundle, who'd both been black crows on the fence when she'd had her Seasons years ago. For an hour Anne listened to gossip regarding every person who walked through the door. Fanning herself, hoping against hope for a breath of air to penetrate the veiling, she watched the clock.

Suddenly, Preston stood before her. He bowed over her hand, his lips not touching the black lace of her glove.

"We need to talk," he whispered. Straightening up, he announced loud enough for her neighbors to hear, "Your sister thoughtfully suggested you might enjoy a turn around the room. I hope you'll allow me to do her this small service by accepting my arm."

Caring more for the chance to escape than for the appropriateness of her actions, Anne stood, excused herself to her shocked companions, and placed her fingertips on his forearm.

"Thank you for your kindness," she said.

He set a slow but steady pace the length and breadth of the large ballroom. Then he deftly steered her behind a potted palm and through a set of doors to a deserted portico.

She threw the veiling back over her head and breathed in the cool night air. Even if she took a chill, the relief she currently felt would be worth it.

"Thank you for rescuing me," she said. "I was about to suffocate in there."

"From the lack of fresh air, the ungodly temperature, or the boring company?"

She laughed. "All three."

He gave her a courtly bow, then hopped up to sit on the stone balustrade. "Letty told me you'd brought her, though I must confess the information was imparted in the form of a complaint."

"You don't have to explain. I'm sure she sent you to change my mind. Did she bother to tell you she agreed to leave after two hours?"

He shrugged, as if Letty's problems mattered little to him.

"I also came to warn you," he said. "Marsfield is here."

"You already told me he—"

"No. Here. At the ball."

Anne gasped at the thought of seeing Marsfield face to face for the first time since her momentous experience. Maybe Preston was mistaken. She hadn't seen Marsfield come in, and the dowagers had missed no one with their barbed comments.

"He's having a drink with the duke right now. He should be announced into the ballroom shortly."

"Bloody hell," she whispered.

"Exactly why I thought you needed a warning. If those biddies you were sitting with heard that comment, no telling what they would have thought. You really must think about cleaning up your language."

Anne whirled in a complete circle. Her heart pounded. "I have to find Letty. I have to leave. I . . . I can't see him . . . let him see me."

"Calm down." He placed his hands on her shoulders and looked into her eyes. "You told me he thinks you are your aunt."

"Yes, but the old crows know I'm not Elizabeth Gordon. They think I'm Dunstan's widow."

"You're making too much of this. If he speaks to you, just turn and walk away."

"I can't give the cut direct to an earl."

"Of course you can. In either persona, you're a respectable widow, and he's the notorious Earl of Marsfield. It is not only possible, he would expect it."

She shook her head. "Not after his kindness to Andrew. He would . . . I don't know what he'd do."

"He'll do nothing," Preston assured her. "You worry too much."

"You don't know Marsfield as well as you think you do," she said with a stern look.

"And you know him better?"

A hot blush crept up her neck. She could only hope it wasn't discernible from the flush anyone would attribute to the stifling heat of the crowded ballroom. She drew the veil back over her face.

"I know he can be relentless in the pursuit of his goal," she said.

"Then you're in luck. In my experience, he has never pursued widows in mourning. In fact, he avoids them like lepers."

A shiver snaked down her spine, and she knew it was from more than the chilly air.

"If you're my friend," she said, "you'll help me find Letty and convince her to leave."

"In this crush, finding anyone could take hours. You can't wait out here. You'll catch your death."

"I don't intend to wait out here. You take the card rooms and the refreshment areas. I'll check the dance floor and the retiring rooms."

Preston escorted her back and left on his errand. Her original seat had been usurped, but she found a place to stand near the end of the long row where she could observe the dancers undisturbed by the necessity for conversation. However, the ballroom was large, and the dancers many. In twenty minutes' time, she hadn't caught a glimpse of her sister.

She decided to check the retiring rooms. Before she could act, the sudden murmuring and tittering of her neighbors alerted her to the fact something unusual was happening. Looking down the fence line of black crows, she discovered Marsfield making his way down the row, greeting and chatting with each and every widow. Avoid them like lepers, hmm? Not one of those oh-so-proper widows cut him, either. They giggled and simpered like schoolgirls when the notorious Lord Marsfield turned on his charm.

Anne fled in the opposite direction.

Letty wasn't in any of the rooms set aside for the women to use. As Anne rounded the top of the stairs and began her descent, she could only hope Preston had found her sister and was waiting at the front door.

Instead, Marsfield leaned against the newel post as if he were expecting her and had every intention of waiting all night if necessary. He looked at her with an unreadable expression. She hesitated, but could not escape once he'd spotted her. Their meeting was now unavoidable. She continued downward with slow steps.

"Good evening, Lord Marsfield." She felt a certain satisfaction that her voice did not betray her quivering insides.

"Lady Gordon. I sought you with a purpose in mind."

"To compliment me on my costume?"

He smiled. "That would normally be an opening conversational gambit at such an event, but I rather thought we might discuss your nephew, if you have a moment to spare. I had intended to call upon you tomorrow. However, since we are both here . . ."

"It is unnecessary for you to refrain from the festivities. Andrew has kept me informed. Unfortunately, I won't be at home tomorrow."

She made to step by him, but he stopped her with a gentle touch on her arm. A touch that sent electric shivers through her. A simple touch, and she wanted to leap into his arms and press her lips and body to his. He could not know—she could not let him know—how fiercely his nearness affected her. She tilted her head toward his hand and waited in silence until he removed it.

"I once ventured the opinion that you played the game of chess well," he said, his voice low and husky, reminding her of intimacies she must somehow forget.

"You are laboring under an incorrect assumption, sir. I do not play games of any sort." She walked past him, heading toward the front door.

"Oh, but, my lady, I think you do," he whispered in the same intimate voice.

She stopped in her tracks and forced herself to turn and face him. He was gone.

Twenty

"I cannot do it," Anne said.

"You can. I'll help you," Preston promised.

"I can't."

"Why?"

She stomped her foot in frustration. She couldn't explain to Preston that it wasn't so much anything Marsfield had said or done, it was her uncontrollable reaction to him she feared.

"Marsfield suspects nothing. Now straighten your cravat." Preston checked his watch. "He'll be here any minute."

Anne automatically looked in the hall mirror and adjusted the knot at her throat. Smoothing back her pomaded hair and pushing her tinted glasses further up her nose, she was unable to dismiss her misgivings as easily as Preston had, but she was willing to let him convince her.

She did look quite different, quite manly in her new cocoa brown coat and fawn breeches, both made with appropriate padding by the understanding little tailor. Maybe she could do this, if only Marsfield wouldn't touch her.

She'd been fine last night until the touch of his hand on her arm had brought back memories of other touches, other places his magic fingers had—

Stop it, she admonished herself. *Think about the gaming hell. Think about boxing.*

"I hope you don't expect me to actually box." She saw

Preston's grin in the reflection and whirled around to face him. "You do. Bloody hell."

He shook his head. "Most of the time you'll be observing my excellent technique as Burke and I spar—"

"I thought Burke had a broken leg?"

"Seems the country doctor erred on the side of caution. It was just a bad muscle pull in his calf. He's hobbling around quite well. Marsfield says Burke needs some exercise after sitting around for weeks."

"Then you can box with him," she stated in a tone meant to settle the matter.

"I will, and Marsfield will point out the basics to you. Then I'll volunteer to be your sparring partner, and you can batter away at me with the gloves for a while. Should prove interesting."

"I wouldn't want to hurt you."

"Don't worry, you won't. At least not in the ring."

The carriage pulled up, and he guided her toward the door. She did an abrupt about-face.

"I can't."

"Yes, you can." He pulled her through the door and pushed her toward the waiting carriage.

Anne stood next to the raised boxing ring while Burke and Marsfield shoved the sparring gloves on her hands. The gloves looked like padded leather mittens to her, and judging from Burke's bloodied nose, they provided little protection from Preston's blows. She fought the urge to grab her coat and cravat from the back of the nearby chair and run from the room.

Marsfield reached for her glasses.

She ducked her head away. "Without my glasses, I won't be able to see my opponent."

"It's all right," Preston called. "I won't hit him in the face."

Marsfield nodded. "Into the ring with you, then." He slapped her on the back hard enough to make her fall forward and have to catch herself on the rope.

A distinguished gentleman approached the small group. "I say, Marsfield, jolly good show." He winked and wiggled his bushy mustache as he harrumphed. "Quite."

"Good afternoon, Colonel," Marsfield said. His expression indicated he expected the man to elucidate on his comment.

The colonel pulled out a copy of her book and thumped it with his knuckles. "Quite good, eh? Knew it was you all along. Told the missus so right off, eh?"

"I haven't the slightest idea what you're talking about." The frigid tone of Marsfield's voice sent the colonel stumbling back a few paces.

"What? Oh. Right-o. My mistake. Abject apologies and all that, eh?" The colonel turned and fled.

"What is going on?" Marsfield asked. "That's the tenth person today who has waved that silly blue book under my nose."

Anne crawled into the boxing ring to get away from the thunderous look on his face.

"While we were away, sir—" Burke started to explain, his voice muffled by the damp cloth he held to his nose.

Marsfield turned away from him. "Preston, in twenty words or less," he demanded.

"Latest rage. Called *A Lover's Manual*. Anonymous account of a scintillating affair between Lord X and Lady Z. Gossips running wild. Seems some have identified you as Lord X."

"Preposterous nonsense," Marsfield growled.

"That was twenty-nine words," Burke pointed out.

"If we'd waited for your explanation, we would have needed to send out for tea," Preston countered.

"What are you going to do?" Anne asked in a small voice.

"Do?" Marsfield turned to face her eye to eye now that she stood on the raised platform. "Nothing. To do anything at all would only fuel the mill. The only choice is to ignore it."

"But they will say—"

"I don't give a bloody fig for the *ton's* opinion."

Her relief was short-lived.

"Put up your dukes, Andrew." Preston assumed the boxer's stance. "It's time you learned to take your licks as well as give them. Time to be a real man."

Marsfield shouted directions from the sideline. "Keep up your guard, Andrew. Right, left, right. Move, damn it."

She put up her fists and danced around like she'd seen the others do. Shuffle, shuffle left. Bob up and down. Shuffle, shuffle right. Rather like a drunk who couldn't remember the steps to the country reel.

"Jab," Marsfield shouted. "Don't let him get in close. Move out of his reach, then step forward quickly and hit him. Right, left, right."

She punched at Preston, but he danced out of her way and her glove only grazed his ear.

"Come on. You punch like a girl," Preston taunted her. "Bend your knees a little. Put your body into it."

"Keep your guard up," Marsfield advised. "He might decide to throw a punch at you," he added in a dry tone.

"You have to hit me," she hissed at her opponent when her back was to Marsfield.

Preston shook his head.

"Do it. He's suspicious." She punched as hard as she could. Right, left, right. One lucky jab caught Preston solidly on the cheek.

His eyebrows shot up in surprise.

Grinning in response, she danced back and forth in front of him, gloating in her triumph.

She didn't even see the punch that doubled her over.

Burke rang the bell and she dropped her arms limply to

her sides. One minute had felt like an eternity. Leaning on the top rope for support, she concentrated on not throwing up her breakfast. Preston whispered his apologies.

She nodded. "That was good," she croaked.

Farrell, the gym's owner, stood facing the ring and conversing with Marsfield. "Not much potential. Skinny arms. No endurance."

"It's his first lesson," Marsfield said. "We'll build up his upper body strength over time."

"Don't overdue the first day," Farrell said, and she silently blessed him for it.

"Just a couple of rounds," Marsfield said with a nod.

She groaned.

Farrell pulled his copy of the book from a back pocket, held it up, and gave Marsfield a wink before he left.

"Bloody hell, does everyone have that blasted book?"

She calculated in her head. If Marsfield had met eleven, that meant only eight thousand eight hundred twenty-nine to go. On this side of the Atlantic.

Anne took the brandy offered by Gaines and sat back in the comfortable chair. She looked around Marsfield's library with interest. You could tell so much about a man by his books. She picked out familiar classics in their original languages, scientific treatises, and political commentary, as well as collected agricultural essays. The occasional slim volumes of poetry and plays looked new, as if they'd never been read. Not a single novel in the lot. She wasn't sure if she was more relieved or insulted.

After separating for dinner engagements, they'd agreed to meet at Marsfield's town house and use his coach for the evening.

Burke opened his watch, and while it played *God Save the Queen* he compared it to the clock on the mantel.

"He's late," Preston said. "Most unusual."

She looked at her friend. Poor Preston. Every time she saw his glorious black eye she felt the insane urge to shed a tear and giggle at the same time. But he'd goaded her in the ring and practically asked for the shiner.

"Don't say it," he warned, then downed his brandy in one gulp.

A commotion at the front door saved her the necessity of a response. Marsfield burst into the library and rushed straight for the brandy bottle, not even waiting to be served. He fell into the nearest chair with a long sigh.

"I thought I'd never make it home," Marsfield said, leaning his head back and closing his eyes.

Burke sat up. "Footpads? Robbers?"

"I wish. It was much worse. Women." Marsfield drank the two fingers of brandy in a single deep gulp. "I have been pursued by women all day."

Preston laughed.

"Doesn't sound so bad to me," Burke said in his stodgy tone. "I've always wanted women to chase me rather than me chase them."

"Not just pursued. Followed, hunted, hounded, stalked, chased down, attacked. And every one of the silly creatures was waving a copy of that blasted book. Pulled them from reticules, sleeves, and bodices. One matron who was old enough to know better lifted her skirt to show me it strapped to her plump thigh."

The three listeners dissolved in fits of laughter at the picture Marsfield painted of the matron baring her secret.

"I had to walk for blocks to find a hack, because they had my carriage barricaded in front of Gunter's. You can laugh, but we won't be going out if my coachman can't get free. In fact, staying in has a particular appeal tonight."

"Nonsense," Preston said. "Where we're going the women don't spend their idle time reading. We can take my carriage." He rose and rang for Gaines to send a message to his coachman.

"I can see, sir, this will complicate your search for the perfect wife," Burke said.

"Ho!" Preston jumped on the comment. "I didn't know you were on the mart."

Marsfield gave Burke a glare. "We had too much time to talk while Burke was laid up." He shrugged. "It seemed like a good idea. Heirs and all that."

Anne saw through his casual nonchalance. He must have spent a lot of time thinking about the perfect wife in order to compile his detailed list of requirements. If he'd finally decided to wed, he'd do it soon. And she would have to face the thought of another woman in his arms.

"That's why he went to the masquerade last night," Burke blurted out, then shrunk back into silence under the force of Marsfield's steady stare.

"Did you meet your ideal?" Preston pushed the subject and grinned into Marsfield's glare. "I thought the Chesterton chit quite comely."

Anne snorted. "Just don't say anything amusing. She laughs like a braying donkey."

"The old duke's granddaughter Caroline," Preston suggested. "Nice portion and seems intelligent."

"Her mother coaches her on three intelligent questions to ask her dance partners," Anne said. "From then on her instructions are to say nothing, only nod and smile demurely."

"The Count d'Atrois's sister," Burke contributed. "Very pretty. Very French."

"Very skinny and very bowlegged beneath all the padding and ruffles," Anne said with sympathetic shake of her head.

Marsfield sat his glass down with a thunk. "How do you know all this?"

Anne scrambled for an explanation. "My cousin Letty tells me everything she learns. It seems women are quite candid with each other in the retiring rooms."

"You mean quite catty," Preston said with a laugh. "I

have three sisters, so I know. I'll never get married if I listen to them."

Marsfield waved their suggestions away. "It was just a notion. The entire crop seems young and silly."

"Is that why you spent so much time on the widows?" Preston asked.

Anne blessed him silently for asking. Now her curiosity might be satisfied.

"Just another notion." Marsfield dismissed the comment with a slight shrug of one shoulder.

"Your aunt is a widow, isn't she?" Preston asked Anne with a sly look.

Now she knew he had brought up the subject simply to make trouble. "Aunt Elizabeth is too old to consider another marriage," she said, with a quelling look in Preston's direction.

"Seemed sprightly enough to me," he responded with a laugh. "And Marsfield is no spring chicken himself."

"That's enough," Marsfield said, standing. "I've been beset by women all day." He paced the length of the room. "I refuse to discuss them all night."

"But there is no more interesting subject," Preston said.

"Then find a dull one."

Preston gave a mock salute, and Anne breathed a sigh of relief.

"Did you read in the *Times* that they've cast a thirteen-and-a-half-ton bell?" Burke asked.

"Yes," the other three companions answered together, and the tension broke with laughter.

The Plump Partridge was packed with men, from professional gamblers to aristocrats to young men out for a thrill. The comparatively few women, dressed in low-cut gowns and gaudy jewels, seemed to serve as the sole decoration. The big wheel clicked as it turned, and a winner cried in triumph when it stopped on an icon of Punch. Players crowded around a long table where one rolled a pair of dice. At other tables, dealers wearing green eye-shades dealt vingt-et-une.

When they passed a table with four empty chairs, Marsfield shook his head. Finally, he spotted a table near the far wall that seemed to meet his requirements. Preston explained to Anne that not only did Marsfield prefer to have his back to the wall, he knew which players cheated and refused to sit at those tables. As the group moved through the crowd, Anne was jostled and elbowed. She could barely breathe for the smoke and the smell of unclean bodies crushed so close together.

No wonder they called these places gaming hells. The heat from all the candles necessary to produce sufficient light to see the cards clearly gave the room an infernal air.

The crowd thinned toward the back of the room. Again Preston explained to Anne that the serious card players preferred the less trafficked area.

Marsfield introduced the group. There were two empty chairs. One poor card player lay slumped on the table.

"Don't mind Weathersby," one of the players said. He signaled for a waiter.

Anne restrained herself from racing around the table to her brother's side. "What's wrong with my cousin?"

"Nothing. He's just sleeping it off."

The waiter arrived and was instructed to put Weathersby in his usual place, a chair in the corner.

"Weathersby is a nice enough chap," the other card player said. "But he can't hold his brandy. Plays a few hands, looses his few quid, then spends the rest of the night in that chair until his friend picks him up about two o'clock."

"Every night?" she asked. "He can't afford that."

"Don't know how he does it, but every night he has another fifty quid to lose. We've become rather fond of his regularity," the player chuckled.

If she'd ever needed evidence she'd failed her brother, it just slapped her in the face. No doubt the so-called friend was Geoffrey. Some friend. But how could she talk? She should have done something to save her brother from this. She'd been so busy thinking of herself, she'd been unaware how much help he really needed.

Marsfield reached into his pocket and pulled out a handful of folded notes. He threw them on the floor.

Preston picked several up. "What's this? Notes from the ladies?"

Marsfield frowned. "I think every woman we passed stuck her hand in my pocket."

"Meet me in my carriage. Signed, *Lady E."* Preston looked around. "Most direct. I wonder which one she is."

Marsfield grabbed it out of his hand and threw is over his shoulder. Preston smiled and picked up another note.

"Roses are red, violets are blue, I know who you are, and I want you. Miss Z. I say, a poetess, no less." When Marsfield grabbed for the note, Preston held it out of reach. "I think I'll save this one."

"I thought we came to play cards," he said, his voice a low growl.

"Yes, of course." Preston nodded to one of the other players. "Your deal, I believe." He winked at Anne.

Normally a very astute whist player, she couldn't concentrate on the cards. She lost the thirty pounds she'd budgeted in successive hands. Then Burke was convinced to take her seat. She stood with her back against the wall and watched the play.

Because she could see Marsfield's cards, she learned he played a rather methodical, conservative game. He bypassed several risky plays she would have made, yet he capitalized on every good hand he was dealt.

That was the same way he dealt with his life. He would be methodical and conservative in looking for a wife, too. She realized with a pang she'd denigrated the candidates

Preston had presented out of jealousy. Yet Marsfield would chose a wife and it wouldn't be her. He didn't even see her as a woman.

Over the next hour, there was little conversation. Marsfield won, slow but steady. Burke lost his bankroll even faster than she had, and Preston wavered back and forth, winning a little more than he lost.

While she watched the game, Anne realized she had seen enough—of the gambling hell, of life as a boy, of London in general. Leaving Marsfield to find his perfect wife would break her heart, but she had no choice. It was time she faced her responsibilities. She would move her family back to the country for the holidays. Letty would undoubtedly throw a tantrum, but she would get over it eventually. Anne would make Robert her pet project. Starting tonight.

She pushed away from the wall.

"I'm taking my bro—cousin home," she said to Marsfield, and he gallantly offered to send for his carriage.

"No, but thank you," she said. She still had a few pounds in her pocket, enough to get them to Grosvenor Square. "We'll be fine in a hack."

Preston volunteered to accompany them. She shook her head, but she took him up on his offer to help get Robert outside.

Marsfield remained quiet when she wished the group a good night. She couldn't tell him good-bye. If she said the word aloud, tears would soon follow. She knew she'd see him in her dreams for the rest of her life.

Once outside in the fresh air, Robert roused somewhat from his drunken stupor. He even managed, with only two false steps, to climb into the carriage by himself. Anne gave the direction to the driver, said good-bye to Preston, and climbed into the conveyance after her brother.

"I say, you look familiar," Robert said, blinking and

squinting as if trying to bring her image into focus. "Do I know you?"

Anne looked at her brother as if he'd grown two heads. Then she remembered she was dressed as a boy. When she'd hatched the plan to get Robert home, she'd assumed he would stay asleep. Now she was in a pickle barrel up to her neck in brine.

"You ain't one of those pixies, are you?" he asked, leaning away from her and nearly falling over on the seat.

"Did you say pixies?" she asked, not sure she'd understood him the way his words all slurred together.

Robert nodded sagely. "Dicken sees pixies when he's foxed. They pinch him." He held up his hands as if to ward her off. "You're not going to pinch me, are you?"

"No, and I'm not a pixie."

"Good." Robert sighed. "I was afraid it was just my luck to draw a giant pixie. Dicken's pixies are this big." He held up his thumb and index finger an inch apart and he belched loudly. Twice.

She crossed her arms and gave him a disgusted look.

"Stop looking at me as if you were my conscience," Robert whined, looking away.

Anne knew a good opportunity when she saw one.

Marsfield massaged his temples. The world had suddenly become cockeyed. Nothing had worked as he'd expected. And he didn't like surprises.

He picked up the reports he'd received from his man of business and his valet Kirby. All the evidence pointed to Robert Weathersby as the villain they sought: Access to supply information through his staff position in the Crimea. An investor in key companies which had profited from the sale of substandard goods. Most importantly, unexplained wealth. Cash with no discernible trail. As the only son of a spendthrift viscount, Robert had inherited a title, entailed lands, and little else.

Yet Marsfield had witnessed with his own eyes Weathersby's lifestyle, fine clothes, nightly gambling. He was not only disappointed his old enemy Lord Fain seemed to be in the clear, but he regretted poor Andrew might suffer the consequences of any punishment meted out to his cousin. Perhaps it was just as well the boy had already left for the continent.

The Dowager Lady Decklesmoor would be forced to retire to the country, that was for certain. He refused to question why that caused him disappointment.

How had his life become such a muddle? That first meeting with Cassandra had started the spiral downward, and now he was spinning faster and faster, totally out of control. Years of organization and planning to achieve the perfect life blasted to smithereens in just a few short months.

Cassandra had disappeared off the face of the earth—again. Instead of being a reason to forget her completely, it gave him hope she would reappear—again. His plan hadn't included a mistress, and yet he found himself dreaming of buying her a secluded house, showering her with jewels, and making love to her through long hot summer nights and on cold winter mornings.

Therefore, his schedule for finding the perfect wife must be delayed. Though many other men kept a mistress and a wife, he had never planned to do so. He couldn't see himself courting a young chit, marrying her, and begetting a child on her when she would pale to insipidness compared to the wild and passionate Cassandra.

Damn her black heart. She'd spoiled him for lesser women. And they were all less than she. If—no, *when* he found her, he didn't know whether he'd throttle her or chain her to his bed and make love to her until they were both senseless.

Blood surged through his body and quickly turned to impotent fury. How could he search for Cassandra in the salons of society when he couldn't venture from his house without being accosted by women? Men who were total strangers seemed compelled to slap him on the back and give him the thumbs-up sign.

All because of that bloody book.

He picked up the second report from his man of business. Marsfield could at least do something about that book. This very afternoon, in fact.

Cold satisfaction stilled his rage. He would take control of his life. He would amend so far as to include a mistress and then see his plans come to fruition. Marsfield laid that page aside and began drafting his own report to the director.

Twenty-one

Anne took a bracing sip of her tea, then set the cup squarely in the center of the saucer. Putting this off would not make it any easier.

"Letty—"

"I can't see what is so important that you rouse me at the crack of dawn." She yawned and stretched, reminding Anne of a kitten in her lovely yellow and orange striped muslin morning dress.

"It's eleven o'clock," Anne said. "Hardly daybreak."

"I suppose it's just as well. It's not as if I could sleep. Why are the servants in such a tizzy?"

"Today is a busy day."

"Don't tell me. I'd rather not know if it's wash day or candle-making day or any other tiresome—"

"It's moving day." Anne closed her eyes against the tirade she knew would follow her announcement. "We're leaving tomorrow morning. Back to the country for the holidays."

The shriek she expected, but the physical attack nearly knocked her off her chair.

"I know you're disappointed—"

"Disappointed?" Letty hugged her again. "This is wonderful." She danced around the parlor. "Absolutely perfect."

Anne blinked and pinched herself on the arm. Ouch. She wasn't dreaming. "Perfect?"

"Oh, yes. Don't you see? We can ask Timothy and his mother for a visit, and she'll see for herself I can run the house. She'll see all the good works I do with the poor, unfortunate orphans. Then she can't object to our marriage in spite of the fact that I'm not an heiress."

Now Anne was thoroughly confused. Letty run the house? Letty work with the orphans? "Timothy who?"

"I knew you weren't listening to me all these weeks." Letty put her hands on her hips. "You never listen to me."

Of course, Anne always tried to listen, but Letty prattled on and on with silly chatter of the latest fashions and gossip. "My apologies for not paying appropriate attention. Timothy who?"

"The man I adore, the love of my life, the man I'm going to marry. That is, if his crotchety old mother approves the match."

"I'm still confused. Timothy who?"

Letty flounced across the room and sat in the chair next to the settee. "Timothy Wentworth, Lord Asterbule, my fiancé."

"You can't get engaged without Robert's blessing."

"Well, I already did."

"Oh, Letty." Anne couldn't contain a sigh of exasperation. "What do you know about this young man?"

"I know he's handsome and good and kind, and he loves me to distraction."

"But there is so much more to be considered in a marriage. Love is important, but—"

"Stop treating me like a child." Letty stood and paced. "I have enough sense to check out his finances and habits. He is currently the Viscount Asterbule, with an estate in Hampshire and a town house in Green Square. Those are both entailed. He neither gambles nor drinks to excess. In addition, he will inherit one hundred thousand pounds upon the birth of an heir. So we'll soon be rich."

"Then why does Lady Asterbule want Timothy to marry an heiress?"

"Because." Her expression clearly said she'd explained this before. "His father thought there was such a thing as too much money. Can you imagine that? Therefore, whatever dowry the wife brings to the family coffers will be subtracted from Timothy's inheritance and therefore added to the Dowager's. If she snags an heiress for him, she stands to gain in her portion."

"Or so Timothy says?"

"Yes, and he should know."

"But if Timothy stands to inherit a fortune, every mama in town must be pushing her daughter at the Asterbules."

"Oh, Lady Asterbule is very particular. The chosen one needs to be rich, but not beautiful enough to have expectations of snagging an earl or a duke. She must be of good family, but not so much so that Lady Asterbule would be outranked at family functions. She must be accomplished enough to impress, interested in charitable good works, and competent enough to run the manse, because Lady Asterbule wants someone to take over her duties."

"And what does Timothy want?"

Letty sank into a chair, an angelic smile on her face. "He wants someone beautiful to love him. So, you see, except for the heiress stipulation, I'm the perfect candidate."

"I rather think Lady Asterbule will not be inclined to overlook that fact."

Letty dismissed her objection with an airy wave. "Timothy is sure he can convince her. He says she has an adequate dowager portion if she would only practice a few simple economies."

Anne pictured the flamboyant dress of the party-loving Lady Asterbule. She remembered meeting the lady, being swept from head to foot by a gaze that calculated the cost of her garments, inventoried her jewelry, and dismissed her as lacking in both categories. Timothy might well be asking for the Stone of Sisyphus. She could see her sister was headed for heartbreak.

"There will be other men, other proposals—"

"I will marry Timothy," Letty insisted.

"If not—"

"You're so negative because you've never been in love. Just because you never married is no reason for you to spoil my happiness. Timothy and I love each other. Nothing else matters." Letty stood. She looked down with her lips thinned to a mutinous line. "I'm going upstairs now to write a note to Timothy. He'll want to call before we leave. Tomorrow, did you say?"

Anne focused her gaze on the vase of flowers at the window. The chill outside was nothing compared to the icy atmosphere in the parlor. She fought the tears that threatened.

"As early in the morning as possible," Anne said. "Binny's bunion is predicting a snowstorm before the day is out."

Letty flounced out without another word.

Despite the multitude of tasks that awaited her, Anne could not make herself move off the settee. She was so tired these days. And Letty's derision had hurt. Her own sister viewed her with pity and contempt. Why not? That was how society viewed a spinster.

But Letty was wrong. Anne had fallen in love. She had known the knee-weakening shivers caused by his smoldering gaze, the intoxicating taste of his passionate kisses, the heart-pounding thrills of his magic hands on—

Stop thinking of him. She might not be able to control her nightly dreams of Marsfield, but during the day she could force her thoughts elsewhere. Her meeting with Robert to convince him the move was for the best. Packing the household goods. Servants to organize. Goods to be ordered for delivery to the estate.

She would probably never see Marsfield again. Her life

would consist of running Robert's house until he, too, married. Then she'd retire to a small cottage, write her stories, and visit her future nieces and nephews on the holidays. Even if another man would accept her, she could not allow any other man to touch her. Because it would not be Marsfield's hands, his lips, his—

She must remind cook to pack a basket of food for the trip. Bread, cheese, fruit, wine. Her family was bound to get hungry on the road. Since she'd taken that chill the night of the masquerade, her own usually hearty appetite had failed. And she must remember to pack a jar of Robert's favorite pickled eggs, not that anyone else ever touched them. But pickled eggs suddenly sounded delicious. In fact, she should see cook right away.

With renewed energy and purpose, she stepped into the hall with a firm stride, only to come to an abrupt halt.

Robert sauntered down the main stair, but her planned conference would have to wait. Geoffrey stood by the front door.

"Good morning, Anne." Robert kissed her on the cheek before he turned to his friend. "This is an unexpected pleasure, Geoffrey. I'd planned to meet you for luncheon as usual after I ran my errands."

"I was driving past and thought I might see if you needed some help." When only silence answered, he continued, "There seems to be a lot of activity at the servant's door. Tradesmen lined up and blocking traffic. Are you giving a party?"

Robert turned his blank look from Geoffrey to Anne.

"No." She wanted to add that if they were, he wouldn't be invited. For the sake of manners, she bit her tongue. This wasn't how she'd planned to tell her brother, but she didn't seem to have a choice. If he argued with her and brought Geoffrey into the discussion for support, she was determined enough to take them both on. This move was in Robert's best interest.

"We are leaving tomorrow morning. We're spending the holidays in the country."

"Jolly good," Robert said.

"You can't!" Geoffrey cried. He coughed. "You can't mean that. We've accepted invitations, made plans."

"Plans can be changed. Just think, Geoffrey. Christmas in the country, like when we were children. Bringing in the Yule log. Sleigh rides. Caroling outside the church."

"Think of London. The balls. The theater."

Robert just shook his head.

Anne watched with interest as the two friends disagreed. This sounded like the old Robert she knew.

"You're on a winning streak," Geoffrey said. "You can't quit now."

This was the first Anne had heard of a winning streak. Considering what she knew, it seemed a greater fiction than anything she'd ever concocted.

Robert put his hand on Geoffrey's shoulder. "Isn't that the first principle of successful gambling? To quit while you're ahead?"

The other man sputtered out a denial. "You really are a plebeian farmer at heart."

Robert laughed at the accusation. "The appeal of waking at noon not knowing how I got to my bed or what I did the previous evening has worn rather thin. When I was in the Crimea dreaming of home, this isn't what I pictured. Yes, I think Christmas at Weathersby is exactly right." He turned to hug her. "Thank you for thinking of it, Sis."

She shut her mouth, which had been hanging open. She had really lit into Robert last night in the carriage, but she hadn't expected quite such a radical result.

Geoffrey straightened his coat. "Well, at least we have tonight. If you bet all your winnings, you can go out in a blaze of glory this town will never forget."

"I'm afraid that's not possible," Robert said. "You see, I had a long talk with my conscience last night. I tell you, it does something to a man to meet his conscience face to face, man to man, so to speak. I'll tell you all about it at luncheon. After my usual trip to the bank—"

Geoffrey stumbled back. "The bank?" he croaked.

"Now, now. I know you have this irrational distrust of banks, but I also know my own weaknesses. If I have money in my pocket, I spend it. It's safer in the bank."

"At least the Bank of England is on the way. You can withdraw enough money to play with."

Robert shook his head. "I'm done with gambling, Geoffrey. I can't control it, so I have to avoid it."

"Don't be a goose. Every gentleman gambles. You don't want to be labeled a bumpkin," he said, sneering. "We can stop at the bank on the way."

"Won't do no good. The money is in Anne's name."

"What?" Geoffrey and Anne said in unison.

Robert smiled at her. "I not only know my weakness, I also know your strengths. You're better at managing money than I am. And I know your dowry and Dunstan's money went into Weathersby Manor. Did you think I didn't notice the improvements?"

"Yes, but—"

"But you've won hundreds of thousands of pounds," Geoffrey sputtered.

Anne blinked at Geoffrey's assertion. The sneaky snob was obviously exaggerating in order to make his point.

"Whatever the amount, I trust Anne to make good use of it."

"Robert, you couldn't have—"

He wouldn't let Anne finish, and he took up both her hands. "You're not going to fail me now, are you, Sis?"

She shook her head.

"I'll have the bank send an accounting, and after the holiday, we'll sit down with your books and sort everything out. Agreed?"

She nodded and tried to swallow the lump in her throat.

Geoffrey walked to the door, his rapid steps clicking a staccato on the tile floor. He paused and turned. "I just remembered an urgent errand. I'll . . . I'll contact you later, Robert." On a gust of frigid air, he was gone.

"Well," she said, not having any other comment.

Robert shook his head. "Sometimes I don't understand him at all." He took her hand and tucked it in the crook of his arm. "But it's just as well. Now I can help you with the traveling arrangements. I'm sure you can use more help than Letty has offered."

She laid her head on his shoulder and felt some of her burden lift. "We should talk about Letty."

He led her toward the dining room. "Food first. I have a feeling I'm going to need sustenance for this discussion."

She returned his smile.

Marsfield looked around the publisher's office and tried not to wince at the disorder. How could a man expect to run a business surrounded by mountains of clutter? Moving a stack of books off a chair, he dusted it with his handkerchief and sat down. The chair creaked and moaned at his bulk, but held.

"I tol' ya. Mr. Blackthorne is not to be disturbed at 'is tea, an' yer ain't allowed in here. It's private. I tol' ya to come back later."

The belligerent young twerp stuck out his pimpled chin and crossed his arms. Marsfield stared at him with one eyebrow raised until the boy took a step back.

"There is nothing wrong with my hearing, and I understand the English language quite well, even butchered as you are wont to speak it. In case you are not similarly blessed, I will repeat myself. Once."

Marsfield paused for deliberate emphasis, and then

spoke in a slow, measured cadence. "Fetch Mr. Blackthorne immediately. I will wait."

He returned his handkerchief to his pocket without breaking eye contact. Suddenly, the boy turned and fled the room. The door slammed, and Marsfield checked the time. Four-fifteen. His patience was worn dangerously thin. He took a deep breath and let it out to the count of ten. No sense botching the deal now just because it had taken longer than expected to get to this point.

Oh, Blackthorne had wanted the loan, needed the money to purchase the materials to meet his production commitments. But with his current successful book, the foreign contracts he had in hand, and the almost guaranteed return, he could have picked from a wide pool of eager investors and named the conditions. It had taken Marsfield three days to convince the other potential investors their best interests lay elsewhere.

It hadn't hurt when they'd assumed he had a vested interest in the publisher. At least the damned book had worked to his advantage this once. Even complete strangers had marked him as the mysterious Lord X. He'd been forced to cover the crest on his coach in order to get around town unhindered. Yet no one in the entire city of London seemed to have the slightest interest in the identity of the scandalous Lady Z—except for Marsfield, of course. So far he had met only women who'd volunteered, in terms graphic enough to make a courtesan blush, to take her place.

If his name were to be linked to hers, at least he should have had the pleasure. He touched his pocket where his copy of the book remained out of sight. His personal theory on the popularity of the book did not say much for the general male population. Marsfield knew not all men enjoyed the variety of lovemaking he did, different places, different positions. Not all men cared if the woman reached climax. Quite a few even believed it was undesirable. Hah. A vision of a particular woman arched in pleasure under his hands caused an immediate hardening in his loins. They obviously had never met Cassandra.

He tried to place the Lady Z of the pictures in the book into his vision, but the woman's face stubbornly remained Cassandra's.

Though he had never exactly made a secret of his principles, he couldn't remember ever having revealed them to a woman. No matter. He would soon know the real name of Lady Z. Much as he hated to bow to the demands of society, in this case a statement from her that he wasn't Lord X would put to rest these rumors and allow him to return to his normal life.

Patience had never come easy to Marsfield. He stood. Without touching anything, he examined Blackthorne's desk for clues to the character of the man. Piles of manuscripts were stacked haphazardly along the length of the front edge, providing a precarious barrier from anyone seated on the single rickety guest chair. In contrast, Blackthorne's throne of padded leather looked comfortable and well worn. The surface of the desk was scattered with correspondence, half-edited pages, and scraps of paper containing cryptic notes. A biscuit tin identified the crumbs as remnants of imported vanilla crisps. Marsfield opened the humidor and sniffed the expensive cigars. Blackthorne was a man in tune with his comforts.

Marsfield checked his watch. Four-twenty. He turned to examine the bookshelves lining the walls, and Blackthorne bustled into the office.

"Now see here—oh, Lord Marsfield." Blackthorne bowed. "What an unexpected pleasure."

He noted with satisfaction that the portly publisher hadn't taken the time to don his hat and gloves, nor had he taken the time to remove the napkin from his collar. An opponent's discomfort could be used to advantage.

"I judged our business to be of sufficient importance to attend you in person." He motioned Blackthorne to his seat and took the rickety guest chair without a hint of his concern for his safety.

The editor fell into his chair without removing his cloak. "Our business, milord?"

"Yes." He removed a packet of papers from his breast pocket and held them out. "Here is a contract stipulating a reasonable percentage of your anticipated profits and my personal bank draft."

When Blackthorne reached for the packet, Marsfield pulled them back. "However, I must request that my man be allowed to examine your books first." He smiled. "Just a formality. I'm sure you understand."

"But the investment pool—"

"There is no pool. Only me. All the other potential investors backed out at the last minute."

Marsfield waited for the wheels to turn in Blackthorne's head. First, Blackthorne would realize the pool he'd attempted to organize had failed. Then he would remember a large shipment of paper was due within days. Not only did he need cash quickly, he wouldn't have time to seek out new investors. The realization of his predicament was obvious on his lined face.

Marsfield laid the contract and money on the desk.

Blackthorne stared at the bank draft. In slow motion, he removed a key from his waistcoat, unlocked a desk drawer, removed a ledger, and handed it over.

Marsfield tucked the ledger under his left arm and reached out to shake hands with his other.

"I'll return on the morrow to sign the contracts and make the draft over to you."

Minutes later, in the carriage, he handed the ledger to his waiting man of business. "Find that name."

Bentley thumbed through the pages, humming under his breath.

Impatient now that he was so close to his goal, Marsfield fidgeted for what seemed an eternity. "Well?"

"The individual books published are coded to a numbered system. The key is in the back of the ledger, but it may take a little time for me to decipher the entries."

"I have just paid an obscene amount of money for a simple bit of information."

"Actually," Bentley said. "It seems you made a very good investment here."

"To hell with the bloody investment. What is her name?"

Bentley flipped the pages back and forth. He closed the book with a worried frown.

"Well?" Marsfield demanded.

"There are three names listed as receiving royalties from *A Manual of Love*. Bernard Tuttle. Seems he's the artist." He pursed his lips, and a frown wrinkled his forehead.

"And the others? Out with it, man."

Bentley flinched and ducked into the corner, holding the ledger up in front of his face as if he expected an explosion.

"Davis Preston and Cassandra Drummond," he said in a rush.

Marsfield turned and looked out the window, forcing himself to remain calm. Preston and Cassandra. Bloody hell. The expected red haze of anger did not appear. Instead, a cold fury settled deep in his gut.

"What is her address?" Marsfield asked.

"Twenty-one Grosvenor Square," Bentley squeaked from behind his barricade.

Marsfield tapped on the roof and gave the driver that familiar direction.

Andrew. The boy and Cassandra lived in the same house. Suddenly, it made sense. Andrew must have given her the list. The rest she'd cobbled together out of her own vast experience. As yet, he didn't understand how Preston fit into the picture, but he would tackle that problem after he confronted Cassandra.

Twenty-two

Weathersby Manor

Anne read the note from her editor immediately because he had marked it urgent. Blackthorne wrote that Marsfield had gotten hold of his accounting book and had then been followed straight to her Grosvenor Square address. Blackthorne guessed her country estate would soon have an irate visitor.

Just what she needed. Another difficult guest.

"Bad news, dear? You look a little pale."

"No, Aunt Elizabeth. Just a note concerning business."

Lady Asterbule selected another bonbon and popped it into her mouth. "You are an example to all young women that business is bad for the complexion."

Anne gritted her teeth. If her complexion was a shade of pale green, it was because she had become rather sensitive to odors lately, and she blamed Lady Asterbule's choice of heavy, cloying scent for her problem.

"More tea, Lady Asterbule?" Anne asked, and gave her houseguest an appropriately bland smile.

"Not for me. Dear Timothy has promised to escort me on a turn through your gardens. He is such a good son to be concerned I might be bored."

"Aunt Elizabeth?"

"No thank you, dear. In fact, I'll excuse myself to rest a bit before dinner. I know you and Lady Asterbule have much to discuss." Elizabeth patted her niece's shoulder on her way out.

Lady Asterbule set her teacup on the tray with a clank. She sat stiff-backed on the edge of her chair, leaning backward as if to distance herself from the coming discussion.

Anne jumped right to the heart of the topic Lady Asterbule had been avoiding all day. "Letty tells me your son has asked for her hand in marriage."

"The impetuousness of youth." Lady Asterbule made a tsking sound as she shook her head back and forth like a disapproving clock pendulum. "Boys his age can be quite rash."

"He is five and twenty. Not so much a boy."

"Much too young to make such a life-altering decision without the advice and approval of a cooler, wiser head. I am quite surprised you have allowed your sister to consider an impassioned plea as a serious offer."

"I think they are lucky to have found a love match involving a suitable partner."

"Of course *you* would think the match suitable."

The woman's attitude grated on Anne's nerves. Letty might not be an heiress, but her bloodlines were just as aristocratic and went back even further than the Asterbules'. No matter what Anne personally thought of the match, Letty was convinced her future happiness depended on being married to Timothy. When Letty decided she wanted something, she neither changed her mind nor let up until she got what she sought.

"Since our brother Robert is the *tenth* Viscount Weathersby, and since Letty is not only beautiful but also accomplished, I had, *of course,* hopes of an earl or even a duke as a brother-in-law. However, one must make allowances for matters of the heart. Is that not so?"

"Precisely the opposite. Passions cool and beauty fades. A successful marriage benefits the family and their progeny. The bedrock of marriage is financial security."

"Really? Then what price would you put on your son's hand in marriage?"

"That is putting it rather crudely."

Anne smiled. "I see no point in dancing around the matter for the next week. Let's you and I at least be honest with each other."

"Very well," Lady Asterbule said. "Ten thousand pounds."

Ann blinked and swallowed hard.

Lady Asterbule looked around the parlor with a calculating gaze, sniffed, and gave Anne a smug little smile.

"That is the absolute minimum dowry I expect."

His mother certainly thought dear Timothy was worth a bloody fortune. Letty and she each had a reasonably adequate dowry of four thousand five hundred pounds. If she put in some of her book earnings and added her own dowry to Letty's . . .

Anne's dowry had become hers to do with as she pleased when she hadn't married by age twenty-five. And it wasn't as if she expected an offer for her hand because of her fortune. As if she even wanted any other man after being with Marsfield. Another man holding her as Marsfield had, kissing her, touching her . . . just the thought of another man . . . doing those things curdled her stomach.

She forced her thoughts back to the matter at hand.

Anne displayed her own smug smile. "How fortunate. That is the exact amount of Letty's dowry."

Lady Asterbule's eyebrows shot up, but she managed a gracious nod nonetheless. "There is still the matter of suitability to consider. I'll have the chance to get to know your sister this week and therefore judge for myself."

Anne also nodded graciously. "May I ask which qualities you find admirable in a young woman?"

"Don't think you can fool me by knowing the criteria in advance."

"I am simply curious," she said with a nonchalance she

didn't feel. Anne shrugged as if the requirements were of little import, as if her sister's happiness did not depend on her passing some test of her abilities. In all probability, Letty would be able to demonstrate nothing on the list.

"Nothing out of the ordinary," Lady Asterbule said. "Modest, temperate, prudent. A graceful and delicate decorum, yet a firm hand with the servants. Talented in music and painting. Desirous of children. Conscious of one's duty to help the less fortunate, within reasonable bounds. And, of course, capable of running a large household efficiently."

Quite simply a paragon of womanhood. Lady Asterbule's litany nearly mirrored Marsfield's list of necessary qualities for a wife. Anne hid her concern for Letty.

"You seem to have thought this through quite carefully," Anne said.

"If you had a son, you would understand."

Anne refrained from asking what Timothy thought of his mother's requirements. Personally, Anne considered his preference as the more important. Her sister would have a difficult time living up to her future mother-in-law's expectations, as would anyone. But they only had to make it through this week and get the marriage contracts signed to ensure her sister's happiness.

"I think Letty will make your son a perfect wife."

One of the objects of their discussion burst through the parlor door. His face was flushed, presumably from the cold air. He bowed to Anne, then swept his mother up by pulling on both her hands.

"Isn't it a glorious day? I apologize for being late, but the ride to the village was positively invigorating. Robert is quite the expert on agriculture. I'm anxious to speak to our steward about some of his scientific techniques. Come. Let me show you the splendid greenhouse."

"Really, Timothy. Your enthusiasm for bucolic pastimes is distressingly plebeian."

He laughed. "Don't worry, Mother. I won't expect you to leave London for the joys of country living."

Mrs. Finch brought in a heavy shawl for Lady Asterbule. Her son wished Anne a good day and escorted his mother out, babbling about the advantages of root crops.

"Lord Marsfield is here," Mrs. Finch said. "We put him in the library."

"Here?" Anne squeaked as she jumped up and ran for the door. She stopped with her hand on the knob. "Did anyone else see him?"

The housekeeper shook her head. "He didn't look none too happy, but he's still there. I figured you didn't want him announced."

Obviously, Anne would have to see him and convince him to leave immediately. Automatically, her hand went up to smooth her hair.

"Please fetch my black cape and the mourning hat with the thick veil," she requested.

She paced the parlor as she waited for Mrs. Finch to return. She had to get rid of him before Robert or Aunt Elizabeth saw him. Or, God forbid, Lady Asterbule. A notorious rake ensconced in the library would start a scandal and ruin everything. She had to make him leave. Anne knew she would need a good story to get out of this predicament.

Mrs. Finch also brought a pair of long gloves to cover the sleeves of her blue wool day dress. Once she was covered from head to toe in concealing black, she hurried across the hall to the library. She hesitated, taking a deep calming breath. It turned into a gasp when the door whipped open in front of her.

Marsfield halted in obvious surprise, his expression thunderous, an empty brandy glass held negligently in his fingers. He stared at her intently, as if to see through her thick veil.

Why did her knees have to turn to jelly in his presence?

His appearance was travel rumpled, and she could still smell the freshness of the cold outdoors mixed with the heady fumes of brandy and his own unique scent. The combination played havoc on her senses, but she couldn't allow her weakness to ruin her plans for Letty. She had to get him out of full view in the hallway, and then out of their lives altogether.

"Another brandy, Lord Marsfield?" she asked, stiffening her spine and taking a step forward.

He backed up to allow her space to sweep through the door.

"I'm surprised you're out on such a miserable day for traveling. I hear we're to expect more snow. I'm sorry your trip to the country has been in vain. I did send you word that Andrew has left for the continent."

"I came to see Cassandra Drummond."

Anne settled herself on the settee, and waved Marsfield to a seat across from her.

"Again I must apologize for your unnecessary journey. Cassandra also has left for the continent."

Not the most creative dissembling she'd ever done, but it would have to do on short notice.

"But she was here? She does live here?"

"Not exactly. What I tell you must be held in the strictest confidence."

He agreed.

The fabrication Anne had prepared just minutes ago seemed to spill out of its own accord. "Cassandra is my cousin. She has lived most of her life in France, and received a somewhat unorthodox upbringing lacking in proper supervision. Her father is an attaché to the diplomatic corps and her mother passed away when she was quite young. She arrived on my doorstep with a letter from my uncle seeking shelter for her from the rumors her imprudent behavior had incited in Paris. You can understand my hesitation to present her or even publicly acknowledge her until the gossip had time to die down. My goal was to then find her a suitable husband as quickly as possible."

She let out a long-suffering sigh, another mimic of her Aunt Elizabeth's behavior.

"Unfortunately, Cassandra's behavior could not be adequately restrained. Rather than threaten Letty's chances for an advantageous match, I had no choice but to send the woman back to her father."

"When? How?"

Anne blinked at the unexpected questions. She scrambled for reasonable travel arrangements for Cassandra.

"The packet from Dover to Marseilles," she said. That should be discouraging enough. She stood. "I hope you make it back to London before the snow starts."

Marsfield also stood. He looked at the glass he still held in his hand, as if wondering how it got there. After a moment, he shook his head as if to clear it and set his glass on the table.

"Thank you for your time, Lady Gordon, and your confidences. If you will excuse me, I have several urgent errands which need my attention."

"Of course," she replied, but she spoke to his retreating back.

She found her handkerchief before the tears fell.

Five minutes later she discarded the sodden square of linen and used her petticoat to wipe the last of the dampness from her cheeks. It wasn't like her to be so weepy, but since her momentous experience she seemed to cry at the drop of a hat. If this was what losing virginity did to women, no wonder they held on to it as long as possible. When she heard a knock on the door, she fought off another wave of fresh tears and called permission to enter.

Mrs. Finch rushed to her employer's side, and Harvey checked the hall before closing the door.

"What's the matter, milady?"

"Nothing. I'm fine. Just a cinder in my eye, that's all."

Mrs. Finch handed over her own handkerchief. "Can I get you anything?"

"We have more important matters to discuss." Harvey stood by the door, his arms crossed, his expression belligerent.

"In a minute," Mrs. Finch said. "Give her a chance to compose herself."

"Minutes count. Marsfield is on his way to Dover to find the mysterious Cassandra."

Anne sat up straight. "But I told him she'd taken the packet to Marseilles. He wouldn't follow her to France."

Harvey looked heavenward as if pleading for help. "You don't know much about men. His pride has been pricked. That demands a rebuttal."

"Revenge?"

"He can't just let it lie. France isn't that far. Some men would go to the ends off the earth to rectify an injury to their pride."

"He probably just wants an explanation from Cassandra herself," Mrs. Finch said, patting Anne's hand.

"How do you know all this?"

Harvey shrugged. "I put one and one together and came up with three. If you'd have let me know your story ahead of time, I could've done better, but as it was . . . at least when he asked for directions to Dover, I gave his coachman the long way around."

"I didn't know the story, as you put it, beforehand." Anne explained the meeting in the library and everything that had been said. "Now what do we do?"

"Well, we know he's headed for Dover, and now we know he's looking for Cassandra. He'll expect to find her there because the next packet won't leave for Marseilles until Thursday."

"Oh." Anne had forgotten the packet sailed only twice

a week. Her mind raced. If he returned to Weathersby after a futile search, it would ruin everything.

"Then he'll have to find Cassandra," Anne said. "She can tell him herself that . . . that . . ."

"That she has accepted an offer of marriage from a member of the French nobility," Mrs. Finch prompted.

Anne smiled. "You're becoming too good at this. It worries me."

Mrs. Finch patted her hand again before she jumped up. "I'll pack a few things for you and Harvey will bring the coach around. We have to beat that man to Dover."

"I'll leave instructions for Finch and cook and have a quick word with Aunt Elizabeth so she can relay the news of a friend's emergency illness to Robert and Letty. That way I won't be missed."

"This is not a good idea," Harvey said. "I told Marsfield's man the roads are getting bad, and that was the truth."

"We'll leave immediately," Anne said. "We can't let a little snow stop us from settling this once and for all."

"It's not just a little snow."

Anne ignored his cryptic comment and practically floated up the stairs. Even a blizzard couldn't deter Cassandra from the chance to see Marsfield again.

Twenty-three

Marsfield cursed himself for his foolishness. Only an idiot or a madman chased a woman cross country in the middle of a snowstorm. Entering the welcoming warmth of the inn's taproom, he stomped off the snow that had caked to his boots on the short walk from the carriage. He hoped the late hour did not preclude a hot meal before he continued his task of checking each and every inn between Weathersby and Dover.

That is, if he didn't come to his senses first.

Removing his gloves and shrugging off his greatcoat, he started toward the huge roaring fire, only to stop short.

A woman sat near the fireplace. Though still wrapped in her hooded cloak, he recognized her hands cupped around a mug of tea as if to gather its warmth. When he was halfway across the room, she looked up and smiled at him through tear-stained eyes.

Relief washed over him, and he knew he would have traveled halfway round the world to see her again. As quickly as the relief had come, unreasoning anger followed—at her for being foolish enough to travel in such weather, at the snowstorm, at himself for behaving like a love-struck fool.

He stomped across the room and stood at her side. "What the bloody hell do you think you're doing?" he growled.

"Going to France," she whispered.

"Not tonight."

And what about tomorrow? Then what? He hadn't thought beyond finding her, seeing her again.

"Your book has caused me untold misery," he said.

She did not even bother to lie about being the author. "It is a work of fiction."

"I know that, but no one else in London seems to."

She shrugged. "I needed the money. I have no control over, nor do I care, what the *ton* chooses to gossip about."

"Easy to say when it's not you."

"It's not you, either."

He nodded his acknowledgment of her riposte. He realized that, aside from the temporary inconvenience the book had caused, he wasn't angry that the *ton* considered him Lord X. He was angry because the book had made him wonder who was.

"But you wrote it. That means—"

"That means I'm a writer," she said, her chin at a stubborn tilt. "Nothing more."

"Are you telling me the woman in the book was a fiction also?"

"I'm allowing you to come to your own conclusions."

He swooped her up into his arms. "Tell me the truth," he said.

Anne lifted her face and leaned into his chest. "Does it matter?" she asked, her lips inches from his.

With Cassandra in his arms, he realized the origins of the book didn't matter. Nothing was as important as the woman he held close to his heart. All thoughts of London gossips, Lord X, everything disappeared as he caught her up in a fiery kiss.

When she pulled away and ducked her head, a blush staining her cheeks, he remembered they were in the public room in full view of the scattered, avidly staring patrons. He whispered an apology in her ear, his lips caressing the delicate lobe in the process, and set her firmly away from him.

"Have you eaten supper?"

She shook her head.

A few minutes later, he'd procured the best room the inn had to offer and ordered a meal delivered. He had to exercise all his self-control in order to escort her up the stairs and converse on inane subjects such as the weather until the servant finished his tasks. He built up the fire, lit the lamp, turned down the bed, and set out two steaming bowls of stew, a loaf of bread, a bottle of wine, and a pot of tea. A wedge of cheese and two apple tarts completed the meal.

All the while Cassandra stood like a statue near the door, as if suddenly shy, suddenly wary of him. He coaxed her to a seat at the small table and took the chair across from her.

"Eat," he urged. "It'll warm you."

"Why did you come after me?" she asked.

"Why do you keep leaving me?" he countered.

She looked down and picked up her spoon. Pushing the chunks of meat and vegetables around in the bowl, she didn't answer for a long moment.

"We cannot be together. You have your life and I have mine. Andrew told me you're to be married soon."

Marsfield shook his head. "Only a notion. It has nothing to do with us."

She laughed, but the sound fell on his ears with a mirthless tone.

"When I get to France, I am to be married, too. Despite what you must think of me, I intend to honor my wedding vows."

"Don't go. Stay with me."

"As your mistress?"

"As my love."

"Whatever name you call it, if you really knew me, you'd know it's impossible."

She sipped her tea, and he had to fight the urge to taste the brew from her lips. He gulped his wine instead.

"I know your kisses intoxicate me," he said. "Your passion inflames me and satisfies me like no other. I know you make me laugh, and that is something sorely missing in my life."

"Stop," she whispered.

Yet he could not. "I can't explain it any other way. If that's selfish, so be it. I don't want to lose you."

She jumped up and paced the small room. "Would you buy me a house in the almost fashionable part of town and bring me presents? Meaningful little tokens when you were forced to break a date?"

"Yes. I'll dress you in the finest clothes, take you to the theater and dancing."

Cassandra shook her head.

"Whatever you want, I'll get for you. Your happiness would be my utmost concern."

She faced him, hands on her hips. "I'm selfish, too. And that's not enough."

Not enough? What did the woman want?

As if he couldn't guess. Every woman seemed to think of marriage as some sort of Holy Grail. He should have known the ruse of finding a bride would come back to haunt him. Well, a man might marry his mistress in France, but not in England. Even if he cared little for the prattle of the *ton,* even if he had tweaked their collective nose more than once, that was a step too far.

He pictured her French fiancé in his mind, seeing a fat old man putting his gnarled, liver-spotted hands on her smooth skin. Marsfield jumped up and strode across the room to face her. She turned away and looked out the small dingy window.

"Is marriage to your old, ugly Frenchman so much better? You'd deny the passion we've found together for the sake of a piece of paper."

Anne whirled around to face Marsfield. "You seem to be laboring under a false pretense, confusing passion with a deeper, more abiding emotion. It so happens I love the man I would marry."

Marsfield did not believe her. Refused to believe her.

"And he is not ugly. He is most handsome, and he is—"

Marsfield leaned over and kissed the tip of her nose. "Your eyes sparkle like the rarest emeralds when you are angry."

She took a half step back. "He is—"

He cut off her words with a gentle brush of his lips.

Shaking her head, Anne tried to concentrate on her story. The whole point of seeing him again as Cassandra was to make him believe she was beyond his reach so he would never seek her out again. But he was too close. She couldn't think when the familiar scent of his cologne fogged her brain and turned her knees to jelly, and the lightest taste of his lips made her hunger for more.

She took a full step back and bumped against the wall. He moved with her, giving her not an inch of respite. Placing his hands on either side of her shoulders, he gave her no room to escape. Without touching her, he'd boxed her in. Only her wits could save her now. Unfortunately, all her blood had headed in the opposite direction from her brain, leaving her decidedly lightheaded.

"The man I love is—"

"Does he kiss you like this?"

Marsfield leaned in slowly, seeming to take forever for his lips to reach hers. With infinite care, he placed quick kisses from one corner of her mouth to the other.

She couldn't protest, afraid to open her mouth with his so close. Instead, she pushed her back into the wall for support, and fisted her hands at her side.

He tilted his head and ducked to reach the sensitive place beneath her ear.

"Does he kiss you here?"

His warm breath tickled her throat. She tried to resist,

but her treacherous body betrayed her. Cursing her weakness, she turned her head to the side.

If he had grabbed at her, she could have fought, but she had no defense against his slow, delicious tenderness. With a sigh, she closed her eyes and leaned her forehead into his shoulder.

If she was truthful with herself, she didn't want to fight him. This was, after all, the last time she would see him. As Cassandra, that is. Once this encounter was over, she would revert to spinster Anne, the dutiful sister dressed in her plain gowns. If she met him again, he wouldn't even notice her. A paragon of virtue to the outside world, even if inside she seethed with passion. In the future, her only outlet would be her writing. Somehow, tonight, that did not seem enough.

With his cupped hands on her face, he directed her to look at him. She stared into the deep midnight blue of his eyes.

"Say you'll stay," he whispered, his voice husky with passion.

She managed to shake her head, but even as she did, she raised her arms and wrapped them around his neck.

With a low growl deep in his chest, he picked her up and carried her to the bed.

Anne hurriedly dressed as best she could in the predawn darkness. Without help she couldn't manage her corset, so she just rolled it up and stuffed it in one of her cloak pockets. Its voluminous folds would hide the fact that without a corset, she'd had to leave a few buttons at her waist undone.

Into the other pocket she put a piece of bread wrapped in a napkin. Though physically ill this morning at the thought of leaving Marsfield, she knew she would be ravenous later. Being in love seemed to have given her the strangest appetites for food.

She paused only a moment at the door to look back at Marsfield, sprawled across the bed in exhausted slumber. Yet she knew she would carry this memory, like all the other wonderful memories he'd given her, close to her heart for the rest of her lonely life.

Slipping down the stairs, she reiterated all the reasons leaving him was for the best. She wasn't the Cassandra he desired. Maybe a part of her was that wild and passionate woman, but she couldn't deny the aspect of herself that accepted duty and responsibility. And that part of her, maybe the biggest part, he would never desire.

Her treacherous heart prompted her to turn around and tell him the truth about Cassandra. Fortunately, Harvey was waiting in the taproom, saving her the humiliation facing Marsfield would have brought. The coachman handed her a steaming mug of tea.

"Drink up, lassie. The mail coach from Dover is due through any minute. I'd like to take advantage of the ruts it made in the snow before the wind blows them away."

Anne held the cup for warmth. Not sure how her upset stomach would react, she took a small tentative sip. The mailcoach would pass through Weathersby by early afternoon, and suddenly she wanted nothing more than to be home.

"If you wouldn't mind going on to Dover alone, I think I'll take the mail coach back," she suggested.

"If you want to go home, I'll be driving you there."

"No. We must complete the ruse for Marsfield to be convinced Cassandra took the packet to France. You're the one who insisted he wouldn't give up looking for her otherwise."

"Mrs. Finch will have my head if I let you go off alone. Since she had to stay and run things for Miss Letty, she entrusted me with your safety. Not that I've done such a good job so far."

Anne patted his arm. "You're not responsible for my behavior. I blame no one but myself."

"Well, I blame that notorious earl. Curse the day we found the scurvy bas—man. I should've never stopped. I should've run over him and kept going."

"Nonsense, Harvey. Knowing Marsfield has done me more good than harm." And she realized it was true. She took another sip of her tea and began to feel more her optimistic self. "Let's just make it through this one last deception. Then we can get back to our normal, quiet life."

What was it Letty once said? Responsibility, respectability, and wretched boredom. And now, thanks to the research Marsfield had inadvertently provided, she could add rich. She would find her satisfaction in making others happy.

Harvey really had no choice but to agree to her plan. He grumbled until she boarded the mail coach, finally satisfied when he saw two respectable women would be her fellow passengers.

Anne stood in front of her cheval mirror in her bedroom and placed her hand on her still flat belly. Marsfield's child nestled within her body, beneath her heart. A thrill whispered up her spine and then slithered back down with dread. A miracle both wonderful and awful at the same time.

Mrs. Finch stepped from behind the bathing screen with a handful of towels, and Anne dropped her hand to her side.

"I see you know," Mrs. Finch said, crossing her arms over her ample chest. "I've been wondering when to say something."

Anne spun around. "Know what?" she asked, with an innocent expression.

Mrs. Finch gave her a don't-take-me-for-a-ninny look. "I've been supplying your rags since you started your monthly flow, and you haven't had the need of them for two months."

"The women on the mail coach discussed their relative pregnancies and births during the entire trip." Anne sat at her dressing table and rested her hands in her head. "What am I going to do?"

"First, you're going to get dressed. You're expected for tea."

"I don't think I can face Aunt Elizabeth. And Lady Asterbule? If she finds out, poor Letty's chances will be ruined."

"No one will be able to tell for another two months, maybe three if we're lucky. Concentrate on getting Letty married as quickly as possible. Then we'll work on the other problem."

"But what can—?"

"I've been thinking I'd like to see a bit of the world. If you were to take an extended trip, say to the continent or even America, I'd be most happy to accompany you."

"And then what?"

"Here I thought you were the one with all the grand schemes and plans."

"I think I've caused enough trouble with my deceptions. I'll never tell another lie," Anne said.

"Maybe just one more." Mrs. Finch took Anne's hand in hers and patted it gently. "Dunstan can come to the rescue one more time, as the father of your baby."

"Dunstan's been dead six months. That won't add up."

"Knowing Marsfield, I'd say the baby will be big for his age and smart as a whip. After a year or two abroad, you'll be able to pass him off as a much older child. Babies all develop at different rates anyway." Mrs. Finch patted her hand again. "Well, you think about it while I lay out your clothes."

As if Anne could think about anything else.

Marsfield had a right to know he'd fathered a child. She pictured herself calling on him at his elegant town house, the plain, dowdy spinster claiming to be carrying his baby. He'd laugh in her face.

If she went to him as Cassandra, he would never be one hundred percent sure the child was his. There would always be a niggling doubt. And he would never marry Cassandra. If there had ever been the tiniest hope he might, last night had stifled that.

She didn't want her child raised with the stigma of being a bastard. Therefore she had no choice. But first she had to take care of Letty's happiness. Her resolve firm, she stood and dressed to face the dragon who was about to become her sister's mother-in-law, whether the woman liked it or not.

Twenty-four

Marsfield stood on the quay next to his heaving, lathered horses and watched the packet from Dover sail away. A few stragglers remained despite the bitter cold, waving their loved ones on their journey as the ship turned and headed toward France. If he squinted, he could see a few hardy souls on board waving back. Was that woman near the prow his Cassandra?

He snorted in disgust. His? Not now. Even if he could get himself across the channel soon, she would probably be wedded before he could get there. If he were her fiancé, he would damned well rush her to the altar before she had time to pull another one of her infamous disappearing acts.

The realization stunned him.

Looking away from the depressing sight of the diminishing ship, he noticed the Weathersby coach finishing its turn for the return home. He leaped in front of it and waved it down.

"Are you crazy, man?" the coachman hollered, yanking on the reins and pulling the confused horses to a stop.

Marsfield clambered up on the wheel. "Tell me where she's headed," he demanded.

"I'm only the coachman. I don't know nothing."

"Servants always know more than they say."

"Are you asking me to repeat servants' gossip, sir?"

"I don't have time for niceties or I'd take you aside, buy

you a pint or two, and pump you for information. I'm desperate for her direction. Do I have to beat it out of you?"

"Wouldn't do no good. I don't know where in France she would go."

Somehow Marsfield knew the coachman spoke true. Not only would he not get the information he desired, he couldn't beat a servant for his loyalty. He slowly climbed down.

"My apologies." Marsfield straightened his coat. "It was a foolish notion."

"Pardon my saying so, milord, but any man who refuses to see the truth when it's right under his nose is a fool."

The coachman snapped his reins and the coach lumbered off.

Marsfield chose a chair in the rear of the seedy tavern, his presence unremarked by the rough crowd due to his disheveled appearance. His coat was filthy from a day of scrounging the waterfront for transportation across the channel. Because the storm had worsened, no small craft sailor was willing to risk his boat and his life by putting out to sea. And no larger vessels were scheduled to sail for several days.

He rubbed the stubble on his chin and ran his hand through his hair. Reverting to tried and true habits, he pulled out his notebook and began listing the circumstances which had brought him to this sorry state. It seemed his life had turned topsy-turvy since that night on the road when he'd been left for dead.

The reminder of his mission was less than welcome. He would have to set aside his impotent pursuit of Cassandra for the greater goal of finding the villain who caused so many deaths in the Crimea.

He'd allowed Cassandra to distract him. Talk about a fool. Robert Weathersby was his prime suspect, and yet

Marsfield had allowed his cousin to distract him from his duty. He downed his ale despite the sour taste and set out to find a fast horse.

Anne couldn't sleep. She listened for sounds of furtive movement as the ormolu clock on the mantelpiece struck eleven-thirty. Moving to her bedroom window, she pulled aside the heavy brocade drapes and wrapped her robe more tightly around her as a chill wafted in.

The Asterbule carriage, carrying Timothy and Letty to Gretna Green, rolled down the drive of Weathersby manor. Anne watched it with mixed emotions. This wasn't the resolution she'd hoped for, but considering Lady Asterbule's attitude and conversation at dinner, it seemed the best possible solution. Though the dragon had agreed to the engagement of Letty and Timothy in principle, she didn't want to announce it until the first ball of next Season. She also proposed plans for an elaborate, extravagant wedding, one that Letty's family would, of course, pay for.

Anne didn't begrudge her sister the wedding of her dreams, but she couldn't afford to wait that long for the nuptials to take place. So when the two lovebirds had approached her with their plans to elope, she'd helped them. The gossips of the *ton* would titter behind their fans, but the marriage itself would quell the rumors in time, and it would survive the inauspicious beginning.

Feeling a bit sad and left out, Anne pushed the drapes further aside to catch a heartening glimpse of the moonlit garden. An unusual golden light lit the trees at the western perimeter of the manor.

Fire! The orphanage was on fire.

She yanked on the servant's bell, but could not wait for Cleeve to rouse a maid. She grabbed the first dress th came to hand, her oldest gown that she wore on clo forays, and pulled it on over her nightdress. Jammir feet into the first shoes she laid her hands on, pink satin dancing slippers, she ran from the room, hollering to wake the house.

Before she cleared the newel post of the main stairs, Cleeve had been sent to ring the fire bell to rouse the neighborhood. Stopping only long enough to tell old Finch to direct everyone to the orphanage, she grabbed a cloak from the rack under the stairs and ran for the stables. Mounted on the first horse saddled, she rode across the bare fields and through the woods.

Slipping off the horse's back, she ran to find Miss Ridley, the headmistress, huddled against the stone garden fence with a score of crying children.

"Is everyone out?" she screamed over the cacophony. When she didn't get a response from the stunned teacher, she shook her by the shoulder. "Are all the children out?"

Miss Ridley, roused from her state of shock, looked around her and tried to count heads. Unable to get an accurate count with all of the children moving around, she lined them up against the wall. She turned back to Anne with an expression of horror.

"Two are missing."

A girl with long blond pigtails stepped forward. "Tommy dared Katie to meet him in the haunted bell tower at midnight. She left the dorm about ten minutes before the fire bell rang."

Anne looked toward the abandoned bell tower. They should have torn it down when they converted the old refectory for the children's use. Flames from the burning roof of the orphanage danced perilously close to the old ⸺ structure.

⸺ oad of volunteers pulled up and started a ⸺ ide.

⸺ wagon and take the children to my house. Tell ⸺ to find blankets and something hot for them to drink. I'll be along directly with Tommy and Katie. Go on," she urged when Miss Ridley hesitated.

"You can't go in there," the headmistress cried. "It's too dangerous."

"I'll be in and out before the flames catch me, don't worry."

"Let one of the men go."

"They're busy. I'll be fine. Now get these children someplace warm before they all catch colds."

Anne scrambled over the wall and headed straight for the bell tower. Ducking beneath the timbers meant to block the door, she called the children's names.

"Help. We're stuck."

"Where are you?" Anne called back.

The flames from the building next door had broken through the east wall in places, providing macabre lighting in the derelict tower.

"I can't see you," she called.

"Up on the ledge where the old bell ringer used to stand. The ladder fell away when Katie twisted her ankle."

Anne searched the floor and found a homemade ladder. The adventuresome boy must have made it himself. Hoping it would hold for one more descent, she maneuvered it into place.

"All right. Come on down," she said, her calm tone not betraying her panic as spots of flame appeared on the roof. She held the ladder steady, but did not feel any sign that the children had put any weight on it.

"Hurry up, children. Miss Ridley will be getting worried about you two."

"Katie can't climb down with her hurt ankle," Tommy called down. "She's afraid."

"I am not."

With satisfaction, Anne heard spunk in the little girl's voice. "Here's what we're going to do. Tommy, you come on down, and then you can hold the ladder while I help Katie."

The boy scrambled down with the ease of long practice. Though Anne had doubts about his ability to hold the ladder steady with his skinny arms, the condition of the roof caused her to hurry. The ladder shook as she ascended, and several rungs sagged when she put her weight on them.

She gave a big sigh of relief when she reached the top.

A crack like thunder preceded a large beam falling from the roof. Anne dived forward and rolled onto the ledge just as a falling beam shattered the ladder. Gathering Katie in her arms and wrapping her cloak around the girl to protect her from flying cinders, she peered over the edge and called to Tommy.

"Are you all right?"

"I'm fine," he answered.

But she heard pain in is voice.

"Can you go for help?"

"My legs are pinned. I can't move."

Katie sobbed into Anne's shoulder, and only Anne's attempts to calm the little girl kept her from breaking into tears herself.

Marsfield's temper, set to boiling once he'd figured out Cassandra's ruse, had not been improved by the long snowy ride. But the time had allowed him to figure out the rest of the clever plan. He now knew Cassandra and the Widow Gordon were one and the same. There was no passage to France. It was only to get him out of the way for a few days until they could clear out.

So the oh-so-proper Widow Gordon had a taste for visiting brothels in the disguise of a prostitute, did she? Well, he would confront her with the truth.

He knocked on the front door of Weathersby Manor disgusted by the sloppy servants who did not immediately appear to take his horse and open the door. Sounds of a wild party echoed from inside the house—high-pitched squeals, feminine giggles, and loud booming male laughter.

He pounded on the door with his fist.

Old Finch answered, with a broad smile on his face.

And a tiny child seated on each foot, their skinny arms wrapped around each leg.

Thoroughly confused, Marsfield asked for Robert. Once informed the lord of the manor wasn't at home, he requested to speak to Lady Gordon. Old Finch took his hat and coat and directed him to the parlor. As Marsfield strode across the hall, giggles caused him to turn. The dignified butler shuffled away, the toddlers on his feet squealing as if riding one of the amusements at Convent Garden. Finch's booming laughter was a second surprise.

When Marsfield entered the parlor unannounced, he was nearly bowled over by two young boys chasing each other. A dozen other children played at various activities around the room. A huge woman dressed in bright red from her frilly nightcap to her bedroom slippers sat on the settee, admonishing the children to sit and be still. The second woman, properly dressed in her black widow's weeds, was bent over another child lying on the second sofa.

Marsfield, tempted to rip off her concealing headgear, settled for calling her name. The woman who faced him, her black mobcap minus the concealing veil within her own home, was not Cassandra.

"My apologies, madam. I was looking for Lady Gordon."

"I am she. Who the devil are you?"

The woman in red heaved herself up and executed a creditable curtsy. "Lord Marsfield, I'm Lady Asterbule. I'm sure you've heard of my family. I had no idea you were acquainted with the Weathersbys."

Lady Gordon snorted her disapproval. "He's not. How did you get in here?"

"I'm here to see Robert." A sudden inspiration, fueled by his investigation, hit. "And his sister."

"Which sister?" Lady Asterbule asked, her eyes narrowed.

"Neither of my nieces are at home to the likes of you," Elizabeth Gordon said, drawing herself up and crossing her arms over her chest.

Marsfield could almost laugh to see the mannerism Cassandra had mimicked so well in her disguise.

"I would like to speak to Cassandra."

"Who?" Lady Asterbule asked.

A child falling off the settee, unhurt but wailing in distress, distracted Lady Gordon.

"Tall, dark blond hair, green eyes," Marsfield said.

"Oh, you mean Anne." Lady Asterbule sounded disappointed. "She's down at the fire with everyone else."

"The fire?"

"Yes. Just my luck for the orphanage to burn while I'm here on a visit. All these children are giving me a headache. There's not a maid to help me dress, and I can't leave because there's no one to ready my carriage. Did you perhaps come in a carriage, sir?"

Marsfield tried to back away as the woman babbled on, but she followed him to the very door of the parlor.

"My apologies, but I came on horseback and must be away."

"Lady Gordon is most remiss in not offering you something to eat. At least a drink?"

"No. No, thank you. I must be going." Marsfield scooped up his outer garments from a nearby chair and practically ran for the door.

Once he reached the front stoop, Marsfield took a deep breath, like a prisoner who'd escaped the torture chamber. As he mounted his horse and rode for the orphanage, he struggled to fit the new piece of information into the puzzle. Could respectable Anne Weathersby really be Cassandra?

When all the possibilities have been eliminated, the impossible must be true.

He spurred his horse to greater speed and reached the pandemonium in the yard around the orphanage in a few minutes. The light and heat from the flames gave a surreal aspect to the scene. Drafted into the bucket brigade, he could only search for her with his eyes. He did not see Cassandra—or Anne, as he now knew her to be—anywhere within his limited field of vision.

Finally, someone called a halt to the never-ending stream of buckets. There was no way to save the building. The line of volunteers collapsed in exhaustion. Except for Marsfield, who walked from person to person asking if anyone had seen Anne Weathersby.

"I know she was here. She's the one who sounded the alarm," a helpful maid replied.

Marsfield questioned everyone.

"Haven't seen her."

"Must be around the back."

"Not here, mate."

"She's probably round to the front o' the building."

Finally, he spotted the coachman who'd driven her to Dover and most likely had driven her right back again. It galled him to think she was probably inside that coach the whole time. He grabbed the coachman by the shoulder and spun him around.

"Where is Anne Weathersby?"

The bandy little man shrugged off his hold. "She's around here somewhere. Why do you want to know?"

"No, she's not here. No one has seen her and I asked just about everyone."

A plump woman came up to the coachman's side and slipped her arm through his. "Miss Weathersby was the first one here and got the children out. She's probably back at the house with them."

"I just came from there."

The older woman paled. "Then it's true. Someone said she went into the burning bell tower after two missing children."

Robert had joined the group. "My sister isn't foolish enough to enter a burning building."

Marsfield barely heard the comment. He was already running toward the bell tower. From what he knew of her, facing him as the widow to demand he honor his pledge, and daring to act as Cassandra, Anne Weathersby was both brave enough and foolish enough attempt such a rescue.

Kicking aside the boards that blocked the door, he entered bellowing her name. Or one of them. He wasn't even conscious of which one he used.

"We're up here," she answered to his great relief. "The ladder broke," she called down from somewhere over his head. "Tommy is down there, injured by a fallen timber."

"I told you, I'm fine," the boy piped up. "I just can't move. Get them down first."

Marsfield moved debris until he found the boy. "That's very gentlemanly of you, but I need you out of the way to give me room to work."

He freed the boy and carried him to the door. "Can you walk?" Marsfield asked after setting the boy on his feet.

Tommy tested his leg with a few steps. Despite a pronounced limp, he said, "Sure."

"Good," Marsfield said. "Find someone from the bucket brigade and tell them to get some water on that west wall, and it will buy us a little more time."

Tommy limped away on his errand.

"If you could possibly expedite your rescue, Marsfield, I would appreciate it," Anne called down. "It is getting rather warm up here, and I forgot to bring my fan."

Though she sounded calm enough, the edge to her

voice and her deep coughing worried him. At least she'd retained her sense of humor despite the situation.

"You are one contrary woman. Everyone else in the county is complaining of the cold, and you're too warm." As he talked, he searched the floor of the deserted building for some means of getting to her.

"How do you feel about jumping?" he asked, trying to keep his tone light to hide his own growing desperation. In the semidarkness he could find nothing useful to effect a rescue. "If you jump, I promise to catch you."

"Actually, I'd rather not. As a child, I once jumped off the roof of the barn, and I've not been fond of heights ever since. I think there's time to find another way. We're stuck up here, and uncomfortable, but not in any immediate danger."

Marsfield found the remnants of the ladder and discarded them as useless. He hoped keeping her talking would help her to remain calm, though truth be told, she was handling the situation remarkably well.

"Why did you go up there in the first place?"

"I had to save Katie," she said as if it made perfect sense. "Her ankle is injured, and Tommy couldn't possibly carry her down the ladder."

"Perhaps next time you'll wait for help."

"I did consider that, but I had no idea when help would arrive, and the building was on fire, you know."

"Still is, in case you hadn't noticed," Marsfield said.

"Oh, I noticed." A rack of coughing interrupted her. "I'm actually quite observant."

He'd just about decided to try coming in over the roof when the long ceiling beam that had fallen gave him an idea. Struggling to stand it upright, he was thankful when helping hands seemed to appear out of nowhere. Tommy had brought help, including a much-needed rope.

Throwing the coil over his shoulder, Marsfield shimmied up the timber. It didn't quite reach the ledge, short by about ten feet. One other roof timber remained intact across the ceiling, and he hoped it would hold their weight.

"Scoot as close to the edge as you can," he directed Anne as he knotted a loop in the rope and threw it over the last remaining roof timber. He couldn't see her face, but her pink satin slippers caught the light as they dangled over the edge of the platform.

"Good. Now put the loop in the rope around your body and under your arms."

"Katie first."

"Fine. Ease her over the edge and swing her over to me."

He caught the tiny girl easily with one arm and sent the rope loop swinging back up to Anne.

"Your turn."

"Surely you do not expect to catch me while you're perched on that beam like crow on a fence rail?"

"No." Marsfield sent the rest of the length of the rope to the men waiting below. "We'll lower you all the way down."

Anne leaned over the edge, her dear face puckered in worry.

"I can't do that," she said.

"Just close your eyes and try not to think of the height."

"It's not that, but you will have to think of another way."

Marsfield shifted the little girl to the other arm and tried to ease the cramp in his leg.

"It is incumbent upon the rescuer to determine the method used, not the one being rescued," he said. "May I remind you that we do not have a lot of choices, and time is of the essence?"

"I am not wearing any petticoats," she confessed in a whisper. "Those men below will see . . . everything."

Marsfield burst into laughter. "Is that all?"

"I do not find it amusing."

"It's quite dark now that most of the flames have been put out by the bucket brigade working solely on the tower. I'm sure they won't be able to see a thing."

She shook her head. "That is an illogical statement. If I can see them, they will be able to see me."

He called down for all the gentlemen below to close their eyes. Anne finally seemed satisfied when he threatened to call out any man who peeked, and slid herself almost off the edge.

"Stay with me, Marsfield," she begged as she swung loose from the ledge.

He did, easing himself down the beam at the same speed the men gently lowered her to the ground. The last bit, he jumped down, handed off the child to a waiting woman, and caught Anne in his arms before her feet touched.

Grubby and soot-stained, her hair singed and mussed, she was the most beautiful sight he'd ever seen. He carried her out of the building and commandeered a carriage to take her home. Even once seated in the carriage, he sat with her in his lap, loath to let her out of his arms.

"Oh, Anne, I thought I'd lost you," he said, smoothing back her hair, caressing her cheek.

She looked up at him, her green eyes sparkling. "You called me Anne."

"Yes. As soon as I settle a few things with your brother, we have to talk."

"What's wrong with right now?"

He shook his head. "Tomorrow when you're rested and we have plenty of time."

"If you are going to ask me to be your mistress again, the answer is still no. Even though you did save my life, and I am grateful."

"Actually, I had something more permanent in mind."

"I'll never sleep if we don't talk tonight."

He looked down into her eager face and realized he

wouldn't sleep either until they'd settled things between them. But first he had to confront Robert. It would be better for Marsfield's future with her if she heard the news of her brother's despicable deeds from his own mouth. There was still the chance she might hate him for bringing her brother to justice, but it was a risk he had to take.

"All right. Later. But I must speak to Robert first."

She settled her head under his chin with a contented sigh.

Marsfield tightened his embrace. She'd misunderstood his intent, but he couldn't bear to disillusion her. Not just yet.

Twenty-five

Marsfield paced among the potted palms and trays of flower pots in the conservatory, the only room in the house not overrun with children. Though it was twelve-thirty, very few of the orphans were asleep. Some of the younger ones had dropped off in exhaustion, but the majority were too keyed up by the excitement of the fire and new surroundings to settle down. When last seen, Harvey and Cleeve had organized the children into a parade, and were marching them around the main rooms of the house, hoping to tire them out. Their raucous makeshift band was one reason Marsfield had sent a note asking Robert to meet him in the conservatory.

Having no change of clothes, Marsfield had settled for a quick wash. Finch had brushed his clothes, though they still smelled of smoke.

He'd arrived in the conservatory a few minutes early, and now had time to worry over what he would say to Robert. Marsfield had every intention of marrying Anne, if she would have him after he ruined her brother. His only chance seemed to be for Robert to confess to his sister. Marsfield's future marital happiness probably depended on it.

At the sound of the door, he spun around, but it wasn't Robert who entered.

Geoffrey Fain sauntered forward, a gun pointed at Marsfield's chest.

"What are you doing here?" Marsfield asked.

"Well, well, if it isn't my old friend," Geoffrey sneered.

"I was never your friend."

Marsfield leaned back on one of the planting tables, crossing his arms and ankles in a casual pose, refusing to give Fain any satisfaction by showing distress.

"No," Geoffrey said, with a sigh. "I suppose enemy is a better word, but it sounds too dramatic. Perhaps adversary."

"What are you doing here?"

"Actually, I should be asking you that, but then you always did have a knack for turning up at the most inopportune times. I'm afraid you're about to ruin the finale of my money-making scheme, and I can't let that happen."

The click of the pistol cocking was audible despite the ambient noise from the rest of the house. Marsfield knew his only chance was to keep Geoffrey talking and hope for a distraction and a chance to get the gun away from him.

"How did you know I was here?"

"I intercepted your note to Robert. You're quite the hero, I hear. I suppose I should thank you for saving my fiancée's life."

"Your fiancée?"

"Oh, Anne doesn't know it yet, but it's inevitable. I've spent too much time and effort setting up her imbecile brother to take the blame for me to let them spoil it all."

"I don't understand."

"Of course you don't. My plan is pure genius, and you followed the path right to Robert as you were supposed to. Just as someone else will after you're dead."

"Then Robert didn't—?"

"Of course Robert didn't mastermind the theft of millions. He can't outthink his beloved farm animals and moronic tenants. I put the money in his pockets and let him think he'd won it gambling. I planned to win it back from him in a very public place, hence giving me a provenance for my wealth and leaving him to ruin."

"Hopefully, I interfered with your plans."

"Don't try to take credit where it isn't due. Admit you were as lost as the rest of the fools trying to trace me. It's that bitch sister of his who ruined everything. Robert is so cowed by her that he put the money in the Bank of England in her name. Now, I'll have to marry the ugly stick to get it."

Marsfield's hackles rose at hearing him speak of Anne that way, but he schooled himself to restraint. The more worked up Fain got, the better the chance he would make a mistake.

"But that is of little matter," Geoffrey continued. "It's easy to rid oneself of a wife. I've done it before. Actually, the fire tonight would have been fortuitous if she had already married me. I shall have to remember that for the future. But you, alas, will not be around to rescue her."

Geoffrey raised the pistol and sighted down the barrel.

As his finger tightened on the trigger, the door opened behind him, and Robert bumbled through. Marsfield dived behind a large pot, the shot grazing his head. He heard a scuffle and a thump and the sound of a large planter crashing.

Anne rushed down the stairs. Though she was anxious to see Marsfield again, she'd taken time with her toilette. A woman should look her best for a marriage proposal, shouldn't she? Surely that was what Marsfield meant when he said he wanted to speak to her brother.

But it wasn't her love who waited at the foot of the stair, only Geoffrey, whom she'd been trying to avoid for days, just as determinedly as he seemed to be trying to get her alone.

"I beg a moment of your time," he said.

"You'll have to excuse me, Geoffrey." She motioned to the children marching through the main hall, wearing folded paper hats and banging on various pots and pans. Grinning servants marched in their wake. "I'm a little busy," she called over the noise.

She couldn't see either Marsfield or Robert, and assumed they were still in the library discussing her nuptials. Since Robert could have no objection to a proposal at her age, there must be a prescribed amount of congratulatory brandy to be drunk, though she'd have preferred, for Robert's sake, that they toast her upcoming wedding with tea.

"This is very important," Geoffrey insisted. "It's about a gambling debt Robert still owes."

"This is the first I've heard of any debt."

"It's a matter of life and death," he said, grabbing up a cloak and looking around nervously. "Something you don't want everyone to know. Let's step outside."

Anne distrusted his dramatics, but if Robert had a serious debt, she should know the details. At least the cold would keep the conversation short and provide her a convenient excuse to come inside if it did not. She took the cloak from Geoffrey, draped it over her shoulders, and preceded him out the door.

Geoffrey followed her out. As soon as the door closed behind him, a smelly horse blanket was thrown over her head, and rough hands lifted her. Though she struggled and screamed, she doubted her muffled cries would be noted over the noise of the children. Thrown against a hard seat, she felt and heard the motion of a carriage as it immediately pulled away.

The blanket loosened, and she thankfully whipped the nasty thing off her head. Geoffrey sat in the opposite seat, his hands crossed over his chest.

"What is the meaning of this?" she demanded.

"We're on our way to be married, my dear."

"Don't be ridiculous. You can't seriously believe I'll marry you, ruined reputation or not."

Geoffrey uncrossed his arms, revealing his pistol. "But I do." He looked down at the gun, back at her, and chuckled. "Don't bother to say marriage to me is worse than death. This isn't for you—at least not yet."

"I will never marry you." She glanced out the window, but could see no landmarks in the darkness.

"If you persist in that uncooperative attitude," Geoffrey said, fondling the pistol, "you'll have the opportunity to choose who dies first. Perhaps your brother. Or dear sweet Letty. Maybe I should start with your beloved retainers? I never liked Old Finch. Should he be first?"

Anne looked away, refusing to dignify his threats with an answer. But that didn't make them any less real. No one at Weathersby would be safe if she refused to comply with his demands.

"Why are you doing this? Why do you want to marry me?"

Geoffrey chuckled. "Believe me, it's not for your severely limited charms, but rather for your bank account."

Now Anne knew how an heiress on the marriage mart must feel. Curse the book for making her rich, if this was what it brought.

"Two million pounds makes you quite attractive."

Anne's mouth dropped open. *A Lover's Manual* had been successful beyond her wildest imagination, and she admitted she had a pretty wild imagination, but two million pounds?

"I don't know where you got the ridiculous idea that I have two—"

"I know exactly how much you have, because I put a portion of it in Robert's pockets every night after he'd passed out at the gaming tables and before I brought him home. I would have won it all back from him at the appropriate time except, more's the pity for you, he stupidly put the entire sum in an account in your name. But no matter. Once we're married, your property will become mine."

Geoffrey didn't have to say she would then become an encumbrance. A disposable encumberance.

Anne knew without asking that his money was ill-gotten gains. As an unexpected bonus, he would also gain control of her writing earnings and her dowry. Somehow the thought of him getting her long hoarded dowry was the worst of all.

The carriage slowed and halted in the yard of a disreputable inn. She had no opportunity to escape as his two burly cohorts escorted her into the main room. He immediately sent one man off on an errand. The other stood guard at her side as she sat near the fireplace.

When the local magistrate appeared, obviously rousted from his bed, Geoffrey produced a special license. He pulled her to her feet and propelled her to stand at his side.

Marsfield blinked the blood from his eyes and stumbled to his feet. He nearly tripped over Robert. Helping the other man to his feet, he got them both to the main hallway.

Children ran screaming from him in every which direction.

"It's Dunstan returned from the dead," Binny shrieked, then fainted in a heap.

"Anne," Marsfield shouted over the din. He dumped a dazed Robert into a nearby chair and let one of the wandering servants tend to him. "Anne."

"She's in her room," Mrs. Finch answered, stepping forward to dab his head with a damp cloth.

He waved her away. "It's nothing. Find Anne."

Once it was determined she wasn't in her room, the house was searched to no avail.

"Did anyone see a horse or carriage leave?" Marsfield bellowed. He got the answer he dreaded. "Get me a horse," he demanded, and a terrified footman scrambled to do his bidding.

"I'll go with you," Robert said, struggling to rise.

Marsfield pushed him back in his chair. "No. You'll only slow me down. You'll have to trust me, Robert. I'll bring your sister back."

Again Marsfield had to push Mrs. Finch and her ministrations aside.

"Thank you, but it's only a scratch. Head wounds bleed a lot. I'm fine."

Old Finch handed him a warm cloak and hat just as he heard horses gallop to the front door. Harvey, the coachman, was mounted on the second horse, lantern in hand, ready to follow the tracks of the carriage in the new-fallen snow.

Marsfield mounted and urged his horse to reckless speed. Once Geoffrey had Anne's signature on a marriage certificate, her life was worthless.

Twenty-six

Marsfield spotted the carriage in the inn courtyard from several hundred feet down the road and immediately had Harvey douse the lantern. After directing Harvey to work his way around to the back of the inn, Marsfield rode slowly into the yard, hunched over his saddle like a weary traveler.

He noted the guard at the door as he dismounted and led his horse into the barn. The carriage horses were still in their traces despite the weather, indicating Geoffrey didn't intend to stay long.

Keeping his head low, Marsfield trudged to the door. Once past the unsuspecting guard, he whirled and knocked him out. Catching him as he fell, he leaned the guard quietly against the building and let him slide to a sitting position.

On the journey, he'd used snow and his handkerchief to scrub the blood off his face once his head had stopped bleeding. He pulled up the collar of his cloak to hide his bloody shirt and stepped in the warmth of the inn.

At two o'clock in the morning, few patrons were in the taproom. Two weary travelers, such as he pretended to be, huddled over a table. Three ragtag die-hard drinkers stared in bleary-eyed fascination as their local magistrate performed a wedding for two members of the *ton*.

Marsfield leaned against the back wall and propped

one foot on a nearby bench. After clearing his throat for attention, he said, "Have you gotten to the part about objections yet?"

Both Anne and Geoffrey whirled around at the sound of his voice. The patrons, sensing danger, backed away, clearing the ten-foot space between the men.

Geoffrey yelled for his guards, to no avail.

"This woman is being forced to marry that man," Marsfield said to the magistrate, though he kept his gaze on Geoffrey.

The patrons grumbled in the background.

"That's not true, is it my dear?" Geoffrey said, putting his arm around Anne's shoulder. "Tell the magistrate and everyone here you're marrying me of your own free will."

She looked into Marsfield's eyes. He saw her plea for forgiveness as she repeated the words in a clear firm voice.

Stunned, Marsfield was forced to believe her.

Until he dropped his gaze and noticed her hands clenched into tight fists.

Something about her hands rang warning bells in his head. She clenched her fists like a boy. Like a boy named Andrew. The final puzzle piece.

Marsfield burst out laughing. He laughed so hard he had to sit down on the bench. He was in love with the most amazing woman. Not only had she successfully disguised herself as a widow and a courtesan, but as a boy she'd learned to make a decent fist.

"What's so funny?" one of the patrons asked.

"I think all women should learn to box," Marsfield explained between chuckles.

"Sir," the magistrate said, puffing up his chest. "This is a solemn occasion, despite the surroundings. I'm a representative of the crown, and you are obviously drunk. Remove yourself from the premises."

"I think not," Marsfield said, standing and drawing his pistol.

Geoffrey moved to step behind Anne, reaching for her waist, but she was too quick for him. She took a step back, assumed the boxer's stance and punched him as hard as she could. Right, left, right, just as she'd learned, putting her body's weight behind each thrust. Her opponent, too surprised to react, took the brunt of each blow with a grunt, then slid into a helpless, moaning puddle on the floor.

Evil genius he might be, but he was a lousy boxer. And he had seriously underestimated Anne. Something Marsfield would never do again, he promised himself as he took her into his arms.

Harvey broke through the back door with a yell, startling everyone and setting the dogs to howling.

Anne, her eyes lit with laughter, looked up into Marsfield's eyes. "You rescued me again."

Marsfield motioned to Geoffrey, who was still whimpering as Harvey and the magistrate carted him away. "You did a pretty good job of rescuing yourself."

"I never would have thought of hitting him if you hadn't reminded me of those lessons."

"Speaking of that, I think we need to talk." He looked around at the gawking audience.

She wrapped her arms around his neck and gave him a passionate kiss. Marsfield kissed her back with love and tenderness.

"With a thank you like that, I'll have to stick around to rescue you more often." He kissed her on the nose. "But two rescues in one day is a bit much, don't you think?"

"Technically, the first rescue happened yesterday because it was before midnight. That's only one rescue per day."

"Still more than my desired quota."

She smiled. "I'll try to remember that."

She kissed him again, to the wild applause of their audience, who had obviously enjoyed the unusual show from start to finish. It was the kind of tale that would be passed on to grandchildren before a winter's fire.

Marsfield commandeered Geoffrey's carriage to take Anne back to her home. In the cozy darkness, she answered honestly his questions about Andrew, the widow, Cassandra, and the book that had caused him so much trouble.

"Now that you know everything, do you hate me?"

"Anne Cassandra Andrew Elizabeth Gordon Weathersby, I love you beyond all reason and cannot bear the thought of facing the rest of my life without you. Will you do me the honor of being my wife?"

"Yes," she answered with joy in her heart.

A passionate kiss sealed their happy pact.

"I have one last question to ask about Cassandra," he said. "If you were a virgin that first night, how did you know enough to pass yourself off as a courtesan?"

"Was I that good?"

"Very good," he admitted with a deep chuckle. "The best."

"Thank you. I simply followed the example of pictures on the wall, sort of a primer even a fool could follow."

"I think you have a natural aptitude," he said nuzzling her neck.

"Probably not," she admitted, determined to be honest with him from now on. "There were quite a few I didn't understand and a few which seemed patently impossible."

She leaned over and in embarrassed whispers described the picture she'd seen at Rose's of the couple making love in the carriage.

Without a moment's hesitation, he swung her over to straddle his lap.

"Are you going to show me how it's done?"

"When are you going to learn to appreciate your future husband? Nothing's impossible with me."

"Now?"

"Anything my lady wishes," he said with a wicked smile.

How she loved it when his eyes deepened to that dark shade of midnight blue.

"Anything?" she asked with a sensuous smile of her own. "There were actually quite a few pictures I didn't understand. I don't know if I remember them all."

"Perhaps you'll have to go back to Rose's for another look."

"That would be wonderful. She and the girls were so nice to me. I would go in the daytime, for tea. And I could wear a disguise."

"Maybe we'll go together," he said with a warning look.

She wiggled in excitement.

Marsfield clamped his hands on her thighs to still her. "If you keep that up, we'll have to make Harvey drive us around for another hour or two."

"Now that's what I like. A man with ideas."

"I can't believe my luck. I've found a woman who not only will make a respectable countess, but who is also a friend and a passionate lover."

"Then I am even luckier than you," she argued. "For I have found a man who can appreciate all the aspects of my true self."

When he demanded they be married within the week, she thought about the baby she carried beneath her heart and readily agreed. She wondered for just a moment before her thoughts were scattered to the stars when should she tell him the rest of the truth about Cassandra.

Epilogue

Though she'd been quite ill on the voyage, the last few days had been glorious. Anne lay on a chaise situated on the sunny palazzo of the villa they'd rented for their honeymoon. She stretched like a lazy cat in the warm Italian sunshine. Ignoring the writing she'd intended to complete, she watched over the low wall as her new husband swam with sure muscular strokes in the bright blue bay.

How well she knew those muscles now, the feel of them, their strength moving beneath her touch. If she looked back to a year ago, she never would have pictured herself here. Only one thought marred her happiness.

The money. Geoffrey's ill-gotten gains were still in her name at the Bank of England. Though it could not be proved as anything but hers, an agent of the government had suggested she turn it over to the crown. But she thought it should go back to the people who had been most hurt by the swindle, the widows and orphans of the Crimean War veterans.

She hadn't discussed it with Marsfield yet, but she wanted to set up homes for them, maybe a village where the children could live with their mothers and go to school without worrying where their next meal would come from. The mothers could go to school, too, if they wanted to learn a skill, and they could work in the shops of the village for spending money so they wouldn't feel like they were accepting charity.

She'd written all her ideas down and hoped Marsfield would volunteer to manage it. She would need help, because their baby would come before the project could be completed.

Marsfield came running up the stairs from the sea, his bare chest already bronzed by the sun. She squealed in pretend horror when he shook droplets of water onto her from his hair.

"I see you have letters from home already," he said, plopping into a chair next to her.

"There's an absolute scandal at home."

"How is that possible without us there?"

She gave him a quelling look. "Binny and Old Finch have pooled their retirement funds and purchased a cottage together. They seem to be happily cohabiting in sin, to the chagrin of his sister and the entire community."

Marsfield chuckled. "Hardly. They've been married for thirty years."

"No? How do you know that? Why wouldn't they say something?"

Marsfield shrugged. "I uncovered it when I was investigating your brother. I guess it's kind of hard to admit after they've kept it secret all these years."

"But why keep it a secret?"

"It was a long time ago. A servant could lose his post if he or she got married."

"I would never do that."

"You weren't in charge thirty years ago."

Even if he was right, it hurt her feelings they hadn't trusted her with the fact. When she got back, she'd make them spill the beans, somehow.

"Any other news?"

She knew he was trying to coax her out of her sulk, and she let him. They day was too nice to brood.

"It looks like Lady Asterbule is going to forgive Letty

and Timothy for eloping. Though Letty did complain that, as usual, she missed all the excitement."

"Timothy is probably just as glad they did."

"At least we provided a good distraction. No one even thought of following them until it was too late."

Marsfield smiled. "You are my distraction," he said, leaning over for a long kiss.

"Preston has accepted a post as secretary to a Royal Scientific Society expedition headed by Sir Richard Burton. He'll be gone by the time we return and doesn't expect to be back for two years."

"Good," he said, smiling.

"Why? I'll miss his friendship."

"He'll write."

"You look like the cat that swallowed the canary. Were you behind this? You can't possibly be jealous. There was never anything—"

"I know. The boy had a crush on you and will grow out of it eventually. I just thought it would be better if he did his growing from a distance."

"You didn't tell him that?" she said with a look of horror.

"Give me some credit. It may have been long ago, but I do remember being at that awkward age."

"Actually, I give you a great deal of credit. In fact, I have an idea for a new book."

He groaned. "As your publisher—

"I'm still not sure I like that."

"I leave all selection of material to Mr. Blackthorne. As your husband, I beg of you, please leave me out of this book. One reason I chose Italy for our honeymoon was that your book has not been distributed here."

"Yet."

"Maybe, after the honeymoon. But remember, we might want to come back. In fact, I'm considering buying this villa. What do you think?"

"I can't leave you out of the book, because you're going to help me write it."

"Me?"

"Yes. It's a manual on fatherhood, tentatively titled, *How To Make a Rake into an Excellent Father.*"

Marsfield looked at her with a stunned expression.

"The answers to your unspoken questions are: yes, I'm sure, the first time we made love, and in the spring."

Marsfield fell to his knees beside her and laid his large tanned hand gently on the slight bulge of her belly. She covered his hand with hers.

"You have made me the happiest man alive. I want a daughter just like you."

Anne laughed. "You know the old saying: Be careful what you wish for. If she has your blue eyes and dimples, heaven help the men of this world twenty years from now."

"If she has your temperament and daring, heaven help us."

Anne rubbed his hand. "A boy would be nice. With your strong chin and noble brow."

Removing his hands and hers, he leaned over and kissed her belly. "Whether you are the next earl or a daughter," he said to her stomach, "I promise to be a good father to you."

"The next Earl of Marsfield," she said with a sigh. "Such a wicked reputation to live up to."

"With you as an example, maybe he'll be satisfied to be a reclusive writer."

She slapped him playfully on the shoulder, and they dissolved into giggles and kisses.

When she finally sat up, he helped her stand with tender care, as if she were aged or infirm. This would never do. She didn't plan to spend the next few months cosseted like a delicate china doll.

"Do you know what I like most about Italy?"

He blinked in response to her quick change of subject, but didn't resist when she led him inside.

"The siestas," she said in answer to her own question.

"I'm not tired," he mumbled.

"I know." And she gave him one of her Cassandra smiles.

Embrace the Romances of

Shannon Drake

__Come the Morning $6.99US/$8.99CAN
  0-8217-6471-3

__Blue Heaven, Black Night $6.50US/$8.00CAN
  0-8217-5982-5

__Conquer the Night $6.99US/$8.99CAN
  0-8217-6639-2

__The King's Pleasure $6.50US/$8.00CAN
  0-8217-5857-8

__Lie Down in Roses $5.99US/$6.99CAN
  0-8217-4749-0

__Tomorrow the Glory $5.99US/$6.99CAN
  0-7860-0021-4

Call toll free **1-888-345-BOOK** to order by phone or use this
coupon to order by mail.

Name_____

Address_____

City_____ State _____ Zip _____

Please send me the books that I have checked above.

I am enclosing $_____
Plus postage and handling* $_____
Sales tax (in New York and Tennessee) $_____
Total amount enclosed $_____

*Add $2.50 for the first book and $.50 for each additional book. Send
check or money order (no cash or CODs) to:
Kensington Publishing Corp., 850 Third Avenue, New York, NY 10022
Prices and numbers subject to change without notice.
All orders subject to availability.
Check out our website at **www.kensingtonbooks.com**.

Discover The Magic of
Romance With
Jo Goodman

__More Than You Know $5.99US/$7.99CAN
0-8217-6569-8

__Crystal Passion $5.99US/$7.50CAN
0-8217-6308-3

__Always in My Dreams $5.50US/$7.00CAN
0-8217-5619-2

__The Captain's Lady $5.99US/$7.50CAN
0-8217-5948-5

__Seaswept Abandon $5.99US/$7.99CAN
0-8217-6709-7

__Only in My Arms $5.99US/$7.50CAN
0-8217-5346-0

Call toll free **1-888-345-BOOK** to order by phone or use this coupon
to order by mail, or order online at **www.kensingtonbooks.com**.

Name_____

Address_____

City_____ State _____ Zip _____

Please send me the books that I have checked above.

I am enclosing $_____

Plus postage and handling* $_____

Sales tax (in New York and Tennessee) $_____

Total amount enclosed $_____

*Add $2.50 for the first book and $.50 for each additional book. Send
check or money order (no cash or CODs) to:

Kensington Publishing Corp., 850 Third Avenue, New York, NY 10022

Prices and numbers subject to change without notice.

All orders subject to availability.

Check out our website at **www.kensingtonbooks.com**.

The Queen of Romance

Cassie Edwards

__Desire's Blossom $5.99US/$7.99CAN
0-8217-6405-5

__Exclusive Ecstasy $5.99US/$7.99CAN
0-8217-6597-3

__Passion's Web $5.99US/$7.50CAN
0-8217-5726-1

__Portrait of Desire $5.99US/$7.50CAN
0-8217-5862-4

__Savage Obsession $5.99US/$7.50CAN
0-8217-5554-4

__Silken Rapture $5.99US/$7.50CAN
0-8217-5999-X

__Rapture's Rendezvous $5.99US/$7.50CAN
0-8217-6115-3

Call toll free **1-888-345-BOOK** to order by phone or use this coupon to order by mail.
Name_____
Address_____
City_____ State _____ Zip _____
Please send me the books that I have checked above.
I am enclosing $_____
Plus postage and handling* $_____
Sales tax (in New York and Tennessee) $_____
Total amount enclosed $_____
*Add $2.50 for the first book and $.50 for each additional book. Send check or money order (no cash or CODs) to:
Kensington Publishing Corp., 850 Third Avenue, New York, NY 10022
Prices and numbers subject to change without notice.
All orders subject to availability.
Check out our website at **www.kensingtonbooks.com**.

Put a Little Romance in Your Life With

Betina Krahn

__Hidden Fire 0-8217-5793-8	$5.99US/$7.50CAN
__Love's Brazen Fire 0-8217-5691-5	$5.99US/$7.50CAN
__Luck Be a Lady 0-8217-7313-5	$5.99US/$6.99CAN
__Passion's Ransom 0-8217-5130-1	$5.99US/$6.99CAN

Call toll free **1-888-345-BOOK** to order by phone or use this coupon to order by mail.

Name _____

Address _____

City _____ State_____ Zip_____

Please send me the books that I checked above.

I am enclosing	$_____
Plus postage and handling*	$_____
Sales tax (in NY and TN)	$_____
Total amount enclosed	$_____

*Add $2.50 for the first book and $.50 for each additional book.
Send check or money order (no cash or CODs) to: **Kensington Publishing Corp., 850 Third Avenue, New York, NY 10022**
Prices and numbers subject to change without notice.
All orders subject to availability.
Visit our website at **www.kensingtonbooks.com**.

<u>BOOK YOUR PLACE ON OUR WEBSITE</u>
<u>AND MAKE THE</u>
<u>READING CONNECTION!</u>

We've created a customized website just for our very special readers, where you can get the inside scoop on everything that's going on with Zebra, Pinnacle and Kensington books.

When you come online, you'll have the exciting opportunity to:

- View covers of upcoming books
- Read sample chapters
- Learn about our future publishing schedule (listed by publication month *and author*)
- Find out when your favorite authors will be visiting a city near you
- Search for and order backlist books from our online catalog
- Check out author bios and background information
- Send e-mail to your favorite authors
- Meet the Kensington staff online
- Join us in weekly chats with authors, readers and other guests
- Get writing guidelines
- AND MUCH MORE!

Visit our website at
http://www.kensingtonbooks.com